MW00753682

The Séance

Also by John Harwood

The Ghost Writer

The Séance

JOHN HARWOOD

Houghton Mifflin Harcourt
Boston · New York
2009

First U.S. edition

www.hmhbooks.com

First published in 2008 by Jonathan Cape

Library of Congress Cataloging-in-Publication Data
Harwood, John.
The séance/John Harwood.—1st ed.
p. cm.
1. Haunted houses—Fiction. 2. Murder—Fiction.
3. Extortion—Fiction. 4. England—Fiction. I. Title.
PR9619.4.H37S43 2008
823'.92—dc22 2007046029
ISBN 978-0-15-101203-9

Text set in Adobe Jenson / Designed by Cathy Riggs

Printed in the United States of America

MP 10 9 8 7 6 5 4 3 2 1

For Robin

To manifest a spirit, take twenty yards of fine silk veiling, at least two yards wide and very gauzy. Wash carefully, and rinse seven times. Prepare a solution of one jar Balmain's Luminous Paint; half a pint of Demar Varnish, one pint odourless benzine and fifty drops lavender oil. Work thoroughly through the fabric while it is still damp, and then allow to dry for three days. Then wash with naphtha soap until all the odour is gone and the fabric is perfectly soft and pliable. In a darkened room, the fabric will appear as a soft, luminous vapour.

—*Revelations of a Spirit Medium* (1891)

Part One

Constance Langton's Narrative

JANUARY 1889

If my sister Alma had lived, I should never have begun the séances. She died of scarlatina, soon after her second birthday, when I was five years old. I remember only fragments from the time before she died: Mama dancing Alma on her knee, and singing as she would never do again; reading my primer aloud to Mama while she rocked Alma's cradle with her foot; walking beside Annie, our nurse, while she pushed the perambulator past the Foundling Hospital with me holding on to the frame. I remember coming home after one of those walks and being allowed to nurse Alma by the drawing-room fire, feeling the heat of the flames on my cheek as I held her. I remember, too—though perhaps I was only told of it—lying in a cot and shivering, looking up at a window which seemed very small and far away, and hearing the sound of weeping, muffled as if through thick cotton wool.

I do not know how long my own illness lasted, but it seems, in memory, as if I woke to find the house shrouded in darkness, and my mother changed beyond recognition. She kept to her room for many months, during which I was allowed only brief visits. The blinds were always drawn; often she seemed scarcely aware of my presence. And when at last she began to sit up, and then to emerge from her room—stooped like an old woman, her hair thin and lank—she remained sunk in lightless misery. Sometimes she would send for me, and then seem not to know why I had appeared, as if the wrong person had answered the summons. Whatever I ventured to say to her would be met with the same lifeless indifference, and if I sat in silence, I would feel the weight of her grief pressing upon me until I feared I would suffocate.

I wish I could say that my father grieved too; but if he did, I saw no sign of it. His manner with Mama was always polite and solicitous, very like that of Dr. Warburton, who would call from time to time and go away shaking his head. Papa was never ill, or cross, or out of sorts, and would no more have raised his voice than appear in public without waxing the points of his moustache. Sometimes in the mornings, after Annie had given me my bread and milk, I would creep downstairs and watch Papa and Mama through a crack in the dining-room door. "I trust you are feeling a little better today, my dear?" Papa would ask, and Mama would rouse herself wearily and say that yes, she supposed that she was, and then he would read *The Times* until it was time for him to set off for the British Museum, where he worked each day on his book. Most evenings he dined out; on Sundays, when the Museum was closed, he worked in his study. He did not go to church because he was busy with his work, and Mama could not go because she was not well enough, and so each Sunday Annie and I went to St. George's by ourselves.

Annie explained that Mama was grieving because God had taken Alma to Heaven, which I thought very cruel of Him; but then, if Alma was happy, and would never be ill again, and we would all be together again one day, why was Mama so dreadfully distressed? Because she loved Alma so dearly, Annie replied, and could not bear to be parted from her; but when the time of mourning was over, Mama would recover her spirits. In the meantime, all we could do was accompany Mama, once she was able to leave the house, to the only place she ever visited, the burial ground near the Foundling Hospital, and arrange fresh flowers on Alma's grave. I wondered why God had left Alma's body here, and taken only her spirit; and whether He was looking after Mama's spirits until she recovered them, but Annie declined to answer these questions, saying that I would understand when I was older.

She had dark brown hair, pulled back very tightly, and dark eyes, and a soft way of speaking; I thought her very pretty, though she insisted she was not. Annie had grown up in a village in Somerset, where her father was a stonemason, and had four brothers and three sisters; five more children had died when they were still very young. I had assumed, when she first told me this, that her mother must have been even more grief-stricken than mine. But no, said Annie, there had been no time for mourning; her mother had been far too busy looking after the rest of them. And no, they had not had a nurse; they had been far too poor for that. Things were much better now, though, because three of her brothers had gone for soldiers, and her two elder sisters were in service like herself, and they were all (except for one of the brothers, who had fallen into bad company) sending money home to their mother.

Whenever the weather was fine, Annie and I would go out for a walk in the afternoon. Our house was in Holborn, and on these walks we would sometimes pause at the Foundling Hospital to watch the foundling girls at play in their white pinafores and brown serge gowns. It looked as grand as a palace with its avenue of lamps, and more windows than you could count, and a statue of an angel before the entrance. The foundlings, Annie told me (she had a friend in service who had grown up here), had been brought here as infants by their mothers, who were too poor, or too ill to care for them. And yes, it was very sad for their mothers to have to give them up, but the foundlings had a much better life at the Hospital. The infants were all sent to good homes in the country until they were five or six years old, and then brought back to the Hospital for their schooling. They had meat for their dinner three days a week, and roast beef on Sundays, and when they were old enough, the boys would be sent for soldiers, and the girls for ladies' maids.

I wanted to know all about the mothers who had given their babies up for foundlings; after all, Annie's mother had been very poor, but she had kept them all at home. Annie seemed reluctant to answer, but eventually she told me that most of the foundlings were here because their fathers had run away and left their mothers alone.

"So if Papa were to run away," I asked, "would I be sent for a foundling?"

"Of course not, my child," said Annie, "your papa's not going to run away, and you've got me to look after you. And besides, you're too old for a foundling."

Later that afternoon, while we were standing beneath the angel, watching the foundling boys playing in their part of the grounds, she told me the story of her friend Sara, whose mother had given her up to the Hospital because her father had run away before she was even born. Sara had kept her mother's name, which was Baker, but could remember nothing of her, whereas she had grown very fond of her nurse, a Mrs. Garrett, in Wiltshire, and had cried very much when the time came for her to return to the Hospital for her schooling. Mr. and Mrs. Garrett would dearly have liked to keep Sara, because all of their own children had died, but they were very poor, and the Hospital wouldn't have paid them to look after Sara once she was old enough for schooling. And yes, the nurses in the country were sometimes allowed to keep the children for their own, but only if they could prove to the Hospital that they had enough money to care for them properly; just as the mothers who had had to give up their children could come and get them back if their fortunes took a turn for the better.

I was, I think, about six or seven years old when it first occurred to me that I too might have been a foundling. It would explain why we lived so close to the Hospital; and we had lived in the country before Alma was born, though I had only dim memories of that time, and Annie could not help, because she had come to us after we moved to London. Of course I might have been another sort of foundling; Annie had told me that there were other Hospitals (and looked at me rather strangely when I asked if we might visit them). I had heard, too, of infants being left on doorsteps in baskets; I might have been one of those. Perhaps Mama had had other children who had died and never been spoken of; or else she had been barren, like Abraham's wife Sarah, and had taken me in as a foundling and decided to keep me. And then the Lord had given her Alma . . . though that made it doubly hard to understand why, if He was a kind and loving God, as Mr. Halstead insisted in his sermons, He had taken her away again so soon. Had He done it to test Mama's faith, as He had tested Job's? "The Lord giveth, and the Lord hath taken away," Job had said. "Blessed be the name of the Lord."

I could not understand it, but nevertheless the suspicion took root and grew. It explained why Mama had loved Alma so much more than me, and why I was never any comfort to her, and even why, as I sometimes guiltily suspected, I did not love her as much as I ought to. Though I prayed constantly for her to be happy again, I dreaded being alone with her in the dark drawing room where she passed her days. I would sit on the sofa beside her, picking at my work or pretending to read, feeling as if a leaden band were slowly tightening around my chest, repeating silently to myself, I am a foundling, she is not my mother; I am a foundling, she is not my mother, until I was allowed to leave; and then I would reproach myself bitterly for want of sympathy. Indeed everything I felt for my mother was compounded of guilt—even guilt at being alive at all—for I knew that she would far rather I had died and Alma had lived. But at least she had not given me back to the Hospital, and since she and Papa had evidently resolved not to tell me that I was a foundling, I knew it would be wrong to ask them.

I tried in all sorts of ways to approach the question with Annie, but somehow she never seemed to take the hint, and the more I tried to steer our talk toward foundlings, the more she seemed to veer away, until, without anything being said, we had ceased to pass the Hospital on our walks: it was always "next week" or "another day." I once asked her whether she thought it was my fault Alma had died, and was frightened by the vehemence of her denial; she asked me quite fiercely who had put such an idea into my head. And what if Mama and Papa had not told her the truth about me? She would think me wicked for imagining such a thing; and besides, I was never quite certain how far I believed it myself.

So long as I had Annie, there was always something to look forward to each day. She had friends who were nurses who would bring their children to play in the square, and I would join in their games, and run about, and laugh, and forget about being a foundling. But listening to their talk of brothers and sisters, uncles and aunts and cousins and grandmothers reminded me that I had never seen any of my own relations. As I grew older, I learned that Papa had a widowed sister in Cambridge, who did not visit because Mama was not well enough, and that Mama had a younger brother called Frederick, whom she had not seen for many years. I had no living grandparents, because Papa and Mama had been quite old when they married; her own father had been ill for a long time, and she had had to stay at home and look after him until she was almost forty.

It never occurred to me that Annie and I would not continue thus indefinitely. But when I was eight years old, she took me into her own room, and sat me down on her bed, and put her arms around me, and told me that I would soon be going to Miss Hale's day school, which was only a short walk from our house. She was trying to make it sound like a treat, but I could hear the sadness in her voice. And then she confessed that she was leaving us; Papa had decided that I had grown too old for a nurse, and that Violet the maid could look after me from now on. I did not like Violet, who was fat, and had cold hands, and smelt like washing which had been left too long in the basket. In vain I pleaded with Papa to let Annie stay; we could not afford to keep her, he said, with Miss Hale's fees to think of. I told him I did not want to go to school, and could learn everything I needed from books, and then Annie would not have to go; but that would not do either. If I stayed at home I would need a governess, which would be even more expensive; and no, Annie could not be my governess because she knew nothing of French, or history, or geography, or any of the things that I would learn at school.

Though I went to Miss Hale's resolved to hate everything about it, I was unprepared for the sheer tedium of the classroom. My reading at home had never been supervised, for Annie knew nothing of books and could scarcely construe a primer. Papa kept his study locked, but not the library next door, a room no larger than a bedchamber, but to me a treasure-house to which I was tacitly admitted, so long as every volume was restored to its exact place before he came home. And so I was quite accustomed to reading books I scarcely understood, puzzling out the sounds and meanings of unfamiliar words with the help of Dr. Johnson's dictionary. Whereas at school everything had to be learned by rote, except for the endless sums in arithmetic, which I found pointless as well as baffling. And again, with the other girls in my form, I was acutely aware of my lack of brothers and sisters and relations; I had nothing to talk about but the books I was reading, and I soon discovered that a premature acquaintance with the works of Shelley and Byron was not something to boast of.

Yet for all the tedium, Miss Hale's became a respite, of sorts, from the darkness which had engulfed my mother. Instead of tea with Annie in the nursery, I had now to join Mama at the dining table, and make effortful conversation—mostly a recital of what I had learned at school that day. And then we would sit silently in the drawing room, Mama stitching mechanically or staring vacantly into the fire while I picked at my own work and listened to the heavy ticking of the mantel clock, counting the quarter hours until I could go up to my bed in the attic, where I would read for as long as I could be sure to blow out my candle before I went to sleep.

In my second year at Miss Hale's, I won a prize for recitation: a book of Greek myths with wonderful pictures. The stories I liked best were those of Theseus and Ariadne, Orpheus and Eurydice, and especially Persephone in the Underworld. Anything to do with the Underworld fascinated me—I used to imagine that it was just under the kitchen floor, and that I would find steps going down to it if I were only strong enough to lift up one of the flagstones. I had a seashell in which I could hear the sound of the sea, which had always comforted me; I would read my book and gaze at the pictures, listening to the sea, and make up my own stories of Persephone in Hades. Six pomegranate seeds did not seem very much of a sin; later I learned from Papa that it was really a story about the seasons, seeds waiting underground for spring to arrive—a clever man at Cambridge had said so—but this seemed so dull and trite, and left out everything interesting, Charon the ferryman and Cerberus with his three heads, and Hades with his helmet of invisibility, in which he could go about the upper world unseen. I asked Papa if the clever man thought the same about Eurydice, but apparently the clever man had not yet made up his mind.

Strangely, perhaps, the souls of the dead had no part in my Underworld. It was a mysterious place of tunnels and secrets, dark and sombre and yet somehow enthralling, in which I would be free to wander if only I could find the way in. I dreamed once of a cave in which I found an elaborately carved chest full of gold and silver and precious stones, from which light poured as you opened it, and this became part of my imagined Underworld, together with its opposite, a plain wooden box which seemed empty at first, but as you watched, darkness began to well up like cold black mist and spill over the sides and across the rocky floor of the cave. There were the Plains of Asphodel, which sounded beautiful and sombre, carpeted—or so I imagined them—with flowers of the richest purple, and when you were weary of tunnels, you could ascend to the Elysian fields, where the sun always shines and music never ceases.

At home, however, my dead sister was always with us. Mama had made a shrine of Alma's room, a small chamber opening off her own bedroom, keeping everything as if Alma might reappear at any moment: the sheet turned down, Alma's favourite rag doll by the pillow, her nightgown laid out, a posy of flowers in a vase upon the dresser. The door was always open, but no one else was allowed across the threshold; Mama did all the dusting and polishing of it herself, which suited Violet well enough, for she was lazy and hated climbing stairs. Violet slept in the attic bedroom across the landing from mine;

sometimes at night I would hear her grumbling and puffing on her way up to bed.

I wonder now why she stayed with us so long, for our house had so many stairs that you could scarcely go anywhere without climbing at least two flights. Apart from Violet, we had only Mrs. Greaves the cook, who lived entirely in the basement. Mrs. Greaves was a widow, grey-headed, stout and red-faced like Violet, but whereas Violet wobbled like a blancmange tied up in a cloth, Mrs. Greaves was as round and solid as a barrel. Though the kitchen had only one grimy window into the area below the street, it was the brightest and warmest place in the house, for Mrs. Greaves kept the gaslight turned as high as it would go, and in winter she would heap up the coals in the range until you could see the red glow pulsing through the cracks around the door. It was she who gave Violet her orders, which were carried out slowly and sullenly, but obeyed nonetheless. There was no laundry; the washing was sent out to a laundress.

Outside of Alma's room, Mama took no more interest in the housekeeping than in anything else, and I suppose that Papa either did not know what gas and coals ought to cost, or did not care so long as his serene existence was not disturbed. Mrs. Greaves slept in a little room behind the pantry, opening onto a dank, high-walled courtyard. The dining and drawing rooms were on the ground floor; and Papa had the first floor to himself, with the library at the front, his study in the middle, then his bedroom, and a bathroom on the landing, so that there was no necessity for him to ascend any higher; at least, I had never seen him do so. Mama's and Alma's rooms were on the next floor up, along with the room that had been Annie's, and above them the attics. My own little room faced eastward, and often on wintry Sunday afternoons, I would climb into bed for warmth and try to lose myself in the sea of slate and blackened brickwork stretching away toward the great dome of St. Paul's, thinking of all the lives going on behind those endless walls.

I had always liked Mrs. Greaves, but so long as I had Annie to speak for me, I had been too shy to say more than "yes," "no," or "thank you." And for a long time after Annie had left us, I missed her too much to want to make advances to Mrs. Greaves. But as the months dragged by, I was drawn to the light and warmth of the kitchen, especially on Saturdays, when Violet had her day off. At first I simply sat on a stool and watched; little by little I began to help, until I became quite proficient at peeling potatoes, rolling pastry and kneading dough. Sometimes I was even allowed to polish the silver, which I thought a great treat; all in all, it seemed to me that the life of a servant was far preferable to that of a lady.

"I think I should like to be a cook when I grow up," I said to Mrs. Greaves one winter's afternoon. It had been raining steadily all day, and through the soft rumble of the stove I could hear water gurgling down the area drain.

"I can see where you might think that," she replied, "but it ain't like this, most places. There's many a poor skivvy shiverin' in the dark, when she's not wearin' her fingers to the bone, because her mistress grudges her an inch of candle or a few coals, never mind gas like we have in here. Besides, you're going to be a lady, with a house and servants of your own, and a husband and children to look after; you won't want to be peelin' spuds then, believe you me."

"I shall never have children," I said passionately, "for one of them might die, and then I should be like Mama, and never be happy again."

Mrs. Greaves regarded me sadly; I had never before spoken so directly of my mother's affliction.

"The country people in Ireland, miss, would say your mother was 'away.'"

I looked at her expectantly.

"Well—'tis only their fancy, mind—they say that when someone is—like that—it's because the fairies have carried her off, and left one of their own in her place."

"And do the fairies ever bring them back?"

"Yes, my child . . . I lost two sons, as you know, and thought my heart would break; I miss them still, but I know they're safe above. And I had others to think of . . ." She paused uncomfortably.

"*How* do you know," I asked, "that they are safe in Heaven? I mean, that there *is* a Heaven? Because the Bible tells us so?"

"Well, yes, miss, that, of course, and . . . because *they* tell me so."

"But *how* can they tell you? Do their ghosts speak to you?"

"Not ghosts, miss; their spirits. Through Mrs. Chivers—she's what they call a spirit medium—do you know what that is?"

I told her I did not, and she explained, somewhat hesitantly at first, about spiritualism, and how she belonged to a Society, which met twice a week in a room in Southampton Row, and all about séances, and how the spirits of the departed could visit us from Heaven, which some people called "Summerland," to speak through a medium to those they loved.

"Then I must tell Mama about Mrs. Chivers," I said, "so she can talk to Alma's spirit, and be happy again."

"No, miss, you mustn't; leastways, you mustn't let on I told you, or I might lose my place. Your Pa don't hold with spiritualists, so I've heard. And ladies don't go to Mrs. Chivers, only cooks and skivvies like me and Violet."

"Are ladies not allowed to be spiritualists, then?"

"It's not that, miss, but they have their own meetings, them that believe. I've heard there's a Society for ladies and gentlemen in Lamb's Conduit Street, but remember, it wasn't me that told you."

I meant to tell Mama that very evening, but the impulse died, as usual, in the face of her leaden indifference, and I was afraid, besides, of getting Mrs. Greaves into trouble. And so, at breakfast the next morning, I asked Papa what spiritualism was, saying I had heard someone mention it at school. I was now considered old enough to breakfast in the dining room, provided I did not speak whilst Papa was reading *The Times;* Mama had not been joining us since Dr. Warburton prescribed her a stronger sleeping-draught.

"Primitive superstition in modern dress," he replied, and opened his newspaper with a disapproving rattle; it was the nearest I had come to seeing him angry. I had already begun to suspect that Papa did not believe in God. He had made no objection when I ceased to attend church after Annie left us, and soon after this I discovered that the book he had been writing for so long was called *Rational Foundations of Morality.* Its purpose, so far as I could gather from the snippets he let fall, was to prove that you ought to be good even if you did not believe that you would burn in torment forever if you were bad; I often wondered why something so obvious needed a book to prove it, but never dared say so. And when next I tried to question Mrs. Greaves about spiritualism, she changed the subject, much as Annie had done with the foundlings. But the idea that the spirits of the dead were all around us, separated only by the thinnest of veils, became part of my private mythology, along with the gods and goddesses of the Underworld.

I remained at Miss Hale's school until I was almost sixteen, growing up in a kind of limbo state in which I was free to read whatever I wished, and walk wherever I wanted, whilst at the same time feeling that nobody would care if I vanished from the face of the earth. My freedom set me apart from the other girls, and since I could not invite any of them to our house, I was seldom invited to theirs. Mama's spirits did not improve; if anything she became more desolate and lethargic as the years passed, dragging herself around the house—which she no longer left at all, even to visit Alma's grave—as if she were being slowly crushed beneath an invisible weight.

Violet gave notice at last, a few months before I left Miss Hale's, and was replaced, on Mrs. Greaves's recommendation, by Lettie, a quick, intelligent girl not much older than myself. Lettie's mother had died when she was twelve and she had been in service ever since. Though she spoke like a London girl, she had Irish and Spanish blood on her father's side, and her skin was quite dark, as were her eyes, which were large and heavy-lidded, with long, curling lashes. Her long fingers were roughened and callused by years of scrubbing, though she rubbed them with pumice every day. I liked her from the first, and would often help her with the dusting and polishing, simply for an excuse to talk. On Saturday afternoons she would join her friends—mostly servants like herself from houses around Holborn and Clerkenwell—in St. George's Gardens and they would go on excursions together; I often wished that I could accompany them.

My life continued in this desultory fashion until one morning at breakfast, when, without the slightest warning, my father announced that he was leaving us. "It is high time you left school," he said to me, or rather to his plate, for he avoided my eyes whilst speaking. "You are old enough now to keep house for your mother, and I must have peace and quiet until I have finished my book. So I am going to Honoria—my sister in Cambridge. I have arranged for you to draw an allowance from the bank, sufficient to maintain this house as at present, and also to provide you with a subscription to Mudie's, though many of my books will remain, and you may have the use of them; I am taking only my working library."

I knew from this that he was never coming back; I had several times begged for a subscription, only to be told that we could not afford it.

"But Papa," I said, "I already keep house for you"—he had been giving me the housekeeping money every Thursday morning for a year or more—"and how could your life be any more peaceful in Cambridge than here?"

Light flashed from the lenses of his pince-nez. "I am sure you know what I mean," he replied, "and I do not think anything is to be gained from further discussion. I have let you have your way in many things, Constance, and you will kindly oblige me in this. I have informed Miss Hale that you will be leaving at the end of this term; she will speak to you about it today."

He folded his paper neatly, rose to his feet, and was gone before I could ask him whether he had told Mama.

The day passed in a kind of stupor; I remember Miss Hale—who was very small and stout, so that she resembled a medicine ball on legs—summoning me to her room, but I cannot recall a word of what she said to me. It was only when I came home that afternoon, and heard, on my way upstairs, the muffled sound of sobbing from Mama's room, that the full horror of my situation struck me. I stood for a small eternity upon the landing, willing the sobs to cease, before I crept on up to my own room.

I had given very little thought to the future, beyond daydreams in which, at the end of my time at school, I would marry an intrepid explorer and travel the world with him, while Mama and Papa went on as they had always done. Now I saw that my father had planned this all along: I would be imprisoned here for the term of my mother's life, unless I could harden my heart enough to abandon her as he was doing. And even that I could not do until I was twenty-one, and able to seek a situation on my own behalf.

Lettie and Mrs. Greaves, though full of sympathy for me, were not nearly as shocked at Papa's desertion as I would have liked. Mrs. Greaves said it was a miracle he had stayed so long, and Lettie remarked that at least he hadn't thrown us all into the street, as her own father had done. And perhaps, said Mrs. Greaves, I could persuade my mother to join the Holborn Spiritualist Society once my father was safely out of the house; it might be just what she needed to cheer her up. Lettie and I exchanged glances at this; Lettie had told me privately that Mrs. Veasey, who sometimes presided at the séances in Lamb's Conduit Street, was given to pumping servants for information about her sitters.

At last I summoned the courage to go upstairs again and knock at my mother's door. I found her crouched on a little low chair that she kept just inside the entrance to Alma's room. Her eyes were swollen from weeping, and she looked so old and shrunken that my conscience smote me. I knelt and put my arm around her stiff, unresponsive shoulders.

"Your father has told you, then?" she said in a low, desolate monotone.

"Yes, Mama."

"It is my punishment."

"For what, Mama?"

"For letting Alma die."

"But Mama, you could not have saved her. And Alma is in Heaven now; you will be with her again one day."

"If only I could be *sure*," she whispered.

"Mama, how can you doubt it? She was an innocent child; how could she not go straight to Heaven?"

"I meant, that there *is* a Heaven."

The idea came to me with the echo of my own question to Mrs. Greaves: Instead of trying to persuade Mama to join the Society, I would summon Alma's spirit myself.

The following morning I avoided my father by breakfasting in the kitchen, and when I came home from school, he was gone. Lettie told me that he had not gone to the Museum that day; two men with a cartload of boxes had arrived at half past nine to pack at my father's direction, and by two he was on his way to St. Pancras. Dr. Warburton had called half an hour later. My father had left me a letter on the hall table; it consisted entirely of instructions except for the final sentence, which read: "You need not write to me except in an emergency. Your affec^{t} father, Theo. Langton."

I do not remember feeling anything at all; I went numbly up to my room and began to rehearse for my séance, watching myself in the mirror through half-closed eyes and trying to recall how Alma used to sound. All that would come was a vague impression of her chanting nonsense words to the tunes of hymns; and I could not tell whether it was a true memory, or something Mama had told me, or a confused recollection of something I had done myself.

My mother seemed less desolate that evening; I wondered if Dr. Warburton had given her a sedative. Sitting in the chair opposite hers, I closed my eyes and allowed myself to drift in the warmth of the fire. Then I began to sing in a thin, piping voice, making up sounds to the tune of "All Things Bright and Beautiful," until I heard my mother speak, in a voice trembling with emotion.

"Alma?"

"Yes, Mama," I replied, in the same childish pipe, keeping my eyes closed.

"Alma, is it really you?"

"Yes, Mama."

"Where are you?"

"Here, Mama. The angel said I could come to you."

"Why could you not come before, my darling? It broke my heart to lose you."

I had not expected the question, and did not know how to reply.

"I wish you would not be sad, Mama," I said at last, "because I am happy in Heaven, and one day you will see me and we will never be parted again."

"Soon, I pray. My life here is a torment; I wish it were over."

"You must try to be happy, Mama," I repeated helplessly. "It makes me sad to see you cry."

"Do you see me all the time, my darling?"

"Yes, Mama."

"Then *why* could you not come before?"

"I could not find the way," I lisped, and to avoid any more questions began to sing again, letting my voice trail gradually away and my breathing slow. A few moments later, I pretended to wake with a start, and opened my eyes to find Mama staring at me in a way I had never seen before.

"I think I have been asleep, Mama; I dreamed of Alma."

"No, child, you were in a trance; Alma was speaking through you."

"What is a trance?" I asked innocently.

"It is—what spiritualists do—I wanted to try, but *he* forbade it—he said he would leave me if I ever went near a séance—and now he has left me anyway—" she choked, and burst into raw, noisy sobbing. I went and put my arms around her, and felt, for the first time in all the years since Alma died, an answering pressure, and my tears mingled with her own.

———

I went to bed that night happier than I could remember, thinking that Mama was at last emerging into the light. But the very next evening she wanted me to resume my trance; I said that I did not know how I had done it, but would try. As I pretended to fall asleep, I struggled to think of something new to say, but could summon only vague images of white-robed figures bathed in golden light. What were people supposed to *do* in Heaven, apart from singing and playing the harp? Mrs. Greaves had spoken of Summerland; perhaps Heaven would be like a perfect summer's day in the country, with Alma riding a celestial pony through fields of beautiful flowers. But if Alma was still only two, waiting for Mama to arrive in Heaven so as not to miss any of her growing up, she would surely be too small for a pony, even a celestial one. . . . In the end I abandoned the attempt and opened my eyes, to see the familiar look of desolation settling over her face.

"Did Alma not come to you?" I asked.

She shook her head wearily.

"But Mama, you *know* now that she is safe in Heaven; you must not be sad anymore."

"But how can I be *sure*? Perhaps you were talking in your sleep—if only I could hear her voice again . . ."

I looked at her with a sinking heart. "I do not know how it happened, Mama, but I will try again tomorrow," I said at last, and soon after excused myself and went upstairs to my room. Already I could feel the black cloud of her misery rising to engulf me, but I knew I could not sustain the deception alone. And so, the following afternoon, I plucked up my courage and went round to Lamb's Conduit Street, where I walked up and down until I discovered a door marked "Holborn Spiritualist Society" in faded gold lettering, set into the wall next to a milliner's shop. I stood irresolute for so long that the milliner came out and, when I said I wished to see Mrs. Veasey, directed me to another house farther down the street. There a maidservant who looked no more than ten asked me to wait, and after a while a stout grey-haired woman, dressed entirely in black, came out to greet me.

"And what might you be wanting, my dear?" she said, in an accent that reminded me a little of Annie's. I began to explain, very hesitantly, about Alma and Mama, whereupon she suggested that we should walk up to the Foundling Hospital, where she liked to sit and watch the children. Something in the way she said it made me wonder if she, too, had lost a child, but when I ventured to ask, she said no, she had never had any. Her husband, a sea captain, had been drowned off the West Indies nearly twenty years ago.

"He still comes to me sometimes," she said. "But spirits can't be commanded, you know."

She sighed and patted my hand; a plain, motherly woman quite unlike my imagination of a spirit medium. As we walked, I told her of Papa's departure, and how he had forbidden us to have anything to do with spiritualism, and by the time we were seated by the statue of the angel, I had resolved to trust her entirely, even as far as my pretence at summoning Alma.

"I know it was wrong to deceive her," I said, "but Mama has been so unhappy for so long, and if only she could be certain that Alma is safe in Heaven, I think she might recover."

"You mustn't reproach yourself, my dear. For all you know, it was your sister's spirit moving you to speak; you might have the true gift and not know it yet."

"How would I know if I did?" I asked uneasily.

"You feel . . . taken up . . . they are so strong, sometimes, you think they will shake you to pieces. And then when they leave you, emptied out . . . like a vessel used and thrown away. . . . When I was young, like you, I was filled with their light . . . now they hardly come to me at all. But you never forget, my dear, you never forget."

She patted my hand again and sighed deeply, and I found tears pricking my own eyes.

"But if they don't come to you—" I ventured. Mrs. Veasey did not immediately reply. On the other side of the railings, the foundling girls were gathered about the yard in two and threes and fours, or playing at jump-rope; they might have been the very same girls that Annie and I had watched ten years before.

"We must help people believe," she said at last, "like your poor Mama. There isn't a medium in London who doesn't pretend, sometimes, and how can it be wrong to bring comfort to them that mourn?"

"And—do people have to pay to come to your séances?"

"Goodness no, my dear; we take up a small collection afterwards, and those that can afford it, give what they can. But no one in need is ever turned away."

"Mrs. Veasey," I said after a pause, "have you ever *seen* a spirit?"

"No, my dear, not with these eyes. The gift didn't take me that way. But you know, my dear, there's something about you . . . I shouldn't be at all surprised if you were chosen."

"But I don't *want* to be chosen," I said, "only for Mama to be happy again."

"That's a sign of a true gift, my dear, not wanting it. And as for your Mama, why don't you bring her to our meeting tomorrow?"

"Mama has not left the house for years," I said, "but I should like to come to you myself, if I may."

At half past six the following evening, therefore, I let myself out of the house, telling Mama that I had a headache and needed to walk. She had sunk further toward her old blank misery, but I did not want to risk another summoning until I had seen how Mrs. Veasey conducted a séance. It was the first week of June, and still broad daylight, but the evening chill was already upon the air. The Society's door was open; I went on up a narrow staircase, as Mrs. Veasey had told me, and into a dim, panelled room in which the curtains were already drawn. The only furniture was a large circular table, around which half a dozen people were already seated, including Mrs. Veasey, who sat with her back to a small fire of coals. She greeted me warmly, introduced me to the circle, and invited me to sit opposite her, between a Mr. Ayrton, whose wife was on the other side of him, and an elderly woman called Miss Rutledge. There was also another middle-aged couple, Mr. and Mrs. Bachelor, and Mr. Carmichael, an immensely fat man whose several chins spilled out onto a vast expanse of waistcoat. He had moist, pale eyes, and wheezed softly as he breathed.

These people, as I would learn, were Mrs. Veasey's regular sitters. Several others appeared during the next few minutes until the last place at the table had been taken, whereupon Mr. Ayrton rose and shut the door. He then invited us to join hands and sing "Abide with Me," which we did rather discordantly, along with several other hymns, whilst Mrs. Veasey slumped lower in her chair and appeared to doze.

Mrs. Veasey had told me about spirit controls, but I was still startled when she began to speak in a gruff man's voice, greeted by Mr. Ayrton as "Captain Veasey." The messages were commonplace but affecting; Mr. Carmichael, for instance, was told that Lucy was watching over him, as always, and that his "present difficulty" would resolve itself very soon, whereupon he gave a great wheezing sigh, almost a sob, and bowed his head. Everyone in the circle received a message, and I saw how the sitters hung upon every word. The message for me was "Alma says you have done right," and even though I knew that Mrs. Veasey's trance was feigned—indeed, I thought her left eye-lid quivered very slightly as she (or rather the Captain) spoke—it still brought a lump to my throat.

She had ceased to speak, and I thought the séance had ended, when her eyes, which had been closed throughout the performance, flew open, apparently fixed upon an invisible object floating somewhere above the table.

"Alma," said the Captain's harsh voice, "Alma will speak through Constance."

There was a collective gasp from the sitters; the hair rose upon the back of my neck. Mrs. Veasey started violently, and seemed to become conscious of her surroundings.

"Miss Langton," she said hoarsely, "you must do as he bids. Close your eyes, and summon the image of your sister."

Her voice was urgent, peremptory; I could not tell whether she was feigning or not. I closed my eyes, feeling my companions' hands trembling in mine, and tried to fix my mind upon Alma. After a little I became aware of a faint buzzing vibration, running up my arms and through my body.

"I can feel the power," said Mrs. Veasey. "Is there anybody here?"

It is only pins and needles, I told myself fearfully, willing the vibration to stop. But it seemed to me that words were welling up in my throat, threatening to choke me if I did not speak, and to forestall the sensation I began to chant in my Alma-voice, as I had done the other evening, sounds to the tune of "All Things Bright and Beautiful," and slowly the tension relaxed, and my hands ceased to tremble.

"Alma," said Mrs. Veasey, "tell us why you have come." The hoarseness had left her voice.

"For Mama," I piped.

"You have a message for your Mama?"

"Tell Mama"—I paused, thinking rapidly—"tell Mama . . . safe in Heaven. Tell Mama to come here."

"We shall. And—would you like to speak to anyone else?"

I did not reply, but lapsed back into my chanting, letting it gradually die away, and a few moments later pretended to wake.

Three days later, my mother emerged blinking into the light. Though she was not yet sixty, she might have been my great-grandmother, clad in a frayed mourning-dress of rusty brown and clinging tightly to my arm. Her expression, as she gazed about her, was bewildered but strangely incurious, and I became aware that she could not actually see the things I was pointing at; she had grown so shortsighted that her world had shrunk to a circle a few feet across.

Mrs. Veasey had told me privately that she felt sure Alma would want to speak through me again, and thus it proved. I felt my mother's hand quivering in mine as I began to sing in my Alma-voice, and though she asked more or less the same questions, and received more or less the same answers, as on the first evening in the drawing room, she was still in tears of joy when the performance ended. We remained for some time afterward talking to Mr. and Mrs. Ayrton, who had lost both their sons to the cholera, and I invited them to tea the following week, thinking that all would be well.

And so for a while it seemed. Mama remained obsessed with Alma to the exclusion of all else—she refused to be fitted with spectacles on the ground that there was nothing she needed to see—but I was so delighted to see her in company, I did not care that the talk was all of bereavements in this world and joyful reunions in the next. The Society met twice a week, and in between séances I would sometimes sit with Mrs. Veasey on the bench outside the Foundling Hospital. There she would instruct me in the arts of mediumship, always on the understanding that we were simply helping the spirits in their task, and suggest messages that Alma might give to other sitters. I came to realise that she had chosen me as her successor, though I was never sure of her motives, just as I was never quite certain whether she believed or not: I suspect that, like me, she had had glimpses of a power, fleeting and uncertain, coming upon you when you least expected it.

There was, she insisted, an affinity between us; but I was aware, too, that we were bound by our mutual confidences; neither could afford to expose the other, and I sometimes wondered if this was why she had chosen me. I noticed, too, that the contributions increased as our partnership developed; all of the money, of course, went to Mrs. Veasey, but though my conscience often troubled me, the deception did not seem wicked, since it was done for Mama's sake. Our Society was far from grand; it admitted both impoverished gentry and respectable women of the housekeeping class, people on the fringe of their station. Most of the sitters, including, of course, Mama, were eager, if not determined, to believe whatever the medium told them, and with Mrs. Veasey's assistance I began to gain a reputation, which was both exhilarating and alarming. I enjoyed, I confess, the power it conferred upon me, to have grown men and women hanging upon my words. And sometimes—though I was never sure of it—I felt that my feigned trance was becoming a real one. Sounds would grow louder: The creaking of the coals in the grate, the faint whistle of Mr. Carmichael's asthmatic breathing, until the blood seemed to wash and boom in my ears, and then the sounds would begin to shape themselves into words, or rather the shadow of words, like conversation heard a long way off. And yet the more I practised, the less I believed in anything like the realm of spirits we invoked with such assurance.

I had hoped that Mama would be content with regular messages from Alma, but as the autumn advanced and the days grew shorter, the old haunted look crept back into her eyes. Hearing Alma's voice was no longer proof enough; my mother wanted to see, to touch, to hold her, and having learned from the other sitters that there were mediums who could make spirits visible, she began to wonder aloud why I would not take her to see one. Mrs. Veasey disapproved of manifestations; the use of the cabinet, she would declare in righteous tones, was a sure sign of trickery. This was not an argument I wished to pursue with Mama; I thought of contriving a message from Alma along the lines of "Blessed are they that have not seen, and yet have believed," but I doubted whether it would subdue her craving. And so I decided to attend a manifestation séance myself, in the hope that I might stumble upon someone who could present a convincing Alma to my mother's fading sight.

Several members of our circle had spoken, though not within Mrs. Veasey's hearing, of a Miss Carver, whose sittings were held in her father's house in Marylebone High Street. Katie Carver was said to be very pretty, and capable of summoning not only her "control," an equally attractive spirit by the name of Arabella Morse, but a whole troop of them. Only after I had secured my place at a sitting, and handed over a guinea ("for charitable causes"), did it strike me that I should have given a false name. Miss Lester, the young woman who had taken my money, showed me into a dimly lit room furnished, like our own in Lamb's Conduit Street, with a large circular table, but richly carpeted. Candles burned upon the table and within an alcove in the far corner. The alcove was about six feet square, with heavy curtains draped from the ceiling to the floor, tied back at the front to show that there was nothing inside except a plain upright chair.

When all the places had been taken (there were, I think, about fifteen of us), Miss Carver herself appeared, and all the gentlemen rose to their feet and bowed. She was certainly pretty; small and buxom and fair, with her hair plaited and wound about her head, and clad in a plain white muslin gown. Miss Lester introduced us one by one; the sitters were more elaborately and expensively dressed than Mrs. Veasey's, but the only name I would recall was that of Mr. Thorne, a tall, fair-haired young man sitting across the table from me. Something in his expression—a hint of sardonic amusement?—attracted my attention, and I noticed that Miss Carver looked very hard at him when his turn came to be introduced.

I knew that in these séances, the medium sat within the cabinet, but I was surprised when, at a signal from Miss Carver, several of the gentlemen (but not Mr. Thorne) accompanied her to the alcove and watched while Miss Lester, using what appeared to be silk scarves, tied her securely to the chair. The knots were examined; the gentlemen returned to their places; Miss Lester extinguished the light in the cabinet, drew the curtains, and asked us all to join hands. "You must not break the circle unless a spirit invites you to," she said. "The manifestations are a great strain for Miss Carver, and she may be harmed if you do not do exactly as instructed." She then invited us to sing "O God, Our Help in Ages Past," took up the candelabra, and went quietly from the room, leaving us in complete darkness.

We had sung perhaps half a dozen hymns, led by a strong baritone voice somewhere on my right, when I became aware of a faint glow from the direction of the cabinet. It brightened into a luminous halo, hovering around the outline of a head, and seemed to unfurl downward into the figure of a woman, veiled in draperies of light. She glided away from the cabinet and began a circuit of the table. As she came nearer I could see the movement of her limbs beneath the veil, and then the gleam of eyes and the suggestion of a smile. Her effect was manifest in the quickened breathing of my companions.

"Arabella," said a male voice from the darkness to my left, "will you come to me?"

She passed behind my chair, trailing a distinct odour of perfume (and, I thought, of flesh), and drifted closer to the table until the man who had spoken was faintly illuminated by the glow of her robes. Then she kissed the top of his bald head, prompting a deep sigh from the audience before she glided away again. She had gone about three-quarters of the way round when I heard a muffled exclamation and the scrape of a chair, and another light floated up from the darkness in front of her: a small phial of radiance, lighting up the face of Mr. Thorne as he stretched out his other hand and grasped the retreating spirit by the wrist.

"There is no need to struggle, Miss Carver," he said drily. "My name is Vernon Raphael, from the Society for Psychical Research. Would you care to explain yourself to the company?"

The room was suddenly in uproar. My hands were released, chairs were overthrown, and several matches flared, showing Mr. Thorne—or, rather, Mr. Raphael—holding at arm's length a very angry Miss Carver, whose stays and drawers were plainly visible beneath diaphanous layers of what appeared to be butter muslin. A second later, she had torn herself free and darted back into the cabinet, wrenching the curtains closed behind her.

I expected the sitters to drag her out again, but to my astonishment, several of the men seized Vernon Raphael instead, calling his intervention an outrage and a violation and a damned disgrace as they propelled him toward the door. On impulse, I rose and followed them. "All right, all right; I'll go quietly," I heard Vernon Raphael say as they hustled him down the front steps. His hat was flung after him into the street. With no one taking the slightest notice of me, I took my cloak and bonnet from the hall-stand and followed him down the steps. There I waited until I heard the door close behind me; Vernon Raphael was walking slowly away, brushing the dirt from his hat.

He looked at me ruefully as I came up beside him.

"Have you too come to reproach me with cruelty to spirits, Miss, er—?"

"Miss Langton. And no, I have not; I only wanted—"

I paused, wondering what exactly I did want of him. In daylight his hair was straw-coloured, with a reddish tinge; his eyes were an intense, rather cold shade of blue, and his face had a slightly vulpine cast, but I liked the humorous edge to his voice. We began to walk again; it was late in the afternoon, and the street was relatively quiet.

"Are you employed by the Society, Mr. Raphael, to seek out fraud?" Mrs. Veasey had warned me against the Society for Psychical Research; sceptics and unbelievers, she called them, with no respect for the departed.

"Well, yes, in a way; I am one of their professional investigators. And you, Miss Langton? What brings you to Miss Carver's parlour?"

Again I wished I had not revealed my name; what if he were to turn his attentions to Holborn? But then it struck me that we had little to fear, now that I knew him.

"Curiosity," I said. "Do you think, Mr. Raphael, that all spirit mediums are cheats?"

"All manifestation mediums, yes."

"And mental mediums?" I had heard the term from Mrs. Veasey.

He looked at me curiously. "I see you know something of the subject. Some are frauds; the others mostly self-deluded."

"Mostly?"

"Well . . . I am a sceptic, not an out-and-out atheist—not yet, at any rate. Gurney and Myers—you know of them?—have assembled some very remarkable cases; they are looking at subjects who claim to have seen the apparition of a friend or relation at the moment of that person's death, but the verdict is not yet in. And you, Miss Langton? What do you believe?"

"I do not know what I believe, but"—I decided after all to risk it—"my sister died when I was five, and my mother has been prostrate with grief ever since. Frankly, Mr. Raphael, if I could find a medium who could convince her that Alma is safe in Heaven, I would want her to have that comfort. And so I wondered—whether there is anyone you could recommend."

"My business, Miss Langton"—he sounded more amused than indignant—"is to expose frauds, not to recommend them."

"It is all very well for you, Mr. Raphael, who are clever and confident and at home in the world, but for those like my mother, who are simply crushed by the weight of grief, why deprive them of the comfort a séance can bring?"

"Because it is *false* comfort."

"That is a harsh doctrine, Mr. Raphael; a man's creed, if I may say so. Have you never lied, or kept silent, to spare the feelings of another? If you had lost a brother, let us say, and your own mother had been prostrated by grief, would you sternly insist—as my father did—that she take no comfort in séances?"

He looked, to do him justice, a little abashed.

"I confess, Miss Langton, that I should be reluctant to disabuse her. But, to take the other side of the coin, what of those mediums who prey unscrupulously—for monetary gain—upon the bereaved? Do you think they should be allowed free rein?"

"I suppose not," I said reluctantly. "But they are not all like that."

"You speak from experience, evidently."

"Only a little . . . so there is no one, then, that you are prepared to name?"

"Surely, Miss Langton, your mother needs the help of a doctor, not a medium."

"A doctor has been seeing her for the last twelve years, without doing her the slightest good."

"I see . . . The difficulty, Miss Langton, is that if I were to direct you to a known, or even a suspected fraud, I would be breaching my duty to the Society. And besides . . . Miss Carver is generally considered the best in London; you have seen for yourself how zealously her admirers defend her."

"But surely," I said, "after today, her reputation is lost forever."

"Not at all," he said cheerfully. "There will be a furore in the spiritualist press, and some of her followers will fall away, but others will replace them. It is all part of the game."

"Is that how it seems to you?"

His reply was lost in the cry of a street-vendor; we were approaching Oxford Street, and the traffic was increasing.

"Miss Langton," he said, "I was on my way back to the Society's rooms in Westminster, but may I escort you home—if that is where you are going?"

"Thank you, no, I am quite used to walking alone."

"Then—may I hope to see you again?"

"I am sorry," I said, "but that would be quite impossible. Goodbye, Mr. Raphael."

I came home resolved to have no more to do with manifestations, but one glance at my mother, huddled upon the drawing-room sofa with the curtains drawn, was enough to change my mind. Vernon Raphael, at least, would not be allowed back into Miss Carver's circle, and with Mama's desolation filling the house like a miasma, I felt I had nothing to lose. And so I returned next day to Marylebone High Street. Miss Lester, as I thought, had not noticed me leaving, and graciously accepted my professions of sympathy for Miss Carver, as well as a donation of three guineas—my entire savings—to the spiritualist cause. I told her of my mother's plight, and asked whether it was true that spirits could materialise at different ages. If only, I said wistfully,

Mama could hold Alma as she had been in infancy, she might find peace at last. Miss Lester asked me, among other things, if I could recall what scent Mama had used when Alma was still with us; perfumes, she said gravely, could be very helpful in summoning spirits. But of course, she added, Miss Carver would want to meet my mother before the séance. Mr. Raphael's shameful deception had gravely imperilled her health, and so, sadly, they would have to be on their guard against disruptive influences.

At eight in the evening on the following Saturday, I was seated beside my mother in Miss Carver's séance room, covertly studying the other faces around the table. I had tried to persuade Mama of the need for secrecy, so as not to hurt Mrs. Veasey's feelings, but I was not at all sure she had understood, and I watched the last of the sitters being shown to their places with the sensation of having added one storey too many to a house of cards.

Miss Carver was bound to her chair, as before. Miss Lester drew the curtains and invited us to join hands and sing "Lead, Kindly Light," and as the lights were extinguished, I felt my mother's hand trembling in mine. We had just reached the end of "The Lord Is My Shepherd" when a faint haze of light heralded Arabella's appearance. The singing died away; I heard a creak of chairs and a quickening of breath; but this time the light remained formless, floating like a will-o-the-wisp in the void. After a few seconds it began to drift away from me, following, I thought, the circumference of the table, though in that utter blackness I would not have known if the walls had dissolved around us.

Then, from somewhere above my head, a voice began to sing in a thin, piping chant, to the tune of "All Things Bright and Beautiful." I had told Miss Lester about Alma's singing, but I shivered nonetheless, and my mother's hand jerked convulsively.

"Alma?" she cried.

The chanting ceased, and the scent of violet water floated down to us; a scent my mother had not worn since the day Alma died. The faint patch of light stirred and brightened and seemed to open like a flower into the glowing form of Arabella facing us across the table; only this time she was cradling something in her arms. Accompanied by murmurs of amazement, she glided around the room until she was standing directly behind us.

"Alma has come from Heaven to comfort her Mama," said a woman's voice from the darkness overhead, "but she may only stay a little while."

The scent of violet water grew stronger. My mother had already released my hand, though I could see only her outline, turning around in her chair and reaching out her arms toward the small, shimmering form, which stirred faintly as my mother received it; no mere doll, but a real infant in luminous swaddling clothes. "Alma," she murmured, "at last, at last, at last." Someone was weeping in the darkness nearby. Tears sprang to my own eyes, and I had to subdue the impulse to whisper my thanks to Miss Carver, stooped so close between us that I could feel the heat of her body. Thus we remained for perhaps twenty seconds before Miss Carver held out her arms again and my mother, to my surprise, surrendered the child with only a deep sigh, echoed around the table as the glowing figure turned and retreated and vanished into the dark.

My mother smiled and wept by turns as we rattled homeward, thanking me over and over again. "At last," she kept saying, "at last I can rest in peace." I remember embracing Lettie as she opened the door to us; I remember, too, wondering how on earth I was to keep Mama from telling our fellow sitters in Lamb's Conduit Street, and whether I ought even to try; perhaps, after this, we would have no more need of séances. I tried to persuade Mama to take a glass of wine with supper, but she declined. "I am perfectly happy, dear Constance, and not in the least hungry. I shall go to bed now, and dream of Alma." And with that she kissed me and went on upstairs, whilst I went down to the kitchen to sup with Lettie and Mrs. Greaves and tell them as much as I dared, and thence to my own room, where I slept more deeply and peacefully than I had in a long time, and woke with autumn sunlight slanting in through my window. Mama did not come down to breakfast, but that was quite usual; Lettie's custom was to take a tray up at about ten, tap lightly on the door, and leave my mother to fetch it when she would. Thus it was not until eleven had struck that I became uneasy. At last we resolved to force the door with a poker, and found her tucked up in bed with Alma's christening gown held to her breast, and a faint smile on her face. There was an empty bottle of laudanum upon the night table beside her, and a note which read: "Forgive me—I could not wait."

The days that followed are mercifully blurred in memory. I can picture—rather than recall—the feeling of leaden blackness filling my body, as if Mama's torment had descended upon me; I remember, too, the conviction that I would never eat or sleep again, but only lie upon my bed and stare dry-eyed into the dark, wondering what was to become of me, and whether, if I went to the police and confessed what I had done, I would be sent to prison. Yet I said nothing of the séances to Dr. Warburton, or to my father, when he appeared in a state of extreme irritation (it was most inconsiderate of Mama, he all but declared, to poison herself just as he was about to begin work on his second volume) and announced that he was giving up the lease on the house.

We were seated, as with every conversation I had ever had with him, at the breakfast table; he did not seem to notice that I had eaten nothing.

"It is a very great nuisance," he said, "but I suppose you will have to live with us in Cambridge. My sister will find work for you around the house, and for the rest you must try to be quiet and cause no further upheaval."

"But what is to become of Lettie and Mrs. Greaves?"

"They must look for new situations, of course."

"But Papa—"

"Kindly do not interrupt me. They will receive the usual month's wages in lieu of notice, which I consider more than generous, and you may give them references, if you choose. And now I have a great deal of business to conduct, thanks to your mother's—to this unfortunate event—no, not a word further, if you please. I shall not be home until late."

To my surprise, Lettie and Mrs. Greaves took the news philosophically. "We'll be all right, my dear," said Mrs. Greaves, "I know you'll give us good characters; but it won't be much of a life for you, in Cambridge." Indeed I felt that I would as soon go to prison, but I had no spirit to protest. I sent Mrs. Veasey a painfully composed letter, saying that Mama had died and that I would not be able to see her or any of the circle again, and wondering, as I struggled with the wording, how long it would be before Miss Carver's circle intersected with Mrs. Veasey's. And so Mama was buried on a bleak October morning with only my father, Mrs. Greaves, Lettie, and myself at her graveside.

A week or so after the burial, I was folding away my mother's clothes, and wondering what I ought to do with Alma's things, when Lettie came up to tell me that a gentleman was here, asking to see me. My father was out, as usual; he claimed to be run off his feet with the business of closing up the house, but I suspected he was spending most of his time at the Museum. I went numbly downstairs expecting someone to do with books or furniture, and found instead a small, stocky man who seemed vaguely familiar, though I was sure I had never seen him before. He was wearing a green velveteen jacket, rather the worse for wear, and grey flannel trousers with a smear of paint on one knee, and looked to be somewhere between fifty and sixty. His head was bald on top, but surrounded by a mane of grey-brown hair, long and unruly at the sides, so that his ears were almost hidden. Tangled whiskers, a beard and a thick moustache obscured his mouth and much of his cheeks; his eyes were dark brown, the lower lids wrinkled and heavily lined, and his skin—what could be seen of it—was much weathered by the sun.

"Miss Langton? My name is Frederick Price, and I think I must be your uncle; I saw the notice of my sister's—your mother's—death in *The Times*, and came to offer my condolences."

I looked at him wonderingly; now that he had said it, I could see a very faint resemblance to my mother.

"Thank you, sir. I am afraid my father will not be back until late—he is very seldom home. Will you have some tea?"

"I really should not disturb you at such a sad time."

"You would not be disturbing me," I said. His voice was low and slightly hesitant, and something in its cadence appealed to me. "I should welcome a change from my thoughts."

I took him into the drawing room, where many of the ornaments had already been packed up; a half-filled box stood beside the fireplace.

"You must wonder," he said, "why we have never met. The fact is, I lost touch with your mother after she married; I had no idea that she was living in London until I saw the funeral notice the other day.

And—well, to be frank, we were never close, partly because I saw so little of her. I quarrelled with our father, you see; he wanted me to preach, and I wanted to paint, and it ended with his cutting me out of his will, and my running off to Italy before I was twenty-one. Poor Hester was left to look after him, and I suppose she must have resented it—who could blame her?—and then, when our father died I couldn't, or at least didn't, come home. The last letter I had from her was to say she was engaged to be married. I hoped she'd be happy at last. . . . And then I came back to London in '75, and took a house in St. John's Wood, where I've had my studio ever since, never knowing I had a niece living not three miles away."

"And I never knew I had an artist for an uncle."

"More a jack-of-all-trades, I should say. In my time I've been—let me see—an illustrator (which is how I make most of my living), a copyist, an engraver, a draughtsman, and a restorer, as well as a painter, of sorts . . . Was it a long illness?—your mother, forgive me."

"Yes, but not in the way you . . . the truth is . . ." And with that I was launched upon my story. He listened gravely and without surprise, even when I came to the séances, and I managed somehow to reach the end without breaking down.

"And so you see, sir—though my father does not know it—I am the cause of my mother's death."

"You judge yourself too harshly," he replied. "From everything you say, the wonder is that she did not choose to end her life long before this. Yours was a generous action, and you ought not reproach yourself."

I did weep, at that, but I saw that it made him most uncomfortable, and controlled myself as soon as I could.

"And now," he said, "you go with your father to your aunt in Cambridge?"

"I have never met her. They don't want me, and I would far rather not, but yes, I must."

"I see." He was silent for a while.

"Constance—if I may"—he said at last—"I am a bachelor—and I know myself well enough to say that I am a selfish man. I like my quiet, and my comforts, and the certainty that I can go to my studio after breakfast and not be disturbed for the next ten hours. I have a cook and a maid, both excellent women, but they will sometimes bother me with questions. Now, if I had someone to keep house for me; someone who would study my likes and dislikes and see that everything ran smoothly—a quiet, reserved young woman, let us say—and especially if her father were disposed to make her an allowance, for I am frankly not well off . . . it wouldn't be an onerous task, and the house is large enough for you to have your own quarters. . . ."

A week later, I was installed in my uncle's house in Elsworthy Walk. I was so relieved not to be going to Cambridge that I should have been glad of a bed in the cellar; to find myself in a room on the top floor, looking eastward up the grassy slope of Primrose Hill, seemed altogether miraculous. The dining table was always strewn with books and papers; my uncle's idea of comfort was being able to leave things exactly where he wanted, and he was happy for us both to read at meals: sometimes a whole day would pass without our exchanging more than "good morning" and "good night." At first I could not leave the house without fearing that I would run into someone from Mrs. Veasey's or Miss Carver's circles, but I never did, and my uncle never referred to the séances again. Instead of the Foundling Hospital, I had Primrose Hill, and often that autumn I would sit by my window and watch the children at play, finding an obscure comfort in the sight.

But even in this tranquil setting, it was many months before the burden of guilt and self-reproach began to lighten, only to be displaced by an increasing restlessness of spirit. My housekeeping duties were indeed far from onerous, leaving me with a great deal of time on my hands. My uncle, I soon realised, shrank from any display of emotion; not, I think, from any essential coldness, but because he feared its effect upon him. From certain things he let fall, I came to suspect that his conscience sometimes troubled him about his neglect of his family, especially my mother, whom he could have traced easily enough, and that taking me in had been his way of making amends. He seemed to like having me in the house; it gave him someone to talk to when he wished to talk, and left him to his own thoughts when he did not, and if he sensed my trouble, he gave no sign of it.

I could not, in any case, have told him what my trouble was. I was accustomed to solitude, and did not miss—or did not think I missed—the society of people my own age; I had no particular talent or ambition, and certainly no desire to marry. And yet there was *something* I craved, a nameless, faceless yearning that could only be assuaged by walking for hours at a time in all kinds of weather, until I knew every street in the district, all the way to the edge of Hampstead, where the houses gave way to lanes and fields. But I never went back to Holborn.

In the end I found a situation as day-governess to the children of a Captain Tremenheere, who was serving with the Royal Horse Artillery at the barracks on Ordnance Hill. My uncle was a little put out by this, but as I reminded him, my allowance from my father would end soon enough, and I could not live upon his charity. I was happier for the occupation, and grew very fond of my three pupils, and yet the restlessness remained; I could not shake off the feeling that I was sleepwalking through my days, waiting for my real life—whatever that might be—to begin.

In the spring of 1888, my father died suddenly of a stroke. I had the news in a letter from my aunt, who wrote that he had left everything to her, with instructions to continue my allowance until I came of age the following January. She did not invite me to attend the funeral, nor did I wish to; I knew that I had meant nothing to him, and grieved, I think, for my own lack of feeling, rather than for the man I had scarcely known.

The ensuing summer was so cold and wet that it scarcely merited the name, and the autumn was overshadowed by the continuing news of the atrocities in Whitechapel. My solitary walks were curtailed; I no longer felt at ease beyond the boundaries of St. John's Wood; and then in December Captain Tremenheere was posted to Aldershot, taking his family with him. My twenty-first birthday had passed without my finding another situation, until one morning after breakfast, whilst I was idly browsing through the personal column in *The Times*, I came upon the following advertisement:

> **If Constance Mary Langton, daughter of the late Hester Jane Langton (née Price), formerly of Bartram's Court, Holborn, will contact Montague and Venning, Commissioners for Oaths, at their offices in Wentworth Road, Aldeburgh, she may learn something to her advantage.**

I had imagined that all would be revealed in Mr. Montague's reply, but his letter merely requested "such proofs as may readily be furnished" that I was indeed the Constance Mary Langton in question. My uncle joked, as he drafted a statement to this effect, that for all he knew I might simply have wandered into the house in Bartram's Court on the day he happened to call—a remark which troubled me more than he realised. I was also required to give the date and place of my birth—for the latter I could only put "in the country near

Cambridge"—and to say whether I had any sisters "or other close female relatives" living, to which I replied that to the best of my knowledge I had none. In response to this, I received a note from Mr. Montague, saying that he would be coming up to London in a few days' time, and would like to call upon me, whenever might be convenient, "regarding a bequest." My uncle thought from the wording of the advertisement that the legacy must have come from someone on my mother's side, but could shed no further light; he had never taken much interest in their history. Most likely, he warned me, it would be a small sum of money, or a few decrepit pieces of furniture, willed to my mother by some forgotten aunt or cousin. But the prospect had reawakened my childhood fancy that there might be some mystery about my birth. I had never mentioned this to my uncle, and was secretly relieved when he declined to attend the interview, saying that it was my own business, now that I was of age; he could always be fetched from his studio if he were needed.

Mr. Montague came to see me on a freezing January morning; I was standing by the window when the maid showed him into the drawing room, and he paused as the door closed behind him, seemingly struck by something in my appearance. He was tall and spare, and slightly stooped, with grey hair receding markedly at the temples. His face was lined as if by suffering or illness; his skin had a greyish tinge, and there were dark shadows like bruises beneath his eyes. He might have been anywhere between fifty and seventy, and yet there was an air of diffidence, even of apprehension about him as I extended my hand—his own was icy cold—and invited him to take a seat by the fire.

"I wonder, Miss Langton," he began, "whether the name Wraxford means anything to you." His voice was low and cultivated, with a faint burr to it.

"Nothing at all, sir."

"I see."

He regarded me in silence for a moment, and then nodded, as if confirming something to himself.

"Very well. I am here, Miss Langton, because a client of mine, a Miss Augusta Wraxford, died some months ago, leaving the bulk of her estate to 'my nearest surviving female relation.' And assuming—forgive me—that you are indeed Constance Mary Langton, and the granddaughter, on your late mother's side, of Maria Lovell and William Lloyd Price, then you are the principal beneficiary of Augusta Wraxford's will, and sole heir to Wraxford Hall."

He sounded as if he were preparing me for news of some grave misfortune.

"The estate consists of a derelict manor house—very large, but quite uninhabitable—on several hundred acres of woodland near the Suffolk coast. The property is heavily encumbered, and will yield, at best, two thousand pounds after the creditors have been satisfied—"

"Two thousand pounds!" I exclaimed.

"I must warn you," he said, in the same troubled tone, "that it will not be easy to find a buyer. Wraxford Hall has a very dark history. But before we come to that, I am obliged to ask you certain questions—though I confess, Miss Langton, that I have only to look at you . . . the resemblance is quite remarkable—"

He broke off suddenly, as if shocked by what he had just said.

"The resemblance . . . ?" I prompted.

"Forgive me, it is only . . . May I ask, Miss Langton, whether you take after your mother? In appearance, I mean?"

"No, sir. My mother was barely five feet tall, and—I do not think I favour her at all. May I ask in turn, sir, how you came to know of my existence?"

"From the notice of your mother's death in *The Times*. Miss Wraxford had instructed me to trace the female line, which proved a long and difficult task; I had got as far as the notice of your parents' marriage, but after that, the trail went cold until my clerk—who goes through all the papers every morning—brought in that death notice. But I was not at liberty to approach you then. Miss Wraxford felt that expectations were bad for the character; and of course, so long as she was alive, there was always the possibility that she might change her will. And by the time she did die, your former house had changed hands several times—hence our advertisement."

He was silent for a moment, gazing into the fire.

"You said in your letter," he resumed, "that you were born somewhere near Cambridge, but you do not know exactly where?"

"No, sir."

"And you have no record of your birth?"

"I am afraid not, sir; it may be amongst my father's papers, with my aunt in Cambridge."

"It is possible that none exists; there is no entry in the register at Somerset House—but it was not then mandatory," he added, seeing the change in my expression, "to notify the Registrar, so you need not be alarmed on that score."

Once again he paused, studying me without seeming to be aware that he was doing so. Despite—or perhaps because of—his talk of a resemblance, I was becoming more apprehensive with every question. Did he suspect—or even possess some evidence—that I was not my parents' child? Should I reveal my own suspicions? I might lose a fortune by speaking out, but to remain silent would surely be wrong, perhaps even criminal. My thought was interrupted by Dora tapping at the door with the tea-tray, and for the next several minutes

I was obliged to make uneasy small-talk, whilst trying to decide what I should do.

"Sir, before you continue," I said as soon as the door had closed behind her, "I think I ought to tell you . . . I have sometimes wondered whether I might have been a foster child—a foundling. My—My parents never said, but it would explain—certain things about my childhood—and if I am not their child by blood, then—"

I broke off, alarmed by Mr. Montague's reaction. What little colour he possessed had drained from his features; his cup rattled against his saucer, and he was obliged to set it down.

"Forgive me, Miss Langton—a momentary indisposition. Are you willing to tell me how you came to this conclusion—to consider the possibility, I mean?"

And so I launched into the story of Alma's death, and my mother's collapse, my walks with Annie by the Foundling Hospital and my father's utter indifference, but leaving out the séances, wondering all the time what had so shaken Mr. Montague. Though the fire was scarcely keeping the cold at bay, I noticed a faint sheen of perspiration on his forehead, and every so often, though he did his best to conceal it, he would wince, as if in pain. He asked various questions, most of which I was quite unable to answer, about my parents' lives before they had married—I did not even know where or how they had met—the sources of my father's income, and whether I had any memories at all of the time before we moved to London.

"None, sir; none that I am sure of."

"I see . . . Let me say at once, Miss Langton, that even if your suspicions were proven, the bequest would stand. You are your mother's legitimate daughter according to law, and that is all that the law requires. And besides . . ."

"Mr. Montague," I ventured, when he did not immediately continue, "you have spoken of a resemblance, and intimated—at least, my heart divines—that you know something which touches upon my suspicions about my birth. Will you not tell me what it is?"

Still he kept silent, as if caught up in some inner debate, glancing from me to the glow of the fire and back again. Pale grey light slanted through the window; the glass was streaked with tears of condensation.

"Miss Langton," he said at last, "I assure you, I know nothing of your history beyond what you have told me. What you divine is—only the wildest of fancies on my part. No—the best advice I can give you is to sell the estate, sight unseen, enjoy whatever wealth it brings you, and let the name of Wraxford vanish from memory."

"But how can I be certain of that," I persisted, emboldened by his hesitation, "if you will not tell me what you suspect—or whom you think that I resemble?"

He seemed more struck by this than I would have expected, and resumed his communion with the flames.

"I confess, Miss Langton," he said finally, "that I do not know how to answer you. You must allow me time to reflect; I shall write to you within the week." And soon after that he took his leave.

My uncle was naturally astounded by the news, but the name Wraxford meant nothing to him, beyond vague associations with some ancient crime or scandal, and the weather remained so bitter that the streets were mired with frozen slush, whilst the hours dragged by in an endless round of speculation until, on the fourth morning after Mr. Montague's visit, a stoutly wrapped parcel arrived for me by registered mail. It contained another package, also sealed; a brief letter, and a chart of the Wraxford genealogy, drawn in the same small, precise hand.

20th Jany 1889

Dear Miss Langton,

You have trusted me with your secret, and I have resolved to trust you with mine. I sealed this packet nearly twenty years ago, and have not opened it since. As you will see, I am placing my reputation in your hands, but I find I do not greatly care. My health is failing; I shall shortly retire from practise; and if anyone has a right to these papers, it is you. When you have read them, you will understand why I say to you: sell the Hall unseen; burn it to the ground and plough the earth with salt, if you will; but never live there.

Yours most sincerely,

John Montague

Part Two

John Montague's Narrative

30 December 1870

I have at last resolved to set down everything I know of the strange and terrible events at Wraxford Hall, in the hope of appeasing my conscience, which has never ceased to trouble me. A fitting enough night for such a decision, for it is bitter cold, and the wind howls about the house as if it will never cease. I shrink from what I must reveal of my own history, but if anyone is ever to understand why I acted as I did—and why else attempt this?—I must not withhold anything of relevance, no matter how painful. I shall feel easier in my mind, I trust, knowing that if the case is ever reopened after I am gone, this account may help uncover the truth about the Wraxford Mystery.

I first met Magnus Wraxford in the spring of 1866—my thirtieth year—in my capacity as solicitor to his uncle Cornelius, a trust I had inherited from my father. Ours was a small family firm in the town of Aldeburgh, and I had followed my father as he had followed his. Like every boy growing up in that part of Suffolk, I had heard tales of Wraxford Hall, which lies at the heart of Monks' Wood, about seven miles to the south of Aldeburgh as the crow flies, but a good deal farther by road. Old Cornelius Wraxford had lived there in complete seclusion for as long as anyone could remember, attended by a handful of servants seemingly chosen for their taciturn qualities, for there appeared to be little else to recommend them, whilst the house slowly decayed around him and the wilderness reclaimed the park. Even poachers avoided the place, for Monks' Wood was said to be haunted by—as one might expect—the ghost of a monk; according to local legend, anyone who saw the apparition would die within the month. Cornelius, besides, was rumoured to keep a pack of dogs so savage they would tear you to pieces if they caught you. Some said that the old miser was guarding an immense hoard of gold and precious stones; others maintained that he had sold his soul to the Devil in exchange for the gift of flight, or the cloak of invisibility, or some such diabolical attribute. Then there was William Brent the poacher, who used to boast that he could hunt as close as he liked to the Hall without arousing the dogs, until the night he saw a malignant face peering down at him from an upstairs window, and was dead within a month; of pleurisy, admittedly, but all the same . . . My father scoffed at the rumours, but could shed no light of his own, as he had met Cornelius only once, at the office, several years before I was born. Even then, he said, Cornelius had looked like an old man; small, wizened and suspicious. All of their business thereafter had been conducted by letter.

As I grew older, I absorbed more of the Hall's history from my father. It had been built in the time of Henry the Eighth, on the site of the monastery which had given Monks' Wood its name. The Wraxfords, like many Catholic families, had renounced their religion during Queen Elizabeth's reign; Wraxford Hall, indeed, had served as a Royalist stronghold throughout the Civil War. Charles the Second himself was said to have hidden in the priest's hole while Henry Wraxford faced down Cromwell's men. At the Restoration, Henry was rewarded with a knighthood, but the title died with him, and for the next hundred or so years, the Hall served as a summer retreat for several generations of Wraxfords, mostly scholars and clerics who seemed to have done nothing whatever of note.

In the 1780s, it passed to one Thomas Wraxford, a man of grander ambitions who had recently married an heiress. He immediately set about extending the house and grounds, with a view to entertaining in the grand style, deaf to warnings about its remoteness and difficulty of access. He spent a good part of his wife's fortune, as well as his own, on this plan, but the great parties never eventuated; the invitations were politely declined, and the newly fitted-out rooms remained unoccupied. And then, around 1795, his only son, Felix, died at the age of ten, in a fall from a gallery above the great hall.

Thomas Wraxford's wife left him soon after the tragedy and went back to her own people. He lived on at the Hall for another thirty years, until one morning, in the spring of 1821, his manservant brought up the hot water at the usual hour and found his master gone. The bed had not been slept in, but there was no sign of struggle or disturbance; the outer doors and windows were all secured as usual; and the only thing missing was the nightshirt he had been wearing when the servant had last seen him the evening before. The house and grounds were thoroughly searched, in vain; Thomas Wraxford had vanished from the face of the earth, and no trace of him was ever found.

It was generally assumed that the old man's wits had finally given way, and that he had somehow got out of the house in his nightshirt (it had been a clear, moonlit night), wandered off into Monks' Wood, and fallen into a pit. The area had been mined for tin many centuries before, and some of the old workings still remained, roofed over by bracken and fallen leaves, as snares for the unwary. A year and a day after Thomas's disappearance, Cornelius Wraxford, his nephew and sole heir, petitioned the county court for a judgement of Thomas Wraxford's decease, which was granted readily enough. And so Cornelius, a reclusive, unmarried scholar, resigned his fellowship at Cambridge and took possession of the Hall. And that was all that my father could tell me, save that over the years, Cornelius had gradually sold off the rest of the land from which the estate had once derived its income, except for Monks' Wood and the Hall itself.

I spent a great deal of time, as a young boy, happily plotting with my companions as to how we might make our way through the forest, evade the dogs, and creep into the Hall through the secret passage which was said to lead from the house to a disused chapel in the woods nearby. None of us had seen more than a distant glimpse of Monks' Wood, and so our imaginations were free to run wild; the terrors we invoked haunted my dreams for years afterward. Our plans, of course, came to nothing; I was sent away to school, where I endured the usual brutalities, until the shock of my dear mother's death left me for a while indifferent to lesser torments.

It was then, I think, that I began to find refuge in sketching and drawing, for which I possessed a natural facility but had never taken very seriously, or received much in the way of instruction. My forte was natural scenery—the wilder the better—houses, castles and, especially, ruins. Something in me was struggling toward the light, but it seemed to have nothing to do with my destiny, which was to read for the law at Corpus Christi, my father's old college at Cambridge. This I duly did; and there, in my second year, I met a young man named Arthur Wilmot. He was reading classics, but his real passion was for painting, and through him I discovered a new world of which

I had been ignorant. It was in his company in London that I saw Turner's work for the first time, and felt that I understood at last those lines of Keats about stout Cortez gazing upon the ocean with a wild surmise. During that long vacation we spent three weeks painting and sketching in the Highlands, and with Arthur's encouragement, I began to believe that my future might lie in a studio rather than a solicitor's office.

Arthur was about my own height, but very slightly built, with fair skin of the sort which burns easily, and delicate features. But the impression of frailty was misleading, as I realised on our first day in Scotland when he went scampering up a steep incline with the agility of a goat whilst I followed, panting, in his wake. He spoke a great deal of Orchard House—a perfect Arcadia, as he made it sound—near Aylesbury, where his father, a clergyman, had a living, and especially of his sister Phoebe, who was plainly very dear to him: he grew anxious if more than a day or two had passed without a letter from her. By the end of our tour, it was settled that instead of returning to Aldeburgh, I should accompany him home and stay at least a fortnight. I had neither brothers nor sisters—my mother had been very ill after my birth—and I knew that my father had been looking forward to having me at home again. But I did not want to disappoint Arthur; or so I told myself in justification.

Orchard House was everything he had promised, and more: a rambling place of thatch and dazzling whitewash, set as its name implied amidst groves of apple and pear trees. Arthur's father, white-haired, genial, rubicund, might have stepped straight from a canvas by Birket Foster (though I did not see it so at the time), as might his mother, a serene, slender, fine-boned woman—one could see where Arthur had gotten his looks—always to be found somewhere in her garden when there was nothing else to attend to. And then there was

Phoebe herself. She was beautiful, yes, with her mother's classical profile and slender figure; she had thick lustrous hair the colour of dark honey, and her eyes were hazel, the eyelids always slightly lowered, though there was nothing coquettish about her. But it was her voice that first enchanted me: low and vibrant, with a kind of tune to it, a singing undertone which made the most commonplace remark seem charged with emotion.

My love for Phoebe was returned; I had her promise soon enough, though consent to our engagement was much longer in coming. I put aside all thought of starving in garrets and applied myself to the law, knowing that the sooner I had secured my articles, the sooner we would be married. Aside from the torments of longing I endured, away from her, swinging between bouts of wild elation and terror lest she should change her mind, the one cloud on our horizon was the question of where we were to live. I was serving my articles with my father in Aldeburgh; to turn my back upon the firm would break his heart, and lead perhaps to a permanent breach between us. But to keep my place with him would mean separating Phoebe from all that she loved best in the world. She and my father had tried to like each other for my sake, but did not quite know how to go about it. I knew, too, that she found our house, a plainly furnished cottage overlooking the strand, windswept and bleak.

In the end we reached an uneasy compromise: we would live in Aldeburgh, but in a house of our own, somewhere away from the sound of the waves which, as Phoebe reluctantly admitted, seemed to her melancholy and oppressive. I would more than once catch her murmuring, half-unconsciously, "Break, break, break, on thy cold grey stones, O sea. . . ." And we were to spend as much time at Orchard House as the demands of my practise would allow.

After three long years we were married, in the spring of 1859; I was just twenty-three years old, and Phoebe a year younger. We spent part of our honeymoon in Devon; I had wished to take her to Rome, but her family were anxious about the journey, and the dangers of disease. Those days and nights alone with her seemed, at the time, the happiest of my life; but by the end of a fortnight she was pining for Orchard House, and thence we returned, with much rejoicing on the part of her family, until the time came for us to begin our life in Aldeburgh.

I had taken a cottage in a picturesque spot by the Aldringham road, about a mile from my father's house and certainly well away from the sound of waves breaking upon shingle, but also rather isolated, leaving Phoebe with only our housekeeper—a kindly woman, but no conversationalist—for company during the day. Within weeks of our arrival, we knew that she was with child, a joy tempered by her increasing homesickness, which she tried in vain to conceal. Arthur came to stay; a relief on the one hand, but his visit also cast a shadow, for he plainly thought me cruel in keeping Phoebe from her family. And so we decided that she should spend the last months of her confinement at Orchard House, little imagining that they would be the last months of her life. I let the cottage go and returned to my father's house, fully resolved to leave the firm and seek a situation in Aylesbury as soon as the child was born. But my father was so pleased to have me at home again that I could not bring myself to tell him, and there matters stood until late one winter's evening I had a wire from Orchard House urging me to come at once. Phoebe's confinement had begun prematurely, and continued all that night, whilst she grew weaker and weaker until a surgeon was sent for. She died, and our son with her, an hour before I arrived.

Useless to dwell on that extremity of grief, or upon its terrible sequel, which is quickly told. I remained at Orchard House a week after her funeral, until the unspoken thought in all our minds—if only I had never crossed their threshold—became too painful to endure. Five months later, in August of the same year, Arthur went climbing in the Welsh mountains and was killed in a fall.

Returning to Aylesbury for the burial was the hardest thing I had ever done. Useless to say to his parents—so ravaged by suffering they were scarcely recognisable—that I would sooner have cut off my right hand, sooner have died; it would not bring Arthur or Phoebe back, or answer the questions that hung like daggers above our heads. Why had Arthur, in the depths of mourning, left his parents alone to go climbing on a whim? His companions swore that he had slipped whilst prospecting a rock-face, but I saw in them the shadow of my own suspicion: that whether or not Arthur had deliberately chosen to end his life, he had embarked on that fatal ascent without caring whether he lived or died.

In the long darkness that followed, the thought of ending my own life was constantly at my elbow. I could not shave without being gripped by the impulse to draw the blade across my throat. Guns beckoned from gun-racks, poisons from shelves, and always there was the sound of the sea, and the image of myself swimming out into the icy deep until my strength failed and I sank beneath the waves. But the thought of what it would do to my father—haunted as I was by the memory of the Wilmots' ravaged faces—always restrained me; that, and as Hamlet says, the dread of something after death: the lines were often in my mind. Gradually I became aware of how heavily the spectacle of my grief was weighing upon my father, and thence to emerge from black night into a grey twilight of the spirit. I resumed my place in the office, and began, almost unwillingly, to take notice of the world around me, and then to draw again, mere pencil sketches at first, until I found myself roaming farther afield in search of new subjects. But my life, or so I imagined, was effectively over, and another four years would pass before anything happened to disturb this melancholy conviction.

Perhaps it is only the indelible impression left by the story of Peter Grimes in "The Borough," but I have noticed that many visitors find something oppressive, even sinister, about the country to the south of Aldeburgh, to which I was drawn perhaps for that very reason. The keep at Orford, especially when framed against a lowering sky, remained a favourite subject, and from Orford it was only another three miles across a lonely stretch of marshland to the edge of Monks' Wood. You can walk that way many times without meeting another human being, attended only by the lonely cries of seabirds and occasional glimpses of a grey and tumbling sea. Because of the way the land lies, the forest remains hidden until you crest a slight rise and find your way barred by a dark expanse of foliage. I was gazing at this prospect on a chill afternoon in the spring of 1864, and wondering whether the dogs were really as savage as I had once believed, when it occurred to me that I now had a legitimate reason to visit the Hall.

I prevailed upon my father to write to Cornelius Wraxford—from whom we had not heard for several years—introducing me as his new man of business and requesting an interview. A week later came the reply: Mr. Wraxford would continue the association for the time being, but saw no necessity of meeting. So far as my father was concerned, that was the end of it. But my old curiosity had been roused, and I began to make enquiries. I had a friend in the poaching line—a man I had met red-handed whilst I was out sketching very early one morning, and had not betrayed—and in a quiet corner of the tap-room at the White Lion I learned that so much of the outer wall had now collapsed that the few remaining dogs were kept chained by the old stables at the rear of the house. The keeper—who acted mostly as groom and coachman—was given to drink and seldom ventured forth at night, or so my informant had heard; the poaching fraternity, he told me, still gave the Hall a wide berth, especially after dark.

The moon that night was almost at the full, and after I left the White Lion I stood for a long time on the strand, watching the play of light upon the water. I had thought that I would never again hear the sound of waves upon shingle without being overwhelmed by grief and remorse, but time had worn away the edge and the lines that came to me were not "Break, break, break," but "the sword outwears its sheath / And the soul wears out the breast. . . ." The night was mild and clear, and it struck me as I stood there that it would be an interesting exercise to sketch the Hall by moonlight. Business was quiet, and my father was always happy to grant me sketching leave, and so I set off the very next day.

It was early in the afternoon before I stood once more upon the ridge overlooking Monks' Wood. From there I made my way northward along the edge of the forest until I came to a rutted track, and plunged beneath the canopy. A few minutes later, I passed between the crumbling pillars which marked the boundary of the estate. The original oaks had been much overrun by firs, which grew very close, shutting out the light. As I went deeper into the wood, I became aware that the usual chatter of birds seemed strangely muted, and if there was game afoot, it kept well out of sight. The conviction that I had taken a wrong turning grew upon me until, without any warning, the path swerved around the trunk of a gigantic oak and emerged onto a ragged expanse of long grass and thistles which must once have been lawn. On the far side of the clearing, perhaps fifty yards off, stood a large manor house in the Elizabethan style, with drab greenish walls crosshatched by blackened timbers and crowned by numerous gables. The sun was already sinking toward the treetops on my left.

The path continued on through the wilderness toward the front entrance, with a branch leading away to my left toward a tumbledown cottage, perhaps the keeper's abode. Behind the cottage was a row of decrepit outbuildings, half-hidden by the encroaching trees; and farther off still, glimpses of stonework and a steeply sloping roof, presumably the chapel. Wraxford Hall, my father had told me, had once possessed a park of several acres, but the forest had swallowed everything except the house and its immediate surroundings. There was no sign of life; all was still and silent.

I turned my attention to the main house. Signs of long neglect were apparent even at this distance: sagging timbers; jagged cracks in the mortar; a wild profusion of nettles and saplings growing right up against the wall in places. All of the windows were shuttered except for a row along the second floor, which appeared to be at least thirty feet above the ground. It struck me that these might be the windows of the gallery from which the boy Felix Wraxford had fallen seventy years ago. The shutters along the second floor were much smaller; and protruding above these were the attics, each in its own gable, and all on different levels. Silhouetted against the brightness of the sky were a dozen or so crumbling chimneys, and jutting above each of these I saw what appeared to be a blackened spear, aimed at the heavens. These were lightning rods: my first glimpse of the Wraxford family's strange obsession.

It is difficult now to separate my first impressions from the knowledge of what was to follow. I felt at once fearful and exhilarated; my accustomed melancholy vanished like smoke upon the wind. The house seemed preternaturally vivid in the afternoon light, as if I had stepped from the waking world into a dream in which I was *meant* to be here and nowhere else. I settled my back against the trunk of the great oak, got out my tablet and my colour box, and set about making the best use of the remaining daylight.

An hour passed with no sign of life; I began to wonder if the dogs were only a figment of my friend's imagination. Perhaps Cornelius himself had died—but no, we had had his letter only last week—yet what did we really know of his movements? He could have closed up the house and gone away immediately after writing to us. Or perhaps there was another, more modest dwelling in a different part of the wood. . . . Slowly the twilight deepened until I could no longer tell one colour from another. I set my materials aside and ate the food I had brought while the outlines of rooftops and chimneys, the spectral branches of the lightning rods, faded with the last glow of evening until the Hall was no more than a dark mass humped against the blackness of the forest.

A pale glow through the foliage behind me heralded the rising of the moon, and I saw that for its light to fall upon my page, I would have to work in the open. Convinced by now that the estate was deserted, I gathered my things and moved cautiously forward into the starlight. About thirty yards from the house I stumbled over the remnant of a low stone wall, where I settled myself with my tablet and pencils. The air was still and cold; somewhere in the distance a fox barked, but no answering cry arose from the blackness opposite.

Minute by minute, the clearing brightened; the Hall seemed to be inching its way upward out of darkness. As the moon rose higher, the proportions of the house appeared to alter until it loomed above me like a precipice. I reached down for my tablet and, as I straightened, saw a light spring up in the window immediately above the main entrance. A flickering yellow glow that began to move to my left, passing from one window to the next until it came to the farthest, then slowly back about half the distance it had come, before it halted and steadied.

All of my childhood terrors swarmed up at the sight, yet in that sinister progress I saw the completion of my picture; saw that if I could master my fear for long enough to fix the scene in memory, I might at last realise a vision that was truly my own. I began working feverishly, even as my skin crawled in anticipation of a malign face rising up against the glass; or the shout—or shot—that would signal my discovery. The light glowed steadily, wavering every so often as if someone had passed close by. It is old Cornelius, I told myself, moving about his domain; so long as his lamp is lit, he will not see me. I seemed to have become two people; the one appalled at my folly and pleading for release, the other indifferent to everything except the task in hand.

Around midnight, when the moon was at its highest, I had done all that I could. Still the light burned in the window; I gathered up my things and withdrew into the shadow of the trees. I had brought a lantern with me, but that would mean announcing my presence to whatever might be abroad in Monks' Wood, and after a hundred yards of stumbling in near darkness, I went a little way off the path, wrapped myself in my greatcoat, and huddled at the foot of another massive oak. There I lay listening to the creepings and rustlings in the thickets around me, the occasional hoot of an owl, drifting in and out of uneasy dreams until I woke in grey twilight.

For the next five days, I scarcely left my studio. I neglected my father shamefully, but the picture would not be denied; whenever I lay down to seek a few hours' sleep, it floated before my inward eye, beckoning, insisting. I worked with an assurance I had never possessed—or rather been possessed by—constantly running up against the limits of my technique and yet guided by a vision so compelling, it seemed almost to make virtues of my limitations; until the morning when I set down my palette for the last time and stepped back to admire what looked like the work of someone far more gifted than myself. It was a scene at once melancholy, sinister, and beautiful, and in that long moment of contemplation, I felt like the God of creation; I looked upon my work and knew that it was good.

My father, though he admired the picture, was more concerned about the prospect of my being arrested for trespass, and exacted a promise that I would not venture uninvited upon the Wraxford estate again. I agreed readily enough, believing that I would be able to apply my newfound talent to any subject I chose. But my next study of the keep at Orford looked markedly inferior to its predecessor, as did my efforts at several other favourite scenes. Something had been lost, an absence as palpable as a drawn tooth and yet impossible to define; some mysterious collaboration of hand and vision, a facility I had not even been conscious of possessing. Where once I had simply painted, all was now laboured, forced, unnatural; and the harder I struggled against this mysterious inhibition, the worse the result. I thought of returning to the Hall, but aside from my promise I was restrained by a superstitious fear that if I tried to repeat my success, *Wraxford Hall by Moonlight* would somehow . . . not dissolve before my eyes, exactly, but reveal itself as flashy and mediocre. Perhaps I really was deluding myself; the thought had occurred to me often enough, and I had not submitted the picture to expert judgement; I felt I could not show it, for fear of alarming my father. Yet my heart insisted that I had done something remarkable, though at a price I would rather not have paid.

Then in October of the following year, all was changed by my father's sudden death from a stroke. Now I was free to devote myself entirely to painting; except that my talent had deserted me, and besides, selling the practise seemed like a betrayal of my father's memory, even his trust. Our clients expected me to carry on; Josiah, our elderly clerk, expected it; and so I went on "just for the time being," as I kept telling myself, unsure whether it was conscience or cowardice that kept me in harness. My sole act of defiance was to hang *Wraxford Hall by Moonlight* upon my office wall (I told anyone who asked that it had been done from an old mezzotint), where it was displayed on the afternoon when I first met Magnus Wraxford.

I had received a note from him to say that he would very much like to meet me; he did not indicate why. I knew from my father's notes to the Wraxford papers that Magnus was the son of Cornelius's younger brother Silas, who had died in 1857. Cornelius had made a new will in 1858, leaving his entire estate to "my nephew Magnus Wraxford of Munster Square, Regent's Park, London." Out of curiosity, I wrote to an acquaintance in London to ask if the name meant anything to him. "Well, yes, as it happens," he wrote. "He is a medical man—studied in Paris, I believe; practices mesmerism, of which as you know there is a great deal of suspicion amongst the established practitioners. Claims to be able to cure heart disease, among other illnesses, through mesmeric treatment. Apparently his patients—especially the women—can't speak too highly of him. Said to be very charming, personally, but nothing much in the way of fortune, which of course compounds the suspicion against him."

I do not know quite what I was expecting, but even as Magnus Wraxford was shown into the room, I knew that I was in the presence of a superior intelligence; yet there was nothing of condescension in his manner. He was about my own height (a shade under six feet), but broader in the shoulders, with thick black hair and a small, pointed beard, neatly trimmed. His hands were almost square, with long, powerful fingers, the nails clipped very close, unadorned except for a fine gold signet ring, bearing the image of a phoenix, on his right hand. But it was the eyes beneath the high, domed forehead that compelled your attention: deep-set, of a very dark brown, and extraordinarily luminous. For all the friendliness of his greeting, I had the unnerving sensation that my innermost thoughts were on display. Which was perhaps why, when his gaze turned to *Wraxford Hall by Moonlight,* I at once admitted my trespass. Far from disapproving, he admired the picture so warmly that I was quite disarmed, the more so when he insisted that any apologies were due to me.

"I am very sorry," he said, "that my uncle put you off so discourteously. He is, as you will have gathered, the most unsociable of men. He tolerates me only because he thinks I can help him in his—researches. But surely you and I have met before? In town, at the Academy last year—the Turner bequest? I am sure I saw you there, at any rate."

His voice, like his gaze, was wonderfully persuasive; I had indeed visited the exhibition, and though I could not recall seeing him, I felt half-convinced that we really must have met. We had both, at any rate, admired *Rain, Steam and Speed,* and deplored the hostile reaction it still inspired amongst the hidebound, and so we settled ourselves by the fire and talked Turner and Ruskin like old friends until Josiah arrived with the tea. It was four in the afternoon on a chill, overcast day, and the light was already fading.

"I see that my uncle was at work that night—unless that sinister glow in the gallery window is your own inspiration," said Magnus, looking again at my picture.

"No, there really was a light; rather unnerving, I confess. People in these parts firmly believe that the Hall is haunted, and your uncle a necromancer."

"I fear," he said, "that there may be some truth in those tales, at least on the second point. . . . You noticed the lightning rods, I see."

I had spoken lightly, which made his reply all the more surprising. For a moment I thought that he must have said "no truth."

"Yes—I have never seen a building with so many. Is your uncle especially afraid of thunderstorms?"

"On the contrary . . . but I should first tell you that the lightning rods were originally installed some eighty years ago, by my great-uncle Thomas."

"Was he," I asked, wondering if I had misheard him again, "the Thomas Wraxford who lost his son in a fall from the gallery and later—vanished?"

"Indeed so; that gallery is now my uncle's workroom. But the rods—quite a novelty then—were fitted at least a decade before the tragedy. And no, your ears did not deceive you a moment ago—"

My surprise at his seeming clairvoyance must have shown on my face.

"The fact is, Mr. Montague, I fear my uncle has embarked on an experiment which may place him, and possibly others, in mortal danger if nothing is done to prevent it. And so I felt I should acquaint you with the situation and—if you are willing—seek your advice."

I assured him that I would be happy to do anything in my power, and pressed him to continue.

"My uncle and I have never been close, you understand; I visit him two or three times a year, and we correspond occasionally. But since my student days, I have tracked down various out-of-the-way books for him, mostly alchemical and occult works. He suffers, I should tell you, from a morbid fear of death, and I sometimes think this accounts for his having shut himself so much away from the world. It has certainly drawn him into strange paths of study; and in particular to the alchemists' quest for the elixir of life; the potion which will supposedly confer immortality upon him who discovers the secret.

"The winter before last, he began dropping hints about a rare alchemical manuscript he had acquired: a comparatively recent work, dating from the late seventeenth century. He would not reveal the author's name, or say where he had got it. My uncle, as you will have gathered, is profoundly suspicious and secretive, but it was clear that he believed he had found something truly remarkable.

"Last autumn, he told me that he intended to renew the cables to the lightning rods, and asked me to find him a copy of Sir William Snow's treatise on thunderstorms. I was not altogether surprised; he had been muttering for some years about the danger of fire started by lightning. You may well wonder why he has done nothing to secure the house against fires of a more terrestrial kind, but his dislike of spending money is as powerful as his fear of death. So I sent him the book, and thought no more about it until I came up to visit him a fortnight ago.

"The lightning rods, I should say, have always been connected to the ground by way of a heavy black cable secured to the side wall. But now I saw that a section about six feet in length had been removed from the cable at the level of the gallery. I thought at first that the cable was being replaced piecemeal: a dangerous business, for if lightning were to strike with that section still missing, the full force of the bolt would explode into the gallery. But as I drew closer, I saw that the appearance of a gap was deceptive: the wall had been pierced in two places, with the cable leading into the first aperture and reappearing about six feet farther down.

"In his letter of invitation, my uncle had said only that he wanted to 'make some dispositions.'" I had no inkling of what that might mean, but as I stood contemplating this bizarre arrangement, I confess to a cold crawling sensation along my backbone.

"I was admitted, as usual, by his manservant Drayton—a melancholy fellow of sixty or more—who informed me that my uncle was engaged in the library and had left word that he was not to be disturbed before dinner. This was not unusual; his invitations are never for more than two days, and he sees me only when he wants something. Indeed, to be frank, if he hadn't made me his heir, I doubt I should have kept up the connection.

"My uncle, I should say, has kept the same few servants for as long as I have known him. There is Grimes the coachman, who also serves as groom and ostler; his wife, who does the cooking (which is spartan in the extreme), an elderly maid, and Drayton. My uncle wears the same threadbare suit, day in, day out; I don't imagine he has dressed for dinner since the day he left Cambridge, which must be forty-five years ago. Most of the house, as you would have observed, is closed up: Grimes and his wife have the keeper's cottage, and the other servants' rooms are on the ground floor, at the rear of the house.

"My uncle's apartment consists of the long gallery"—again he indicated the lighted windows in my picture—"and the library and study which adjoin it.

"As you enter the gallery by the main doors, you see, at the far end of the room, an immense fireplace. But no fire has burned in it for centuries; the space within is occupied by what at first appears to be an immense cabin trunk. It is in fact a sarcophagus made of copper, so corroded and tarnished with age that only traces of the original scrollwork remain. It was commissioned by Sir Henry Wraxford, around the year 1640, as a species of *memento mori:* his remains are interred therein.

"In the alcove between the fireplace and the library wall stands a massive suit of armour, curiously blackened as if by fire. You would think it the work of some mediaeval craftsman, but as you approach you see that, from the waist down, it resembles one of those Egyptian coffins in the shape of a man. It was built in Augsburg, less than a hundred years ago, at around the same time as von Kempelen's celebrated chess-playing automaton; Thomas Wraxford brought it back from Germany as part of the refurbishment of the Hall.

"The gallery is otherwise bare of furnishings, except for a couple of straight-backed chairs and a long table—which serves as my uncle's workbench—beneath the windows where the light shows in your picture. Portraits of Wraxfords past hang above the table; the opposite wall is adorned with the usual array of ancient weapons, trophies, and faded tapestries, compounding the air of desolation. A cold, bleak, echoing place, smelling of damp and decay.

"The library next door is a typical country gentleman's miscellany, crammed with works that no one would ever wish to read. Whenever he lets me in, the table is always clear of books and papers; he keeps his alchemical works in a locked press. The study is also his bedroom; there is a camp bed in one corner, and he takes all his meals there, so far as I know, except when I visit him. Beyond that is nothing but dust and empty corridors; I don't suppose anyone has set foot on the upper floors since the last century.

"I had a couple of hours to fill before my uncle emerged from the library at seven. And so I let myself out of the house again for a closer look at the lightning conductors.

"This time I noticed that the gallery window nearest to the main cable was slightly ajar; the fault of the workmen, presumably, for the casements are too high for my uncle to reach. And though I could not be certain, I felt pretty sure that the suit of armour stood beneath that window. Half-formed suspicions kept flitting through my mind, and yet I could not put a name to them. I made a complete circuit of the Hall, but nothing else had changed."

I had become so absorbed that a tapping at the door made me start; it was Josiah coming to light the lamps and build up the fire, and I saw that it had grown quite dark outside.

"I am sorry," said Magnus. "I am taking up a great deal of your time, and perhaps you have other business . . ."

I assured him that I had none. He possessed an extraordinary knack of adjusting his speech to the idiom and rhythm of one's own, so subtly that you were scarcely aware of it, and yet I already felt, within scarcely an hour of our meeting, that I was in the company of an old and trusted friend. And so, having established that he was staying at the White Lion, I pressed him to dine at my house—to which, after the usual demurrals, he warmly agreed—and in the meantime take some refreshment and continue his narrative.

"As a rule," he said, "meals with my uncle are taken in a small breakfast room at the rear of the house. But on this occasion Drayton had laid two places in the cavernous dining room, a musty, dark-panelled mausoleum of a place, directly below the library. There was no fire. My uncle appeared in a muffler and thick woollen mittens; I would have been glad of my greatcoat. We dined by the light of a few candles, at a table intended for forty, with Drayton hovering somewhere in the darkness at my back. My uncle's gaze kept sidling up to mine, and then flickering away; a dozen times I thought he was on the verge of speaking, until at last he cleared his throat, waved Drayton from the room, and drew a sheaf of papers from inside his coat.

"'You know,' said my uncle, tapping the document, 'that I have made you my heir. Now there is a service I require of *you*. If I should die in the normal way'—I wanted to ask what other mode of dying he had in mind, but refrained—'I have a number of instructions regarding the estate that I particularly want you to note.' And he began to list the items which should on no account be sold or removed from the house, beginning with the table at which we were dining. He went through the contents of the dining and drawing rooms, ticking them off on his fingers, but mechanically, perfunctorily, as if his mind was elsewhere.

"But when he came to what he calls 'my apartments'—meaning the gallery, library, and study upstairs—his demeanour changed entirely. The suit of armour in the gallery was to be left exactly as found, for as long as the Hall remained in the family. This was said with the utmost intensity, and in a tone that brooked no contradiction: he told me that he intended to make it a condition of the bequest. Though I don't know, and perhaps it would be improper to ask, whether . . ."

"We have heard nothing from your uncle for years," I said. "Of course, he could have consulted someone else."

"No; I'm sure he would come to you. He made the same stipulation about the library, but the fire had gone out of him, and after listing the contents of a few more rooms, he said he would write it all down as a codicil to his will.

"Again my uncle fell silent, drumming his mittened fingers on the table.

"'If I should vanish,' he said abruptly, 'that is to say, in the event that I should seem to have disappeared . . . if Drayton, for example, should inform you that I cannot be found, then no one is to enter my apartments. *No one*, you understand. No search is to be made; no authority is to be informed; nothing is to be done, until three days and nights have passed. Thereafter, if there has been no communication from me, you may enter my workroom and—do whatever is necessary. But nothing is to be removed, I say again; nothing, or your inheritance will be forfeit. Do you accept? Answer yes, or no.'

"He picked up the document, which was evidently his will, and grasped it with both hands, as if prepared to rend it into pieces if my answer did not suit him.

"'Well, yes,' I replied, 'but surely Mr. Montague would be more suitable.'

"At this he snarled—if you will pardon me—'I don't trust lawyers, and besides, you've more to lose than he has. Have I your word of honour?—Very well. And now I must get on with my work. Drayton will look after you, and see to your breakfast in the morning. I am sure you will want to be on your way as early as possible.'

"He rose, folded away his papers, and left the room without a backward glance."

"Forgive me," I could not help asking, "but is your uncle always so—abrupt?"

"So offensive, rather; though you are too polite to say so. Well, no; even by his standards, this was exceptionally uncivil, but in truth I barely noticed. I remained for some time alone at the table, brooding over his strange demand, while the candles burned lower and the air grew colder still. Had my uncle slipped from eccentricity into outright madness? That was the obvious conclusion, and yet I did not quite feel that I had been in the presence of a lunatic. Or had he brooded upon the disappearance of his predecessor, until . . . but until what? The answer must lie in the gallery, if anywhere; but how was I to gain entry? When my uncle retires for the night, he locks and bolts all the doors to the landing. I had given it up as hopeless, and was about to retire myself, when I thought of the cable.

"The moon was in its second quarter; provided the sky remained clear, it would be bright enough to see by. I told Drayton I needed some air, and not to wait up for me; I would lock up when I returned. From the shadow of the old coach house, I watched while the hours dragged by. Midnight came and went; it was one thirty before the light in my uncle's study window went out. I waited another half-hour, returned to the side of the house, and set about scaling the wall.

"Though the night was perfectly calm, with only a few wisps of cloud drifting across the face of the moon, I cast more than one apprehensive glance at the heavens as I drew on a pair of gauntlets and began to climb. The wall was uneven enough to provide some purchase for my feet, but despite the chill I was dripping with perspiration before I reached the narrow parapet which runs roughly level with the gallery floor. A little above the ledge, the cable disappeared into the wall. The windowsill was at least seven feet above the parapet; to reach the next section of cable, I would have to rise to my full height whilst balancing on the ledge, grasp the cable with my left hand and swing across to open the casement with my right.

"Crouched on the parapet, I dared not look down. Those lines about the man gathering samphire on the dreadful cliff sprang into my head and came near to paralysing me. I did the last of the climb in one desperate, lunging rush and lay gasping across the sill.

"Moonlight was shining down upon the dark bulk of the armour, which stood almost directly below me. The doors into the library were closed, to my relief, and no light showed beneath. I lowered myself down beside the helmeted figure and waited until my breathing had slowed to its normal pace.

"My uncle, I should say, had always been most reluctant to admit me to the gallery. He could not deny me the right to view my ancestors' portraits, but he had never left me alone with them; thus, I had seen the armour only at a distance. It stands upon a metal plinth, its mailed right hand upon the pommel of a drawn sword, point downward in the ground, as it were. But I had eyes only for the two lengths of cable emerging from the wall, the one connected to the back of the helmet, the other to the plinth: so that if lightning were to strike the Hall, the full force of the current would pass directly through the suit.

"Needing more light, I decided to risk the candle I had brought. In that flickering glow, the armour looked unnervingly watchful. The sword gleamed beneath its mailed right hand; the tip of the blade, I saw, passed through a slot in the metal plinth. On impulse, I took hold of the hilt.

"The sword moved like a lever in my grasp, bringing the metal hand with it. As I drew it slowly toward me, a shiver ran through the armour. I recoiled in horror, but my sleeve caught in the hilt and the sword swung to the end of its travel. The armour seemed to explode into life: the blackened plates burst open, as if some monstrous occupant were forcing its way out.

"But there was only emptiness within. Bringing the light closer, I saw that the plates had been hinged on both sides so that the whole of the front half—with the exception of the arms—opened outward. As I moved the sword back to the upright position, the plates closed again with barely a sound. The joints were scarcely visible; it must have taken a skilled armourer months of painstaking work.

"I had found out my uncle's secret, but what did it mean? What did he believe would happen when, sooner or later, lightning struck the Hall? Did he intend to bribe or deceive some innocent person into occupying the suit—or coffin—during a storm, so that he could observe the result? 'If I should *seem* to have disappeared,' he had said, 'no one is to enter my apartments until three days and three nights have passed.' Was this to give him time to escape if his victim died?

"Or was he expecting something to *emerge*? I confess that the hair rose on the back of my neck at the thought—and at the vista it opened upon my uncle's mental state. But I was now determined to discover his purpose, and began to look around for clues. I had thought there was nothing of interest on the long table, but in the shadows at the far end, I came upon a slender folio volume, bound in vellum.

"It was not a printed book, but a manuscript, written in a crabbed, gothic hand. The title page said only: 'Trithemius. *On the Power of*

Lightning. 1697.' Slips of paper had been inserted in several places; this, surely, was the mysterious alchemical work that had so excited my uncle. The original Trithemius, as you may know (I had to look him up in the British Museum when I returned to London), was the Abbot of Sponheim in the late fifteenth century, a supposed magician accused of 'divilish worke'; he is said to have invented an 'ever-burning fire.' But our Trithemius, the author of the manuscript, does not appear in the catalogue, suggesting that my uncle possesses the only copy—or one of very few.

"I tried to read from the beginning, but though the work is in English, it proved almost impenetrable, and so I turned to one of the pages marked by my uncle. The illustration I found there set my skin crawling afresh. It consisted of four stylised panels, the first depicting a suit of armour—you could not tell whether it was occupied or empty—with a long pole or rod projecting vertically upward from the helmet. In the second, a jagged bolt of lightning was shown striking the tip of the rod; in the third, the armour was surrounded by a halo of light. In the last you saw—though the artist's skill was unequal to the task—a glowing figure beginning to separate itself from the armour; or perhaps the two were merging, I could not tell.

"I turned back to the first of the passages marked, thinking I had better read in order, and knew at once that I must note it down. This is a fair copy of what I found," he said, handing me a sheet of foolscap:

> As a Lodestone doth seek the North, so I have found by Tryall that a *Thunderbolt* may be Drawn by a Rodd of Iron set upon the Crown of an Hill. And so, to the Question put by the Lord to Job, I dare answer in the Affirmative:
>
> Canst thou send *Lightnings*, that they may go, and say unto thee, Here we *are*?

For it is written in the Book of Judgement:

> And the Angel took the Censer, and filled it with Fire of the Altar, and cast it into the earth, and there were Voyces, and *Thunderings*, and *Lightnings*, &c.

Thus, a Man who could command the Power of *Lightning* would be as the Avenging Angel upon that Dreadful Day—the Dark as much as the Light, for in this we must Reckon as the *Gnostics*—and have Dominion over the Souls of the Living and the Dead: Power to Bind and Loose, & Raise Up, and Cast Down, & if he be a true *Adept*, to Perform that *Rite* of which I have written Elsewhere. For as a young *Tree* may be Grafted upon an *Old*, so

"I fear there is no more," he said, when I looked up expectantly. "I was about to turn the page when I heard a noise from the direction of the library: the sound of a key turning in a lock. I blew out the candle, closed the book, and moved as quickly as I dared toward the main entrance. But footsteps were already approaching the door from the library, and I knew that the landing doors could not be opened in a hurry without making a great deal of noise. Nor was there time to haul myself up and over the ledge and close the window after me. I could have crouched beneath the long table, but the thought of being discovered, and having to crawl ignominiously out to face my uncle . . . No; there was only one possible hiding-place. I grasped the sword, drew it toward me, and stepped into the armour, sliding my right arm into its metal counterpart as I did so. The suit closed around me, and I was plunged into absolute darkness.

"There was very little air, even at first, and it soon grew stiflingly hot. As my eyes adjusted to the dark, I became aware of a faint glimmer, and discovered that by standing upon tiptoe I could see, through the slits in the visor, the glow of my uncle's candle—at least, I assumed it was my uncle—moving around the room. Once it paused directly in front of me—even on tiptoe, I could only see upward—and I waited for what seemed like minutes for the plates to spring open. At last the light retreated, and then vanished in a muffled clatter of locks and bolts. But I dared not move immediately. As the silence returned, I was seized by a creeping, mortal dread, coiled around the words I had just copied: 'For as a young *Tree* may be grafted upon an *Old* . . .' I imagined black clouds boiling up above the Hall . . .

"But enough of that. I mention it only to explain why, when I at last emerged from that suffocating confinement, I thought only of escape. Suffice to say that the descent proved even more precarious than the climb, and that I reached the ground a good deal scraped and bloodied. My uncle did not, to my relief, come in search of me the next morning. I thought of taking Drayton into my confidence, but I doubted his ability to conceal anything from his master, and so I confined myself to saying that I was worried about my uncle's health. Drayton has promised to wire me in London if anything untoward occurs.

"Which brings me, at last, to the purpose of my visit. As you may know, I have a particular interest in heart disease, and am often called away from town when an opinion is wanted. So I can't always be found at short notice, in which case Drayton would of course come straight to you. But beyond acquainting you with the situation, I wonder—though perhaps, as my uncle's representative, you may think it improper to advise me—whether you can suggest any legal means by which we might forestall disaster, rather than simply waiting—the phrase comes all too aptly—for the storm to break."

The fire had burned low; I vaguely recalled having heard Josiah depart some time ago.

"I don't think it at all improper," I said as I refilled our glasses, "to advise you, given the extraordinary circumstances. But the only course that suggests itself is the very drastic one of committing him to an asylum; and of course, the risk, from your point of view, is that if the attempt didn't succeed he might very well take his revenge by disinheriting you. Do you think that two of your colleagues—as the prospective heir, you couldn't very well be party to it yourself—would be likely to sign a certificate?"

"I'm not at all certain they would," he replied. "We can't prove that he means to use the armour for any sinister purpose; he could plausibly claim to be engaged in a scientific investigation into the effects of lightning. As for his demand that no one enter his domain for three days after he (presumably) ceases to answer his door, supposing he does put that in writing; am I legally bound either to abide by it, or lose the estate?"

"If he brought such a provision to me," I said, after thinking it over for some time, "I would refuse to write it into the will, because it's contradictory. A will has no force until proven; it can't be proven until the testator is dead; you can't know whether he's dead or not until you enter the gallery, which he wants to forbid you to do; but if you believe he's ill or dying, you have a moral duty—which the law would certainly recognise—to go to his assistance. The risk you face, of course, is that if you break in and he *isn't* dead, he could well carry out his threat to disinherit you. In fact . . . supposing Drayton came to me, and said that he was anxious about your uncle, it would be better if *I* broke in. The worst he could do is dismiss me, assuming he was still alive; and if he was dead, well, it would avoid any complications. . . ."

It struck me as I made the offer that I was being rather reckless, but Magnus thanked me so warmly that it would have seemed churlish to retract. There we left the matter for the time being, and went out into the chill night air to walk the few hundred yards up to my house.

I had grown unused to company, but Magnus drew me out that night; I found myself speaking of Phoebe and Arthur as I had not done in years, and of the great darkness of spirit that had followed their deaths. I spoke, too, of the strange loss of facility that had followed the painting of *Wraxford Hall by Moonlight,* and of how, in my efforts to outflank the inhibition—or curse, as I sometimes thought of it—I had abandoned first oils, then watercolours, and eventually confined myself to pencil and charcoal, as if relinquishing all but the plainest of techniques might somehow break its grip.

"I am sure you are on the right track," said Magnus. "Indeed, I have had similar thoughts about my own profession. For all our talk of progress, I cannot see that medicine has advanced very far since the time of Galen. We can inoculate against smallpox, or remove a gangrenous limb in thirty seconds; but when it comes to many diseases, we are no better equipped than an old village woman with a cupboard full of simples. And we—that is to say, the majority of my colleagues—seem positively to spurn any treatment, however effective, for which we cannot account in material terms.

"Consider mesmerism, for example: all the rage twenty years ago; now dismissed by many in the profession as no more scientific than spirit rapping; yet it offers incalculable benefits in the relief of pain, and quite possibly in the cure of chronic illness, including heart disease. I have had remarkable results with some of my patients, yet I would hesitate to describe them in print; I am regarded as quite enough of a mountebank as it is."

We had taken our coffee and brandy into the study—Magnus, like myself, did not smoke—and settled ourselves in armchairs by the fire. Two candles burned on the mantelpiece; the rest of the room was in darkness.

"Consider," he said, "that your mind influences the action of your heart, whether or not you are aware of the effect. If you are possessed by fearful thoughts, for instance, your pulse accelerates; your breathing becomes shallower and more rapid. We are accustomed to think of such reactions as involuntary, but cause and effect are here reversible: you could conjure up a fearful scene *in order* to accelerate your pulse. The fakirs of India have extended this control—as we may call it—a great deal further, so that all the bodily processes we regard as autonomous can be brought under conscious command: not only the action of heart and lungs, but digestion, sensation, the temperature of the body, and so on. Thus a Hindu monk can walk unharmed over a bed of red-hot coals; or place himself in a state akin to hibernation, remain buried alive for hours, or even days, and emerge unscathed, where you or I would suffocate within a few minutes.

"Consider, too, that a mesmerised subject can be commanded not to feel pain, and will feel none: it is often done on stage, and can be just as effective in surgery. Now it does not seem so fanciful, does it, to suppose that if I suggest to a subject that his blood will circulate more freely *after* he wakes from the trance, a real improvement will follow? Indeed, I see no reason why, on the same principle, a malignant tumour could not be commanded to shrink, as happens spontaneously from time to time."

"But if this is true," I exclaimed, "and you say that you have had remarkable results with your patients, you have made a great discovery. Why is it not generally accepted?"

"Well, first, it is not my discovery. Elliotson said as much thirty years ago, but he made a circus of his demonstrations and was forced to resign his post. Second, and principally, because we do not know *how* the mind influences the body; we can speak of electrobiological influence, or ideomotor force, but these are mere labels applied to a mystery. I can see the improvement; my patients feel the benefit of the treatment, but to a sceptic, it is mere spontaneous healing, and I cannot prove otherwise. Until a physical mechanism is discovered, anatomised and dissected, it will never be accepted by the profession."

"But won't the sceptics' patients all desert them and come to you?"

"Let me put a question in return: if you had felt out of sorts this morning, and a mesmerist had offered his services, would you have accepted?"

"Well, no—"

"Precisely; you would have dismissed him as a charlatan."

"But now that I know—"

"You know only because you have met me; if you were to ask your physician, he would most likely assure you that the whole thing had been discredited years ago. Besides, there are numerous cases where orthodox methods must be applied; you would be most ill-advised to command an inflamed appendix not to burst, rather than removing it on the spot."

I went on to ask what were doubtless the usual questions about mesmerism, and was assured that no, a person could not be mesmerised against their will, or compelled to do anything they would not consent to do in waking life. In the deepest state of trance, however, a subject could be instructed to see scenes and persons who were not actually present.

"So if you were to mesmerise me," I said, a trifle uneasily, "you could suggest to me that Arthur Wilmot"—I had wanted to say "Phoebe," but feared I might break down—"was about to enter this room, and he would then appear—very much as spirit mediums claim to be able to summon the dead."

I could not help glancing into the shadows beyond the firelight as I spoke.

"Yes," said Magnus, "but the man you saw in a state of trance would not be a spirit. He would be an image composed of your memories of him."

"But would I be able to talk to him? Touch him? Hear him speak? Would he appear to me as a living man?"

"As in a dream, yes; but as with a dream, he would vanish at the instant of waking."

"But supposing," I persisted, "you instructed me to wake from the trance, whilst retaining the facility of seeing—"

"It could not be done. The facility, as you call it, is as specific to the state of trance as dreaming is to sleep. Supposing you were now in a trance, I could suggest that upon waking you would rise, go to the shelf over there, and bring me a certain volume; and most likely you would do so, and then be puzzled as to why you had done it. But I could not command you to wake and find your friend entering the room; or rather, I could command it, but he would not appear . . . I fear the subject is distressing to you."

I assured him it was not, even as I struggled to subdue the emotion which had threatened to overwhelm me.

"Tell me," he asked after a pause, "have you ever attended a séance?"

A spark of firelight caught on his gold signet ring as he raised his glass.

"No," I said, "though I have been tempted. I lost what remained of my faith when Phoebe and Arthur died, and yet I cannot altogether relinquish the feeling that something of us survives beyond the grave. So much depends upon the circumstances. That night I spent sketching at the Hall, for example . . . it would be very easy, there, to believe that ghosts walk."

"Indeed," said Magnus. "As you may have heard, the gallery where my uncle works is supposedly haunted by the ghost of the boy Felix,

Thomas Wraxford's son. Curiously enough—" he broke off, as if suddenly struck by something.

"Curiously enough?" I prompted.

"Well, only that the boy died during a thunderstorm, or so my uncle once told me."

The room seemed suddenly darker; I noticed that one of the candles had sunk to a thin blue flame.

"How old was your uncle when Felix died?" I asked.

"About eleven; he was a year older than Felix. He says that Thomas Wraxford left an account of his son's death, but I have never seen it."

"How exactly did he die—according to your uncle?" I asked.

"One of the servants happened to be polishing the banister on the main staircase as the storm broke. She saw the boy rush from the gallery and hurtle across the landing as if the Devil himself were after him. He ran straight into the railing with such force that it gave way, and he broke his neck in the fall."

"What could have frightened him so badly?"

"My uncle did not say; he comes out with these snippets at odd times, but he will never answer a direct question. Quite possibly the storm itself—assuming the story is true—it was Thomas Wraxford, you recall, who had the lightning rods installed in the first place, and perhaps he communicated his own fear to his son."

"And—the haunting?"

"Sarah, the maid, claims that she has twice heard footsteps running across the gallery floor whilst she was in the dining room below; followed, on both occasions, by a peal of thunder. But the story of the footsteps has come down from the previous generation of servants."

"Do you think . . . is it possible that your uncle was actually present—I mean, at the Hall—when Felix Wraxford died?"

"He did not say so, but yes, it is possible; I believe the estrangement between Thomas and his brother Nathaniel—Cornelius's father—did not begin until after the tragedy. Are you suggesting that my uncle might have been responsible for his cousin's death?"

I had not meant to imply as much, but he had divined my thought.

"Well, I hardly like to—"

"Pray don't apologise; the same thing should have occurred to me, but my mind was running on other lines. I can well imagine my uncle, as a child, devising some scheme to terrify his cousin. . . ."

He fell silent, contemplating the dying fire. I found myself imagining Cornelius as a boy in rusty black clothes, with a wizened old man's face, crouched behind the armour; the darkening sky outside; another boy, pale and fearful, moving through the gallery . . . and then a pounce, a clatter of running feet, a shriek, drowned in the crash of thunder. I thought of Cornelius, decades later, drawing out his life alone in that same gallery. If it had happened thus, the gallery was haunted indeed. Had Cornelius, even as a child, coveted the Hall, and understood that only Felix stood between him and eventual possession of it?

Magnus leaned forward to stir the coals, breaking my reverie.

"You said your thoughts were running on other lines," I ventured.

"I was wondering—again, it should have occurred to me sooner—whether my uncle did not purchase that manuscript, as he professed, but discovered it somewhere in the house . . . wondering, in other words, whether Thomas Wraxford was also acquainted with Trithemius . . ."

A fearful presentiment crossed my mind.

"What were the words you copied?" I asked. "About the young tree and the old?"

Magnus drew the paper from his coat.

"'. . . if he be a true *Adept,* to Perform that *Rite* of which I have written Elsewhere. For as a young *Tree* may be Grafted upon an *Old,* so . . .'"

I seemed to read my own apprehension in his glance.

"Surely," I said, "no man would set out to sacrifice his own son—" realising, as I spoke, that Abraham had set out to do precisely that.

"Surely not," said Magnus. "It is a thousand to one the boy died in a tragic accident." But he did not sound altogether persuaded.

"And Thomas Wraxford's disappearance?" I persisted. "What do you make of that, in the light of your uncle's talk of vanishing?"

"I see your drift," said Magnus, "but without further evidence, we can only speculate. As for my uncle . . . there are, at any rate, no children at the Hall now. Beyond that, I fear you are right; all we can do is watch, and wait. And now, my dear fellow, it is growing late, and I must not keep you up any longer."

I could not quite recall having advised him thus, but could think of no alternative, and though I pressed him to stay, he insisted that he must be going. We compromised upon my walking back with him to the White Lion; the sky had cleared, and the night air was still and very cold, with no sound but the faint rattle of pebbles from the starlit shore away to our left. Magnus turned the conversation back to painting as we walked, saying that he hoped I would one day be able to make another study of the Hall in happier circumstances. But the horrors we had summoned were not so easily dispelled, and my dreams that night were haunted by the sound of running footsteps, and a manikin with a wizened face.

For the next fortnight or so, I was gripped by foreboding whenever the sky darkened, or the glass fell farther than usual. I had received a note from Magnus on his return to London, saying how delighted he had been to make my acquaintance, and thanking me again for my offer to go out to the Hall if it should prove necessary, but nothing further. We had parted like intimate friends; yet when I looked back I realised that I had learned nothing of his history, or of his interests and aspirations apart from his work, whereas I had revealed a great deal about myself. Our encounter had left me restless, unsettled, with no idea of what to do about it.

April proved cold and blustery, and May was well advanced before a prolonged spell of fine weather brought out the last of the blossom. Day after day I walked down to the office under a dazzling blue sky, wishing that my spirits would rise accordingly. *Wraxford Hall by Moonlight* still hung on my office wall, reminding me of the power I could not recapture, and of Cornelius in his haunted gallery. The weather grew warmer still, until one hot and airless morning I emerged to find the sky already overcast, the sea flat and still, but with an ominous leaden sheen. My anxiety grew until, early in the afternoon, I wired Magnus to say that a severe storm was brewing. There was no reply, and I spent the rest of the day reproaching myself for sending it.

All afternoon the heat pressed down and the barometer continued to drop, until darkness fell without a breath of wind. Too restless to read, I sat out in the garden, staring into the night. Then away on the seaward horizon came the first faint flicker of lightning, branching and multiplying in dumb show until the air began to stir, and the distant muttering of thunder rose above the shrilling of the insects. The storm, approaching gradually at first, seemed to gather pace as it came nearer, until the sky to the south was a searing tapestry of light. The words of Trithemius came back to me amidst the tumult: "Thus, a Man who could command the Power of *Lightning* would be as the Avenging Angel upon that Dreadful Day . . ." I thought of the blackened suit of armour in the gallery: if Cornelius had been mad enough to occupy it, he must already be ashes. No one but a lunatic would consent to such a thing, no matter what the inducement . . . but supposing consent had not been asked—or given? If anyone is dead, I thought, it will be on my conscience; we should have tried to stop him, regardless of the risk to Magnus's prospects. But the thought was interrupted by a rush of wind, accompanied by a flash, a deafening blast, and a torrent of rain; I was drenched before I had left my chair.

I sat up long after the lightning had ceased and the wind had died away, listening to the steady patter of rain on the leaves outside. Whatever I ought to have done, it was too late now; unless the Hall had been spared, in which case, was I simply going to wait for the next storm to strike? Or try to persuade Magnus to have his uncle certified; and if that failed, at least to warn Cornelius that we knew what he was up to? Except that we did not know; the only certainty here was any such intervention would lose Magnus the estate, and me my client, if not my professional reputation. I went over and over the ground until the small hours, without reaching any conclusion whatever.

Nevertheless, I was early at the office next day, and spent most of the morning pacing up and down my room, peering out at the rain-swept street, and plaguing Josiah with queries about wires and messengers. My uneasy conscience forbade me to mention the name Wraxford, and by the time I departed for a hasty luncheon at the Cross Keys Inn, he was plainly concerned for my sanity. But no message was waiting on my return. And then at half past three, just as I had convinced myself that nothing would happen, Josiah announced that a Mr. Drayton wished to see me on urgent business.

I had pictured Drayton as a tall man, but he turned out to be several inches shorter than myself, frail and stooped in a suit of rusty black, with a long, pallid face and the eyes of an anxious spaniel. His hands were visibly trembling.

"Mr. Montague, sir; forgive me for troubling you, but Dr. Wraxford—Mr. Magnus, that is—said I should come to you if . . . well, it's the master, Mr. Montague. He didn't come out for his breakfast tray this morning, or his luncheon, and he won't answer when I knock, so I thought . . ."

"Quite right," I said. "Have you informed Dr. Wraxford?"

"I sent a wire on my way here, sir, but the reply will have to come from Woodbridge, so it won't reach the Hall until six at the earliest, even if he answers by return."

"I see . . . I take it you would like me to come out to the Hall, and see if—if everything is all right." I tried to sound calm and assured, but an icy knot was forming in the pit of my stomach.

"Thank you, sir, if you could, it would be much appreciated. Grimes is outside with the carriage, sir, but I'm afraid it's open, so you will need to wrap up warm."

Ten minutes later we were on our way. The rain had all but ceased, but grey, swirling cloud hung low over the sodden landscape. Grimes—a dour, prognathous individual, all too appropriately named—sat slumped in his greatcoat, swaying like a sack of meal; he appeared to have sunk into a deep sleep before we had passed the first milepost. Drayton sat beside me in the body of the ancient vehicle; I tried at first to draw him out, but in vain; he had seen nothing, heard nothing, noticed nothing unusual until this morning. The master had dismissed him at seven the previous evening—well before the storm began—saying he would need nothing more until breakfast. The storm had been very loud, but he had been in his room all evening, and could not say whether a lightning bolt might have struck the Hall; he showed not the slightest curiosity on that score. I asked him whether he found the lightning conductors a comfort; he did not seem to know what a lightning conductor was. He had been forty years at the Hall, and everything, it seemed, had been exactly the same from the day he arrived until this morning. At that I gave up, and huddled deeper into my own greatcoat.

For two and a half interminable hours we splashed and jolted past empty fields and marshes and patches of woodland. The horses plodded steadily onward, never varying their pace; they seemed to know every turn along the way, for Grimes did not stir throughout the journey, and Drayton, too, dozed, his head lolling on his breast, once I had ceased to question him. Despite my heavy coat and muffler, the chill seeped into my bones, slowing my thoughts to a dull trance of apprehension until I sank into a dream in which I seemed to be conscious of every creak and rattle of the carriage, yet somehow safe and warm at my own fireside, only to wake, half-frozen, in the gloom of Monks' Wood. I fumbled for my watch and saw that it was already past six o'clock. Another fifteen minutes passed before the massive oak loomed ahead of us, and Grimes roused himself from the depths of his greatcoat to announce, in the tones of one relishing another's misfortune, "Wraxford 'All."

Shrouded in vapour, the lightning rods all but concealed in the mist that swirled just above the treetops, the Hall looked even darker and more ruinous than my memory of it, the grounds more wildly overgrown. The only sign of life was a trickle of smoke from the chimney of Grimes's cottage, barely rising in the saturated air.

We pulled up amongst the weeds by the front door. I stretched my cramped limbs and descended upon feet so numb they could scarcely feel the ground beneath them. Drayton was in even worse case; I had to help him down in spite of his protests, wondering how on earth he managed in the depths of winter. Grimes remained slumped in his seat, seemingly oblivious, only to drive off the instant we had alighted.

The uncertainty of my position struck me with full force as Drayton struggled with the lock (opening the door was evidently not part of the maid's duties), and ushered me into a vast, echoing chamber dominated by a staircase ascending into the gloom. Far above my head, I could just make out the landing from which Felix Wraxford must have hurtled to his death. The floor was bare, uneven flagstones, the walls dark-panelled oak, pitted with wormholes. Everything smelled of age and damp and decay; a dead chill lay upon the air.

"Perhaps," I said to Drayton, trying to subdue the quaver in my voice, "you should go up ahead of me; it is possible, after all, that your master has merely overslept." He responded with a look of such fearful entreaty that I felt obliged to accompany him, wishing to God I had never made this foolhardy offer, as he moved slowly up the stairs, past canvases so darkened with age and grime that their subjects were unidentifiable. We passed the turning; as we came up onto the landing I knew from Magnus's description that we were facing the study, and that the two sets of double doors in the dark-panelled wall away to our left led to the library and the gallery. Grey mist swirled against the high windows above our heads and at the far end of the landing; there was still a fair amount of light, but it was fading fast.

"I think you should knock once more," I said to Drayton. He raised a trembling hand and rapped feebly; there was no reply. I came up beside him and rapped in turn, more and more loudly until the echoes rang like gunshots up and down the stairwell. I tried the handle, but the door would not budge.

"It's this one, sir," said Drayton. His face was ashen pale; the keys danced and jangled as he handed them to me. The key would not go into the lock; there was evidently a key on the inside, turned so that it could not be dislodged.

"Very sorry, sir," said Drayton faintly. "I'm afraid I shall 'ave to . . ." indicating a chair against the wall to our right.

"Where is the maid?" I asked as I helped him over to it. He mumbled something unintelligible.

"And Mrs. Grimes?—never mind," I said, "show me the keys to the other doors." He indicated them with a shaking finger and sank down on the chair, one hand pressed against his heart.

The pounding of my own heart seemed unnaturally loud as I approached the entrance to the library. Again the doors would not budge, and the key would not enter the lock. Which left only the gallery. The threadbare carpet had worn right through in places, and I did not like the way the echoes rebounded, sounding unnervingly like running footsteps. I glanced at the railing as I came to the last set of doors; the repairs, at least, had been done well enough to leave no trace of the accident—if such it was.

Once again the doors were locked from the inside. I hammered on the panelling, again with no result but a fusillade of echoes. I could go in search of Grimes, but how long would that take?—and would he obey me if I found him? I did not want to enter Cornelius's domain by candlelight.

Of the three entrances, the door to the study had felt a little less solid than the others. I retraced my steps toward Drayton, who had slumped lower on his chair and seemed barely conscious, set my shoulder against the upper panel, and felt it give. I drew off a little and threw my full weight against the door, expecting the panel to fracture; instead the door burst open with a rending crash, pitching me across the threshold as lock and bolts tore from their sockets; the jamb had been rotten with woodworm.

There was no one in the study, which was perhaps twelve feet by ten, with a fireplace at the far end. Against the wall to my left stood a camp bed, neatly made up, beneath rows of theological works. Further along that wall, another door stood open, concealing whatever lay beyond. On my right, beneath the windows, a desk, a tin chest and, incongruously, a washstand. Despite the cold, the air smelled frowsty and stale. And there was something else: a faint odour of ash, which grew stronger as I moved uneasily toward the other door. It was coming from a blackened, calcined mass of paper in the fireplace.

The room beyond was, as Magnus had said, a typical country gentleman's library, with tall cases on three sides, a ladder for the high shelves, more dark oak panelling, threadbare carpet, leather chairs, a vast fireplace in the end wall. And no sign of Cornelius, even when I braced myself to glance around the corner, into the alcove behind the study wall: nothing but a large, empty table; no books or papers on it, or on any of the tables or chairs. Both the doors in the wall adjoining the gallery were closed.

If I should vanish . . . Swallowing hard, I strode across to the nearest of the two and grasped the handle, hoping it would be locked. But the door swung inward with a creak and groan of hinges, opening onto an expanse of bare wooden floorboards, a long table beneath darkening windows. There was the massive fireplace framing the sarcophagus and flanked by the dark bulk of the armour, exactly as Magnus had described . . . but no wizened manikin sprawled upon the floor, and nowhere, as Magnus had said, for him to hide; nowhere but the blackened figure that loomed higher and higher as I approached until it seemed at least seven feet tall.

Shuddering as if I were about to grasp a serpent, I reached for the sword hilt. As my fingers touched the icy metal, I heard a choking sound, followed by a thud, somewhere at my back. It broke the last of my nerve and sent me retreating headlong through the library. As I burst onto the landing, with the sound of my footsteps reverberating around me, I heard another cry from the darkness below. For an instant I thought it was Drayton, until I saw him sprawled in the shadows beside his chair, and realised that he had answered his last summons.

I remember finding the elderly maid Sarah trembling at the foot of the stairs, thinking the ghost had returned (she received the news of her master's vanishing with indifference, but burst into tears when I told her about Drayton); stumbling out to the cottage and railing in vain at Grimes, who was already in drink; seizing a lantern from his wife and setting off to walk the five miles to Melton in the dark. But the chill would not leave my bones, and the shivering grew worse as I walked until my teeth were rattling in my head. I think I must have crouched for hours beside the fire at the Coach and Horses, unable to stop my teeth from chattering, with the odd sensation of looking down at myself from somewhere near the ceiling; and then I was shivering in a strange bed, with the dead face of Drayton circling through nightmares whilst I burned and froze by turns. Other faces came and went in my delirium, Magnus's amongst them, but I could not tell which were real and which mere hallucinations.

The fever broke on the fourth day, leaving me very weak but otherwise unscathed. The doctor attending me—George Barton from Woodbridge, a genial, commonsense fellow of five-and-forty or thereabouts—told me that the Hall and Monks' Wood had been thoroughly searched, without result. I dared not ask whether they had opened the suit of armour; his bluff, hearty manner did not encourage talk of alchemy and supernatural rites.

Magnus came to see me the next morning, full of apologies for my ordeal; he had been in Devon when the alarm was raised, and had not arrived until late on the following day. There was still no news of Cornelius.

"Have you been out to the Hall?" I asked.

"Yes, I spent yesterday there. Inspector Roper from Woodbridge—are you acquainted with him?—thought that I should look through my uncle's papers to see if they afforded any clue."

"And did they?"

"I fear not. He seems to have burned a great many—you noticed the ashes in the grate?—including, I believe, the manuscript of Trithemius. There were fragments—I thought I recognised the hand—but it all fell to pieces at a touch."

I'll burn my book . . . The words of Faustus came involuntarily to my lips.

"I confess," said Magnus, "that the same thought occurred to me."

"And—the armour?"

"Empty. I showed Roper the mechanism, and told him something of my uncle's alchemical obsession, but he dismissed the whole business as mediaeval make-believe. He takes the view that Drayton was mistaken in thinking he saw my uncle retire—and yes, I know that you found all the doors secured on the inside, but Roper insists that the door you forced must have been jammed, rather than locked."

I realised, as I opened my mouth to dispute this, that I could not positively swear to it; the fever had blurred my memory.

"It isn't easy, as you see, to argue with rugged common sense. Roper, just to complete his theory, thinks that my uncle left the house sometime during the previous afternoon—at any rate, no later than dusk—and was caught in the forest when the storm broke. As he says, you could pass within three feet of a body in Monks' Wood and never know it was there."

"And you?" I asked. "What do *you* believe?"

"I am half-inclined to agree with Roper, if only because the alternative seems too monstrous to contemplate. . . . And now, my dear fellow, I must tax your strength no further. Whatever has become of my uncle, I shall have to apply for a judgement of decease, and if you see no conflict, I shall be delighted if you will act for me. I wonder, by the way, since Roper seems determined to ignore the darker possibilities, whether the business of Trithemius and the armour might remain confidential between us; the Hall's reputation is sinister enough as it is."

I assured him that it would remain a secret between us, and on that inconclusive note we parted. I scarcely knew Magnus Wraxford, and yet I could not help thinking of him as an intimate friend, an intimacy forged around the secret we shared.

Cornelius had not, it transpired, written down any of the strange provisions he had mentioned in his final interview with Magnus, and the terms of the 1858 will remained unaltered, though it would be another two years, as things turned out, before the judgement of decease was granted. He had left one hundred pounds to Grimes and Eliza, and another hundred to Drayton and Sarah (who had evidently been Drayton's common-law wife; I learned afterward that his lawful wife had left him many years before). My father had not mentioned these bequests, and I was surprised by their generosity. Everything else went to Magnus: a millstone rather than a windfall, for the estate was heavily encumbered.

There was a strange coda to Cornelius's disappearance. A few weeks after the event, I was conversing with Dr. Dawson, who had charge of the parish infirmary, and he told me the story of a patient who had recently died there. This man, an itinerant stonemason, had been abroad in Monks' Wood on the afternoon of the great storm (possibly to check the contents of certain snares, but that was by the by). At any rate, he had missed his way, and wandered until he came to the old Wraxford chapel. Oppressed by the airless heat, he lay down to rest a little way from the entrance, fell into a deep sleep, and woke in pitch darkness. The storm had not yet broken, but with the stars entirely obscured, he dared not move; he could not see his hand in front of his face.

Then a spark of light appeared in the blackness, flickering amongst the trees as it came toward him. He thought of calling out for help, but—though he was not a local man, and knew nothing of the Hall's reputation—something about its silent, purposeful approach unnerved him. As it came closer still, he could make out a human figure—whether a man or a woman he could not tell—with a lantern in its hand. Again he was about to call out, when he saw that the figure was shrouded, not in a greatcoat but a monk's habit, with the hood drawn over its head. Now he feared for his soul and would have fled blindly into the wood, but his limbs were frozen with dread. Twigs crackled beneath its feet as the figure passed within a few yards of him; it was tall, he said, too tall for a mortal man, and as it went by he caught a glimpse of dead-white flesh—or was it bone?—beneath the hood.

It did not pause, but went straight up to the chapel door. He heard the scrape of a key, the rasp and snap of a lock, and then a creaking of hinges as the door swung inward and the figure passed into the chapel, closing the door behind it. The glow of the lantern shone out through a barred window at the side.

Now was his chance to flee; he knew that if the figure emerged again, it would see him. But he could move only as far as the light from the window would guide him, for fear of falling and having the creature rush upon him. He began to creep around the side of the chapel, keeping to the edge of the dim semicircle of light. Then he saw that the glass had gone from the window, leaving only four rusty bars between himself and the scene within.

The hooded figure stood with its back to him, facing a stone coffin by the opposite wall: the lantern hung upon a bracket overhead. Even as he watched, it leaned forward and raised the lid of the sarcophagus with a grinding of stone on stone. Again his limbs failed him; he could only watch as the creature took down its lantern, slipped over the edge, and in one swirling movement lay down within the tomb, lowering the lid as it went, until only a thin line of yellow light remained. A moment later, that, too, was extinguished, and he was plunged once more into absolute darkness.

Then his nerve gave way altogether and he fled blindly into the wood, stumbling and rebounding from one obstacle to another until he ran headfirst into a tree trunk, to be roused an indefinite time later by a gigantic crash of thunder. Even beneath the trees he was drenched to the skin, and when he finally stumbled out of Monks' Wood the next morning, he was in a worse case than I had been. He was taken to the infirmary, where he survived the first bout of fever, and was able to relate his strange tale to Dr. Dawson, but his lungs never recovered, and another infection carried him off within the month.

Dawson, though he thought it picturesque enough to be worth relating, naturally dismissed the unfortunate man's story as a delirious dream. Of course I agreed with him, but it reminded me uncomfortably of the old superstition about the Hall, and the image of the shrouded figure with the lantern troubled my imagination for many months to come.

Part Three

Eleanor Unwin's Narrative

1866

It began with a fall, soon after my twenty-first birthday, though I recall nothing between going to bed as usual and waking as if from a long, dreamless sleep. I was found, early on a winter's morning, lying at the foot of the stairs in my nightgown, and was carried back to my room, where I lay unconscious, scarcely breathing, for the rest of that day and all of the following night, until I woke to find old Dr. Stevenson bending over me. His head was surrounded by the most extraordinary halo of light, suffused with all the colours of the rainbow, a radiance so subtle and yet so vibrant as to make me feel I had never seen colour before. I lay entranced by the beauty of it, too absorbed to follow what he was saying. And for a while longer—minutes, hours, I did not know—everyone who came to my bedside was bathed in paradisial light, as if my mother and my sister Sophie had stepped from the pages of an old manuscript book I had once seen. For each of them the light was subtly different, the colours shimmering and changing as they moved and spoke. A verse kept running through my mind: "Even Solomon in all his glory was not arrayed like one of these." But then my head began to ache, worse and worse until I was forced to close my eyes and wait for the sleeping draught to take effect, and when I woke again, the radiance had gone.

Everyone assumed that I had fallen whilst sleepwalking, which I had done often enough as a child for my mother to threaten to lock me in her room, though I had never injured myself before. Indeed, Mama was far from sympathetic: it was, she declared, one more sign of my selfish and obstinate nature that I should contrive to fall down the stairs a week after my sister had accepted an offer of marriage. Sophie's being the younger by a year only compounded the offence, for if I had worked at making myself agreeable, instead of hiding away with a book, I, too, might now be engaged. I thought her fiancé a vacuous booby; but I could not deny that I had always been a great trial to my mother.

Though I was, in waking life, far bolder than Sophie, I had been prone to nightmares, as well as sleepwalking, for as long as I could recall. As I grew older, I walked less frequently in my sleep, but the nightmares became more frequent and oppressive. There was one in particular, which recurred many times, of a vast, echoing house I was sure I had never seen. It was not at all like the redbrick villa in Highgate where we had always lived, and never exactly the same from one dream to the next, and yet I knew whenever I was there. I was always alone, acutely aware of the silence, feeling that the house itself was alive, watchful, aware of my presence. The ceilings were immensely high, with dark-panelled walls, and though there were windows I could never see anything beyond the glass.

Sometimes I would be there only for a brief space and wake thinking, "I have been in the house again," but when the dream ran its full course, I would be compelled to move from one deserted room to the next, fearful and yet powerless to stop, knowing that I must come to a flight of stairs—sometimes grand and opulent, in other dreams narrow and worn—and thence to a room at the end of a corridor: a long room furnished with carved chests and screens in a dark, oily wood, covered with elaborate designs picked out in gold. In one such dream I was drawn farther into the room until I came to a low dais, upon which stood a statue of a beast like a panther about to spring, cast in dark, gleaming metal. Cold blue light began to glow around it; a vibration like the buzzing of a gigantic insect filled my body, and I woke to my own cry of horror.

In another sort of nightmare, quieter and yet in its way still more fearful, I would dream that I awoke—it seemed always to be twilight, just before dawn—in my own room, everything in its familiar place, except that my hearing was unnaturally acute: The blood surging in my ears sounded as loud as waves breaking upon the shore. Then I would sense the approach of some malignant being, coming up the passage or hovering at my window; my heart would begin to pound until I feared it would tear itself out of my breast, and I would wake with my heart still beating violently.

A few months before the fall, I was woken, as I thought, in the early morning, by hearing my name called softly. I rose and went to my door in my nightgown, but there was no one in the passage. The voice had sounded like Sophie's, but when I came to her door, it was closed. All was silent; the bathroom door stood slightly open; there was my mother's room beyond; then the landing and the staircase, exactly as in waking life. I heard my name called again, only this time the voice boomed like a gong inside my head; the light failed, as if a candle had been snuffed, and something rushed at me out of the gloom. I screamed and struggled until the light came back with the sound of running feet and I realised that the demon who had seized me was, in fact, my mother.

Mama was justifiably enraged, and I could only agree that I belonged in a madhouse, and should certainly be sent to one if I persisted with this hysterical nonsense. It was all very well to say that I could not help it: Sophie had never walked in her sleep, or woken the household with her screams, so why was I so lacking in self-control? Because I was wilful, obstinate, selfish, and contrary, and a great deal more besides. I was accustomed to Mama's tirades, but this one was so violent and, I felt, so thoroughly deserved, that I resolved to lock myself in my room and hide the key in a different place each night, in the hope that my dreaming self would not remember where I had put it. As the weeks passed without a relapse, I began to believe myself cured of the nightmares as well as the sleepwalking, and gave up locking my door, until the morning when Elspeth, our maid, found me sprawled at the foot of the stairs.

A fortnight or so later—certainly, after the doctor had pronounced me well on the way to recovery—I was sitting up in bed reading when my grandmother came into the room and sat down in the chair beside me, looking exactly as she had when I was a little girl: the same elaborate black silk dress and tightly pinned white hair, the same familiar scent of lavender and violet water. The chair creaked as she settled herself in it, smiled at me and took up her work, just as if she had only been gone five minutes, rather than resting in Kensal Green Cemetery for the past fifteen years. I was vaguely aware that Grandmama was supposed to be dead, but somehow this did not matter; her presence at my bedside seemed entirely natural and comforting. And though my own tranquil acceptance of the visit would later seem, to me, as strange as the visit itself, we sat in companionable silence for an indefinite interval until my grandmother gathered up her work, smiled once more at me and went slowly from the room.

Mama came in so soon after that I thought they must have passed each other in the hall, so I asked, "Did you see Grandmama?" I saw from her look of consternation that I had best not pursue the subject, and agreed that I must have been dreaming. As with the strange radiance, Grandmama's appearance was followed by one of the worst headaches I had ever endured. But I felt certain I had been wide awake.

Even after the strangeness of the experience had become fully apparent to me, I found I could not think of my visitant as a ghost. My reading in sensational literature had enhanced an already vivid imagination of how ghosts ought to conduct themselves: a hint of transparency and one or two bloodcurdling groans was surely the least that could be expected, whereas Grandmama had been—well, just Grandmama. And though nothing like this had ever happened to me before, I had not felt in the slightest afraid.

Dr. Stevenson had declared me well enough to get up, and the memory of my grandmother's visit had faded to the point where I could almost believe it *had* been a dream, when one evening after dinner I saw my father crossing the hall ahead of me. He was no more than ten paces away. I heard the floor creak under his tread, smelt the smoke of his cigar. Looking neither right nor left, he entered his study and closed the door behind him, just as he would have done in life. Again I felt no fear; only an overwhelming impulse to go up to his door and knock. When there was no answer I tried the handle. The door opened readily, but there was no one there, only the familiar cracked brown leather armchairs on the worn Persian rug, the elaborate desk with its feet carved into the fierce faces of tigers that had so fascinated me as a child, the bookshelves crammed with Blue Books and army lists and regimental histories and accounts of old campaigns, the lingering faint odours of tobacco and leather and old bindings. I remained in the doorway for a long time, lost in a trance of recollection.

My father had spent a great deal of his life, or at least the latter part of it, in this room; he had met Mama while he was home on leave after many years' service with the army in Bengal. He had thick white whiskers, streaked with grey, and a beard which jutted out when he walked, making him look very fierce. His skin was a strange shade of yellow, for he had been very ill with fever, and his bald head shone so brightly that I used to wonder if he polished it in secret. Once in a while, he would take us for a long walk by ourselves; and if we found a quiet field where there was no one watching, he would drill us like soldiers, making us march up and down in time, and stand to attention and salute. I loved this game, and used to march Sophie around the back garden until Mama put a stop to it; she did not approve of little girls playing at soldiers.

As the youngest daughter in her family, Mama had been obliged to stay at home nursing her own father, a confirmed invalid, until he died, and by then she was almost thirty. She was very pale and slender, and grew thinner as the years passed, so that her pale blue eyes appeared to grow even larger as the bones of her face became more prominent. The house in Highgate, I came to understand, had been a compromise between Papa, who would rather have lived in the country, right away from London, and Mama, who longed to be part of Society. I had, as a child, no very clear idea of what Society might be, but it seemed that Highgate stood on the outermost fringe of it. We did not want for company: Major James Paget, an old friend and comrade of Papa's, had taken a house only a few minutes' walk from their own, and I had been fast friends with their daughter Ada since she was seven years old. But somehow the Pagets did not count as Society.

Ada and I were often taken for sisters, for we were both quite tall and strongly featured, and much darker in colouring than Sophie, who was fair-haired, fair-skinned, and by any conventional standard the beauty of the family. Sophie had always been my mother's favourite, for she loved balls and parties and gossip, and would happily sit for half a day in front of her mirror, time which I far preferred to spend with my nose buried in a book, as Mama despairingly put it. As I grew older, I came to realise that my parents were deeply estranged, living quite separate lives and avoiding one another as far as possible. So long as the Pagets—a devoted and loving couple to the end—had remained nearby, it had not seemed to matter so much. But soon after my eighteenth birthday, James Paget had died suddenly, followed a few months later by my own father.

And now Ada's mother was living with relations on the Isle of Wight, and Ada herself was married to a clergyman, a hundred miles away in a remote Suffolk village, while I was still at home, restless, unhappy, and constantly at loggerheads with my mother. I had worked at my sketching and music, and was competent at both, but no more; I had tried my hand at a novel and got as far as the third chapter before disbelief in my own creation pulled me up. I had pleaded to be allowed to seek a position as a governess, but my mother would not hear of it. Sophie's success in snaring Arthur Carstairs had only heightened Mama's disappointment in me, whom she was wont to characterise as unfeeling, ungrateful, insolent, obstinate, sullen, and contrary. For all the unfairness of her tirades, I could not altogether disagree, oppressed as I was by the sense of my own worthlessness, of life slipping through my fingers.

As with Grandmama's appearance at my bedside, the apparition of my father was followed, after a peculiarly tranquil interval, by the onset of a blinding headache. I had not made any connection between the first visitation—the word that seemed the least unsatisfactory—and the fall. But now I began to wonder; I had heard people described as "cracked," and perhaps the application was more literal than I had supposed. Could the fall have opened some fissure in my consciousness, admitting perceptions which were meant to be kept out? But that implied that the appearances were in some way real, whereas if no one else could see them . . . though of course they could not, if I alone had stumbled upon some special power of sight.

I knew better than to say anything to my mother and sister, and could not bring myself to write of it even to Ada, whom I had told about the fall, and the strange radiance afterward, but nothing more; whether because I did not want to trouble her happiness, or for fear of being thought mad, I was not sure. As the days passed without further visitations, I tried to convince myself that nothing more would follow. But something in the quality of my inward life had altered, subtly but unmistakably; it was like walking into a room and feeling that the colour of the walls, or the pattern of the carpet, had changed, without being able to say precisely how. Familiar scents and tastes seemed suddenly heightened; it was springtime, admittedly, but there was more to it than that, a sense of—not exactly apprehension, but of something impending. On several occasions I had, very powerfully, the sensation of knowing what everyone in the room would say for the next few moments. And once, when Mama complained of losing the stone from a favourite pendant, I got up, walked straight to the other end of the house, turned into the drawing room, reached under a cabinet in the darkest corner, and drew out the lost stone, which was jet. I was at a loss to understand how I had done this, and glad that my mother had not witnessed quite how remarkable the feat had been.

Several weeks had passed in this uneasy state when Mama announced that Arthur Carstairs's mother and sisters would shortly be coming to tea. On the afternoon in question, I came down to join the others and await our visitors' arrival. As I entered the drawing room, I saw a young man seated on the sofa opposite Sophie and Mama. I had never seen him before. He was just a slender, dark-haired young man, sombrely dressed in what looked like a suit of mourning, and apparently absorbed in a study of the carpet at his feet. He seemed to be averting his gaze out of modesty, as if he did not want to be noticed, but otherwise appeared quite at his ease. I stood uncertainly in the doorway, waiting to be introduced, but neither of the others seemed to be paying him the slightest attention.

"Do sit down, Eleanor," said my mother, pointing to the sofa. She seemed to be indicating the place immediately next to the young man.

"But—will you not introduce me?" I stammered.

"To whom?" replied my mother, staring.

"To—" I gestured helplessly toward the young man.

"I do not know what you mean," Mama said sharply, "and I am in no mood for frivolity. Be seated, and let us have no more nonsense."

Throughout this exchange, the young man continued to gaze quietly at the floor, still with that self-effacing air. I stood transfixed, aware that my mother and Sophie were both speaking to me, but unable to take my eyes off the young man, who, as if suddenly conscious of my plight, rose from the sofa and began to walk toward me. I heard the rustle of his clothing, the sound of his tread upon the floor. He paused a couple of paces from me, still with his head bowed; automatically, I stepped away from the door to allow him to pass. But then—as if a painted figure had stepped from a canvas and, turning aside, revealed itself as a mere film of pigment floating upon the air—he seemed to shrink sideways into himself, until he was nothing but a jagged sliver of blackness, edged with greenish light. Then that, too, vanished and I was left dumbstruck, with the sound of the doorbell ringing in my ears.

I must not faint, I told myself, and summoning all my resolve, managed to gasp out some excuse and stumble away down the corridor until I reached the safety of the back parlour. There I collapsed onto a couch, with my head already beginning to throb. The pain soon became so excruciating that I lost all sense of time until someone, I could not tell who, brought me a sleeping draught, and I sank at last into merciful oblivion.

Next morning, I was at first bewildered to find myself fully dressed upon the parlour sofa. Elspeth brought me a cup of tea and Mama's instruction to remain where I was until the doctor had called, but neither Sophie nor Mama came in to see me. When Dr. Stevenson finally appeared, looking unwontedly stern, it was clear from the tenor of his questions that the others had seen nothing whatever unusual. All I could think to tell him was that I had been deceived by a trick of the light, and the sudden onset of a headache, into thinking I had seen someone sitting on the sofa, but really it was nothing, just a momentary confusion. He did not seem interested in the headache, and after he had left me, a long interval passed before I heard the front door close behind him.

I was prepared for a tirade, but not for the icy contempt with which Mama dismissed my abject apologies. "You are doing your best to destroy your sister's happiness," she declared, "and as for these headaches, you inflict them upon us out of wickedness and spite. It is moral insanity; Dr. Stevenson has said so, brought on by jealousy of your sister. There are surgeons who know how to cure wilful, hysterical girls like you; and if that should fail, you will have be confined to an asylum."

"I am dreadfully sorry, Mama," I said, "but truly I do not do it on purpose. No one would *want* to endure such pain—"

"The pain is nothing to what you have caused your sister. And how dare you contradict me, after such a display at the very instant Mrs. Carstairs and her daughters were expected?"

"Were they very put out?" I asked humbly.

"As you set out to ruin their visit, I fail to see that it is any of your business. Now listen to me: if it were not for Sophie, I should have you sent to a surgeon at once. But if the Carstairs suspect any taint of insanity in our family, Arthur may cry off. If he does, I shall have you locked away forever, though that would be no consolation to poor Sophie. I shall give you one last chance: mend your ways, or have the wickedness cut out of you."

My mother was apt, when enraged, to hurl the most extravagant threats, but the words had been uttered with cold, biting restraint; and whilst I had no idea what a surgeon might do to an hysterical girl, the final phrase had set my skin crawling with fear. I was of age; but I had read too many novels in which innocent heroines were confined to asylums to doubt my mother's power in that regard, and perhaps the same power could compel me to submit to the surgeon's knife. I had no money of my own, and no way of earning my living. I did not even know the terms of my father's will, save that the income from his estate, according to Mama's repeated laments, was barely enough to keep us.

And at any moment, another visitation might come upon me, even more ruinously timed than the last. If the young man had appeared to me ten minutes later, I might now be on my way to the surgeon—or the madhouse. He had looked so meek, so harmless, until the instant of his dissolution; but *was* it mere coincidence that he had appeared just as the Carstairs were arriving . . . ? The prospect was too appalling to confront alone. I retreated to my room and began a long letter to Ada, and did not pause until I had finished and sealed it and consigned it to the post.

At dinner that night, Sophie informed me, very coldly, that she and Mama had managed to conceal their agitation from the Carstairs and pretend that I had suffered a relapse of concussion from the fall. But that was all; for the remainder of the meal, Sophie and Mama exchanged pointedly trivial remarks, and I left the table as soon as politeness allowed, feeling that I was already condemned. And so it came as an immense relief when Ada replied by return, pressing me to visit as soon as possible.

It took all of my courage to ask leave of my mother who, thankfully, made no objection. "Perhaps it will be best," she declared with the utmost coldness, "if you keep away from us until Sophia is safely married; I shall write to see whether you can be trusted to attend the wedding when the time comes." Throughout my preparations, I was sick with terror that my freedom would be snatched away by another visitation; I kept, as far as possible, to my room until my trunk was safely aboard the hansom. The cloud of dread accompanied me all the way through the squalor of Spitalfields and Bethnal Green to Shoreditch Station, and was only really dispelled by the sight of George Woodward on the platform at Chalford. Even in a crowd, he would have been impossible to miss, because of the shock of coarse orange hair (no other word could do justice to the colour) which always made him look as if he had just come in out of a strong wind. He and Ada had met in London, and married, after the briefest of courtships, when the living at Chalford was unexpectedly offered him.

Chalford rectory—a large, dilapidated house of grey stone with a walled garden (or "yerd," in the idiom of the parish)—seemed to me the most charming place I had ever stayed in. "You would not think so," said Ada, "if you came to us in January, with an east wind howling about the house and snow heaped against the walls; I used to think London winters cold, until I came here." But in mild June weather, with everything in leaf and flower, Chalford was paradise enough. The rectory stood close by the churchyard, surrounded by fields and patches of woodland, and away from the village itself: Old Chalford had been stricken by the Black Death, its cottages burned to kill the plague, and a new settlement built a quarter of a mile off. The population of the village had been reduced by enclosures to little more than a hundred souls, mostly farming people whose great-grandfathers had tilled the same acres in much the same fashion. To the north and west of the parish were farmlands; to the east grazing, with gorse and marshland as you drew nearer the sea.

Within the space of a week, my colour had returned, and I was sleeping so soundly that I was scarcely aware of my dreams. Ada and I walked miles each day, and I began to see the country with new eyes. Every field, every path, even every hedgerow in the village had its own name and its own history, from Gravel Pit Walk on the western boundary to Roman Kiln Field by the river on the eastern edge. On our very first excursion I found a hag-stone—a flint with a hole through it, much prized by the farming people as an omen of good luck—and placed it beneath my pillow, as an amulet against further visitations.

Though there was no question of Ada's repenting at leisure, as my mother had unkindly prophesied, I could see how isolated her life had become. She longed very much for a child, but after a year of marriage she had still not conceived, and had begun to fear that she might be barren. And George, she confided, was increasingly troubled by doubts about his vocation. "I can listen, and question, and follow, I think, much of what he tells me, but he misses the society of thinking men like himself. He has read Lyell, and Renan, and the *Vestiges*, as well as Darwin, and has begun to wonder what, if anything, can be saved for belief. He prefers not to speak of it, but it troubles his conscience that he is living upon the tithes of people who expect and assume—especially in a country parish such as this—that he accepts the literal truth of Scripture. But he believes in goodness, kindness, and tolerance, and practices what he preaches, which is more than can be said for many churchmen who call themselves devout."

I had been in Chalford a fortnight when George proposed an expedition to see the old Norman keep at Orford, a small coastal settlement about four miles away. George himself had been there only once, but seemed perfectly sure of the way as we set out on a still, overcast afternoon. We had walked perhaps a mile before he admitted that this was not the road he had taken before. "Still," he said confidently, "we are heading more or less southeast, so we shouldn't go too far wrong."

Even I had to concede that there was something desolate about the prospect, once we had left the farmland behind. There seemed to be no one abroad, and no sign of habitation; only sheep wandering through the gorse, and occasional glimpses of a leaden grey sea. After another half-hour the path began to climb, with the ground falling away on both sides. Dense green bushes encircled the lower slopes, but the crown of the hill, as we approached it, was almost bare, cropped close by the sheep, and bunched like a counterpane—the image that came to me—into curious folds and mounds, which did not look at all natural, as if some huge burrowing creature had been tunnelling just below the surface. I was about to ask what had made them when we reached the top of the rise, and a dark expanse of woodland loomed before us.

"That can only be Monks' Wood," said George. "We are much farther south than I supposed. It is by far the oldest—and largest—forest in this part of the country."

"Is there a monastery within?" I asked. From where we stood, the dense green canopy seemed quite unbroken, stretching away to the south as far as the eye could follow.

"There was once, yes," said George, "but it was sacked by Henry the Eighth's men."

"And after that?"

"The land went to the Wraxford family for services to the Crown, and has been in the family ever since. Wraxford Hall was built on the foundations of the monastery; it is now almost a ruin, I believe; I have not seen it."

"Does anyone live there now?"

"No; not since . . . that is to say, it has been empty for some time."

"And how far is the Hall from here?" I persisted.

"I don't know," said George repressively. "The Wood is private; it belongs to the estate."

"But if there is no one living there . . . ? I should so love to see it."

"We should be trespassing. And the Wood has a bad reputation hereabouts; even poachers avoid it at night."

"Do you mean it is haunted?"

"Supposedly. There are tales—"

He was silenced by an anxious glance from Ada.

"Truly," I said, "I do not mind talk of ghosts. I do not even think of my—my visitants as ghosts, and besides I am quite recovered. I want to hear all about the Hall; it sounds most romantic. And look, there is a path leading down to the forest—"

"No," said George firmly, "we must be getting on to Orford."

"Then if you will not take us there," I said, "I insist that you tell me all about it."

"There is very little to tell," said George as we set off again. "According to local superstition, the Wood is haunted by the ghost of a monk, who appears whenever a Wraxford is about to die; it is said that anyone who sees the apparition will die within the month. I shouldn't be surprised if the Wraxfords started the rumour themselves to keep people away. The family have played no part in local affairs for as long as anyone can remember, but there is nothing unusual in that. No; the only genuine oddity is that the last two owners have disappeared."

"What do you mean, disappeared?"

"Exactly that; no more, no less. Mind you, the two incidents happened nearly fifty years apart. The first was a Thomas Wraxford, a widower; he had great plans for the Hall when he inherited it, somewhere in the 1780s, I think, but then his only son died in an accident, and his wife returned to her family. He lived alone at the Hall for many years, until he was quite an old man; then one evening he went to bed as usual, and when his valet came to wake him the next morning, he wasn't there. There had been a heavy downpour, with thunder and lightning, not long after he retired, but then it cleared to a fine moonlit night. His bed hadn't been slept in, and there was no sign of a struggle; so it was generally assumed that he'd wandered off into the forest—disoriented by the storm, perhaps—and fallen into a pit or something of the sort. The Wood is very much overgrown, you see, and there are various old workings—it was mined for tin centuries ago—a very easy place to come to grief in."

"And—the other?" I asked with a slight shiver. The path had descended again, and now ran parallel to the edge of the forest, which looked very dense indeed, so choked with creeper and fallen branches that you could see only a few yards within.

"Cornelius Wraxford—Thomas's nephew, the nearest surviving male relative—petitioned the Court of Chancery to find that Thomas was legally deceased. He—Cornelius—was a fellow at some obscure Cambridge college, but he resigned as soon as judgement was given—and took possession of the Hall. Where he remained for another forty-five years, living the life of a complete recluse, until the spring of this year, when the same thing happened; he retired as usual—again, by a strange coincidence, on the night of a violent electrical storm—and was never seen again."

"But—what do you think became of him?"

"No one knows. Of course it caused a good deal of talk; the general opinion at the Ship was that both of them had been carried off by the Devil. I wonder myself if Thomas Wraxford's fate could have played upon his nephew's mind until his wits finally gave way, and, under the influence of the storm—he felt compelled to follow his uncle's example."

"Like King Lear on the heath," said Ada. "I remember that storm very well; he must have been mad indeed if he went out in it."

"And what will become of the Hall now?" I asked.

"I believe that the heir—a Magnus Wraxford; I know nothing of him—has applied for a judgement of decease. It may raise a few eyebrows on the bench, but I don't suppose he'll have much trouble getting it; Cornelius must have been at least eighty years old."

"And now," said Ada, "it is high time we spoke of something more cheerful."

I did not press the topic any further, but the image of an old man stumbling through a dark forest remained vivid in my mind, long after Monks' Wood had vanished from sight.

An hour or so later, we came within sight of Orford Keep, a massive, turreted edifice of jagged brown brick and greyish mortar. It stood on a high earthen mound, with a few scattered cottages beyond, though the settlement seemed quite deserted. As we came nearer, I noticed an easel standing a little way from the keep. It bore a stretched canvas, but there was no sign of the artist, who had presumably retired to one of the cottages. I could not resist the impulse to examine the picture.

It was, as I expected, a study of the keep, but in oils, not watercolour, and it reminded me of a place I knew but could not immediately identify. The artist had caught the bulk and mass of the tower, the way it seemed to lean over you, but there was more, something ominous, a sense of impending menace. The closely paired windows below the battlements made you think of eyes . . . that was it, it was like the house of my dream, alert, alive, listening . . .

"That's—er—very striking," said George, coming up beside me.

"Very sinister," said Ada in turn.

"I think it is wonderful," I said.

"I'm delighted you think so," said a voice seemingly from the earth behind me. I spun round as a figure rose from the long grass a few feet away. A man—a young man—slender, not especially tall, wearing tweed trousers and a collarless shirt, rather the worse for paint.

"I am sorry to have startled you," he said, brushing grass seeds from his clothes. "I was asleep, and your voices got into my dream. Edward Ravenscroft, at your service."

As with the picture, I was reminded of someone I had seen before, but I could not think who or where, and I had never heard the name before. He was certainly handsome, with dark brown hair falling across his forehead, fair skin, a little roughened and reddened by the sun; dark, heavy-lidded eyes; a long, prominent nose, straight as a blade, and a most engaging smile.

"It is we who should apologise," I said, as soon as George had made the introductions, "for intruding upon your picture—and your dream."

"Not at all—a delightful awakening," he replied, still smiling at me. "It strikes you as finished, then?"

"Oh yes, it is perfect; it reminds me of a dream I used to have—a nightmare, I must confess."

"Very gratifying—though I shouldn't want to trouble your sleep. Knowing when to stop is the hardest part; I cleaned my palette an hour ago, for fear I might spoil it."

We stood for a while in conversation, during which it emerged that he was on a walking tour of the county, sketching and painting as he went; that he was an artist by profession, subsisting for the time being upon small commissions, mostly pictures of country houses; and that he was a bachelor, with a widowed father in Cumbria. He had been staying for the past few days at an inn near Aldeburgh, making forays up and down the coast.

I already knew that I wanted to see more of Edward Ravenscroft, and began singing the praises of Chalford, in the hope that he might pay us a visit. And indeed he liked the sound of Chalford so much that he asked if he might accompany us back there, and put up at the Ship while he explored the countryside around. George had by now recognised the road by which we ought to have come, and so the journey homeward took us nowhere near Monks' Wood. It needed only an exchange of speaking looks with Ada for Edward to be invited, long before Roman Kiln Field came into sight, to stay for a few days as a guest at the rectory.

Edward's few days became a week, which we spent—or so it seems in memory—entirely in each other's company, walking for hours each day or talking in the "yerd." Beyond his talent for painting, he was not especially learned, or well read; he had no great interest in religion or philosophy; but he was beautiful—the word that came to me from the first, rather than "handsome"—and had a gift of enjoyment which brought the world alive for me, and I loved him. On the fourth day he kissed me, and declared his love for me—or perhaps it was the other way round, I cannot recall—and from that moment onward—I shall write it, immodest or worse as it will sound—I desired him to make love to me, without even knowing exactly what it meant, beyond his kissing me and drawing me closer until I felt I should dissolve in bliss.

I would happily have married Edward that same week, but he told me from the first he could not afford to marry—he subsisted upon a small allowance from his father, a retired schoolmaster—until he had made his name. "Until I saw you," he told me, "I lived only for my painting" (I was not entirely convinced of this; the assurance with which he embraced me suggested that I was not the first woman he had ever made love to, but I was too happy to care)—"now I think only of the day when we can be wholly together, and the sooner I produce a masterpiece, the sooner that will be."

Ada and George were naturally uneasy about the speed of our courtship, and also about keeping the news of our betrothal—as I thought of it—from my mother. Ada had ceased to chaperone us after the first few days, not without misgivings, privately expressed to me, about what Mama would say if ever she found out.

"Mama will never approve," I replied. "You know what she thinks of artists; it will mean a complete breach between us. And there is no reason to tell her yet; not until we can afford to marry."

"Perhaps not," she said, "but you must think of the scandal that would follow if—if it appeared that Edward had seduced you under our roof. If your mother ever found out, she would certainly write to the bishop, and George would lose his living."

"But he has *not* seduced me! I am of age, and I adore him, and I do not need Mama's consent to marry him—"

"That would not prevent her from making a scandal. And besides, a man—even a good man, as I am sure he is—can take advantage of a woman's love for him, especially when they are thrown very much together, as you are here, with no immediate prospect of marriage. Do not think me unfeeling, dearest; I know very well what it means to—to long to be with the one you love—but you have only known him a week, and it is simply too soon to be sure of him, or even of yourself—especially when you are still convalescing."

"Yes, but I have already seen far more of him than Sophie has ever seen of Arthur Carstairs. I will never be surer than I am now; and the visitations, I am sure, were only brought on by the strain of things at home. . . . Do you mean that Edward cannot remain with us?"

"I fear not—not until you have told your mother that you are engaged."

"Then I shall tell her," I said, "though I am sure she will not give us her blessing. But please let Edward stay—a few more weeks at least."

And so, despite Ada's misgivings, it was agreed that Edward could remain for the present. He insisted upon contributing as much as he could afford to the household expenses, as I had done with the pound a week my mother had allowed me for the visit. Though still very poor, he was beginning to make his name as a painter. Several of his pictures had been sold by a private gallery, "at the wrong end of Bond Street," as he cheerfully put it, but Bond Street nonetheless. Beyond his study of Orford Keep, I had seen only a few recent canvases sent on from the inn at Aldeburgh, all of them studies of ruins or wild places, and all displaying the same qualities of seeming verisimilitude and dreamlike immediacy. Ada had offered him a choice of rooms—the rectory had evidently been built with an immense family in mind—and he had taken a disused sitting-room on the first floor with high windows and a good north light, which would serve as both bedroom and studio. And within days of our engagement, he was back at work in earnest. Though he spoke lightly of producing masterpieces, I knew how deeply he longed for recognition; he was sure of his talent, and needed only the world's acknowledgement to set the seal upon it.

I thought a good deal about how I might bring the day closer by earning some money of my own, but to no purpose. Taking a situation as governess or companion—even if one were offered me—would mean being parted from Edward, and from my friends, yet I knew I could not live on George's charity indefinitely, much as I dreaded returning to Highgate. Which in turn raised the fearful prospect of writing to tell my mother, for to delay much longer would not be fair to Ada and George, now the whole village knew that Edward and I were betrothed. Yet delay I did, for every time I sat down to begin, the thought of my mother's fury would rear up like a thundercloud, blotting out all else. I had told Edward of my difficulties with Mama, even the threats of confinement to an asylum, but attributed these to my sleepwalking rather than the visitations, the one thing I could not bring myself to speak of; I did not quite know why. Did I doubt his love? I would ask myself.—No, of course not.—Then why not tell him? My conscience seemed to think I ought; but then he would only worry about me, and really there was no need, now that I was well again.

My only other cause of anxiety was the recurring sense that I had met Edward somewhere before, and that it was important—I did not know why—that I should remember where. I would sometimes find myself gazing at my beloved, thinking, where *have* I seen you? Feeling the answer hovering like a forgotten word upon the tip of my tongue, but unable to summon it. Nor did I understand why this preoccupation should be linked to an uneasy feeling that everything—save the impending confrontation with my mother—was *too* perfect, my happiness too complete: a vague, superstitious dread that only troubled me when I was alone. I sought to convince myself that these anxieties were merely the shadow of my former indisposition—which was now, of course, entirely cured.

A few weeks later, Edward decided to visit his father in Cumbria. I would have loved to go with him, but to travel together unchaperoned, without my mother's permission, was out of the question. Edward wanted to tell his father in person, and so I set myself to the business of writing to my mother on the morning after his departure. I had tried and discarded half a dozen variations upon "I know you will not approve . . ." or "I fear you will be displeased . . ." before I settled upon "You will be surprised but not, I hope, displeased, to hear that I am engaged to be married to Mr. Edward Ravenscroft, the artist." It seemed best not to mention that Edward was staying at the rectory; the difficulty, indeed, was to think of anything whatever that would not simply heighten my mother's displeasure.

I was still struggling with my letter when George returned from a visit to Aldeburgh with the news that he had run into John Montague, an acquaintance of whom he had spoken, in the company of a very agreeable man who turned out to be Magnus Wraxford, the prospective owner of Wraxford Hall; so agreeable, indeed, that George had invited them both to dine with us the following evening. I was sorry that Edward would miss the occasion, for Mr. Montague was a keen amateur painter as well as solicitor to the Wraxford estate, but Dr. Wraxford was only in town for a few days, to attend a hearing into his uncle's disappearance.

Ada, despite the lack of notice, was pleased for George's sake. "He has so little opportunity to talk to men of ideas," she said, "and whilst Edward is always delightful company . . ." I could not disagree, for Edward's theology went no further than "If, when I die, I discover there is an afterlife, I shall be pleasantly surprised—at least, I trust the surprise will be a pleasant one—if not, it will be mere oblivion. *Carpe diem* for me, I'm afraid." But rather than seizing the day, I used the welter of preparation as an excuse to set my letter aside, with the result that it was not finished until the following morning, and then only because Ada insisted that if we were to speak of my engagement before Dr. Wraxford—a London physician with, presumably, a large acquaintance—the letter must absolutely be in the post to my mother before the gentlemen arrived.

Ada and I were standing by the drawing-room window, as our guests were shown in. I was wearing a plain white gown of which my mother deeply disapproved (on the ground that it was so out of fashion it might have been worn in the last century); Ada was in deep blue, and I suppose with the last of the evening sun picking up the lights in our hair, we made something of a picture. But I was quite unprepared for its effect—my effect, as I soon realised—upon Mr. Montague.

At first glance, however, my attention was captured by Magnus Wraxford. He was only an inch or two taller than John Montague, though broader in the shoulders, but beside him Mr. Montague seemed to be moving in deep shadow as they advanced across the carpet. Magnus Wraxford looked no more than thirty-five, with thick black hair, a clipped black beard which gave him a slightly Mephistophelian air, and dark eyes of remarkable luminosity. Though George had said he was handsome, the sheer force of his presence took me by surprise. The saying that eyes are the windows of the soul flitted across my mind as I extended my hand, but I had the discomfiting sensation, as our fingers touched, that my own soul had become momentarily transparent to his gaze.

"I am delighted to make your acquaintance, Miss Unwin." His voice was low and resonant, reminding me of someone, I was not sure whom.

"And this is Mr. John Montague," said George.

I turned to greet him—a spare, dark-suited man with brown hair already receding—and realised that he was deeply agitated. John Montague was staring at me—and struggling, as our eyes met, to conceal his emotion—as if I had been a ghost. Something in his haunted expression brought back a fleeting memory of my last visitation, an ominous shadow from which I recoiled as swiftly. The hand that clasped mine was cold, and trembled perceptibly.

"And I, too, Miss—Unwin, am—am very much delighted," he said, stumbling over the words.

"Thank you, sir. I am only sorry that my—my fiancé, Mr. Ravenscroft, could not be here to meet you."

I had not meant to declare my engagement so precipitately, but his agitation compelled me to it. He started visibly at the word "fiancé," and seemed to make a great effort to bring his emotions under control.

"Mr. Ravenscroft is an artist by profession," said Ada, "and travels a great deal in search of subjects."

"Most remarkable," said Mr. Montague, with his gaze still fixed upon me. "I mean . . . that is to say . . ." There was an awkward pause while we waited for him to continue.

"Miss Unwin," he said at last, "you must forgive me. The fact is—you bear an extraordinary likeness to my late wife Phoebe, and it has rather shaken me."

"I am very sorry to hear of her death," I replied. "Was it very recent?"

"No—she died five years ago."

"I am very sorry to hear it," I repeated, and could not think of anything else to say; at that distance, his shock at the resemblance was all the more unnerving. Ada, to my relief, led him a little away from the rest of us, and Dr. Wraxford began to converse with me.

"Does Mr. Ravenscroft live in this part of the country?"

"Not always," I said uncomfortably. "As Ada mentioned, Edward travels a great deal. He has gone to Cumbria to visit his father."

"Edward Ravenscroft . . . I don't think I know his name, but I wonder if I have seen some of his work."

"Perhaps not yet," I said. "Edward is still making his way in the world—he is only twenty-six, you see—though I am sure he will succeed."

"Then I shall look forward to seeing the fruits of it. I take a keen interest in painting, Miss Unwin, especially in the work of my contemporaries."

"As it happens, sir," I said hesitantly, "we have one of his pictures here; I am sure he would not mind your seeing it—and Mr. Montague also, if he would like to."

Edward's study of the keep at Orford had been framed, and was hanging in the sitting room opposite. Both men—John Montague had by now recovered his composure, though I sensed his gaze straying toward me whenever he thought I was unaware of it—examined the picture in silence for some time whilst George and I awaited the verdict; Ada had gone to see about the dinner.

"This is very fine—very fine indeed," said Dr. Wraxford at last. "And most original—has Mr. Ravenscroft been to Paris?"

"No," I replied, "though he hopes to, before very long." Edward was determined that we should go there for our honeymoon; I felt my colour rising at the thought of it.

"Even more impressive, in that case. Don't you think so, Montague?"

"Er, yes, yes—very fine, as you say. I must have made a dozen attempts at this very subject—none half so accomplished as this."

"Come, come, my dear fellow," said Dr. Wraxford, "you know that your picture of the Hall can stand in any company—in fact, there's something about this that reminds me of it. Mr. Montague," he explained, "has painted a superb study of Wraxford Hall by moonlight."

"Which I fear will be my swan song. You may have heard, Mr. Woodward, of the superstition amongst the poaching fraternity: that anyone who sees the ghost of the monk will die within the month. In my case (though I saw no ghost), it seems to have been my talent, such as it was, that died." He spoke lightly, but the undertone of bitterness was plain.

"I am sure," said George, "that your talent only needs to lie fallow for a while. Besides, you are a professional man, with many calls upon your time; you cannot expect to outdo the work of men who do nothing all day but paint."

Mr. Montague's expression suggested that he did not at all agree, but whatever reply he had been contemplating was forestalled by the bell announcing dinner.

By the time the fish service had been cleared, it was quite dark outside. George was sitting at the head of the table, his back to the unlit fire, with Ada and Magnus Wraxford on his right, and myself and John Montague on his left, facing the windows, an arrangement for which I was grateful, as I did not have to meet his gaze unless he addressed me directly, which he seldom did. I was still struggling to shake off the foreboding he had inspired.

The conversation thus far had ranged from Mr. Millais' recent election to the Royal Academy, to the new Biblical scholarship, to the efficacy of mesmerism in alleviating pain and even curing disease, a practise which, according to Dr. Wraxford, had been prematurely rejected by the medical profession. He spoke for some time about the nature of mesmeric suggestion, and how it could influence even the action of the heart.

"For all our talk of progress," he said in conclusion, "we—that is to say, the majority of my colleagues—seem positively to spurn any treatment, however effective, for which we cannot account in material terms. Such is the great difficulty with mesmerism; that, and its misuse by mountebanks and quacks. You must forgive me, Montague—he has heard me on this theme before."

John Montague murmured something I did not catch.

"Is it possible," asked George, "to mesmerise someone against his will?"

"Possible, yes, given an impressionable subject; but only a charlatan would attempt it."

"And once mesmerised, is the subject compelled to do whatever the mesmerist commands?"

"I doubt whether a mature, rational individual could be compelled to act against his deepest instincts: further than that I shouldn't care to go."

"You remarked, I think," said Ada, "that in a state of trance, a subject can be instructed to see persons who are not actually present?"

I divined, from the way she avoided my glance, that she was asking on my behalf.

"Yes—quite correct."

"And might this explain, do you think, how spiritualists—spirit mediums—believe they can have commerce with the dead?"

"It might indeed, Mrs. Woodward—at least, those who are not simply perpetrating a fraud, which is regrettably common in spiritualist circles."

"And is it possible," I asked, striving to keep my voice steady, "for a person to fall into a trance without being aware of it, and thus to see—people who are not there?"

Dr. Wraxford regarded me for a moment before answering. I felt that he was seeking to divine the thought behind the question; it was quite unsettling, the way his dark eyes held the candlelight.

"Possible, yes. But for a subject to become deeply entranced without being aware of it; that would be most uncommon, Miss Unwin, unless you mean that state between sleeping and waking?"

"No," I replied, summoning my courage. "I suppose I mean . . . a friend once told me of a strange experience: she walked into a room one afternoon where her mother and sisters were sitting, and saw a young man upon the sofa, a young man she had never seen before. But then she realised that he was invisible to the others. He got up and walked toward her—she was not afraid—and then—seemed to dissolve into the air. And so I wondered . . . whether she might have fallen into a trance."

"I don't think trance will explain it—and you are presumably sure your friend was not deceiving herself, or . . ."

"I am certain the experience was exactly as she described it."

"And your friend was not afraid—that is most unusual."

"Not afraid of the young man—she said she did not think of him as a ghost because he seemed so ordinary—she could hear the sound of his tread upon the floor. But it left her very shaken, knowing the others had not seen him."

The room was suddenly very quiet. I was aware of John Montague glancing from me to Dr. Wraxford and back again.

"And was that your friend's only such experience?"

"I believe so . . . It was some weeks after a bad fall, which left her unconscious for many hours."

Again I felt the pressure of Dr. Wraxford's scrutiny, as if he knew what I was leaving out.

"It may well be—of course I would have to examine the young lady to be sure—that your friend has suffered a lesion of the brain, which will probably heal itself in time."

"I am sure she will be very relieved to hear it, sir."

"Relieved, Miss Unwin?"

"That it will heal, I meant."

"I see."

Dr. Wraxford continued to regard me with speculative interest. I felt that he was willing me to say more, until Ada broke the silence by asking if there was any news of the hearing into his uncle's disappearance.

"I believe, Mrs. Woodward, that the judgement of his decease will be granted fairly shortly. But Mr. Montague is better placed to answer you."

"It ought to be straightforward," said John Montague. "In a case such as this, where there are no conflicting interests—no one, that is, who stands to lose by a ruling of decease—the business of the court is simply to decide whether, on the evidence available, it is overwhelmingly probable that the missing person is dead. And given that Cornelius Wraxford was a frail, elderly man, the fact that he has not been seen since the night of the storm three months ago is alone sufficient: however he got out of the house, he could not have survived a night in the forest.

"The only real difficulty is to explain how he got out of his apartment at all. Drayton, his manservant, told me that he saw him retire at seven that evening, before the storm broke. When I arrived some twenty-four hours later, all of the doors appeared to be locked and bolted from the inside, so that I was obliged to break down the door to the study. All of the windows were certainly shut and latched—and they are in any case far too high for him to have reached. So either he left by way of some secret passage—though a careful search revealed no trace of any such thing—or Drayton and I were mistaken. Drayton is beyond questioning: he collapsed and died, as you may have heard, whilst I was making my search. I have since wondered whether the gallery doors—which I opened from inside the room, in a state of considerable agitation—might simply have been stuck, rather than secured, as the inspector of police believed; it is easier to doubt my own recollection than to believe that a man simply vanished into thin air; and that, I expect, will be the finding of the court."

"I had wondered myself," said George, "whether the disappearance of his own uncle, in—er—similar circumstances, might have preyed upon his mind."

"Quite possibly," said Dr. Wraxford. "My uncle's mental condition was, at best, fragile, and the shock of the storm . . ."

He and John Montague exchanged glances, and I thought he was about to continue, when Hetty the parlourmaid brought in the joint. George busied himself with carving, and Ada turned the conversation to lighter topics.

Reassured by Dr. Wraxford's diagnosis (as I thought of it), I resolved to enjoy the rest of the evening. It would, I thought, have been perfect if only Edward were beside me instead of Mr. Montague; but then, I reflected, I should not have dared question Dr. Wraxford about the visitations. The curtains had not been drawn, and the reflected gold of the candle flames floated amongst the outlines of shrubs and trees; the blurred image of my own features hovered beyond Ada's shoulder, mirrored in darkening glass. Absorbed in this shadow-play, my attention wandered, until I became aware that Dr. Wraxford had been speaking for some time.

". . . whether or not we survive death," he was saying, "and if so in what form, is surely the great question of the day. It can never, I think, be settled in the negative, because it is always open to us to suppose that the dead survive, but can have no communion with us. Whereas one undeniable instance of communication from beyond would establish the truth once and for all. Imagine what a discovery that would be! The man who made it would stand beside Newton and Galileo. For those who have the gift of faith, it is not, of course, a question"—George looked a little uncomfortable at this—"but for those who must see before they can believe . . . I trust, Mr. Woodward, you don't find these speculations offensive."

"Not at all," said George, "I find them fascinating. But what, in your view, would constitute proof? A communication from beyond the grave that could not have come from any other source? Spiritualists, I believe, often claim to have received such messages."

"Therein lies the difficulty. No amount of spirit rapping will ever convince a sceptic. And if you have ever attended a séance—as for my sins have I, in order to expose a fraud—you will know that most of the communications received through spirit mediums are of such staggering banality as to suggest that the life beyond would be unendurable."

"Would you say, then, that all such manifestations can be explained either as fraud or delusion?"

"The great majority, yes; I should hesitate to say all, if only because I like to keep an open mind. From a scientific point of view, there is no necessary connection between Christian doctrine—or that of any religion—and the nature of the afterlife, if such exists. All religions, so far as I know, hold out the promise of some sort of afterlife, whether it be the paradise of the Christian or the Mohammedan, the eternal cycle of return proposed in the various religions of India and the Far East, or the limbo state of the Shaman. Every race has its own deity, and rivers of blood have been shed over which is the true God; yet it is possible that they are *all* mistaken—or that all these beliefs have a common origin. Logically speaking, proof of survival would not, of itself, prove the existence of a God, nor would it follow that the afterlife was eternal. Indeed, to be entirely logical, it would not even follow that every human being would necessarily survive death."

"There you do depart, very fundamentally, from Christian doctrine," said George. "That all are equal in the sight of God is, I would say, one of the linchpins of Christianity."

"Very true; but from my position of scientific scepticism I, alas, can take nothing for granted. Speaking from my experience as a mesmerist, it is not difficult to believe that Heaven and Hell, gods, demons, ghosts and spirits are all contained within the mind—with the proviso that this does not make them any the less real or powerful than in the old dispensation. We think of the mind as enclosed within the narrow compass of the skull, but we could equally imagine a cavern filled with dark water and connected by some subterranean passage, to the limitless depths of the ocean, and think of each individual mind as a droplet of one great oceanic Mind which contains everything: all the gods and demons, the paradises and underworlds of every religion on earth, all history, all knowledge, everything that has ever happened. A mind upon which it could truly be said that nothing is lost, not so much as the fall of a sparrow . . ."

He paused, turning the stem of his wineglass between finger and thumb, dark crimson light swirling within the crystal.

"But these are mere speculations, and we were speaking of the quest for proof. Supposing, for the sake of argument, that communication from beyond the grave is possible, and that there is such a thing as clairvoyance—by which I mean, specifically, the power to perceive and communicate with spirits, for want of a better word. We know—since we have not a single proven instance—that genuine clairvoyance must be exceedingly rare. But suppose, nevertheless, that we have stumbled upon someone who seems to possess that power.

"Let us take—if you'll allow it, Miss Unwin—the case of your friend's experience. Now if a young man of that exact description had lately (or subsequently) died, and your friend, without knowing anything of him, had recognised him from a portrait—that would be worth pursuing. And if she had had not one but several such experiences, then we would have a prima facie case of clairvoyance."

I clasped my hands in my lap, and struggled to control my breathing. Had George spoken privately to Dr. Wraxford about my visitations? Surely not; they had met only the previous day.

"The obvious difficulty, regarding proof, is that no one else can see the spirits. But this evening, under the stimulus of our conversation, I begin to see how it might be done. We know that, in the mesmeric trance, a subject may acquire unusual mental powers; the Frenchman Didier, who could read minds, play cards blindfolded, and identify the contents of sealed containers with great accuracy, is only the best-known instance. If the power of clairvoyance exists, therefore, it might be possible to induce it by mesmeric suggestion.

"So: we take a group of subjects and mesmerise them, telling them that they have acquired the power to see spirits, but giving them no instruction as to what, if anything, they are to see. We put them in a promising location with our presumed clairvoyant (who has not, of course, been mesmerised) and at least two reliable observers who have also not been mesmerised. Now if the clairvoyant and the mesmerised subjects all report the same experience, while the observers see nothing, but are aware of the others all looking in the same direction, reacting to a common stimulus—that, I submit, would be as close to objective proof as we are ever likely to come, short of capturing a spirit and questioning it before the Royal Society."

"What would you regard as a promising location?" asked George, who, like Mr. Montague, had been listening with the utmost fascination.

"I confess I can think of nowhere better than the Hall. Ancient houses, it has always seemed to me, are like Leyden jars, quietly accumulating the influences of the past. . . . Most likely, of course, it would all come to nothing, but it would be an interesting experiment to try—if only we had our clairvoyant."

Once more I felt his speculative gaze upon me.

"Do you think, Miss Unwin, that—supposing your friend's experiences were to develop along the lines I've sketched—she would be willing to participate?"

"I am afraid she would not, sir," I said breathlessly, feeling my colour rising despite my best efforts. "I know her well enough to say that if she were unfortunate enough to—see anything further—she would want only to be cured of her affliction."

"Precisely so," he said sadly. I looked at him with some surprise. "I had always imagined that the hallmark of a true clairvoyant would be a desire to be rid of the gift at any cost. Which is not, of course, to say that your friend is thus afflicted, as you so vividly put it."

"Most interesting," said Ada firmly. "And now I think it is time that Miss Unwin and I retired, and left you gentlemen to drink your wine in peace."

"I am dreadfully sorry, dearest," said Ada as soon as we were safely upstairs. "I should never have broached the subject."

"You must not be," I said. "I chose to question him, and if it had not been for the last part . . . Tell me, did George say anything to him yesterday, about my visitations?"

"No," she replied, "I am certain he didn't. But Dr. Wraxford is an acute observer, and would have guessed, I think, that you and your friend are one and the same."

"I wish I had not betrayed myself in front of Mr. Montague! It was most unnerving, his taking me for his wife. But I still do not want

Edward to know about the visitations. Do you think Dr. Wraxford might have been joking, about the experiment at the Hall?"

"I don't know," said Ada. "He seems to throw ideas on and off like coats. He sounded entirely in earnest, until he made that remark about the Royal Society. He is a very clever man, I am sure of that: George is entirely captivated. And now, dearest, you must go to bed, and think no more of it; you look quite worn out."

Nevertheless, I lay awake into the small hours, alternately reproaching myself for deceiving Edward—what would I say, if Mr. Montague or Dr. Wraxford were to speak of my "friend" in his presence?—and worrying over my letter to my mother. These anxieties became more and more nightmarish until I sank into a troubled sleep, from which I emerged, as it seemed, into a vivid dream. I was wandering through a vast, deserted mansion, which I knew to be Wraxford Hall, searching for a precious jewel Edward had given me. The jewel had been lost; I did not know how, but I knew that my own carelessness was to blame. To make matters worse, I could not remember what kind of stone it was, for as I went from room to room, a voice in my head kept chanting, "Emerald, sapphire, ruby, diamond," over and over, and none of them seemed right, because the lost stone was a different, a more beautiful colour than any of those, and I knew I ought to be able to picture it, and thus recall its name, but I could not.

In the dream, the Hall was absolutely silent; the light throughout, even in corridors where there were no windows, was a pale, uniform grey like that of an overcast sky. The rooms were mostly bare of furniture; each one seemed to have its own miniature flight of stairs, up or down two or three steps, and the corridors kept changing levels in similar fashion. Though the house itself was not especially sinister, my anxiety over the fate of the jewel grew steadily more acute until it had risen to an unbearable pitch.

Then it occurred to me that I still had not searched the dining room. The thought precipitated a vertiginous change of scene; the light sank to a dim, murky brown, and I was standing in the doorway of the room where we had dined that night. The curtains were drawn, the candles snuffed; the room seemed to be empty, but as I crept toward the table, I saw, above the back of the chair in which George had sat, the dark outline of a head. I knew somehow that the head was Dr. Wraxford's. There was still time for me to slip away quietly; but perhaps the jewel had fallen into the lining of my chair, and if I were to tiptoe forward, I might be able to see it. I was within two feet of the motionless figure when a voice spoke from the doorway behind me, a word that rang like a gong, louder and louder until it became my own cry of "No!" and I woke in grey dawn light to find myself standing at the head of the stairs.

Our guests had stayed the night, but I could not face them again, and kept to my room until they had driven away. I had meant to tell Ada about my dream, if not the sleepwalking, but all thought of it was driven from my head by the delivery of a wire from my mother, consisting of just two words: "Return immediately." I knew at once that I would have to defy her, and pleaded with Ada to allow me to leave all my things at the rectory, and return that evening, if the trains allowed it.

"But then we will be in open conflict with her," said Ada, "and she may write to the bishop. Her accusations need not be true for George to lose his living."

"Then I must find a way of stopping her," I said. "The thing she fears most is losing Arthur Carstairs. And no matter what happens, I will never live with her again; if I cannot stay with you, I will seek a situation. I would rather be a parlourmaid than live with Mama."

"You do not know what you are saying," said Ada. "But of course you may come back to us; and perhaps it will not be as bad as you fear."

On the way to London, I tried to imagine every possible threat Mama might employ, and think of some counter to it. But as the cab rumbled up Highgate Hill I still felt utterly unprepared for the ordeal ahead. I realised, too, that pretty as Highgate was, it had ceased to be home to me. I thought of my father, lying in his grave a few hundred yards away—though of course he was not there, only his mortal remains; and if he had not simply ceased to be, where was his spirit?—which reminded me of my visitations, and of how I had walked in my sleep last night for the first time in many months; and of my mother's threat to have me confined; until I was set down at the familiar black-painted door, trembling so that I was scarcely able to stand.

A maid I had never seen led me past the drawing room to the parlour at the far end of the passage, where my mother sat waiting. She did not speak, but motioned me to an upright chair facing her own, as if I were an errant child about to be punished. She wore a black crepe dress, so that I wondered for a moment if some relation had died, and her pale hair was drawn back even more tightly than usual, making the bones of her face stand out against the tautened skin. As the door closed behind the maid, I saw that my mother was holding my letter between the finger and thumb of her left hand.

"Am I to take it," she said, dangling the letter as if the mere touch of it disgusted her, "that you are utterly determined to be the ruin of us all?"

"No, Mama—"

"Then you repent of this foolishness?"

"No, Mama—"

"Then you *are* resolved to ruin us. This—this Ravenscroft; where did you meet him?"

"At Orford, Mama. He was painting—"

"I am not interested in painting; only in how Mr. Woodward could have allowed this disgraceful liaison to develop. He has failed shamefully in his duty, and I shall write to his bishop to say so—"

"Mama, that is most—"

"*Do not interrupt me.* I wish to know where, and on what occasions, you met this libertine and allowed him to seduce you."

"Edward is not a libertine, Mama, and he has not seduced me; he is a respectable gentleman—"

"I thought you said that he was an artist."

"Yes, Mama, a very fine—"

"Very fine indeed! Of course he is a libertine, to take advantage of a wilful, selfish girl run wild. It is moral insanity, just as Dr. Stevenson said; I should have had you quietly confined before you disgraced us. Now listen to me. There will, of course, be no engagement. I forbid you to hold any further communication with this Ravenscroft, or to return to Mr. Woodward's house. Dr. Stevenson will examine you tomorrow, and then we will see—what is to be done with you. Do I make myself clear?"

I had sat, thus far, unable to move, transfixed by her furious stare. My tongue seemed to cleave to the roof of my mouth; the words I was struggling to utter emerged as inarticulate sounds.

"Sophie is not at home," said my mother, in answer to whatever she thought I had said. "She does not wish to see you until you have repented of this wickedness. She said to me, when she read your letter, 'I did not think any sister could be so cruel.'"

"That is not fair!" I cried. "I care very much for Sophie's happiness. Are you afraid, Mama, that the Carstairs will break the engagement if they hear that I am engaged to Edward?"

"Afraid? Afraid! Are you quite mad, Eleanor? At the merest hint that my elder daughter proposes to throw herself away upon a penniless libertine, of course they will cry off."

"And when is Sophie to be married, Mama?"

"The wedding is planned for November."

"Very well," I said, summoning my courage, "then Edward and I will not announce—we will not publish our engagement until after Sophie is married." I remembered as I spoke that I had already told Mr. Montague and Dr. Wraxford.

"How dare you bargain with me? Did you not hear me? You will not marry this Ravenscroft at all."

"You forget, Mama, that I am of age, and may marry whom I choose."

My mother seemed to swell in the dim light.

"If you do not obey me," she hissed, "I shall cut off your allowance. And I doubt that Mr. Woodward will receive you again, if he wishes to keep his living."

"If you do that, Mama," I said breathlessly, "Edward and I might as well marry at once—and then what will become of Sophie's engagement?"

She rose to her feet, eyes bulging. I thought she meant to fling herself upon me like a wild beast, and sprang up in turn, almost knocking over my chair. If she had had a dagger in her hand, I am sure she would have laid me dead on the carpet; yet, as we stood face to face, I realised, as if for the first time, that I was taller than my mother.

"Let us understand one another," I said, in a voice I scarcely recognised as my own. "Edward and I will not announce our engagement until Sophie is married, and in return you will continue my allowance until *I* am married, and promise not to write to the bishop. Shall we agree?"

She stared at me, speechless, for several seconds, while I braced myself for another onslaught. But instead she spoke with freezing disdain, pausing every few words for emphasis; and at every pause she tore my letter into smaller and smaller pieces, and let the fragments scatter at my feet.

"I see, Eleanor, that you are utterly beyond redemption. Very well: we will tell the Carstairs that you are ill, and have been sent for a long convalescence in the country. You will, of course, be too ill to attend Sophia's wedding; your allowance will cease from that day. I will have the rest of your things sent on to Mr. Woodward. Henceforth I have only one daughter. No—not one word more. You may leave this house now; you will not return."

She let fall the last scraps of paper and turned toward the door, ringing for the maid as she opened it.

"Our visitor is leaving us," I heard her say. "You may show her to the door." Her footsteps receded along the passage and up the stairs.

"Will you kindly summon me a cab?" I said as the girl appeared. "I am feeling faint, and must have a moment. . . ."

She took the coin I offered her, glancing fearfully toward the ceiling, and left. *I must get away from here,* I told myself, and moved unsteadily to the door and along the hall as far as the entrance to the drawing room. There I was forced to stop, grasping the frame for support. The door stood open, as it had been on the fateful afternoon of the Carstairs' visit. There was the sofa where Mama and Sophie had been sitting; there was the place opposite where my mother had asked me to sit. I saw, as if it were yesterday, the slender young man in his dark suit of mourning, and I realised with horror exactly where I had first seen Edward Ravenscroft.

I cannot recall how I got out of the house. I suppose the maid must have helped me into the cab, but there is only a blank interval between that moment and finding myself jolting through the reeking streets of Shoreditch. The train journey passed in a haze of numbness, during which I seemed mercifully incapable of thought, and it was only when I saw Ada standing at the rectory door that the emotions of the day came flooding back. The interview with my mother was more than enough to justify my distress, and recounting it to Ada served, at least, to reduce the memory of what I had seen to a small, cold weight in the pit of my stomach. But alone in my room that night, with the bed seemingly swaying like the carriage, and the clack and rattle of the train still ringing in my ears, I was forced to confront the image of the young man upon the sofa.

Superficially, the two were quite different: Edward's hair was long and unruly, whereas the young man's had been short and scrupulously brushed; his complexion had been smooth and pale, whereas Edward's was roughened by wind and sunshine; the young man had sat very straight and still, with his hands clasped upon his knees, whereas Edward tended to sprawl. But their faces were the same: they were the same height, and had the same figure. You had only to imagine that one had gone into the law and the other into art to see that the young man might have been Edward's identical twin brother. How the likeness had eluded me I could not now imagine, unless some protective instinct had shrouded my memory.

If a young man of that exact description were to die . . . Of course Edward is not going to die, I told myself desperately; it is all coincidence; I was overwrought after the scene with Mama; I have exaggerated the likeness. But dread would not release its grip. Would I ever be able to look at Edward again without seeing the apparition's face in his?—or fearing that Edward himself might be—not what he seemed? We knew nothing of him, after all; he had sprung, seemingly, from the earth; I did not know for certain that the address he had given me in Cumbria was indeed his father's . . . or even that he *had* a father. Absurd, absurd, said the voice of reason: it is not clairvoyance, I said to myself, only—what did Dr. Wraxford say?—a lesion of the brain, and will heal itself in time. But the phrase went spinning from one fearful thought to the next—a lesion of the brain, a lesion of the brain—until it became the sound of train wheels clattering through a dream in which I was compelled to return again and again to London.

If Ada had asked me directly whether something else was troubling me, I think I should have spoken, but she naturally blamed my anxiety and depression of spirits upon the confrontation with my mother. I said nothing about the apparition in my long letter to Edward, and endured several days of foreboding—he had warned me that he was a very poor correspondent—before a cheerful note from Cumbria banished the wildest of my fears. All was well, he wrote; he was sure that his father would give us his blessing, and that my mother would "come round in time." "I have begun a new canvas," he wrote, "for which I have great hopes—it may be another fortnight before I see you again, my darling girl, but do write every day, and forgive me if I do not—I shall make it up to you when I return."

For Ada, who had always been on the most affectionate terms with her own mother and sisters, the idea of a permanent breach was almost unthinkable.

"You must try and make it up with her, Nell," she said, as we were walking back from the village one day. "It would be a terrible thing, to lose your mother forever, no matter what has passed between you."

"But she has forced me to choose between her and Edward," I said. "Blood is not always thicker than water—it sounds strange, when you turn it that way round, but Sophie and I have not been close since we were children, and I have been nothing but a disappointment to Mama. What I really fear is that she will make trouble with the bishop once Sophie is married; I shall never forgive myself if George loses his living because of me."

"I don't think she will do that," said Ada. "Making a scandal after the wedding would still be an embarrassment to Sophie. You must see, Nell, that there is nothing unreasonable, from Society's point of view, in her wanting you both to make good marriages—don't frown, dearest, you know very well what I mean. I know how difficult she can be, but I pray, nonetheless, that you will be reconciled. If something were to happen to George and me—"

"But you just said you don't think she will make trouble," I replied uneasily. "And I would rather live upon bread and water in a hovel with Edward than go back to Mama, even if she would have me."

"You would not speak so lightly of hovels if you had a child," said Ada quietly. "What I meant was: supposing you were left quite alone in the world, you would bitterly regret this estrangement."

I thought of her own sorrow, and changed the subject, but I could not help wondering if Ada felt I had treated my mother harshly, whereas I could not see what else I could have done, for her sake as much as my own, and so the question hung between us like an unspoken reproach. Which was perhaps why, the following afternoon, I broke with our usual custom of walking together after luncheon, and slipped quietly out of the house on my own.

Though it was still supposedly high summer, the air was cool and damp, the sky a steely grey. I let my feet carry me where they chose, which turned out to be southward, along the path George had taken us on the day we first met Edward. Absorbed in my thoughts, I did not notice how far I had come until the path began to climb, and I realised that Monks' Wood lay just beyond the skyline. Gorse and tussocky grass stretched away from me on every side; there was no sign or sound of life except for the distant bleating of sheep and the desolate cries of birds. In George and Ada's company, the loneliness had seemed merely picturesque; now I felt suddenly small and conspicuous.

As I stood wondering whether to go on or retreat, a figure on horseback appeared upon the ridge ahead of me, heading away to my left, then paused, as if the rider were surveying the prospect. To my alarm, he turned and began to descend, making directly for me. Not knowing what to do, I stood motionless, with my heart beating very fast as the horse drew nearer, until the figure in the saddle resolved itself first as a tall man with a short black beard, and then as Magnus Wraxford.

"I thought I recognised you, Miss Unwin. This is a lonely place to be walking," he said as he drew up a few paces from me. He was dressed like a country gentleman on his way to the hunt, in a short black riding jacket and white stock, russet-coloured breeches and polished boots.

"I wished to be alone," I said, and immediately regretted the words as too intimate.

"Then I apologise for disturbing your solitude," he said, smiling down at me, but making no move to turn his horse. Again I had the uncomfortable sensation that my thoughts were on display.

"I did not mean that, sir, only . . ." I did not know what else to say.

"Then, if I am not intruding, may I accompany you?"

"I thank you, sir, but I have come far enough today. I must return to Chalford, which would take you far out of your way."

"Not in the least, Miss Unwin; I shall be delighted, if you will permit me, and my horse will be glad of the rest." He means to question me about my "friend," I thought. It was on the tip of my tongue to decline, when I realised I must ask him not to speak of my engagement, and so agreed, whereupon he dismounted and began to walk beside me, leading his horse by the bridle. I was relieved that he did not press me to take his arm.

At first we—or rather he—made small-talk, whilst I tried to summon the courage to say what I must, for Ada and George's sake.

He had just been out to the Hall, he told me, to see what might be done with it; the judgement in the case of his uncle Cornelius's decease was now imminent, though it would be many months before probate was settled. I remembered him saying that the Hall would be an ideal setting for his experiment into clairvoyance, which unnerved me further. Yet in spite of my unease, it struck me that here was an opportunity which might never come again. He had talked of the power of mesmerism in curing nervous illness; he had divined, I felt sure, that I had been speaking of myself; so why not ask him if he knew of some treatment which might prevent any further visitations? My replies became more and more distracted as the idea grew upon me, until it was only natural for him to ask whether something was troubling me.

Hesitantly and with many misgivings, I told him all about my visitations, from the sleepwalking and the fall to the moment of recognition in the drawing room a week ago. He listened intently—indeed, it seemed to me, with admiration—asking very few questions until I had finished.

"I hope you will understand, sir," I said in conclusion, "that this—this affliction—is profoundly distressing to me. You mentioned, when you dined with us, the possibility of a lesion of the brain, which would heal itself in time, but if there is any immediate remedy for these visitations, I should be very grateful to hear of it. I have very little money, and most likely could not afford to be treated, but it would be a relief, at least, to *know*—"

"My dear Miss Unwin," he broke in, sounding almost offended, "let me assure you that my professional knowledge is entirely at your disposal. All other considerations aside, your case is unique in my experience, and it will be an honour and a privilege to assist you in any way I can.

"Let me confess at once that if you were not resolved to be rid of these visitations, as you call them, I should be fascinated to see what followed. I spoke, the other evening, of an injury to the brain, and later of clairvoyance: listening to your much fuller account today, I am more than ever convinced that the two are not necessarily incompatible. Of course we do not even know, for certain, that clairvoyance exists—these are uncharted waters—but do not fear, Miss Unwin, I shall do my best to ensure that your visitations do not recur. Mesmeric suggestion is, I think, the most promising avenue, though I shall have to give some thought as to exactly what to suggest . . . I shall be staying with Mr. Montague for another few days; if it suited you, I could call at the rectory—and no, I insist, the only question is whether you will allow me to try the treatment, knowing that I cannot absolutely guarantee its success."

He waved away all of my objections to inconveniencing him or taking up his time, and assured me that everything would be in the strictest confidence between us; he suggested, indeed, that if I did not want George and Ada to be anxious on my behalf, I could tell them that the treatment was for my headaches, and it ended with my agreeing that he should call at the rectory at three o'clock on the day after tomorrow.

"There is one other kindness I would ask of you, sir," I said. "For—for various reasons, I feel it will be best if Mr. Ravenscroft and I do not formally announce our engagement until after my sister's marriage in November, and so I should be grateful if the news could be kept within our small circle here—"

"But of course," he replied, "and, if you like, I will mention it to Mr. Montague. And now that St. Mary's is in sight, I shall trespass no further upon your solitude. Until Friday, Miss Unwin—my compliments to Mr. and Mrs. Woodward." Waving away my thanks once more, he swung himself up into the saddle and spurred his horse in the direction of the Aldeburgh road. I had expected him to accompany me all the way to the rectory, and was relieved that I would not have to explain his presence immediately, and yet his sudden departure left me feeling there had been something clandestine about our meeting. It was not until he was almost out of sight that I realised he could not possibly have recognised me at that distance.

At three o'clock precisely on Friday afternoon, Dr. Wraxford appeared at the rectory, dressed this time in a dark suit, high collar, and tall hat. I had spent much of the interval regretting my impulse to confide in him; Ada had asked me several times if I was sure my trouble had not returned, and reproached me for recklessness in venturing so far alone into the marshlands. I did not like keeping secrets from her; still less the feeling that I had betrayed Edward by revealing more about myself to Dr. Wraxford than I was willing to reveal to him; and Dr. Wraxford's insistence on treating me as a friend rather than a patient had made me all the more uneasy. But it was done now, and all I could hope was that his treatment would prove effective.

Hetty showed him into the small sitting room where I had chosen to wait; Ada had tactfully remained upstairs, saying she would join me when the consultation was over. But as the door closed behind Hetty, I felt so uncomfortable that I was sorely tempted to run upstairs, confess everything, and ask Ada to sit with me during the treatment.

"Now, Miss Unwin," he said, as if in answer to the thought, "I assure you that you have nothing to fear. The very worst thing that can happen is that my suggestion will not help; in which case you are no worse off. All that is necessary is for you to allow me to mesmerise you. And then, in essence, I will instruct your mind to reject any extrasensuous data which may be presented to it—in the waking state, that is—no matter what the source. You will not be conscious of my instruction at the time, nor will you recall anything of it when you are woken from your trance. It may be necessary to repeat the treatment on several occasions before it becomes fully effective, but the principle is straightforward.

"There is one potential obstacle," he continued. "For the treatment to succeed, you must place your entire trust in me; otherwise your mind will not be receptive to mesmeric suggestion. Therefore, if you have any reservation about placing yourself in my hands, pray speak now."

"No, sir, I have every confidence in you," I said hesitantly, "only—I am a little apprehensive about the mesmerism. Might Ada sit with me whilst you—?"

"There, I fear, we reach an impasse. Your awareness of her presence, even in the trance, would prevent you from attending solely to my suggestions, and so render them ineffective. Stage mesmerists, of course, perform in front of an audience, but when it is done for a serious purpose . . ."

"I see," I said. "Then I shall try my hardest to compose myself."

"You must, rather, seek to relax your will, just as if you were tired and wished to go to sleep; all you need do is watch, and listen."

At his direction, I settled myself in an armchair, with my arms resting along the sides and my head supported by a cushion. He placed a small occasional table immediately before me, with a straight-backed chair on the other side of it, directly facing me. Then he took a single candle from the mantelpiece, lit it, and set it in the centre of the table between us before drawing the curtains and taking his own seat. Dazzled by the flame of the candle, I could see nothing beyond the circle of light in which we sat. Dr. Wraxford's face seem to hang unsupported in the darkness opposite me. The light accentuated the contours of his cheekbones and eye sockets; the pupils of his eyes were as black as polished jet, holding the twinned reflections of the candle flame.

Something flashed and glittered and began to revolve above the flame between us. It seemed to be a gold coin, about the size of a shilling, but embossed on both sides with a strange geometrical pattern I could not identify. Did he carry it with him wherever he went? I heard his voice instructing me to follow the movement of the coin. "Round and round, round and round . . . you are becoming sleepy," chanted the voice. "Round and round . . . your eyelids feel heavy . . ." But a part of my mind remained alert, and would not surrender. I tried closing my eyes, but they opened again of their own accord; the tension would not leave me; it was as if I could hear a warning bell sounding in time to the oscillations of the coin.

"I am sorry," I said eventually. "I cannot do it."

"So I perceive," said the disembodied face opposite. "Trust cannot be commanded, Miss Unwin, but without it, I cannot help you."

"I am sorry," I repeated helplessly, "I do not know what to do."

He rose, opened the curtains, and set the room to rights.

"We may have proceeded too hastily. If you are willing to try again, I shall return at the same time tomorrow—"

"I thank you, sir," I said, "but I must impose no further upon your generosity. No, sir, I beg you—I should be utterly mortified if you were to waste another journey on my behalf. And now, will you take tea with us? Ada especially invites you."

"Thank you in turn, Miss Unwin, but I must be off; it occurred to me on the way here that I might return by way of the Hall, and so I shall look forward to seeing you when next we meet, and Mr. Ravenscroft, of course, when he returns from Cumbria."

And with that he departed, leaving me devoutly wishing I had never said a word about my visitations.

Edward returned a week later, and my fear that the apparition would come between us was swept away in the joy of our first embrace, and the news that one of his pictures had sold for thirty guineas, the highest price he had yet commanded. One more success like this, he assured me, and we could be married as soon as Sophie was safely wed.

I had hoped Dr. Wraxford would have returned to London, but the very next day we received a note from John Montague, inviting us all to luncheon at his house in a week's time; Magnus Wraxford was eager to meet Edward and would come up from London especially. To make matters worse, George and Ada were already engaged for that day. Edward, of course, was eager to go, and so I was forced to tell him that Dr. Wraxford had tried to cure my headaches, and answer all his questions about mesmerism, and insist that it had not worked simply because I was such a bad subject. On the day of the luncheon I feigned illness at the last moment, and passed a long and miserable day at the rectory before Edward returned at dusk, in a state of high excitement.

"The luncheon was a success, then?" I asked. We were sitting in the "yerd," beneath a beech tree which was just beginning to shed its leaves, on what ought to have been a perfect evening.

"Not the luncheon, exactly; that was rather mixed. Wraxford and I are fast friends already—he's a remarkable man, as you said—but John Montague seems to have taken a dislike to me. I don't understand it—I was very complimentary about his picture of the Hall, but he simply wouldn't thaw. They were very sorry to miss you, Dr. Wraxford especially; you've made quite a conquest there, you know. He and I went for a long walk along the strand after luncheon, but Montague declined to join us, and I'm sure it was because of me.

"No, the great thing is that in looking at Montague's picture, I had an idea for a series of studies of the Hall—it's a wonderfully sinister subject—moving from day to night. The set piece will be the Hall at the height of a storm, lit by a jagged bolt of lightning. He told me all about his uncle's disappearance, you see, and it made a great impression. . . . I gather the Hall is still in some sort of legal limbo, but it's bound to go to Wraxford in the end. Anyway, I talked it over with him, and he says he doesn't mind in the least, and that he'll square it with Montague; I asked him if he knew why Montague had taken against me, but he wouldn't say; just told me not to take it to heart . . . You look worried, my darling, is something the matter?"

"No, only that . . . the Hall is an unlucky place, and such a long way to go."

"Oh, I shan't go traipsing back and forth, I'll do all my studies at one stretch—doss down in the old stables or something of the sort. Wraxford's given me the lie of the land. I just hope we get at least one good storm before the nights get too cold. You musn't fret, dearest girl; I'm used to sleeping rough, and I *know*—I can feel it—this is going to make my name, and speed us to the altar into the bargain."

Edward spent an entire week—the longest of my life, as I thought then—sketching at the Hall. Ada was troubled by my agitation, and suggested several times that we should walk down to Monks' Wood. But I knew that Edward hated being observed while he was working; it seemed like giving in to superstition; I worried that he might think me a silly hysterical girl; and—though I did not like to admit it, even to myself—I was afraid we might run into Magnus Wraxford. I hated his knowing more about me than Edward; it preyed upon me as if we had had a guilty liaison, and yet I could not make up my mind to tell Edward (or even Ada) about the apparition.

Would it have made any difference if I had? He would have called me his darling girl, and told me it was all the fault of my over-vivid imagination, and distracted me with kisses, and gone cheerfully off to the Hall—from which he returned in the best of spirits, with a great roll of sketches under his arm, and set to work in his studio. The weather continued fine, growing, if anything, warmer as September advanced and the fallen leaves heaped up beneath the trees, and my foreboding slowly diminished, until Edward announced on a still, humid evening that he had finished the first of his canvases.

I had heard enough about the Hall to anticipate bats circling a crooked tower at dusk, but the sky above the treetops was a pale, almost cloudless blue, permeated with fine streaks and swirls of creamy vapour. Everything about the sky suggested an idyllic afternoon scene, but that was not at all the impression left by the house itself. The sunlight seemed only to accentuate the darkness of the encroaching forest, and to deepen the shadows within the window frames. And somehow—even though I had not seen the original—the proportions of the building seemed to have gone subtly wrong, as if I were looking at it through water.

"I'm very pleased with it myself," said Edward after we had all congratulated him, "and I rather hope Magnus Wraxford will be, too; he's back in Aldeburgh—did I not tell you? I had a note from him yesterday; he'll be here at least another week."

"Excellent," said George, "we must ask him to dine again—and John Montague, of course."

"Yes, indeed," said Edward, as Ada and I exchanged helpless glances. "I'm sure, my darling, you will be able to charm Montague into affability." He had told the others of John Montague's coldness toward him; George put it down to envy of Edward's talent and freedom to paint, but I feared that my strange resemblance to Mr. Montague's dead wife might also be to blame.

"I should much rather he didn't come," I said. "Why should we invite him, when he has been so unpleasant to you?"

"It wasn't as bad as all that," said Edward. "I'd rather mend fences than break them, and besides, I shouldn't want to miss seeing Magnus."

An invitation to dine in five days' time was accordingly despatched to Aldeburgh, leaving me to repent all the more bitterly of ever having mentioned the visitations. But the very next afternoon, whilst I was seated in the shade of an elm, attempting to concentrate on my book, I heard the crunch of hooves on gravel, and saw Magnus Wraxford, dressed as if for the hunt, dismounting at the gate. Ada and George were out, and I knew I ought to rise and greet him, but I did not move, and a moment later he had passed out of sight on his way to the front door. As the minutes passed without Hetty coming to fetch me, I realised he must have asked for Edward, and so I waited uncomfortably, expecting to be summoned at any moment, until Magnus at last reappeared, strode across the drive without a glance in my direction, swung up onto his horse, and spurred it away up the hill.

The sound of his hooves had scarcely faded before Edward emerged onto the lawn and came running toward me.

"Our fortune is made!" he cried. "Did you not see him?"

"See whom? I think I must have been asleep."

"Magnus," he said, sweeping me into his arms. "He is going to buy the picture—for fifty guineas—and he wants the other three at fifty apiece, sight unseen! Is it not wonderful? I wanted to come and find you at once, but he said he couldn't stay. We can be married as soon as your sister is safely wed—and who knows?—your mother may even relent and welcome me into the family, now that I'm a man of means."

I felt briefly ashamed of having hidden from Magnus, but the thought was swept aside in a rush of emotion. Until that moment, I realised, I had never quite believed the day would come; now I even allowed myself to hope that Edward might be right about my mother. The celebration that night extended to several bottles of champagne, over which we all sat talking until very late, and when I did go to bed, I lay awake for a long time, perfectly happy, but too excited to sleep until, as dawn was breaking, exhaustion finally overtook me.

It might have been the fault of the champagne, or the oppressive and quite unseasonable heat; at any rate, I woke very late, with the beginnings of a headache which, for all my efforts to subdue it, grew steadily worse. The humidity was quite extraordinary. George returned from the village saying that no one could remember anything like it; Edward was sure we would be cooler inside a Turkish bath. There was not the faintest breath of wind outside; thick grey clouds hung low and motionless overhead, darkening slowly as the hours passed. By three o'clock, my head felt as if steel pincers were being driven through my temples, and I knew I must retire to my room.

After an indefinite interval, the pain began to ease. I was in the midst of a dream that vanished beyond recall as I was jolted wide awake by a searing flash lighting up the room even through drawn curtains, followed a few seconds later by a deafening crack of thunder which rolled and rumbled and reverberated, shaking the house to its foundations. Within seconds I heard a great rush of wind, a spatter of raindrops against the windowpane, and then the roar of a deluge upon the gravel below.

My headache was quite gone; I felt my way to the door, where I found the lamps in the passage lit and saw that it was almost half past eight. I ran downstairs to join the others, and found George and Ada standing by the drawing-room window. I knew from Ada's expression, even before she spoke, where Edward had gone.

"He left soon after you went upstairs. I told him you would worry dreadfully, but he wouldn't listen; he said he hoped you'd sleep right through the night, so he'd be back before you woke."

"At least," said George, "he will have reached the Hall long before the storm broke; at his pace, he'd have got there by half past five. So he'll have taken shelter. You must try not to—"

The rest of his reply was lost in a blinding flash and a clap of thunder right above the house, after which the lightning flashed continuously, bolt after jagged bolt accompanied by a tumult so deafening it seemed the roof must give way at any moment. Speech was impossible for many minutes, until gradually the lightning died away and the wind dropped until there was no sound but the rush of steady, drenching rain.

The night passed unimaginably slowly. I came downstairs again at first light; the rain had ceased, the air was chill and damp and laden with the scents of bruised and broken foliage. Debris was strewn across the garden, from sodden twigs and leaves to great branches, and water lay in pools across the grass.

George followed soon after, dressed in his waterproof and sou'wester.

"I shall drive down to the Hall," he said, "to save him the walk back."

"I shall come, too," I said.

"No; you must stay—in case I miss him on the road."

Fifteen minutes later, he was gone. Ada came down, trying her hardest to seem cheerful and unworried, but I could tell from her pallor that she had not slept either. Six o'clock struck; then seven; then eight; at nine I could bear it no longer, and said I would walk as far as the village. But I had not even reached the church before I heard a clatter of approaching hooves, and George's trap came over the rise and started down the hill toward me. He had no passenger with him, and I knew, the instant I caught sight of his face, that there was no hope at all.

Three days later, Edward was laid to rest in St. Mary's churchyard. George had found him lying at the foot of the side wall, directly beneath the cable which connected the lightning rods to the ground. His satchel with his sketching things in it was around his neck; it seemed most likely that he had tried to climb the cable, presumably well before the storm broke, and fallen to his death. But why he had done this, no one could say. Edward had not made a will, and so his few belongings, including his pictures, were to go to his father, who was so crushed by the news that he could not even attend the funeral.

I remember the weeks that followed as a dark, dry abyss; I could not weep, even at his grave, and wished only to die. Magnus Wraxford called several times, as did John Montague, but I refused to see them. Ada told me that George had written to my mother, but received no reply; the announcement of Sophie's wedding came as a printed card.

The worst anguish of all was the knowledge that Edward had met his doom in meeting me. Ada insisted that anyone who lost a fiancé or a husband could say the same; of course, Edward would not have stayed in Chalford if he hadn't met me, but I was not to blame for that.

"It is not the same," I said at last, one wintry afternoon. "I had a premonition—a vision of his death—before I even met him."

I told her the story of the visitation, thinking she would understand at last how culpable I was, but she could not see it at all.

"You didn't even notice this resemblance," she said, "until that dreadful scene with your mother; you were shocked and distraught; of course you would put the darkest interpretation upon what was—a mere waking dream, dearest, nothing to do with Edward at all. Edward died because he was fearless—fearless to the point of recklessness—he would have laughed at your vision; you know he would . . ."

"Yes," I said bleakly, "but I saw the apparition; and he died; and nothing anyone can say can change that."

I had begun by then to take some notice of the world around me, though it seemed, except for Ada and George, utterly void of light or hope, and when John Montague called again a few days later, I decided I might as well see him. When Ada brought him into the drawing room, I saw that he was dressed in mourning, and asked, without much interest, if he had lost someone close to him. His jaw seemed longer and narrower than I recalled, the lines around his mouth more deeply etched, his eyes more darkly shadowed.

"No," he said uncomfortably. "I—I wore it as mark of respect."

"That is kind of you, sir; especially as I know you disliked him," I said with some asperity.

"Did he tell you that?" He did not seem able even to say Edward's name.

"Yes, he did."

"I am very sorry I gave him that impression. . . . Miss Unwin, I came to say that if there is anything, anything in this world that I can do, any way I may serve you, I pray you, never hesitate to ask." His voice was suddenly quivering with emotion.

"I thank you, sir, but no, there is nothing."

"And—will you remain in Chalford, Miss Unwin?"

"I do not know." A heavy silence fell, and after a little he rose and took his leave; George told us a few weeks later that he had gone abroad.

But the question lingered: what *was* I to do? My allowance had ceased with Sophie's marriage; I had no money of my own, and could not live on George's charity forever, no matter how warmly they insisted I must stay. I had more or less decided to seek a post as a governess in Aldeburgh, where at least I would not be utterly separated from them, when George secured, through a cousin in the north of England, appointment to a small parish in Yorkshire, to begin in a few months' time. It was not, Ada assured me, anything to do with my mother—though she admitted the stipend would be smaller—only that the incumbent of St. Mary's had recovered his health and would return late next spring. And of course I must come with them; anything else was not to be thought of, especially not so soon after Edward's death.

I think I might have been persuaded, had it not been for a darker fear: I dreaded above all things being visited by an apparition with George's or Ada's face. It was all very well for George to say wisely that such fears were only to be expected after so great a loss; he had not seen the visitant upon the sofa. I knew, rationally, that my living with George and Ada could not endanger them, but there was nothing rational about the visitations. And if I did become a governess, and grew to love the children in my charge . . . Did I not have a responsibility to warn my prospective employers?—and who would ever employ me if I did?

On a damp January morning, I went alone to St. Mary's churchyard. The air was laden with the scent of decaying leaves; thin strands of mist drifted amongst the tombstones. Edward's grave had lost its raw, newly dug appearance, but the pain of loss was as keen as ever. I had been standing there for some time, lost in melancholy reflection, when I heard footsteps on the gravel path behind me, and turned to see Magnus Wraxford approaching.

"Miss Unwin; forgive me for disturbing you."

"No; I am glad to see you," I said. He was not in his riding clothes this time, but formally dressed in a dark suit and white stock. "I am sorry I was not well enough—when you kindly called before."

"You must not apologise; I came only to offer my deepest sympathy. Mr. Ravenscroft's death has weighed very heavily upon my mind."

"You were very kind to him, sir; it was your generosity that would have enabled us to marry, if only . . ."

"Not generosity, Miss Unwin; recognition of a remarkable talent, which the world . . . forgive me; the last thing I want is to distress you any further. I fear I was in part responsible; I have wished many times that I had not encouraged him to paint the Hall."

"You must not blame yourself, sir," I said, thinking how brightly his spirit shone in comparison to Mr. Montague's. "Even if you had forbidden him, Edward would have found his way there somehow; it was none of your fault."

"That is very kind of you, Miss Unwin."

We stood for a little in silence, gazing at Edward's tombstone, upon which was inscribed "Gone into the world of light."

"The worst thing," I said, not looking at him, "is knowing that he met his death in meeting me—the visitation, I mean; I never told him."

"Do you think it would have made any difference if you had?" he asked, echoing Ada.

"Perhaps not—but it might have. You said yourself, that if a young man of that exact description were to die, it would prove that I was clairvoyant—"

"Suggest rather than prove, Miss Unwin. But yes; I think you are brave enough to face the fact that you probably are."

"No," I said passionately, "I am *not*—not brave enough, I mean. How can I live with anyone I care for—let alone love—after this? It is an evil thing, a vile, malignant affliction; I would cut off my hand to be rid of it—" And with that I burst out weeping.

If he had tried to comfort me, I think I should have recoiled, but he did not; he stood quietly at my side, not moving or fidgeting, until I had recovered myself.

"Miss Unwin," he said at last, "if you would allow me once more to try to mesmerise you, and thus, I hope, prevent any recurrence, I should be deeply honoured. I am staying, as it happens, at the Ship—this business of the estate, you know—and have no pressing commitments in London. I am entirely at your service."

I thought again of his generosity to Edward, and of my own ingratitude in hiding from him that day and, after a brief hesitation, accepted. He said he would call tomorrow, bowed, and strode away, leaving me wondering whether he, too, had come to visit Edward's grave, and why he was staying in Chalford, when his solicitor—now, presumably, Mr. Montague's partner—was ten miles away in Aldeburgh.

At two o'clock the following afternoon, Magnus Wraxford was again shown into the small sitting room at the front of the house. It was a raw, dismal day outside; I had slept badly, and spent the morning pacing about the house, trying to prepare myself for his arrival. Reassured by the knowledge that Ada—who now knew exactly why he was here—was reading in the dining room next door, I declared myself ready to begin at once. But my apprehension returned as he drew the curtains. I tried to concentrate upon the oscillating coin, to feel myself becoming sleepy, but fell prey to the illusion that Magnus Wraxford had transformed himself into a disembodied face with candle flames for eyes, and a severed hand floating above the table. I tried to imagine Ada's hand in mine, but knowing that she was on the other side of the wall somehow made this impossible. My eyes refused to close; I found myself attending to an odd, vibrating undertone in his voice, rather than to the words he was chanting. A chill draught touched my cheek. The candle flared and almost blew out, so that the bodiless features opposite seemed to writhe and convulse, the eyes blazing.

I cannot go on, I thought. And then I heard Edward saying, "Extraordinary eyes the man has—if I were a portrait painter, I should certainly want him for a subject." Often when I tried to summon Edward's face in memory, he would come to me only as a blur; then, at other times, he would appear unbidden, as vivid to my inner eye as if he were standing next to me. This was one of those times; I heard the exact accents of his voice: his face came back to me, alight with joy and hope, and yet I felt no grief; I could feel his presence here, now, beside me in the dark room. I remained vaguely conscious of the glittering coin, and of Magnus Wraxford's features floating behind it, but Edward was calling me into the clear light of day, speaking what I knew to be words of great comfort, words I strained to hear but could not quite distinguish, and his presence remained with me until, with no perceptible transition, I found myself in grey twilight, with the acrid scent of a snuffed candle in my nostrils, and Magnus Wraxford looking down at me. Through the open curtains I saw mist swirling against the window.

"I am sorry," I said. "I *did* try . . ."

"Indeed you did, Miss Unwin, but . . . frankly, I have never seen anything quite like it. You appeared to go into a deep trance, but then did not respond to any of my suggestions; it seemed to me that you did not even hear them."

"I'm afraid not," I said. "I had a dream—at least I *think* it was a dream—of Edward; he was speaking, but I could not make out what he said."

"I see." There was an edge of frustration to his tone, for which I could scarcely blame him; he was plainly not accustomed to failure. "Then perhaps you really *did* fall asleep, though it did not seem so."

"I am truly sorry, sir," I repeated, "to have wasted so much of your time."

"Not in the least," he said, recovering his good humour with a rueful smile. "I am only dismayed at my own incompetence. Shall we try again tomorrow?"

"Sir, I could not possibly—" I began, but he waved away my protest, declined the offer of tea, and was gone before I remembered that I was supposed to ask him to dine.

That evening I spoke of the difficulty to Ada and George.

"I am sure," I said, "that if Ada were allowed to sit with me, I should fall quite easily into a trance, but he says it would interfere with my concentration."

"I see," said George. "I hadn't thought the presence of a third party would be an obstacle, but then I know nothing of the science of mesmerism. To speak frankly: are you afraid that he will abuse your trust?"

"Perhaps I am, though I don't feel exactly that; I don't know what it is that unnerves me."

"It seems to me," said Ada hesitantly, "that if his intentions were dishonourable, he would insist upon seeing you somewhere else. He would be taking a very great risk, here—"

"Yes, you are right," I said.

"I wonder if it's his eyes," said George, "the way they hold the light. I'm sure it's what makes him a good mesmerist, but it is a little unnerving."

"I think it must be," I said, and resolved not to allow my nerves to inconvenience him any further.

My unease returned, nonetheless, as the room darkened and Magnus Wraxford again assumed the appearance of a severed head and hand floating above the candle flame. *I must not fear him,* I told myself sternly, and found that by narrowing my eyes slightly I could focus more exclusively upon the glittering coin, and then that if I concentrated on breathing deeply and regularly, I became gradually less aware of the disturbing undertones in his voice, so that it seemed as if I were telling myself to relax, and become sleepier and sleepier, deeper and deeper until I woke to daylight and the dwindling spiral of smoke from the snuffed candle and no recollection of anything beyond *I must not fear him.*

I thought for a moment I had failed him again, but then I saw that he was smiling at me; his entire demeanour—even his appearance—seemed subtly different.

"Well done, Miss Unwin; you have been in a deep trance for the past twenty minutes."

"And—do you think I am cured?"

"I can't guarantee it, I'm afraid, but yes; I am very optimistic; and of course you know that you can call on me at any time."

It was strange, the way he had altered; he seemed gentler, less intimidating. He leaned toward me; we were seated facing each other, only two feet apart, and for a moment I thought he meant to kiss me, until I saw that he was only picking up the gold coin. I was startled, then shocked; surely I could not have *wanted* him to kiss me, with Edward scarcely four months dead?

Magnus, as I had begun to think of him, came to dine that night at George's invitation and was altogether charming; there was no talk of hauntings or séances, only of books and paintings, with much affectionate remembrance of Edward, and for the first time since his death I felt almost at peace—though a little uneasy with myself for feeling so. Magnus seemed to be in no hurry to get back to London, and I was relieved—for reasons I preferred not to examine too closely—that George did not invite him to spend the rest of his stay in Chalford with us.

I woke the following morning to find the sun, which we had scarcely seen for weeks, streaming through my bedroom window. It was one of those rare, still January days when for a few brief hours the world is bathed in dazzling light, and you half-believe it will never be grey and wet again. The accustomed pain of waking was still there, but my grief had lost its raw, lacerating edge; or rather, I became aware that it had been imperceptibly dwindling for some time.

I was sitting in the garden with my book upon my lap, not reading or even thinking, but simply absorbing the warmth of the sun, when a shadow fell across my chair. I looked up to find Magnus standing a few feet away from me.

"Forgive me," he said, "I didn't mean to startle you."

"You didn't," I said, " but I'm afraid George and Ada are out."

"The maid told me; it is you I have come to see."

The sun was in my eyes, so that I could not make out his expression, but my heart was suddenly beating much faster.

"Won't you sit down?" I said.

"Thank you," he said, moving the chair in which Ada had been sitting so that he was facing me. He was dressed as on the day we had spoken in the churchyard, his stock and shirtfront glowing in the sunlight.

"Miss Unwin—Eleanor, if I may"—sounding uncharacteristically hesitant—"I wonder if you have any idea of what I have come to say?"

I shook my head wordlessly.

"I know you will say it is too soon—but Eleanor, I have grown not only to admire you, but to love you; you are a woman of rare courage, intelligence, and beauty, and—and in short, I have come to ask you to be my wife."

I regarded him speechlessly for a long moment.

"Sir," I stammered at last, "Dr. Wraxford—I am greatly honoured—you do me far more honour than I deserve—and I am deeply grateful for all your kindness to—to Edward as well as to me. But I must decline—it is too soon, as you say, but most of all because I do not think I could ever love you, or any man, as I loved Edward, and it would not be fair or right to accept, even if—that is to say—it would not be fair," I ended rather weakly.

"I do not ask so much," he replied. "I should not want or expect to take Edward's place in your heart; only to hope that you will come to love me in a different way."

Even as I sought for the right words of refusal, I could not help contemplating all the advantages of accepting. He was learned, cultivated, handsome, and perhaps rich; and if he had not cured me of the visitations, he would be on hand if ever they recurred. . . .

"I am sorry," I said at last, "but I cannot—you must seek a woman who will love you with her whole heart, as I loved Edward. And besides—supposing my affliction recurs—if I were to see an apparition of you—" Yet I knew, even as I spoke, that he was somehow proof against the visitations.

"I can only say, Eleanor, that it will be you, or no one. I was happy as a bachelor; I had no plans to marry; but you have possessed my imagination as I thought no woman would ever do. And as for your affliction, as you call it, you are right: We cannot be certain you are cured; there is a power in you, like it or not, that perhaps can only be contained. I do not fear it, but many people do"—he leaned over and took my hand—his own was surprisingly cold—and fixed me with his luminous gaze—"and I dread your falling into the hands of those who, if they knew of it, would simply confine you—as you once told me your own mother threatened to do."

"But I can't marry you simply because . . . you must give me time—" I broke off suddenly, realising what I had said.

"Of course," he said, smiling, "all the time in the world; and I shall dare, at least, to hope."

Ada and George were surprised, but not altogether astounded, to hear of his proposal, and we sat up talking very late that night. "If you are not sure of your feeling," Ada kept saying, "you must not accept; you will always have a home with us." And I went to bed resolved to refuse him. But I knew that I could not burden them much longer; Ada still hoped and longed for a child, and a stipend that might just support three would certainly not be enough for four. I tossed and turned for hours, as it seemed, before drifting into uneasy dreams, of which I remember only the last.

I woke—or dreamed I woke—at dawn, thinking I had heard my mother call my name. There was nothing odd about her presence in the rectory; I lay there listening for some time, but the call was not repeated. At last I got out of bed, went to the door in my nightgown and looked out. There was no one in the passage, in which everything appeared to be just as in waking life, but I was suddenly seized by fearful apprehension. My heart began to pound, more and more loudly, until I became aware that I was dreaming—and found myself standing in pitch darkness, with no idea where I was. I felt carpet beneath my bare feet, with a ridge running across it. With my heart still thudding violently, I stretched out my hand until it struck something wooden—a post of some sort—then slid one foot forward until it passed over an edge into empty space. I had come within an inch of plunging headfirst down the stairs.

The following morning, Magnus Wraxford returned and renewed his proposal; and this time, I accepted.

On a grey spring morning, a few hours before I was to be married to Magnus Wraxford, I stood once more beside Edward's grave. My doubts had begun that same afternoon; telling Ada and George, I had heard the note of forced happiness in my own voice, and seen my unease reflected in their faces. Why had I not told him, the very next day, that I had changed my mind?—it was a woman's prerogative, after all. Because I had given my word; because I had refused him the first time; because he had reposed his trust in me; the reasons multiplied like the heads upon the Hydra. I had torn up dozens of attempts at a letter saying I could not marry him because I did not love him as a wife should love her husband; every time I reached "because," I would hear him replying, "I do not expect so much; I hope only that you will grow to love me."

I could not understand how I had agreed, in the course of a single hour in the rectory garden, not only to accept a man I scarcely knew, but to name a day less than three months off. Magnus had said that whilst he would be perfectly willing to be married in church, it would be hypocritical of him not to declare his lack of Christian faith, and somehow in conceding this I had found myself agreeing to a civil ceremony, performed by special licence on the last Saturday in March, and before I had collected my wits, he was gone, with the touch of his lips lingering upon my forehead. And when he had called the following day, it was to offer me a wedding tour anywhere in the world, for as long as I should wish, and I had said no, I would prefer to embark upon our ordinary married life straightaway, thinking that at least I would not be utterly alone with him so soon; but then the thought struck me as so uncharitable, when he was willing to put aside his work for my pleasure, that I found myself unable to declare my doubts as I had resolved.

Indeed, he seemed to want nothing more of me than that I should be his wife and share his fortune, and live more or less as I pleased whilst he got on with his work—nothing, that is, except that I should bear him a son. I shrank from contemplating what that implied, but I also blamed myself for shrinking. Edward was gone, and I would never love any other man in that way; what I might learn to feel for Magnus would be utterly different, and perhaps it would be better not to have any comparison. Not all women who were contentedly married loved their husbands as I had loved Edward—that was plain—but they adored their children just the same. And besides, what was the alternative, if I broke my promise to him? I could not stay with George and Ada, and then I would be utterly alone in the world. All I had received from my mother, in reply to my painfully composed letter, was a cold note of congratulation, regretting that I had chosen a date upon which it was quite impossible that either she or Sophie could attend, since Sophie was now "in a delicate condition"—the euphemism could only have been intended as a calculated insult—and would by then be unable to leave London; and of course my mother could not think of leaving Sophie's side to attend a civil ceremony at such a time.

Magnus's generosity shone all the more brightly alongside my mother's conduct. And yet my apprehension had grown until Ada, who had, as always, divined my distress, offered to speak to Magnus on my behalf.

"But what am I to do if I break my promise to him?" I cried. It was scarcely a fortnight since I had made it.

"Stay with us," said Ada.

"No, I could not. If I break my promise, I must go away from here—it would too bad of me to stay and—"

"Are you afraid," asked Ada gently, "that if you do not marry him, he will not be here to help you, should your trouble return?"

"Perhaps I am."

"That is not enough to marry on, Nell. Let me speak to him—or let George, if you would rather."

"No—you must not."

"Then can you not tell him that your heart still belongs to Edward?"

"I have—I did—the first time he asked me—he says he does not mind."

"But Nell, you told me that he wants children—you *do* understand what that means?"

"Yes, but let us not talk of it—not yet."

"Then at least ask him for more time," said Ada.

"I will try to," I said.

"No: promise me that you will."

"I promise, then."

But somehow the moment never came. Magnus was very much occupied with his patients during the next couple of months, and could manage only brief visits to Chalford; I strove to cherish these last weeks of freedom, but the shadow of my impending marriage hung over them all. Repeatedly, George and Ada tried to persuade me to break off the engagement, but in all of these exchanges I felt compelled to assume the role of Magnus's advocate, countering every argument with recitals of his virtues and my own failings. And when he appeared three weeks before the day, already in possession of the marriage licence, the final preparations took on an inevitability of their own.

Not that there was much to prepare, for I had already said that I wanted only the smallest and simplest of weddings, and in this, as in everything else, he had taken me exactly at my word. The approaching ceremony was, by any ordinary measure, a travesty of what was supposed to be the happiest day of my life, and from there it had seemed only a short step to a reception for four (since I could think of no one apart from George and Ada whom I wished to invite, and Magnus's friends all seemed to be scattered to the most inaccessible corners of the world). Ada and George had, of course, offered the rectory, but I did not want that, or anything that I might have had in marrying Edward. Happiness lay buried in St. Mary's churchyard, and beside that fact, no breach of custom, however extreme, seemed to matter in the slightest.

Ada had once, in desperation, taxed me with betraying Edward's memory.

"If I have betrayed him, it is done," I replied, "and breaking my promise will not undo it."

These words came back to me as I stood beside Edward's grave on the morning of the wedding. In truth, I could not feel I had been false to him, because this marriage was so little what I wanted for myself, and so much a matter of a kind of moral compulsion—I had given my word to Magnus in a moment of self-forgetfulness, having convinced myself that I could bring warmth and happiness into his life in exchange for all he had done for me. And if I had ever since felt like one who wakes from a dream in which he has signed away a precious inheritance, to find himself in his solicitor's office, pen in hand, with the ink drying upon his signature, well, my word was no less my word for that. "He will never take your place," I said silently to Edward. "Never." And then, almost angrily, "If only you had heeded me, and kept away from the Hall. . . ." But again the feeling of his presence eluded me. "Forgive me," I said aloud, as I set the flowers I had gathered, forget-me-nots and bluebells, lilacs and hyacinths, upon his grave, and blindly turned away.

Part Four

Nell Wraxford's Journal

WRAXFORD HALL
TUESDAY, 26 SEPTEMBER 1868

Darkness has fallen—I do not know what time it is. Clara sleeps soundly in her cradle; so soundly I am compelled to look to make sure she is still breathing. I am utterly fatigued, but I know I will not sleep. My head swarms like a cage of rats; I cannot think, and yet I must, for her sake. I have three days before Magnus arrives: three days in which to set down everything that has happened, and prepare myself for what I fear will come.

At least I have found the perfect hiding-place for this journal. I dared not begin in London, for fear that Magnus would find it. If he were to learn—but I will not come to that yet. I must not *assume* the worst, or I shall lose all hope.

I shall begin by describing this room, or rather two, for Clara sleeps in a small chamber, once a box room or closet, I suppose, opening off this one. We are on the first floor, about halfway down a passage which twists and turns so often that you cannot tell where you are. I had to go back and count three times to establish that there are fourteen rooms on this corridor. The servants' stairs are at the back of the house, with a door leading to the main part of the Hall at the front.

The panelling has been scrubbed, and new carpets laid, which would be reassuring if I did not suspect it had been done for Mrs. Bryant's sake, rather than my own. Since I am to preside at her séance, appearances must be kept up—not that she is likely to set foot in here. The floor creaks wherever I move, no matter how softly I tread. The bed is an ancient four-poster, with the canopy removed—doubtless it had decayed to shreds—the bedding, at least, is fresh and dry. There is a chest, a washstand, a dressing table, all in very old, dark wood. The writing desk at which I sit . . . again, I do not know whether to find its presence reassuring or sinister. Was it here already, or did Magnus order that a desk be brought in?—as if to say: "I know, my dear, exactly what you intend to write, so do not imagine you can keep me from reading it"?

The writing desk stands beneath the window, which by day looks down—a long way down—upon a ragged expanse of grass, so recently scythed, as I saw this afternoon, that the stalks are pale yellowish-white. The trees crowding upon it are so tall they blot out half the sky. But now there is nothing but my candle flame reflected beneath a blurred image of my face; beyond that, the darkness is absolute.

I have asked myself endlessly whether, on the one occasion Magnus succeeded in mesmerising me, he subdued my will, or shrouded my perception, for long enough to obtain my promise. But if he did, the memory is lost beyond recall, and I am still to blame for marrying him. I knew I did not love him, and should have told him I had changed my mind, as Ada pleaded with me to do. I remember her white, stricken face at the wedding; I have not seen her since. I say in my letters that I am perfectly happy, and she pretends to believe it; and so our letters have grown less and less frequent. But I will not confide in her; she has sorrows enough of her own.

How could I have imagined that I would come to desire him as he plainly desired me? It seems to me now that even before we were married, I shrank from his touch, but it cannot have been so, unless desire makes men altogether blind—even a man as subtle and discerning as Magnus. On the night of our wedding—I *shall* write it—I found the act immensely painful (would it have been thus with Edward? I cannot believe it) but my distress seemed to excite him further. The assault was renewed the next night, and the next (of the intervening days I have scarcely any memory at all) and I tried to pretend, to persuade myself I would grow used to it, but though the physical pain diminished somewhat, the sense of violation only increased. Because I had refused a wedding tour, we had gone straight to his house in Munster Square. My bedchamber was on the second floor; his was on the first, but for those first days—or was it weeks?—he regarded my room as his own, until the morning when all was changed irrevocably.

I must have come down to breakfast first, though I do not recall dressing, or pinning up my hair, only—just as if I had been sleepwalking, and found myself suddenly wide awake at the breakfast table—seeing the maid at the sideboard, just as Magnus appeared in the doorway. The maid's name was Sophie, like my sister, a girl of about sixteen, small and shy and fair. Magnus came up beside me and laid his hand upon the nape of my neck, and—I could not help it—I shuddered violently at his touch. Sophie saw, and blushed, and scurried from the room.

The hand on my neck seemed to turn to stone. There was a moment of absolute stillness; then the hand was removed, and I looked up fearfully. Magnus's face was utterly expressionless. For another small eternity, we remained thus; he nodded slowly, confirming something to himself, and then—as if a blind had been swiftly and silently drawn—reverted to his usual manner, and said, as though nothing whatever had happened, "I trust you slept well, my dear."

He went out soon after and did not return until late in the day. All evening he kept up the pretence that nothing had occurred; and when it came time to retire, he did not touch me, but bowed and said good night and withdrew to his own room. I lay awake half the night, dreading the sound of his tread upon the stair, but next morning it was the same; I would not have known that anything was wrong, except that again he did not touch me. Sophie gave in her notice soon afterward, but if she had been forced to do so, she did not admit it to me. Day after day he went on playing the devoted husband, in company and before the servants, and I felt compelled to follow his lead, not knowing what else to do. The mask never slipped, even when we were alone together, though that was never for long. He was out most days seeing patients—or so he told me—and in the evenings, if we had dined at home, he would excuse himself with the utmost courtesy as soon as the plates had been cleared, and I would not see him again until he appeared at the breakfast table.

If he had shown any emotion—even fury—I think I should have felt for him. Perhaps I should have abased myself, and pleaded for his forgiveness, but the mere prospect set my flesh crawling, for I was now afraid of whatever waited behind that smiling façade. And a few weeks later, I discovered that I was with child.

I thought that the news was bound to change our situation, but when at last I gathered the courage to tell him—one morning at breakfast whilst the maid was out of the room—all he said was, "So I am to have a son. I congratulate you, my dear. You will need to look after your health, which has been a little uncertain, of late." I dared not question his certainty that the child would be male.

I was ill for much of my confinement, which passed in a sort of limbo state, days and weeks blurring together. Magnus was often away for days at a time; he did not, to my relief, insist on treating me himself, but engaged an elderly physician much like Dr. Stevenson. I had little to do but rest as I was bid, and read, and try for the child's sake to subdue the dread that clung like ice about my heart. When I felt well enough, I would walk with my maid Lucy—the one servant I was allowed to engage myself—in Regent's Park, a few hundred yards from the house in Munster Square.

Lucy is—though I may never see her again—a quiet, soft-spoken girl; she had the nursemaid's room along the landing from mine. She was keen to improve her reading, and became quite fluent by the time Clara was born; I thought of her more as a friend than a servant, though I strove to conceal this from the others. The household is run by Magnus's manservant Bolton and Mrs. Ryecott, the cook; every so often they make a pretence of consulting me, and I tell them to do as they think best. I think of Bolton as Magnus's familiar: a dark, fleshless, thin-faced man in a suit of black. We disliked each other on sight, and I am always aware of his mistrust. Mrs. Ryecott is a gaunt woman in middle age, equally devoted to Magnus; she, too, regards me as an interloper. For the rest, there is Alfred the groom and footman, a boy of seventeen or so, and the two maids, Carrie and Bertha, who live in fear of Mrs. Ryecott's wrath. They are all here, now, at the Hall—all except Lucy, who has gone to Hereford to nurse her mother, who is very ill. She stayed with me until the very last—I wanted her to go straight to Paddington this morning, but she insisted upon coming all the way to Shoreditch to help with Clara, and making the long journey back alone.

Without Lucy's company, I think the loneliness of my confinement would have been unbearable. I had hoped to find new friends in Magnus's circle, but our estrangement, and the sickness of those first months, put paid to that. I knew nothing of where he went, or whom he saw, or what, if anything, he said of me, beyond what he chose to tell me, and no way of knowing whether any of it was true; whereas I had all too much time to brood upon his intentions. Was he only waiting for his son—as he always referred to the child—to be born before he had me locked away in an asylum?—which he could do easily enough, knowing my history. Or if the child should be a girl, would he force himself upon me? There were days, too, when I doubted—as part of me still doubts—my own perception: perhaps he was leaving me alone out of delicacy, and my apprehension was entirely misplaced. But why had he married me? He had desired me, certainly—but there were many young women more beautiful than myself, women of family and fortune who would have been far more compliant. I feared, even then, that my gift, as he calls it, had been the deciding factor.

Yet there was one certainty to which I clung: that the birth of my child would precipitate whatever action he intended to take. On the freezing January morning when I first held Clara in my arms, I vowed to protect her, even at the cost of Magnus's renewed embraces. The doctor and the midwife had gone; I had suckled Clara for the first time, and slept a little myself, and thought I had better send Lucy to ask if Magnus wished to see her. But it seemed that Magnus had left the house soon after the doctor, and I heard nothing more until the following morning, when Lucy returned with a message from Bolton: "The master sends his compliments to Mrs. Wraxford, and regrets that he is obliged to leave immediately for Paris on urgent business."

He was gone a fortnight, leaving me prey to forebodings made all the more fearful by my delight in Clara. The one thing I did not imagine was that he would continue exactly as before. On the day of his return, he stood for a little beside Clara's cradle, regarding her with a sort of mild interest, rather as a man might absently contemplate the child of a distant relative for politeness' sake; thereafter he referred to her as "your daughter," and would ask after her at breakfast with his usual courteous detachment. A month passed; two, and then three; often at night, when I was awake with Clara, I expected to hear his footsteps approaching, but he did not appear. Many times I braced myself to ask him, "What do you intend to do with me?" But the question always died upon my lips; the perfection of his manner compelled assent. And yet the sense of impending crisis was as palpable as the ticking of a clock.

My thought has just been broken by Clara stirring in her sleep. She looks so utterly peaceful. Knowing I must be brave for her sake is all that keeps the fear from overwhelming me. If the worst happens, everyone will say that I should have left her in London, but I could not bear to, with Lucy gone. And since this last visitation I dare not be parted from her.

If anyone—other than Magnus, who will surely destroy it on sight—if anyone should read this, they may wonder why I did not simply take Clara and flee. I am not a prisoner—or was not, before I came here. But I have no money of my own, and nowhere to go. I am so utterly estranged from my mother and sister that I do not even know their address. (I assume that Mama has gone to live with Sophie and her husband.) And even if Ada and I were still close, she and George could not take us in: Clara and I are Magnus's lawful possessions, and he would reclaim us soon enough. Even without the visitations, my flight would be taken as proof of madness, for I have absolutely nothing to complain of: Magnus has never struck me, or ill-treated me in any way; he has never so much as raised his voice to me. True, he cares nothing for Clara, but I have heard that many men respond thus when their hopes of an heir are dashed. He is in every respect a model husband, except that his mere presence fills me with dread.

I must not *assume* that I am to be a prisoner here. There is no infant carriage, of course, and Clara has grown so that I cannot carry her for more than half an hour without my back aching badly. But if Magnus took no precautions against my escape in London, why should he care if I were to summon Alfred and demand to be driven to Aldeburgh? The only person I know there is Mr. Montague, who admires Magnus above all other men; even if I were to trust him, which I do not, he would tell me that my suspicions were groundless, and advise me to return at once.

Yet there are limits to my freedom. The library and the old gallery from which Cornelius Wraxford vanished are locked, for reasons of safety, according to Bolton—he says that Magnus holds all of the keys. And all of the rooms above this floor are closed, the stairs roped off and all the landing doors locked—or so again says Bolton; of course I have not tried them. Some of the boards are rotten, he explained. All perfectly reasonable; except for that very slight air of insolence, of his being my keeper in waiting. The rooms Mrs. Bryant will occupy are directly across the landing from the library—a vast bedchamber, with its own drawing and dining rooms. She says she finds ruins romantic, but what a woman who travels with her personal physician will make of this desolate place, I cannot imagine.

I did not even know of her existence until the morning a few weeks ago when Magnus informed me that "Mrs. Diana Bryant, a patient of mine" had invited us to tea at her house in Grosvenor Street in three days' time. Except for my walks in Regent's Park with Lucy, I had scarcely left the house since the beginning of my confinement, and

Magnus had accepted all invitations on his own behalf: "I am sure that in your delicate state of health, my dear, you would prefer to remain at home" had been his standard refrain.

"May I ask—why you wish me to know her?" I said, trying to keep my voice from quavering.

"Well, my dear," he replied, affecting surprise, "it is surely time you began to go out in Society. Mrs. Bryant—she was widowed some years ago—is a woman of considerable wealth. She suffers from weakness of the heart; my treatment has succeeded where others have failed, and she has become a great advocate of my methods. I am sure you will find much to talk about."

His tone was as courteous as ever, but there was a glint in his eye which discouraged any further questions.

The weather that week had been stiflingly hot—Lucy was obliged to sprinkle chloride of lime on the sills, and pack the nursery casements with brown paper to keep out the stench—and continued so until the morning of the visit to Mrs. Bryant, when the heat was dispelled with a great clap of thunder and a deluge. In any other circumstances, I should have enjoyed a drive through streets washed clean by the rain, but as Magnus followed me into the carriage, I felt only deepening apprehension.

I had pictured Mrs. Bryant as an elderly widow, but she proved to be a handsome woman of perhaps forty-five; tall and statuesque, I imagine men would call her; elaborately and expensively dressed, with a great mass of coiffed auburn hair, not all of which was her own. Her complexion was very pale, with a bluish tinge to it. I had deliberately chosen a plain grey high-necked gown which would not have embarrassed a Quaker, and she looked me up and down with ostentatious pity. She had a loud contralto voice, coquettish when she was speaking to Magnus, condescending when she addressed herself to me.

The only other guest was her physician, Dr. Godwin Rhys, a Welshman, small and slightly built, with very large, prominent blue eyes—almost turquoise, indeed—giving him a permanently startled expression. He looked no more than twenty-five, but was already married with a son and an infant daughter. It seemed to me that he was a little ashamed of his role as a sort of medical lapdog, but he was plainly in thrall to Magnus. Mrs. Bryant launched into an account of her trials at the hands of the medical profession: Magnus, it seemed, had been mesmerising her for some time, with Dr. Rhys's entire approbation. Despite Mrs. Bryant's studied disdain, I did not feel as uncomfortable as I had expected, until I became aware that Dr. Rhys was studying me with professional curiosity, glancing every so often toward Magnus, who was seated beside and a little behind me. *Magnus has told him of my visitations,* I thought, and then, *two doctors must sign a certificate of insanity.*

My cup and saucer rattled in my hand; Mrs. Bryant paused in mid-sentence and asked me, with a look of displeasure, whether I was unwell.

"No," I replied, "only a little—that is to say, no, not at all."

"I am glad to hear it. You are most fortunate," she said pointedly, "to be the wife of such a gifted practitioner, and be able to call upon his services at any hour of the day."

I forced myself to smile and murmur something appropriate. On the excuse of setting down my cup, I moved my chair a little so as to bring Magnus within my field of vision. Behind the affable mask, I thought I detected a gleam of amusement. *I must be calm,* I thought, *I will not play into his hands;* but her next remark unsettled me further.

"Your husband tells me, Mrs. Wraxford, that he is now master of Wraxford Hall. After all this unnecessary delay, you must be delighted."

When I agreed to marry Magnus, I had told him I wished never to see or hear of the Hall again; and I had sometimes wondered, since our estrangement, why he kept silent on the subject when it had power to hurt. Now it struck me, with a sudden freezing sensation, that they were all acting in concert, seeking to goad me into an hysterical outburst that would justify my incarceration. The walls of Mrs. Bryant's opulent, overdecorated drawing room seemed to close around me. I inclined my head, not trusting myself to speak.

"The Hall, of course, is in a very run-down state," said Magnus smoothly. "But I am sure that rooms can be made habitable for our—experiment. Mrs. Wraxford has heard nothing of this," he continued. "I did not like to trouble her with it until the estate was settled."

I waited for him to continue, but he did not. All eyes turned to me, as if I were an actress who had missed her cue.

"Experiment?" I said, hating the tremor in my voice.

"Yes, my dear," said Magnus. "You will recall, I am sure, the evening of our first meeting, when I remarked that the Hall would be the ideal setting for a séance—to be conducted on strictly scientific principles—which might settle, once and for all, the question of survival after death. Mrs. Bryant takes a great interest in spiritualism, and is very keen to participate, as is Dr. Rhys."

"Indeed I am." Dr. Rhys glanced at Mrs. Bryant, made a show of consulting his watch, and rose to his feet. "And now, if you will excuse me, I am afraid I must leave you—an urgent appointment, you know. Delighted to have met you, Mrs. Wraxford; I look forward to renewing our acquaintance very soon."

His departure was too obviously contrived for me to take any comfort in the fact that there were no longer two physicians in the room. I expected Magnus to continue, but instead Mrs. Bryant addressed herself to me.

"With so much unthinking prejudice abroad, Mrs. Wraxford, this is an opportunity not to be missed. Do you know that my own son sought to have me confined to an asylum, simply for attending Mr. Harper's sittings?"

I shook my head mechanically.

"And so, Mrs. Wraxford," she persisted, "I am sure you see our difficulty. I have been so grievously disappointed by spirit mediums—including Mr. Harper, though that does not excuse my son's monstrous behaviour—that I had almost despaired of ever communicating with my dear father again, until your husband . . . so refreshing, to meet a man of science with a genuinely open mind . . . but to the point. I understand, Mrs. Wraxford, that you are a gifted medium, yet you refuse to exercise your gift."

For a long moment I was speechless, while Mrs. Bryant regarded me with feigned concern. Then the blood rushed to my face, and I found that I was speaking.

"No, Mrs. Bryant, you are mistaken. It is a curse, not a gift; I cannot control it, and would not exercise it if I could. And now you must excuse me; I shall wait in the carriage."

I rose and turned without a glance at Magnus and walked toward the door on legs that would barely support me, praying I would not collapse before I passed through it. Anger carried me down the staircase and out onto the pavement, where a bewildered Alfred ushered me into the carriage. Only when I was seated, and trembling violently from the reaction, did I realise that I had played right into Magnus's hands. I realised, too, that I had compounded my humiliation by saying I would wait, but before I could make up my mind to tell Alfred to drive off, Magnus had appeared on the front steps.

To my surprise, he seemed positively cheerful as he settled himself beside me.

"I must apologise, my dear," he said amiably, "for Mrs. Bryant's lack of tact. She is accustomed, as you see, to having her own way."

"Why did you—how could you—" I was about to say "humiliate me so," but the words died at the thought of the humiliation I had inflicted upon him.

"I thought, my dear, given that relations between us have been a little—strained, that the request might come better from Mrs. Bryant than from me."

"How could you possibly think that?" I cried. "I should far rather you had asked me yourself—not that I should have agreed—than betray me to that vain, vulgar woman—" I was about to add, "who is either your mistress, or wishes to be," but restrained myself in time.

"Vain and vulgar she may be, my dear, but she is also our patron. She has already contributed generously to my work, and if we are fortunate enough to witness a genuine manifestation at the Hall, her largesse will be assured . . . which is why I should like you to reconsider your refusal."

"You wish me, in other words, to be party to a fraud."

"You of all people, my dear, should know me better than that. This is to be a scientific experiment, conducted before witnesses; it requires only your presence, I assure you."

"You expect me, then, to accompany you to that unholy place, where my—where Edward died."

"Yes, my dear." He spoke in the same genial tone, but now there was an edge to his voice like the whisper of steel on steel, a sword eased in its sheath.

"And—if I refuse?"

"I am sure you will not, my dear. Your health is still delicate; I think you need a little time in the country."

"But I am nursing Clara and cannot be parted from her, and the Hall is no place for an infant."

"Then perhaps it is time you weaned her. That is one of your symptoms, my dear, your unnecessary anxiety over the child. I have not asked anything of you, before this; you will agree, I am sure, that I could not have been a more indulgent husband."

He waited for me to contradict him, but this time I dared not.

"Very well, then; I shall leave it to you to decide about the child. You may bring her with you if you wish, and speak to Bolton about what you require in the way of rooms. He and I shall be going down tomorrow to prepare for Mrs. Bryant's visit in three weeks' time."

"And—after this? How many more séances shall you require me to attend?"

"With luck, my dear, none. And if all goes as I hope, perhaps we can then discuss—our future living arrangements. Ah—I see we are approaching Cavendish Square. There is a gentleman here I need to consult. Until this evening, my dear."

Magnus did not return until late, and had left for the Hall before I came down to breakfast the following morning. Several times during that day, I gathered Clara in my arms with the intention of fleeing, only to remind myself that I had nowhere to flee to. Lucy was plainly aware of my distress, but I had never confided in her, and dared not now. Though Magnus had made his threat as plain as if he had waved a certificate of insanity under my nose, he could have spoken those words before witnesses, and denied on oath that he intended any such thing—as easily as he could deny, if he chose, that he had held out the promise of a separation.

But if he was planning a fraud, how could my presence possibly help him? Mrs. Bryant had behaved abominably, but how could he be sure I would not secretly warn her? Or betray him after the event? There was only one way he could be certain of that. Unless it was *not* to be a fraud, and Magnus truly believed that a spirit would appear: I had foreseen Edward's death in a visitation, and he had died at the Hall . . . I tried to push the thought away, but it hovered all day in the darkest corners of my mind, and in this uneasy state, I went to bed.

I woke—as I thought—at dawn, with a terrible sense of foreboding. The room was like my old bedroom at Highgate, but I knew somehow that I was in Wraxford Hall. Then I recalled, with a jolt of horror that seemed to tear my heart out of my chest, that I had been walking with Clara in Monks' Wood the previous afternoon, and had left her asleep beneath a tree. I flung myself out of bed, threw open the door, and began to run along the passage. I had passed Lucy's door before I realised that I was now awake in fact, and standing at the head of the stairs in grey twilight, with my heart pounding violently.

The house was completely silent. I stole back along the corridor to the nursery—which was between Lucy's room and my own—and softly opened the door.

A woman was leaning over the cradle. She had her back to me, but I could see that she was young, with hair very like mine, and wearing a pale blue gown that looked strangely familiar. As I stood petrified in the doorway, she lifted Clara in her arms and turned to face me. She was myself. For a long, frozen moment we remained thus, and then she and Clara began to shrink into themselves, just as the apparition in the drawing room had done, until there was nothing but a streak of livid green light floating between me and the cradle. Then that, too, vanished; the floor swung up and struck me on the temple, and I heard, in the far distance, the sound of Clara's crying before darkness swallowed me.

Wednesday evening

Today I stood at the place where Edward died. The cable he tried to climb is thick with rust, which runs in a dark stain down the wall.

When I first saw the Hall yesterday, I thought it had been painted a dingy shade of green, but the walls are covered in lichen, speckled with mould and riven with cracks; the ground beneath is strewn with fragments of mortar. I was resolved not to weep, knowing that Bolton would be watching me, though there was no one in sight.

If Edward had never met me, he would be alive today. So I torment myself, but if he had kept his promise, and never come near this place, we would be married now, and Clara would be his child. (I wrote that unthinkingly, but the thought is often with me: I have never seen anything of Magnus in her, whereas I often fancy she has Edward's eyes—the same shade of hazel, flecked with a darker brown.) I will not—*must* not—believe that he was doomed to die—or that Clara and I are doomed because of this last visitation. Perhaps I was mad to bring her here—but what else could I have done? If I had left her at Munster Square with a nurse I did not know, and something had happened to her . . . no, I could not.

Why did he do it? Was it mere curiosity—to see what was in the gallery? A light where no light should have been? Or was he fleeing from something? The forest is dark enough even in daylight; by moonlight it would be all too easy to imagine terrors—as I keep imagining I can hear soft footsteps moving across the floor above my head. But when I lay down my pen to listen, I hear only the beating of my heart.

Thursday evening

Mr. Montague called this afternoon. I thought at first that Magnus had sent him to spy on me, but he said he had come of his own accord. I had just settled Clara to sleep, and rather than converse in the gloom downstairs (with Bolton lurking in the shadows), I suggested we walk around to a seat beneath my window, where I could hear

Clara if she cried. He is markedly thinner than when I saw him last, and his hair is streaked with grey.

He told me that Magnus has invited him to witness the séance, which is to take place this Saturday evening; he was startled to learn that I did not know this. I do not think he and Magnus are as close as formerly: the invitation came by way of a brief note, which said nothing of Mrs. Bryant or Dr. Rhys, or of what is to take place. But he spoke warmly of Edward, and confessed that his apparent dislike had been propelled by envy—of his youth, his talent, and his good looks, and so I feel more kindly toward him. He is plainly uneasy—as who would not be?—about the séance. I believe he is an honest and scrupulous man, and I feel a little less fearful, knowing he will be present.

All the time we were speaking, there was no sound from the house at my back, but I was acutely aware of row upon row of windows looking down upon us. As he walked away across the ragged grass, a faint movement in the shadow of the old coach house caught my eye. It was Bolton, watching from the entrance; when he saw that I had observed him, he slipped behind a wall and disappeared.

FRIDAY—ABOUT 9 P.M.

Mrs. Bryant arrived by coach at about three o'clock this afternoon, escorted by Magnus on horseback. I watched from the window of her sitting room for long enough to see who had accompanied her. Apart from Dr. Rhys, there were only her two maids, a footman, and the coachman. The maids are to share a small bedroom across from the vast chamber prepared for her; Dr. Rhys will have the room at the head of this corridor, so that he, too, will be within call if required.

I was resolved to keep to my room until Magnus summoned me, and for three very long hours I waited, with my heart pounding whenever I heard footsteps in the passage outside, but no one knocked. Clara woke and was fretful for a while; which helped at least to distract me. At around six there came a tapping at my door, but it was only Carrie to say that "the master" would like me to join our guests in the old gallery at half past seven: dinner would be served at half past eight. And so I endured another anxious vigil while the light faded above the treetops beyond my window. Surely, I thought, Magnus will want to instruct me as to how I am to behave, but still he did not appear. At seven Clara was still wakeful, and I had no choice but to give her a spoonful of Godfrey's Cordial, not knowing how long I would have to be away from her.

Carrie returned at a quarter past seven to help me dress, not that much help was required, for I had deliberately chosen the same grey gown, without hoops or bustle, that I had worn to Mrs. Bryant's house a month before. By the time the half hour had struck, the last of the twilight had faded from my window.

Until this evening, the passage outside my room had been pitch-dark. Now candles had been lit in the sconces along the wall, but the glass was so blackened that they yielded only a dim, murky light. The air was stale and close. Expecting at every turn to find Magnus awaiting me with a smile, I made my way through the gloom to the landing. The double doors to the gallery stood open.

Along each wall, a row of wavering flames receded. High windows shone with a faint cold light; higher still, the ceiling was shrouded in darkness. Some twenty feet away from me, more candles burned upon a small round table, lighting up the faces of Magnus, Mrs. Bryant, and Dr. Rhys, so that they seemed to hang in the air above the flames.

"Ah, there you are, my dear," said Magnus, just as if he had last seen me five minutes—rather than several days—ago. I moved reluctantly to join them. Mrs. Bryant, resplendent in crimson silk and displaying a large expanse of white bosom, greeted me with disdain; Godwin Rhys bowed awkwardly.

Behind them, the wall at the far end of the gallery was dominated by an immense fireplace. But nothing had prepared me for the sheer bulk of the armour towering in the shadows beside it. The sword glittered beneath its gloved hand; in the shifting light it seemed alert, alive, watchful. Within the fireplace stood a massive chest of dark metal: the tomb of Sir Henry Wraxford. *I have been here before,* I thought, but the flicker of recognition was gone before I could catch it.

"Dr. Wraxford was about to tell us," said Mrs. Bryant impatiently, "of a discovery he has made amongst his late uncle's papers." She spoke as if I had kept them all waiting, and I realised that Magnus had deliberately arranged matters thus.

"Indeed I was." His tone was as cordial as ever, but with an edge of anticipation. His teeth caught the light as he smiled; the pupils of his eyes shone like twin flames. "But perhaps we should return to the mystery of his disappearance—all the more baffling to anyone who has stood where we are standing now. To recapitulate: my uncle's man, Drayton, saw him retire to the study next door at about seven on the night of the storm. When Mr. Montague arrived the following evening, he was obliged to break in, and found all the doors to the landing locked and bolted on the inside, with the keys still in the locks. We have tried in vain to lock—let alone, bolt—any of those doors from the outside. There is, to the best of our knowledge, no secret passage, trapdoor, priest's hole, or anything of the kind. The flues of the chimneys are too narrow for a grown man—even a man as small as my uncle—to pass. What, therefore, became of him?

"The only rational explanation—the only one that I can see—is that he somehow got out of that window"—indicating the one above the suit of armour—"climbed down the cable, stumbled away into the forest, and fell, as his predecessor, Thomas Wraxford, is supposed to have done, into one of the old mine workings. It is not impossible—we found that casement closed, but not latched—only incredible, to suppose that a frail elderly man could have done all that in pitch darkness, on the night of a violent storm. I have made the climb myself, in far better conditions, and I can assure you it was not a pleasant experience."

His gaze flicked toward me as he said this. I clenched my fingers until the nails dug into my palms, struggling to conceal my distress. For a year and a half I had feared him; now I knew that I hated him.

"But if we eliminate the window, we are forced to consider—less-rational possibilities. As you know, my uncle burned a great many papers, including the manuscript of Trithemius, on the night of his disappearance."

Again Magnus glanced toward me, as if to say, "I know perfectly well, my dear, that you have never heard of Trithemius."

"You have heard, too, of my uncle's strange conviction—derived from Trithemius, and possibly from Thomas Wraxford—that the power of lightning might be harnessed to summon a spirit, using that suit of armour to contain the force of the bolt. Now, in going through his study the other day, I found a page of notes—scrawled in haste, and sometimes quite impenetrable—which had slipped behind a row of books."

He drew from his coat a crumpled sheet of paper.

"I shall not weary you with the tale of my efforts to decipher this. The first legible phrase is 'divined T's meaning at last'; whether 'T' is Thomas or Trithemius, we cannot tell. He then refers to the armour as a *portal* (the word is heavily underscored)—which may be used either to 'summon' or to 'pass without need of dying'—and prays for 'strength to endure the trial.' He believed, in other words, that if he were inside the armour when lightning struck, he would pass unharmed into the next world, just as the risen body, according to Scripture, will ascend to Heaven upon the day of judgement."

"But surely," said Dr. Rhys, "anyone foolhardy enough to occupy that suit during a thunderstorm would be struck dead . . . indeed, is it not possible that your uncle did exactly what you suggest, and was reduced to ashes, or even vapour, by the force of the blast?"

"Possible, yes. But we found no trace of ash, or evidence of burning, on the inside of the suit. Men have been struck by lightning and survived"—he paused, as if struck by a sudden thought—"others have died instantly and been badly charred; but I know of no case in which the victim simply vanished from the face of the earth.

"All of this, I agree, would seem utterly incredible, were it not for the inconvenient fact of my uncle's disappearance. For a scientist, there is surely but one course: test the hypothesis."

"But my dear Dr. Wraxford," said Mrs. Bryant, "we cannot sit here for days or weeks, waiting for it to thunder."

"Fortunately, there is no necessity of that. I have managed to secure an influence machine—a device for generating a powerful electrical current—which Bolton will operate from the library, so as not to disturb us; the current will be conveyed to the armour by means of wires passed under the connecting door. Though not as formidable as lightning, the charge is continuous.

"There is a theory, you know, that the basis of spirit may be electrical. For spirits to communicate with the living—the question we shall try tomorrow night—they must surely be composed of *something*. A something which is able to store energy, yet clearly not material. For a scientist, then, it is natural to think in terms of the electrical and magnetic forces.

"I have even begun to wonder whether my uncle's obsession was not, perhaps, quite as mad as I assumed. Gods are often said to wield lightning; and whilst this represents primitive awe at the power of nature, it may also shroud a genuine intuition. The same applies to the spiritualist practice of linking hands around a table. Ghosts and spirits are generally depicted as emanations of light; one thinks of St. Elmo's fire or the very rare phenomenon of ball lightning . . . a far-fetched analogy, you may say, but just as a magnetic field will cause a heap of iron filings to arrange themselves into a complex pattern, so the soul, the vital principle—call it what you will—animates the earthly body. Might it not be that the vital principle is electrical, perhaps in some subtler form that science has not yet grasped?

"These are, as I say, mere theories, but there will certainly never be a better opportunity to test them. Tomorrow night we will seek to summon a spirit; but if that should fail, I am willing to try a bolder experiment. I shall instruct Bolton to operate the influence machine at full power, and occupy the armour myself."

"But my dear Magnus," said Mrs. Bryant, forgetting her discretion, "that is surely too great a risk."

"I confess," said Magnus, "that it would take a good deal more courage to try it during a storm. But that is how science advances. And if we succeed—if there is genuinely something in this business of the portal—then your dream will become a reality. . . . You may not have heard, my dear"—turning to me with his most charming smile, whilst Mrs. Bryant looked on in triumph—"that Mrs. Bryant wishes to endow a retreat for spiritualists: a place where conditions are peculiarly favourable, sheltered from the hustle and bustle of daily life . . ."

I looked from one to the other of them in disbelief.

"It is a magnificent house, Mrs. Wraxford," said Godwin Rhys, "sadly in need of refurbishment, of course, but it could be the pride of the county. And such a picturesque history—the disappearance of two owners only adds to its *cachet*—"

"Evidently, Dr. Rhys," I heard myself saying, "my husband has not told you that my late fiancé, Mr. Edward Ravenscroft, died here two years ago, or you would not speak so lightly of this accursed place. I will attend your séance, Magnus, because you command it, but I will not dine with you. And now you must excuse me."

I had forgotten the threat of the asylum, forgotten, for a moment, even Clara. Dr. Rhys's mouth opened, but no sound came out; Mrs. Bryant regarded me with apprehension. I glanced toward Magnus as I turned away, but instead of fury I saw only triumph. The after-image of his smile accompanied me to the door.

Ten o'clock has just struck; my hand still trembles as I write. Clara has not stirred; she scarcely breathes. It was wicked of me to give her laudanum, but what else could I have done?

Once again I fear my temper has betrayed me into doing exactly as Magnus intended. I half-expected a summons to the dining room, but Carrie came up with a tray at about quarter to nine, which only confirmed my suspicion. He was goading me, and I did not see it—just as Mrs. Bryant and Dr. Rhys do not see that he plays upon them like puppets. But *what* does he intend? Why, after making so much of my "gift," did he not so much as mention it tonight? And if the séance is to be a fraud, why does he want me here? The others are entirely under his spell, and he must know that if his scheme miscarried, I would be the first to expose him. It makes no sense.

But if Magnus truly believes in this monstrous business with the armour, then that must mean

10.15 P.M.

Someone has slipped a message under my door. Within the last few minutes; it was certainly not there when I went to look at Clara. A plain sheet of paper, folded once, no address or signature. The hand is feminine—it could almost be my own.

Come to the gallery at midnight—I have found out the secret, and must speak with you privately. Destroy this, and tell no one.

Who can it be? Surely not Mrs. Bryant. Even if she had made some appalling discovery about Magnus, I am the last person she would turn to. One of the servants? I cannot think so. None of them would dare—or want—to offend Magnus. It *could* be Dr. Rhys—but he would surely go to Mrs. Bryant, not to me.

Could somebody be hiding in the house? The footsteps I thought I heard the other night . . . but who, and why?

Or else it is a trap.

But if someone truly wishes to help me . . . I could go early, and hide behind one of the hangings—but then I would have no way of escape. No; I shall go to the library, and open one of the connecting doors a fraction, and watch from there. The moon has risen; I shall not need a light. And if I am caught, I can say that I have come in search of something to read.

I must take the chance.

Part Five

John Montague's Narrative

If Magnus and I had not met George Woodward that morning in Aldeburgh, I might never have met Eleanor Unwin; nor, perhaps, would Magnus, and she might now be happily married to Edward Ravenscroft. I would certainly never have seen her as I did that first evening at the rectory: a girl in a plain white gown with a mass of dark brown hair pinned up, framed against the setting sun, transporting me back to Orchard House and my first glimpse of Phoebe standing beside her mother on a summer's evening.

It is, of course, impossible, but I would swear I stood motionless for several minutes, caught in a kind of double vision in which I knew dimly where I was, and yet had only to cross the floor to begin my life with Phoebe over again. The vision faded as Magnus and I came forward, and I saw that Eleanor Unwin was markedly taller than Phoebe had been, and that her features were sparer, the bones more prominent, her hair a darker shade of brown. As her bare fingers touched mine, I felt a small, sharp shock, as when you cross a carpet in stockinged feet and recoil from the first thing you touch. She did not appear to notice; I realised that I was staring at her as if I had indeed seen a ghost; and then I heard her say that she was engaged.

It is true that I envied Edward Ravenscroft; I told myself at the time that he was a coxcomb, that his work was flashy and superficial, that he could not possibly deserve her. I saw Nell—as I always thought of her, once I realised that everyone who loved her called her by that name—only one more time before she married Magnus; a brief, painful interview in which her dislike of me was abundantly clear.

I decided to go abroad, and apply myself once more to painting. I sold *Wraxford Hall by Moonlight* to Magnus, as he had several times requested; had I known at the time that he intended to marry her, I should never have agreed to it. But the attempt at exorcism proved vain, for I soon discovered, as I passed from one magnificent spectacle to the next, that I had lost all interest in landscape, and could only say, with Coleridge,

> *I see them all so excellently fair,*
> *I see, not feel, how beautiful they are!*

The only subject that called to me was Nell herself; instead of forgetting her, as I had hoped, I found myself recalling the smallest nuance of her expression, the subtle turn at the corners of her mouth, the slight asymmetry of her face, the movement of her hands, the faint strands of hair escaping from her chignon. I tried endlessly to sketch her face from memory, and though none of my efforts ever satisfied me, I could not bear to burn or discard her image, and kept every one until I had filled an entire case.

I returned to Aldeburgh a year later, knowing of course that she was now married—I assumed happily—to Magnus. The business of Cornelius Wraxford's estate was still unresolved; I should have left the trust in my partner's hands, but could not bear to relinquish my last link to Nell—not that there was anything to link us. Magnus's letters were always cordial in tone, but said nothing of Nell beyond formal compliments, and guilt at my feeling forbade me to ask. In February of 1868 he mentioned that "Mrs. Wraxford had given birth to a daughter"; I was struck even then by the remoteness of the phrasing. I sent my warmest compliments and pressed him for details, but nothing further followed. The Wraxford estate passed into Magnus's hands in August; early in September, he called at the office to collect the keys, as genial as ever but in a great hurry to get on; I heard that he and his man were staying there. I expected a visit or an invitation, but none came, until I received a note:

> *My dear Montague,*
>
> *I am very sorry to have neglected you. You may recall that evening in Chalford, when I outlined a psychical experiment; I am pleased to say that it will proceed next Saturday evening, and would be delighted if you could attend as an impartial witness. Mrs. Wraxford will be staying at the Hall this week; business keeps me in town until Friday.*
>
> *I remain, very sincerely yours,*
>
> *Magnus Wraxford*

I knew it would be most unwise, but the thought of seeing Nell again—even if she sent me away on the instant—overpowered me. Though I had lately acquired a pony and trap, I did not drive all the way to the Hall, but tethered my horse on the edge of Monks' Wood and continued on foot. It was a perfect autumn day, warm and cool by turns, but I scarcely noticed, moving through the forest at a jog until the perspiration was dripping off my forehead.

I had expected, at the very least, to see the timbers repainted, but the only visible change was that the long grass and weeds around the house had been scythed, and only recently, for the remnant was raw and ragged, bristling with the dead stalks of thistles and nettles. Bathed in afternoon sunshine, the Hall appeared, for once, more picturesque than menacing.

I saw at once that Nell had changed. Her face was thinner, the shadows beneath her eyes were darker; yet none of my thousand sketches had done her justice. I halted a few paces off.

"Mrs. Wraxford," I said, "I—er—heard you were already in residence, and thought I should pay my respects."

"That is very kind of you, sir. I take it my husband has asked you to call?"

"Well, no," I replied uncomfortably. "He has invited me, as you know, to witness the—er—experiment on Saturday night—but—he mentioned you were here, and so . . ." I trailed off, regarding her with helpless appeal. She was wearing a plain gown of creamy-grey stuff, her dark hair plaited and wound about her head as I remembered. Though the day outside was mild, the air of the great hall was deathly cold as always, laden with musty smells of damp horsehair and decaying fabric. She glanced toward Bolton hovering in the gloom nearby, and suggested we take a turn about the grounds.

"I am very sorry," I said as the front door closed behind us. "I called upon impulse, but if I am inconveniencing you . . ."

"No," she said. "I was only a little surprised. My husband did not, in fact, mention that you would be joining us; I did not even know that his experiment was planned for Saturday."

"I see . . . I did not realise . . ."

"There is a seat on the other side of the house, beneath my window. I shall be able to hear Clara—my daughter—if she cries."

I realised as we set off along the weed-strewn path that we would pass the place where Edward Ravenscroft fell. My footsteps crunched loudly on the gravel.

"Magnus told me—that you had had a child. I should have written to congratulate you, but I did not . . . I was not . . ." Again I trailed off, glancing toward the encircling trees.

"This is a desolate place. . . . You said you needed to be near your child—does she not have a nurse?"

"No—my maid was obliged to leave me, just before we came here. I am caring for Clara myself—by my own choice, because I will not trust her to a stranger," she added, seeing my startled expression. "And yes, it is a desolate place—it took the life of the man I loved most in the world."

We had turned the corner of the house as she was speaking. I saw the black cable, the rusty stain like blood running down the wall behind it.

"I know," I said abruptly, "that you think I disliked Edward Ravenscroft. The truth is, to my shame, I envied him—his youth, his exuberance, his talent, and above all . . . enough to say that if the loss of my own life would restore him to you, it is a sacrifice I should gladly make."

My voice broke at the last phrase, and tears sprang to my eyes. She took my arm and led me across the ragged grass to the bench—a mere slab of moss-encrusted stone.

"That is a very generous sentiment, Mr. Montague," she said when I had recovered my composure, "and I am glad to know that you did not—look down upon Edward, as I had assumed."

"On the contrary; envy springs from looking up, not down. . . . Forgive me, but—you intimated that you are not here by choice."

"This is the last place on earth I should ever want to visit, Mr. Montague. But Magnus wishes it, and I must obey him. May I ask, in turn, what he has told you about his experiment, as he calls it?"

"Only a note saying he looks forward to renewing our acquaintance on Saturday, when he intends to try the experiment he outlined that night—the night I first saw you, at the rectory."

"Did he say anything of my part in it?"

"Nothing at all—only that Mrs. Wraxford sent her compliments. He did not even say whether you would be present."

"And did he mention Mrs. Bryant?"

"Again, no—only that there would be company. But—the maid told me that Magnus would not be arriving until tomorrow afternoon. May I ask why you are here alone with your child?"

"Magnus wished me to come down earlier—to give me time to settle in, since I would not be parted from Clara."

"I see. And—er—who is Mrs. Bryant?"

"A wealthy widow—a spiritualist. Magnus calls her his patron."

I glanced at her questioningly, then looked hastily away again.

"I know nothing of their relations, Mr. Montague. Tell me—have you and Magnus remained close friends?"

"Not as we were—as I thought we were. Since—since your marriage, I have seen him only twice—did he not mention it? I have always asked to be remembered to you—about the business of the estate. He is as cordial as ever, but there is a distance—a reluctance, in particular, to speak of you." I had been gazing toward the wreck of the old chapel, half-buried beneath a canopy of nettles, but now turned directly to face her.

"May I ask," I said, "though I have no right to, why you decided to marry Magnus?"

"Out of fear, Mr. Montague—or so it seems now. Will you give me your word of honour, never to speak of this?"

"My life upon it."

"The friend I spoke of—that night at the rectory—was myself. I had a vision—saw an apparition—which foretold Edward's death, though not where or when or how he would die; it was before I even met him. And after—Magnus said he could rid me of the visitations, as I called them—he tried to mesmerise me, but could not, at first. He warned me that if the visitations returned, I might be confined to an asylum, as my mother had already threatened to do, unless I married someone sympathetic, who could protect me—meaning himself. Our marriage was a mistake—for both of us, though Magnus has never admitted as much. He pretends that nothing is wrong, but I fear he hates me—and I must do what he wishes, for Clara's sake. . . ."

The words came tumbling out, and her tears with them. I became aware that I had taken her hand in both of mine; with a great effort, she regained control of herself, and gently disengaged my fingers.

"Nell"—I said her name without meaning to—"if I had only known . . . Does he mistreat you?"

"No," she said, "he leaves me entirely to myself. This is the first thing he has asked of me since—the first thing he has asked. He believes, you see, that I have some power of clairvoyance—"

"And do you believe it?"

"I do not want to; I strive not to. The visitations are a curse, an affliction; it was my longing to be rid of them that betrayed me into marrying him, and that is why I am here. He says the séance—that is what he intends—requires only my presence; I do not know whether to believe him."

"But to compel you, against your will—and to bring an infant child here, of all places—"

"I cannot blame him for that; he wanted me to leave Clara in London, and I refused. You may think it selfish and wrong of me, but Magnus does not care for her—he wanted a son—and if I defy him, he will have me confined. Mrs. Bryant's physician is under his spell, and would sign the certificate, I am sure of it—"

"But you do not behave like a madwoman. Do you still suffer from this—affliction?"

She shook her head mutely.

"Then he has no ground—and besides a physician ought not, and in law should not, seek to certify his own wife. Has he threatened to confine you?"

"Not in as many words, no—only by insinuation."

"Forgive me, but are you quite certain, in that case—?"

"No, Mr. Montague, I am not. That is the curse of my situation. Magnus is utterly opaque to me; I do not know what he really thinks, or feels, or believes. But it makes no difference. I cannot risk defying him, for Clara's sake. And he has said—or at least implied—that if the séance is a success, he may agree to a separation."

"And if it is not a success?"

"He has not said, and I have not dared ask."

I remained silent for a little while, staring at the gravel around my feet.

"If there is anything I can do—" I said.

"There is one thing," she said. "I have a journal; an account of my life until my marriage. I brought it with me, not knowing what else to do, but I should rather it was in safe keeping. Would you take it for me, and promise to keep it, and never show it to anyone, unless you hear from me?"

"Upon my life," I said.

"Then I shall fetch it—no, stay here—I shall be only a few minutes."

She walked swiftly away, glancing around the empty clearing as she went, whilst I sat wishing to God I had confessed my jealousy of Edward that wintry afternoon at the rectory. Was it possible, if she and Magnus were to separate . . . ? I found that I, too, was scanning the clearing, and especially the tumbledown row of outbuildings away to my right. Something had attracted my attention; something dark, moving in the shadow of the old stables. I felt suddenly conspicuous, an intruder upon Magnus's domain.

A door creaked behind me, and Nell reappeared with a packet in her hand. As I took it from her, a sudden current of sympathy flowed between us; her face lifted toward mine, and our lips brushed before she whispered, "You must go." I looked back once, as I walked away across the ragged grass, in time to see the door close behind her.

I returned to Aldeburgh consumed by the wildest imaginings, all my senses inflamed by that intoxicating moment. The next day dragged by in an agony of hope and fear; I thought of Magnus arriving, and tormented myself with wondering how far "he leaves me entirely to myself" might be construed. I had more or less forgotten that I was going to attend a séance, and thought only of seeing Nell again. At midday on Saturday, unable to bear the confines of my house, I walked down to the Cross Keys Inn and there heard the news which was already the talk of the district. Mrs. Bryant was dead, and Nell and her child had vanished during the night.

The principal witness to these events was Godwin Rhys. According to his testimony at the inquest (which I give here more or less in his own words), he had joined Magnus and Mrs. Bryant in the old gallery at about a quarter past seven that evening. They discussed their plans for the séance the following evening; Mrs. Wraxford joined them some twenty minutes later. She seemed apprehensive and ill at ease. When Dr. Rhys, in his own words, "inadvertently reminded her of her late fiancé's death at the Hall some two years previously," she became distressed and left the gallery. The others continued their discussion over dinner until about ten o'clock, when Dr. Rhys and Mrs. Bryant retired to their rooms, leaving Magnus downstairs.

Dr. Rhys (a poor sleeper, by his own account) went to bed at around eleven, but was still awake when the half hour struck. Soon after that, he heard soft footsteps—a woman's, he thought; he assumed it was one of the servants—moving past his door. His room was at the head of a corridor, just off the landing. A quarter to twelve had sounded, and he had begun to doze, when he was awakened by the sound of a key turning in a lock. Though his window was in shadow, it was bright moonlight outside. He opened his door a little and saw Mrs. Bryant, wrapped in what appeared to be a dark cloak, pass the entrance to the corridor in the direction of the landing, shielding the flame of her candle with her hand. Her expression made him wonder if she was walking in her sleep.

The lights along the passage had been extinguished, and so he was able to follow her as far as the landing without risk of being seen. Mrs. Bryant snuffed her candle and continued on, all the way to the gallery, where she passed through the open doors and out of sight. He remained where he was, about forty paces away, looking over the black pit of the stairwell.

Faint sounds, as of someone moving about in stockinged feet, came from the gallery. The shuffling ceased; he held his breath, straining to make out another, even fainter sound; a muffled creaking of hinges, as of a door being slowly and stealthily opened.

The scream that followed seemed to explode inside his head; a prolonged shriek of terror and repulsion that rose to an intolerable pitch, reverberating up and down the stairwell in a cacophony of echoes. For several seconds he stood paralysed, until the sounds of opening doors and hurrying feet brought him to his senses.

Dr. Rhys was the first to enter the gallery. He found Mrs. Bryant sprawled on the floor between the round table and the suit of armour, stone dead, her eyes open and her features contorted in an expression of the utmost horror. Mrs. Bryant's two maids ran in as he was kneeling beside the body, followed a few moments later by Bolton and some of the other servants. Magnus (as was later attested by Alfred the footman) had gone out for a stroll in the moonlight; he heard the scream from two hundred yards away, and came running back to the house.

Magnus, therefore, did not arrive at the gallery for some minutes after Dr. Rhys. His first question upon seeing the corpse was, "Where is my wife?" The maid Carrie was sent immediately to Mrs. Wraxford's room, where she knocked for some time before her mistress came to the door in her nightgown. Alone of all the household, she had slept right through Mrs. Bryant's scream. When informed by Carrie that Mrs. Bryant was dead, she replied, "There is nothing I can do; tell my husband I will see him in the morning," and closed her door again; Carrie heard her turn the key in the lock.

Mrs. Bryant's body was then carried back to her room, where Dr. Rhys made the examination. He found no trace of injury; on every indication, she had died of heart failure induced by shock. But what had caused that shock? A search of the gallery and library revealed nothing untoward; the seal which Magnus had placed upon the armour in anticipation of the séance remained unbroken; the movements of everyone in the house had been accounted for. Magnus and Dr. Rhys decided to wait until first light before dispatching a messenger to the telegraph office in Woodbridge, and the household retired for a few hours' uneasy sleep.

At around eight thirty the next morning, Bolton returned from Woodbridge with the news that he could not find a doctor willing to attend; all had said, upon hearing that Mrs. Bryant's physician was already at the Hall, that he could perfectly well sign the certificate himself. Dr. Rhys, therefore, despite considerable misgivings, certified the immediate cause as heart failure brought on by shock, with advanced heart disease as a contributing cause. It was quite possible, as Magnus observed, that Mrs. Bryant had indeed been walking in her sleep, and that the fatal spasm had been precipitated by the shock of finding herself in the gallery.

Magnus and Dr. Rhys were still at breakfast (since Mrs. Wraxford had taken all her meals in her room, they were not expecting her) when a horseman arrived with instructions from Mrs. Bryant's son. An undertaker and his men would follow within two hours to collect the body and convey it directly to London for examination by a distinguished pathologist. Dr. Rhys, upon hearing this, wanted to tear up his certificate, but Magnus dissuaded him, saying that it would give the impression they had something to hide.

Magnus had already decided to close up the Hall and return to London that day, and Carrie was accordingly sent to pack her mistress's things. But she found the door locked, and an untouched tray still in the passage where she had left it half an hour before. (Her instructions were to tap on the door and leave the tray without waiting for Mrs. Wraxford to emerge.)

At Magnus's request, Dr. Rhys accompanied him upstairs to the room, where the door was forced—there was no bolt, but the key was lying upon a little table beside the bed. They found—or rather Magnus, observed by Dr. Rhys, found—a diary open upon the writing table, with a pen lying across the page, as if the writer had been interrupted, and beside it the stub of a candle which had burnt down to its socket. The bed was turned back, the pillow dishevelled. In the child's room beyond (it had no independent exit), the blanket on the cot was turned back in the same fashion. There was soiled linen in the pail, water in the basin; nothing to suggest struggle or sudden flight, or an alarm of any kind. And according to Carrie—though she could not be certain, because of her mistress's secretive habits—the only things missing were Mrs. Wraxford's nightdress and the child's swaddling gown.

It seemed to Dr. Rhys, as they were waiting for the door to be forced, that Magnus was striving to conceal anger, rather than anxiety. Several times he nodded to himself, as if to say, "This is just what I should have expected of my wife." But as he began to leaf through the diary, his expression changed. The colour drained from his face; his hand trembled; a cold sweat appeared on his brow. For a minute or two he read on, oblivious to his surroundings; then he closed the book with a snap and slid it, without explanation, into his coat pocket.

"Search the house!" he directed Bolton, who was hovering by the doorway. "And send for a party to comb the wood. With the child, she cannot have gone far. . . . Perhaps, Rhys, you might assist with the search whilst I look around in here."

It was a command—not a request—and Dr. Rhys spent the next few hours stumbling fruitlessly from room to dusty room, without any clear idea of why he was doing so.

A quarter of an hour after I heard the news, I was driving at brisk pace along the Aldringham road. The day was warm and close, and I was obliged to rest my horse more than once, so that it was well after two before I reached Monks' Wood. As I drew nearer the Hall, I heard voices hallooing in the woods around me.

At the front of the house, several vehicles waited on the gravel, their horses harnessed as if for immediate departure. Servants were running between them, stowing boxes and bags and bundles of clothing. A slight, fair-haired young man in tweeds was hovering by the largest of the carriages, attempting to direct the loading of it. He looked at me fearfully as I approached, and began to explain that the undertakers had already left; I thought for a ghastly moment they had left with Nell. Such was his agitation that it took me several attempts to establish that he was Dr. Rhys, and convince him that I was not a surgeon, and several minutes more to extract from him a summary of the night's events. I was about to ask him why on earth the servants were packing up the house, instead of joining in the search, when I saw Magnus over by the stables, conferring with a group of men. I left Godwin Rhys wringing his hands beside the carriage, and went uneasily to join him.

Magnus walked away from the group—labourers and small farmers, some of whom I recognised—as I drew near. Bolton was distributing coins amongst them, and for an instant my hopes flared.

"What news?" I cried, forgetting everything but my anxiety for Nell. "Have you found her?"

"No, Montague, we have not," he said coldly. "I was rather hoping that *you* might have news for *me*."

Bolton glanced toward me. He was twenty feet away—too far, I hoped, for him to overhear—but the sneer on his face was enough to tell me who had been watching from the shadows.

"I have no news," I replied, holding his gaze as best I could. "If she is not found, why are you leaving?"

"Because my wife is not here. I believe she left here—by arrangement—early this morning. Someone must have been waiting with a dogcart—or something of the sort," he said, glancing at my own vehicle, "and driven away with her."

"Do you mean she was *seen*—?"

"No, but it is the only explanation. She is not in the house; she could not have gone very far in the wood, carrying the child . . . though the search for the child must obviously continue—"

"What do you mean?"

"It is possible—especially if she has fled with a lover—" he added, "that she has abandoned or even made away with the child—"

"That is monstrous!" I exclaimed. "You cannot believe that; she would never—"

"I am aware, Montague, that you are on intimate terms with my wife. But I doubt that your intimacy extends to an understanding of her mental condition, which is precarious, at best. So unless you can tell me where, and with whom, she has gone, there is nothing more for you to do here."

"Magnus, I assure you there is nothing . . ." My words withered under his stare. "Her safety is all that matters now. Suppose your theory is wrong, and they are lost somewhere out there—how can you risk abandoning her?"

"I think it far more likely that *she* has abandoned *me*. Some of the men, as I have said, will continue to search the wood for another hour or so. I shall remain here, on the chance that she may return; everyone else will leave for London within the hour. Which reminds me: you will, I am sure, agree that it would be inappropriate for you to continue as solicitor to the estate. Kindly arrange for the deed-box, the keys, and the other Wraxford papers to be conveyed to Mr. Veitch of Gray's Inn at your earliest convenience. Good day to you."

He strode away toward the house with Bolton, still smirking, trailing after him.

I spent, or rather endured that night consumed by visions of Nell strangling her child, burying the body in Monks' Wood, and fleeing with her lover (whom I could not help picturing as Edward Ravenscroft). I would fight off these ghastly images, only to be possessed by the conviction that Magnus had murdered her and the child in a jealous fury, with the intention of casting suspicion on me: At any moment, the police might come knocking with a warrant for my arrest. But what if she had left him for *me*? That soft tapping at the door (which I would have sworn I heard a dozen times during the night, though there was never anyone there) might be Nell, with Clara in her arms; and so on, round and round, until I drifted into nightmares worse than my darkest imaginings.

On Sunday morning, I learned that the search had been abandoned at around half past three, just as Magnus had intimated. He had addressed the remnant of the search party, along with the departing servants, to the effect that he now believed that Mrs. Wraxford, distressed by Mrs. Bryant's sudden death, had taken the child on a visit to friends, forgetting to inform anyone of her destination. The search, he assured them, had been merely a precaution. He himself would remain at the Hall for another day or two, in case she should return there; the rest of the household would return immediately to London. I could find no one who had actually been at the Hall when Magnus spoke, and yet everyone assured me—claiming to have heard it from somebody who *had* been present—that his manner had been that of a gallant gentleman shielding his wife. Aldeburgh was abuzz with the rumour that Eleanor Wraxford had poisoned Mrs. Bryant, smothered her infant daughter, buried the body in Monks' Wood, and eloped with a lover.

I insisted, to everyone I met, that this was a terrible slander upon an innocent woman, who was quite possibly herself in mortal danger, but my protestations were met with raised eyebrows and knowing looks. If Eleanor Wraxford was innocent, then why had the search for her been abandoned so soon? And if Mrs. Bryant had died of natural causes, why had her body been whisked away to London for an autopsy? Several people wondered aloud why I was not at the Hall with Magnus (for whom there was universal sympathy); to which I could only, and lamely, reply that he preferred to be alone; I did not dare ask what rumour had been saying of *me.*

The weather continued close and still until Monday afternoon, when there was a distant rumble of thunder and a play of lightning on the southern horizon, followed by heavy rain. I learned later that people in Chalford had seen, on the Sunday night before, a single flash of lightning from the direction of Monks' Wood, followed half a minute later by a faint sound that might have been thunder.

Tuesday and Wednesday dragged by; I could not face the task of bundling up the Wraxford papers, nor could I bring myself to instruct Joseph to do it. I told my partner I thought I was sickening for something, but it cannot have sounded altogether convincing, since I spent most of my time roaming the district in search of news. I felt myself an object of general suspicion, and imagined that people were whispering behind my back wherever I went; but to sit shut up in my house was more than I could bear.

On Thursday morning I woke very late, after drinking more whisky than was good for me, and was making a pretence at breakfast when my housekeeper came in to say that Inspector Roper from Woodbridge was here to see me.

"Show him in," I muttered, dabbing at the perspiration which had sprung up on my brow.

I had a nodding acquaintance with Roper, a barrel-chested man in his fifties, but at the sound of his heavy tread I rose to my feet, fighting down a mad impulse to flee. His lugubrious face, the colour and consistency of risen dough, gave an initial impression of stupidity, until you became aware of his eyes—small, deep-set, shrewd—regarding you watchfully.

"Beg pardon, sir, but your clerk said you were at home, so I took the liberty of calling."

"Not at all," I said faintly. "Would you care for some tea? What can I do for you?"

"Thank you, sir, but I had my tea at the station. And as you might guess, sir, it's about the Hall."

"In—indeed? Have you found—is there news of Mrs. Wraxford?"

"No, sir. Visiting friends, is the story we were given." The note of scepticism was all too plain. "You don't look very well, sir, if I may say so."

"I fear you are right," I said hoarsely, sinking back into my chair. "This business at the Hall—won't you sit down?—has shaken me considerably . . . been with my family for generations, you know. . . ." I trailed off, conscious of having said exactly the wrong thing.

"Well, indeed, sir, and that's why I'm here," he said, taking a seat. "You see, we've had a wire from Dr. Wraxford's London residence. He was expected home Monday, and then they thought maybe he'd stayed a day longer, in case Mrs. Wraxford . . . but when it came Wednesday afternoon and still no sign of him, they thought they'd better ask us to go out to the Hall and take a look around. Which we did, but my man found the house all closed up, no sign of anyone, and no horse, either. So of course we inquired of Pettingshill at the livery stable, to see when Dr. Wraxford brought his horse back."

"And had he?"

"That's the odd thing, sir. The horse came back, all right. The stable boy found him waiting at the gate on Monday morning—outside, you understand—saddle still on him, reins tied to the pommel, and a guinea in the saddlebag. So Pettingshill assumed he'd taken the early train, and thought no more about it. But he hadn't. Dr. Wraxford hasn't been seen since Saturday, when they left him at the Hall."

"I—er—I see. Have you any theory, Inspector, as to what might have happened to him?"

"That's where I hoped, sir, that you might be able to help"—my heart lurched sickeningly—"you being solicitor to the estate—and a friend of the family and all."

His small eyes flickered like a lizard's. Even as I shrank from the insinuation (real or imagined, I could not tell), my mind was suddenly racing.

"I've heard nothing, I'm afraid. . . . Did Bolton—Dr. Wraxford's man—suggest that you call on me?"

"Well, no, sir, I came of my own initiative. You see, sir, I think we ought to look *inside* the Hall, just to be on the safe side. But it's private property, and—well, supposing Dr. Wraxford was still there, he might not appreciate the police barging in, if you see what I mean. So I was wondering whether you might have a set of keys . . ."

"I do, yes, at the office. . . . Would you like me to drive out to the Hall and—see if everything's all right?"

I heard, as I spoke, the echo of my words to Drayton on that rainy afternoon a lifetime ago. But instinct was urging me to seize the chance of investigating the Hall alone—the chance, however slender, that I might come upon some clue that would lead me to Nell.

"Well, yes, sir, that would be very helpful indeed. Will you need me to accompany you?"

I understood at last that Roper had no suspicion of me at all.

"I don't think that will be necessary, Inspector; I'm sure you have a great deal to do. Unless, of course, you feel you should be there."

"I'm hard-pressed, sir, it's true, and ought to be on the next train back to Woodbridge. . . ."

"Then I shall leave straightaway; the fresh air will do me good. If I should find anything—untoward—I shall come straight on to Woodbridge and let you know. I shall wire, in any case, as soon as I get back to Aldeburgh."

"Very good, sir, and thank you; I'm much obliged."

It was after midday when I set off. Low, swirling clouds hung over the fields, still damp from the night's rain, and a chill wind blew from the sea: all too reminiscent of my journey with Drayton. I was aware, too, that my position was questionable, at best. If Magnus had told Bolton, or for that matter, Dr. Rhys, that he had dismissed me . . . I had received nothing in writing, but it would raise eyebrows all the same.

On Saturday, with the forecourt crowded with carriages, I had been too shaken by my encounter with Magnus to think of anything but Nell, and had given little thought to the Hall's sinister history. But now those primeval fears returned with a vengeance. It was all very well to tell myself that this was the age of steam engine and the electric telegraph, and that science had banished those terrors; here, I might as well have been a thousand miles from civilisation.

The front door was bolted on the inside, but I found a smaller door, close by the stone bench where I had sat with Nell, which let me into an unfamiliar part of the house. I took a stub of candle from a blackened glass chimney, and made my way through the gloom to the great hall and up the stairs to the landing, where I stood listening to the silence.

The study was locked, but not from the inside. Cornelius's camp bed and the washstand had gone; a leather writing chair was drawn up to the desk. There were rows of volumes around the walls, but nothing on the desk itself. The damp, ammoniacal smell of books left untended for too many winters caught at my throat. The only sign of recent occupation was a greatcoat, which I recognised as Magnus's—hanging from a hook on the back of the door I had just opened.

In the right-hand pocket was an oblong package, sealed with Magnus's phoenix seal and addressed in his hand to Jabez Veitch, Esq., of Veitch, Oldcastle and Veitch, Gray's Inn Square, Holborn. As I stood there trying to divine the contents—which felt like a slender volume, about eight inches by five, and a letter or document of some kind—it struck me that this would be Magnus's advice to Mr. Veitch of my dismissal. I slipped the package into my own greatcoat and turned out the other pockets, in which I found a penknife, a pair of riding gloves, and a purse containing four sovereigns.

Of course, Magnus might simply have forgotten his coat.

I went on through the library, where I saw something that looked like a massive spinning wheel, with half a dozen glass discs, a handle, and wires trailing away beneath the door leading into the gallery. The door was locked, but this time from the outside; I turned the key and entered.

In the middle of the floor, a small round table had been overturned, with several chairs scattered around it, two of them lying on their sides. The tomb of Sir Henry Wraxford sat like a stone in the throat of the fireplace. Wires from the machine in the library trailed past my feet, joining to those which connected the armour to the lightning rods. I became aware, beneath the odours of ancient timber and mildewed fabric, of a faint, cold, acrid smell of burning.

The armour was closed. As I drew nearer, with every nerve urging me to turn and flee, I saw, where the sword blade entered the plinth, a rusty dagger thrust into the slot, jamming the mechanism. Caught between the plates was a piece of dove-grey fabric that might have been torn from the hem of a woman's dress—like the one Nell had been wearing that afternoon a week ago. The cloth was charred along the line where it vanished into the armour.

I stood petrified, remembering the story from Chalford of that single brilliant flash, lighting up the sky above Monks' Wood on Sunday night, and staring at the torn fabric until I realised that the dress had been caught from the outside. Lying in the shadows behind the armour was a small jewelled pistol, such as a woman might use.

Rain spattered against the windows overhead. I dropped the pistol into my pocket, stooped to free the dagger, and then, shuddering as if I were grasping a serpent, took hold of the sword-hilt.

A grey, inchoate form engulfed me; something struck my foot and boiled up around me in a coarse grey cloud, filling my mouth and nostrils with the gritty taste of ash. There were ashes in my hair and upon my clothes, and as the cloud settled, I saw that my feet were surrounded by shards and splinters of greyish bone. Glinting amongst them were several tiny pellets of gold—one still embedded in the remnant of a tooth—and the misshapen shell of a signet ring, blackened and distorted but still recognisable, melted onto a fractured cylinder of bone.

I do not remember thinking, "Nell has done this." I no longer felt afraid; I no longer felt anything at all. I went numbly back through the library and study and down the grand staircase to the front door, which I unbolted and unlocked, and let myself out of the house.

The rain had more or less ceased. My horse waited patiently, his head hanging down. The prospect of confronting Roper was intolerable; I wanted only to go home and huddle by my fireside until it came time to sleep, never to wake again. I reached into the side pocket of my coat and took out the pistol—a derringer, no more than five inches long, with a single barrel—*but 'tis enough, 'twill serve.* I clicked back the hammer, raised the gun, still without conscious intent, and pressed the cold muzzle to my temple, wondering with a sort of detached curiosity what the sensation would be. The movement made me aware that something was pressing against my chest; the corner of the package in my breast pocket.

Awareness flooded back to me; I lowered the pistol, meaning to uncock it, but my hand was seized by a spasm of trembling. The pistol jumped like a live thing; a spurt of muddy water flew up at my feet; my horse threw up his head in alarm as the report echoed around the clearing.

Shaking more violently than ever, I put away the gun and drew out the package. To Jabez Veitch, Esq. But what if Magnus had told him *why* he was dismissing me? I stepped back into the shelter of the portico and broke the seal.

Inside was a small blue notebook, and a letter in Magnus's hand, the latter part of it blotched and spattered with ink.

Wraxford Hall
30 Sept 1868

My dear Veitch,

I am alone at the Hall—the servants left an hour ago. You will hear of my wife's disappearance long before this reaches you. I fear she has committed a terrible crime—perhaps several—and must make up my mind what to do.

I found this diary in my wife's room when we forced the door this morning. It is proof, I fear, that her sanity has given way, as you will see from her terrible animus against me, who has striven so long to keep her from the madhouse. I confess I converted Mrs. Bryant's money into diamonds, in the hope of winning back Eleanor's love—I have just discovered that the diamonds are not in the drawer where I left them last night. And as I learned only yesterday, my wife has formed a clandestine attachment to John Montague, whom I trusted, as you know, implicitly. I dismissed him on the spot when he had the effrontery to call this afternoon; you should receive the papers &c from him some time this week, unless he has already fled with her.

Whether Montague was party to the theft, or to the death of Mrs. Bryant—in which I suspect my wife had a hand—I do not know, but I fear my daughter is already dead

There is someone moving on the floor above.

In haste: I have just seen a woman on the upper landing. The light was bad but I am certain it was my wife—she had a pistol in her hand. I thought she meant to fire, but she vanished into the dark.

The light is fading fast. I shall hide this package and then attempt to find her—perhaps she will listen to reason.

Yours, MW

I remember thinking quite dispassionately, as I slid the letter back into the packet, that I was holding everything required to make me an accessory to Magnus's murder, for which I would very likely hang along with Nell.

Darkness was falling by the time I reached Woodbridge, and such was my state of mind that I did not think to hide, let alone burn the package, which was still in my pocket as I climbed the steps of the police station like a man ascending the scaffold. Roper was still in his office, and received me with the utmost sympathy; it plainly never occurred to him to doubt my story. I handed over the keys, and the pistol (which had discharged, I told him, when I dropped it on my way out), and within twenty minutes was installed in a room at the Woodbridge Arms. There I read and re-read Nell's journal, and sank at last into a drugged, hallucinatory sleep, stepping up to the armour over and over again, knowing what was coming but unable to stop myself grasping the lever. It did not even occur to me until morning, when I was sitting huddled beside my window, watching the grey water flowing past the Tide Mill, that the ashes in the armour might be Nell's. Magnus's letter could have been contrived to hang us both; it could even have been quite sincere, except that in the ensuing pursuit it had been Nell—not Magnus—who had died.

My duty was plain: to hand over the package immediately. It was not too late to pretend that I had been too shaken to remember it; I could even pretend that I had broken the seal in my agitation. Except that no one would believe me, and in trying to persuade Roper that the ashes were Nell's, I would only tighten the noose around my neck.

Back in Aldeburgh, I awaited the inquest—which was delayed some days to allow several London experts time to come up and examine the scene—as if it were my own trial for murder. Bolton was bound to be called, and his evidence alone would be damning. I knew I should burn the package, but every time I took up the matches, I would imagine policemen bursting in upon me, just as I steeled myself a dozen times to confess all to Roper, and in the end, like a man caught in a nightmare, did nothing but pace endlessly about my study at home—I could not face the office—while the jaws of the trap closed inexorably around me.

I was thus engaged, the day before the inquest was due to begin in Woodbridge, when my housekeeper knocked to say that a Mr. Bolton was asking to see me.

"Show him into the drawing room," I said, and spent the next few minutes struggling vainly to compose myself.

He was seated upon the sofa when I came in. His dress was modelled upon Magnus's: black suit, white stock, tall hat and gloves; the expression on his pale, fleshless face was perfectly deferential, and though he rose and bowed as soon as I appeared, it was plain who was the master.

"Very kind of you to see me, Mr. Montague, sir; I'm up for the inquest."

"Er—yes," I said, swallowing. "This—your master's death came as a great shock to me—as it must have been for you all."

"Indeed, sir; and as I'm sure you understand, we're all wondering what is to become of us. In fact, if I may take the liberty of asking, you wouldn't happen to know whether the master made any sort of provision for me?"

"I'm afraid not," I said. "His will is with Mr. Veitch in London; and you understand, of course, that nothing can be done until the coroner has handed down his findings?"

"Oh I quite understand that, sir."

An appraising silence followed; though the room was chilly, I could feel the perspiration trickling down my forehead.

"Er—is there anything else I can do for you?" I asked.

"Well, yes, sir, as a matter of fact there is. You see, sir—not that I wasn't very happy in Dr. Wraxford's service—my ambition lies in the way of photography. I should like to start a little business of my own . . . but of course I'm in want of capital, and it occurred to me, sir—you being such a close friend of the family—that you might see your way to advancing me a loan."

"I see. Er—how much did you have in mind?" I added far too quickly.

"Two hundred and fifty pounds, sir, would set me up very nicely."

"I see. And—for what term?"

"Hard to say, sir. Perhaps we could make it—an informal arrangement. I'm sure I should be very grateful."

"Very well," I said, dabbing at my forehead.

"Thank you, sir, I'm very much obliged. Now I don't suppose, sir, you could favour me with a cheque today . . . ?"

The note of menace was unmistakable.

"Very well," I repeated, avoiding his insinuating gaze. "If you could return at three . . . I shall be out, but the cheque will be waiting for you."

"Thank you again, sir, you won't regret it, I'm sure. No need to ring, sir, I'll see myself out."

My state of mind at the inquest can readily be imagined. I was one of the first to be called before the coroner—a florid-faced gentleman from Ipswich by the name of Bright—and thought my knees would give way before I had taken the oath. But as with Roper, my haggard appearance attracted sympathy rather than suspicion, and I was on the witness stand only a few minutes.

Next came the question of identification. The charred signet was identified by Bolton (who studiously avoided my eye). He also confirmed that Magnus had had five teeth filled with gold. The distinguished pathologist Sir Douglas Keir testified, on the basis of the larger fragments, that the remains were those of a man, probably taller than average, in the prime of life. Further than that he could not go, owing to the extreme heat to which the bones had been subjected—sufficient to reduce flesh and soft tissue to a fine powdery ash. As to whether lightning could have inflicted the damage, he was not qualified to say.

Professor Ernest Dingwall, Mr. John Barrett, FRS, and Dr. Francis Iremonger were called to testify on this point. The effects of being struck by lightning in the open—there appeared to be no precedent for the manner of Magnus's death—varied considerably. Some had survived, with burns of varying degrees; in one case, a man was rendered unconscious, and when he recovered, walked away from the scene with no recollection of having been struck. Others had died instantly; in one case, a man's skull had been reduced to fine fragments, with no apparent injury to the skin. No one could cite anything like the annihilation of Dr. Wraxford, but Mr. Barrett gave it as his opinion that the force of the bolt could have been greatly concentrated by the armour. Dr. Iremonger took a diametrically opposite view, maintaining that the suit of armour would have acted as a "Faraday cage"—i.e., the entire force of the blast would travel around the outside of the suit, leaving the person inside unharmed.

The coroner inquired, with a good deal of sarcasm, whether the learned gentleman would care to try the experiment himself. The learned gentleman confessed that he would not.

It was clear, from that moment onward, that the coroner had made up his mind that Nell Wraxford was guilty. He remarked in his summation to the jury that "the lightning strike upon the Hall was mere chance, and very long odds at that, the salient point being that if Magnus Wraxford was not already dead when his murderer forced him into the armour at gunpoint—Mr. Montague's testimony alone seems to me decisive upon this point, though of course you must make up your own minds—if, as I say, Magnus Wraxford was not already dead, he had been left there to starve. You may well consider, gentlemen of the jury, that jamming the mechanism was as culpable, and far crueller, an act of murder than shooting him dead would have been.

"Furthermore," he continued, "an infant child is missing in circumstances which can only point to the mother's guilt. Why would Mrs. Wraxford not allow anyone else near her child? You may well conclude, gentlemen, that her insistence on caring for the infant alone is already evidence of unsound mind. You have Dr. Rhys's testimony as to her extreme agitation on the night of Mrs. Bryant's death; the curious fact of her being the only person, on her own account, not to be woken by that lady's death-cry, which was heard two hundred yards away. You have heard, too, that a crumpled note was found by the police on the floor of Mrs. Bryant's room—a note inviting her to come to the gallery at midnight—which is when and where she died. The hand appears to be that of Mrs. Wraxford. We are not charged with investigating this death, but it is suggestive, all the same, of a dangerous predisposition to violence on Mrs. Wraxford's part.

"Then there is the matter of the necklace. You have heard from Dr. Rhys that Mrs. Wraxford appeared to be deeply estranged from the deceased. You have heard, from the representative of the Bond Street firm who furnished the necklace, that the deceased purchased this very extravagant gift for his wife for the sum of ten thousand pounds—which suggests an uxorious, even infatuated husband willing to go to the most extravagant lengths to win back his wife's regard. You have heard that the empty jewel-case was found by the police beneath a floorboard in Mrs. Wraxford's room. The necklace is nowhere to be found."

He said a great deal more in the same vein. After brief deliberation, the jury returned a verdict of wilful murder by person or persons unknown, and a warrant was immediately sworn for Eleanor Wraxford's arrest.

The post-mortem on Mrs. Bryant revealed that she had indeed been suffering from advanced heart disease and had died of heart failure, probably as a result of a severe shock. But the family were not satisfied; her estranged son now became his mother's champion, and rumours that began to circulate in London, to the effect that Dr. Rhys and the Wraxfords had conspired to murder her—and that Eleanor Wraxford had then disposed of her husband and child and fled with the diamonds.

Magnus Wraxford, in a will dated some months before his death, had left his entire estate to his cousin Augusta Wraxford, a spinster nearly forty years older than himself, making no provision for Nell or Clara, or any of his servants. Mr. Veitch wrote to me in the most cordial terms to make certain that Magnus had not left any later will with me. The estate, however, consisted entirely of debts: the contents of the Munster Square house had to be sold to reduce them; and at the end of the proceedings, the servants (with the exception of Bolton, from whom I never heard again) were thrown onto the street to look for new situations. The bequest to Augusta Wraxford—who had, as I would later learn, nurtured a lifelong resentment against her male relations for bringing ruin upon the estate—seemed like a satiric act of malice.

I continued to act as solicitor to the estate, partly out of fear of what someone else might discover, and partly in the vain hope of hearing some news of Nell. Augusta Wraxford—a fierce old lady of decidedly eccentric views—came to see me as soon as Magnus's will had been proven, and instructed me to locate her nearest female relative. Thus began the long and weary process of constructing and testing a genealogy, in the course of which I discovered that Nell had been distantly related to Magnus, though neither appeared to have known, which made the tragedy seem even darker. And though Augusta Wraxford had long coveted the Hall, she could not afford to render it habitable; the most she could do was reduce the burden of debt. But neither was she willing to sell, and so the house was once again closed up, and left to its long decay.

My confession is done. It has tormented me day and night, not knowing what to believe. When I summon Nell's face, I cannot imagine her a murderess. But then I think of the evidence, and am confronted once again with what I know would be the world's verdict: that she deceived me utterly, and made me, through my own foolish infatuation, an accessory to murder.

Wraxford Genealogy as Compiled by John Montague

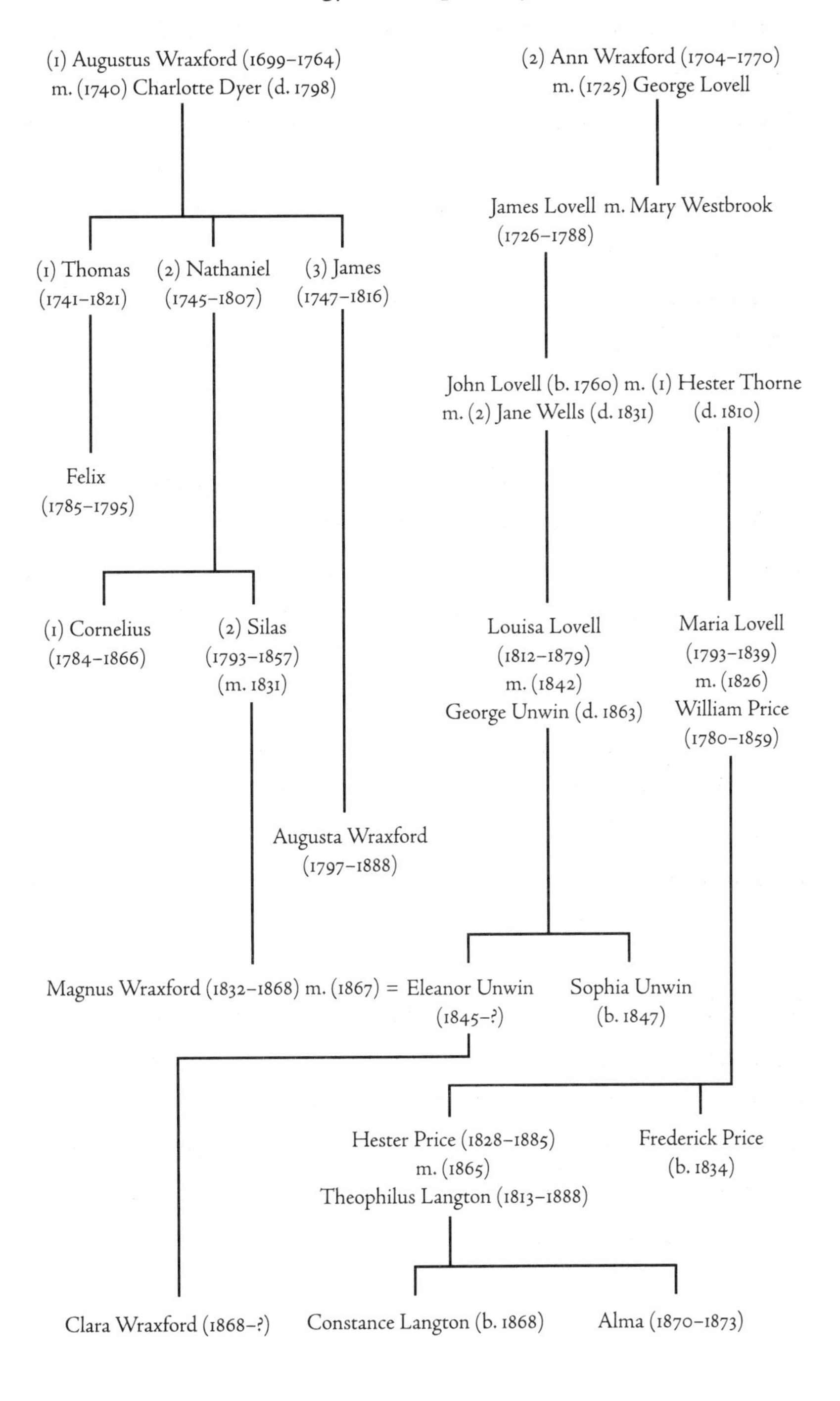

Part Six

Constance Langton's Narrative

All day whilst I read, the rain fell steadily, splashing on the gravel beneath the sitting-room window and lying in pools upon the sodden grass. Except for an occasional glimpse of bare branches gliding through the mist, there was nothing to be seen beyond the top of the wall but grey, swirling vapour; I looked up more than once from the pages of John Montague's narrative and felt the hair rise on the back of my neck before the warmth of the fire brought me back to Elsworthy Walk.

I knew, long before I reached the end, that it could only be my resemblance to Nell that had so shaken him; that, and the "wild fancy," as he had put it, that I might be Clara Wraxford. My heart had accepted—indeed, seized upon—the possibility before my head had even begun to comprehend what it might mean, beyond the conviction that Nell could never have harmed her child. There were so many questions I wanted to ask Mr. Montague, and yet there was a strange finality about his letter, a note of farewell, as if he did not expect to hear from me again.

My uncle (rather to my relief, for I could not decide how much, if anything, I ought to tell him) had decided to brave the weather in order to dine with some artist acquaintances, and so I took my supper on a tray by the fireside whilst studying the genealogy that John Montague had compiled. A wind had risen and was rattling the casements, sending gusts of rain lashing against the glass.

The chart had been drawn so that Clara Wraxford (1868–?) and Constance Langton (b. 1868) were side by side at the foot of the page. All my life I had thought of myself as separate, cut off from the rest of the world. Dr. Donne's saying that "No man is an island" had always inspired in me the opposite sentiment; our house in Holborn *had* been, sadly, an island, entire unto itself, and Alma's death had diminished us all the more because of it. To many, I suppose, the Wraxford connection would have seemed profoundly undesirable, but for all its dark and sinister history, my world felt suddenly enlarged.

Supposing, I thought, staring at the faint tracery of lines connecting us, just supposing I *am* Clara Wraxford: what would follow from that? First, that Nell was innocent of the worst of the crimes laid at her door—but her journal alone was proof enough for me, just as I felt certain she had had nothing to do with Mrs. Bryant's death. And if she really had shut Magnus in the armour, she had done it in fear of her life—and Clara's. I wondered if Mr. Montague had made a grave mistake in not handing those journals to the police.

But if, on the other hand, John Montague had chosen to conceal not only the package he had found in Magnus's greatcoat pocket, but the dagger, the pistol, and the fragment of cloth, Magnus's death would have been judged an accident, the result of a bizarre experiment—a phrase he himself had used in speaking of his uncle Cornelius—and then, if Nell *had* escaped with Clara, there would have been no need for her to hide, once the news was out.

What *had* happened on the night of Mrs. Bryant's death? Nell had said, in her last entry, that she meant to watch from the library and find out who had summoned her. Perhaps in the end she had thought better of it; perhaps she really *had* been asleep when the maid knocked at her door with news of Mrs. Bryant's death. And then, some time later that night, she and Clara had disappeared from the room.

I would not, I told myself sternly, allow my mind to dwell upon phrases such as *carried off body and soul.*

And of course Nell had not been carried off, because Magnus had seen her—or said he had seen her—on the stair, after everyone else had left the Hall.

But if Nell had trapped him in the armour (and I could not, in my heart of hearts, really believe otherwise) she must have returned to the house after everyone else had left; or else she had been hiding there all the time. Alone, she might have evaded the search, but not if she had been carrying Clara. And if she had left the Hall early that morning, she would never have brought Clara back.

Especially not if she had planned to escape all along. Suppose she had arranged for someone to meet her at dawn—a few hundred yards along the path, maybe—and drive her and Clara to safety? Suppose, in other words, that Mrs. Bryant's death had been, from Nell's point of view, a ghastly coincidence, and that she had never intended to be at the séance at all?

But why, with freedom so close, would she ever have returned to the Hall?

Because she had forgotten her journal. Even as the words formed themselves in my mind, I saw how it must have been: lying awake through the small hours, waiting fearfully for the first glimmer of dawn (she would not have dared show a light), dressing hastily—no, she would have been fully dressed already—gathering up her sleeping child, still drugged by the laudanum—then locking the door behind her, in terror lest the snap of the lock give her away, but knowing it would give her more time to get away from the Hall. No wonder she had left her journal behind; the only mystery was why she had risked going back for it.

Yes; she had *meant* to recover her journal, but by then the household was already stirring; Nell had been trapped in the Hall; and her accomplice had been obliged to drive away with the child.

I realised that I had forgotten about the diamonds; the jewel-case the police had found beneath the floorboard. I simply did not believe she would have gone looking for them—she did not even know of their existence—on that night of all nights.

But she might have taken them, for Clara's sake, after that final confrontation with Magnus. Supposing Nell had hidden in the upper part of the house, somehow evading the searchers—perhaps by moving from room to room ahead of them—until they gave up. Then she had waited until the last of the carriages had left and made for the stairs—only to see Magnus on the landing below. He pursued her; she evaded him; but now she was effectively a prisoner again. And so, in desperation, she had confronted him with the pistol (had she been carrying it all along?) and ordered him into the armour. And fled, leaving Magnus to starve—but how could she be sure that he would not break free? More likely he had sprung at her as she was closing the panels, and she had shot him in self-defence, and wedged the mechanism for fear of his revival—or of what, in death, he might become.

Then . . . had she run to her room to collect her journal, only to find it gone? Surely her instinct would have been to flee, knowing that her own life was forfeit, thinking only of Clara. Perhaps he had tried to buy his life with the diamonds, when he saw that she meant to fire . . . I still could not imagine her hiding the jewel-case under the floorboard, but in that necklace she might have seen Clara's future beckoning, even as her own dissolved.

The fire was burning low. The rain had more or less ceased, but the wind was moaning faintly in the chimney. Shivering, I added the last of the coals.

Magnus had said, in his last letter to Mr. Veitch, that daylight was fading as he wrote. By the time of that terrible confrontation, it must have been almost dark. To remain another night at the Hall would have been unthinkable; but where could she have gone? Not to Clara; that would have made whoever was minding the child an accessory to murder.

What would I have done, in Nell's place? I recalled, with a visceral pang, the sick feeling of horror that had consumed me after Mama's death. For Nell it must have been infinitely worse, with the gallows looming over her, and knowing that if she were taken, Clara would be condemned to grow up as the daughter of a murderess, outcast from society.

But Nell had not been caught. The more I thought about it, the more likely it seemed that she had, as John Montague had feared, ended her life in some inaccessible part of Monks' Wood. For how could she have escaped, with the whole country on the watch for her?

And if Clara had survived, she must have been brought up under another name, never even knowing, perhaps, that Nell had been her mother.

Some trusted friend—a woman, surely—had taken Clara away from the Hall, early on that fateful Saturday. And then waited in vain for five days, wondering what had become of Nell, before the news of John Montague's grisly discovery had broken.

Or else Nell had lived; and had written, saying, "I am lost; I pray you ensure that Clara is raised knowing nothing of this; I will send money for her if I can—"meaning, "when I have disposed of the diamonds."

And supposing the friend had been unable to keep Clara herself, but had known that Nell had a distant cousin named Hester Langton, a childless woman of forty, from an estranged branch of the Lovell family, living with her husband near Cambridge . . .

Preposterous, said the rational part of my mind. But John Montague had been shaken by the resemblance; and there were the two names, side by side on the chart, born in the same month of the same year, their Christian names beginning with the same initial letter. And a year or so after Nell's disappearance, Theophilus Langton had given up his fellowship at Cambridge and moved to London, as if he had suddenly acquired a private income.

They need not have been told that the orphaned girl in question was Clara Wraxford; only that she was a child with a tragic history and a mysterious benefactor, who desired them to raise the child as their own.

A wild fancy, yes; but it explained everything, and all of the pieces seemed to fit, even my being drawn to the séance room. And it explained, most of all, the affinity I had felt for Nell from the first pages of her narrative, as if the voice I had heard in those pages was already familiar to me.

I went downstairs the next morning still unsure of what I should reveal to my uncle, only to find that he had heard all about the Wraxford Mystery from his friends, and was eager to impart his knowledge to me.

"You will be startled to learn, my dear, that this house of yours is notorious in the annals of crime. Mrs. Wraxford puts Lady Macbeth quite in the shade; she murdered not only her patroness and her husband, but her infant daughter, and got clean away with a diamond necklace worth ten thousand pounds—"

"None of that was ever proven, Uncle. I spent yesterday reading Mr. Montague's private account of the tragedy, and I do not believe she was guilty; except, perhaps of causing her husband's death in self-defence."

"Rather a large exception," he replied. "Upon what evidence, may I ask, does Mr. Montague base his conclusions? From Erskine's account of the inquest into Magnus Wraxford's murder—he has promised to look out the cuttings for me—it sounded like an open-and-shut case."

"It is my own conclusion, Uncle, but—I fear I oughtn't say too much, or show you Mr. Montague's narrative, without first asking permission."

"Well, if I am not even allowed to see the evidence," he said tartly, "you can scarcely blame me if I prefer the verdict of the coroner's jury, the police, and the public at large."

And with that he stalked off to his studio. For all his bohemian ways, I could see that my uncle's pride had been wounded by Miss Wraxford's leaving the estate to me rather than to him—her nearest surviving *male* relation—and indeed I could not blame him for feeling affronted. And so I wrote at once to Mr. Montague, asking if I might show the papers to my uncle, and saying how much I should like to speak to him again, whenever he might next to be in London. But as the days passed without a reply, I began to wonder if I had offended him; or had my letter gone astray? My uncle studiously avoided any mention of Wraxfords, but the awkwardness between us remained until, ten days after I had written to Mr. Montague, a letter postmarked Aldeburgh arrived, addressed to me in an unfamiliar hand:

Dear Miss Langton,

It is with great regret that I write to inform you of the death of my esteemed colleague, John Montague, Esq., on the 21st inst. Pray be assured of my devotion to your interest in the matter of the Wraxford estate; you may have seen the notice of the bequest which I placed in

The Times on your behalf, as Mr. Montague would, I am sure, have wished me to do; and believe me ever to be, Miss Langton,

Your most obedient serv^t,

Bartholomew Craik

P.S. Since your recent comm^n *to Mr. Montague was marked "Personal and Confidential," I return it to you unopened under separate cover, together with another comm*^{n} *which has lately reached us concerning the Wraxford estate.*

John Montague had died the day after posting his confession to me. But *how* had he died? My uncle, upon reading Mr. Craik's letter, volunteered to take a cab down to the British Museum and look through the Suffolk papers for the previous week, only to return with the news that John Montague had drowned.

"It seems he was in the habit of sea-bathing, even in the most inclement weather, but on this occasion the cold—or so it is assumed—proved too much for him: his body was washed up on the strand the following morning. There was an inquest, of course: the coroner's finding was death by misadventure, but he did append a warning about the dangers of sea-bathing in such extreme conditions."

I recalled, with fearful vividness, John Montague's words about "swimming out into the icy deep until my strength failed and I sank beneath the waves."

"But did no one suspect that—he might have drowned himself on purpose?"

"No, my dear; why should you imagine it? Swimming in January may not be your idea of healthful exercise, but some people think it does wonders for the circulation."

"I do not believe it," I said wretchedly. The burden was suddenly too heavy to bear alone, and so I gave him the entire bundle of papers on a promise of secrecy, and endured another long and oppressive interval, wondering if I were to blame for John Montague's death, before my uncle reappeared late in the afternoon, looking unwontedly sombre.

"I see now," he said, "why you thought at once of suicide; I'm afraid it looks very much that way. The mystery to me is why he sent you these papers in the first place."

"He thought—he said I reminded him of Eleanor Wraxford."

"But there's nothing surprising in that; you were related, after all."

"I meant—he wanted me to know that she was innocent, because—"

"But how can you possibly think that?" exclaimed my uncle. "If there was ever any doubt of her guilt, these papers set the seal on it."

I looked at him in astonishment.

"Don't you see, Uncle, that Nell could *never* have harmed Clara, or murdered Mrs. Bryant? And as I said to you yesterday, if she *did* shut Magnus in the armour, she would only have done it in fear of her life—and Clara's." And my existence may be proof of it, I wanted to add, but I was afraid he would laugh at me.

"Is this simply feminine fellow-feeling, my dear? I don't understand you."

"I suppose I feel—an affinity for her," I said hesitantly. "More than that, I trust her. Everything she did—even agreeing to go to that terrible place—was done for Clara's sake. She did not invite Mrs. Bryant to the Hall, Magnus Wraxford did, and he was an evil man. . . . Can you not see it?"

"No, my dear, I cannot. Mad people can be very plausible, you know, and yet impelled by grand delusions that they manage to conceal until it's too late. She said herself she suffered from hallucinations—"

"She called them 'visitations,' Uncle."

"It is the same thing. Understand me: she may sincerely have believed everything she wrote in those journals, but that does not mean that *we* should believe her. Even John Montague admits the possibility, and he was utterly infatuated—don't frown, my dear, the point is undeniable—and you must remember that he greatly admired Magnus Wraxford, up until the day he went to visit Eleanor at the Hall.

"Indeed, I don't see why you are so set against Magnus. If you consider the marriage from *his* point of view, she herself admits that he behaved with admirable restraint. He did not beat her, or threaten her, or force her; she says she is mortally afraid of him, but surely he was doing his best to placate a dangerously disturbed young woman. And then—as if any further proof were needed—he says in his last letter that he saw her on the stair."

"So you believe, then, Uncle, that she murdered all three: her husband, her child, and Mrs. Bryant?"

"In Magnus's case it is not a question of believing: the coroner's jury found as much, and if further proof is needed, you hold it in your hands. Mrs. Bryant may well have died of fright, but is it not overwhelmingly likely that Nell was the occasion of it? And as for the child, who else could—or would—have made away with her?

"You shake your head at me, my dear, but what of the diamonds? You don't, I take it, dispute that Magnus bought them for her—or that she stole them? The most charitable supposition is that she made away with herself and the child in a fit of remorse—perhaps while Magnus himself was still alive, but entombed—and that their remains lie in some inaccessible pit at the heart of Monks' Wood. How else can you explain the sequence of events?"

"If Magnus truly cared for her," I said, "why did he allow Mrs. Bryant to insult her, let alone insist that she be present at his séance—and at that evil house, of all places? We don't know that she took the diamonds, and we have only Magnus's word that he meant to give them to her; perhaps he bought them for Mrs. Bryant. And when Magnus and Dr. Rhys broke into her room that morning . . ."

I trailed off, remembering Nell's last visitation. She had foreseen Edward Ravenscroft's death—and then her own disappearance, and Clara's. I leafed back through John Montague's pages:

> Thus, a Man who could command the Power of *Lightning* would be as the Avenging Angel upon that Dreadful Day . . .

"Does it not strike you, Uncle," I said uneasily, "that nearly *everyone* who went anywhere near that suit of armour has either disappeared, or died in some unnatural fashion? Thomas, Felix, and Cornelius Wraxford; Mrs. Bryant, Nell, Magnus himself . . . and Magnus could have been mistaken—or lying—about the woman he saw on the stair."

"My dear, surely you are not invoking evil spirits in Eleanor Wraxford's defence? You don't seriously think that a spirit stole the diamonds, or caught its dress in the armour?"

"No, Uncle. But someone else might have done it. Supposing Magnus was engaged in some evil rite . . . helped by some accomplice, who turned on him—"

A coal burst, startling me with a loud crack and a shower of sparks.

"Now, really, my dear, this is clutching at straws; you will give yourself nightmares if you are not careful. People do not dissolve into empty air. However sinister the business with the armour may sound, there are many learned gentlemen currently engaged in much the same sort of pursuit—the Society for Psychical Research, for example—without obvious ill-effect. As for Magnus's insisting that Nell accompany him to the Hall, again I remind you that we have only her version of those events. You must not let your imagination run away with you. It was really very wrong of Mr. Montague to send you those papers; strictly speaking, we should hand them over to the police."

"Uncle, you *promised*—"

"I know, and I don't propose to; it would make a circus of our existence. But in keeping silent, you must realise, we are suppressing evidence in a murder case. If Mr. Montague *did* drown himself, that is surely why: he was placing not only his reputation, but his life, in your hands . . . unless his health was worse than he admits in that letter."

"I fear it was," I said, remembering his ashen complexion. It was now pitch-dark outside. I rose and drew the curtains, shivering at the chill that radiated from the glass, and stirred the coals.

"The best thing you can do with those papers," said my uncle, "is throw them on the fire."

"But, Uncle, I could never do that! I owe it to Mr. Montague's memory to try to discover what really happened at the Hall"—I had not realised I felt thus, until I heard myself speak the words—"and what became of Nell, and besides, I could never destroy her diaries; they might be—"

I stopped short at the look of alarm on my uncle's face. He threw up his hands in a pantomime of despair, and I said no more about the Wraxford Mystery until the letter forwarded by Mr. Craik arrived in the next morning's post.

18 Priory Road,
Clapham SW
25th Jany 1889

Miss C. M. Langton
c/o Montague and Craik, Commissioners for Oaths
Wentworth Road,
Aldeburgh

Dear Miss Langton,

I beg you to forgive this approach from a complete stranger. My name is Edwin Rhys, and I am the only son of the late Godwin Rhys,

M.D. My father was physician to Diana Bryant, who died at Wraxford Hall in the autumn of 1868. He certified her death as due to heart failure, and, despite the absence of evidence to the contrary, was ruined by the ensuing campaign of rumour and innuendo. In the winter of 1870, broken in mind and body, he died by his own hand.

I have always believed in my father's innocence, and it remains my ambition to clear his name. Hence, as you will have divined, this letter. I understand from yesterday's notice in The Times *that you will shortly take possession of the Wraxford estate. It is my hope that amongst the Wraxford papers, or at the Hall itself, evidence may survive that will erase the stain from my father's memory. I wrote on several occasions to Miss Augusta Wraxford, requesting the favour of an interview, but received no reply; I venture to hope that you will take a different view. If you will consent to see me, when and wherever should be convenient to you, I shall be eternally in your debt.*

I remain, Miss Langton, your most obedient servant,

Edwin Rhys

Edwin Rhys replied by return to my note, thanking me warmly and (much to my uncle's unease) accepting my invitation to tea in two days' time. I had realised that he must be relatively young, but the man Dora showed into the sitting room looked no more than twenty. He was only a couple of inches taller than myself, slightly built, with fair, longish hair combed back, an oval face rounding to a strong chin, and a complexion many women might have envied.

"It is extremely kind of you to see me, Miss Langton." His voice was low and cultivated, and his dress—a dark blue velveteen jacket, grey flannel trousers, soft white shirt, and cravat—was very much what I imagined a young gentleman down from Oxford or Cambridge might wear. His boots were still damp from the rain.

"I was very sorry," I said, once we were settled by the fire, "to hear of your father's death in—such sad circumstances. The Wraxford Mystery has blighted many lives."

"Indeed it has, Miss Langton."

"You say in your letter," I went on, "that you hope to clear his name. . . . Perhaps you could tell me a little more about your father."

"I was only six years old when he died; most of what I know comes from my mother and grandfather. My father, as you know, was personal physician to Mrs. Bryant, who seems to have been a thoroughly unpleasant woman. His role was simply to agree with her and indulge her various whims. An older colleague had introduced him to her; it seemed like a good turn at the time, but of course the man simply wanted to be rid of her. My mother met her only once, and loathed her."

"I can well imagine," I said. He glanced at me curiously, and I realised I would have to be more careful.

"My mother thinks," he resumed, "that Magnus Wraxford appeared on the scene about six months before the fatal visit to the Hall. She never met him, but my father was captivated—as, of course, was Mrs. Bryant—"

This time I bit my lip and said nothing.

"—and could talk of nothing but Dr. Wraxford, though his role as physician was more than ever superfluous—my mother says that he might as well have been her lapdog." I remembered that Nell had used exactly that image in her journal. "Mrs. Bryant made no secret of the fact that she had given Dr. Wraxford ten thousand pounds for his Sanatorium, long before she had seen the Hall. He was mesmerising her regularly, and I wonder how much influence he might have exerted. Most medical men nowadays regard mesmerism as pure charlatanry.

"My father's fatal error was to sign that death certificate, against his better judgement. The autopsy found nothing, but Mrs. Bryant's son was convinced that my father had conspired with the Wraxfords and poisoned her for the money. The son had even persuaded himself that she had come to regret the ten thousand and would have demanded it back if she hadn't died that night. And so the rumours began to circulate.

"If my father had had an established practice, he might have weathered the storm. But for a man with no patients to fall back upon, the insinuations were fatal. My grandfather—on my mother's side—might have helped, though he had opposed the marriage, but my father managed to conceal the extent of his debts for over a year. When the creditors could no longer be appeased, he shot himself. It took him three days to die."

"I am truly sorry to hear it," I repeated, thinking how utterly inadequate the words sounded. "And—what became of you and your mother and sister?"

"My grandfather took us to live with him. . . . May I ask, Miss Langton, how you know that I have a sister?"

Again I realised I had read it in Nell's journal.

"I—er—I think Mr. Montague, the solicitor—he drowned, you know, most tragically, a fortnight ago—must have told me. Tell me, Mr. Rhys, how do you believe that Mrs. Bryant died?"

"I do not know what to believe. My friend and colleague Vernon Raphael, whom I believe you know—are you unwell, Miss Langton?"

"No, no, only a momentary indisposition"—I heard myself echoing John Montague—"your colleague in what, pray tell?"

"The Society for Psychical Research. Forgive me, Miss Langton, but you really don't look well."

"It is nothing, I assure you. Did Mr. Raphael, by any chance, explain the circumstances in which we met?"

"No, indeed." Edwin Rhys blushed scarlet. "Nothing of the kind; he said only, when I told him I was coming here, that you and he were acquainted."

I saw that only the truth—or as much of it as I could bear to tell—would dispel his misunderstanding.

"It is not what you think, Mr. Rhys. I met Mr. Raphael only once, in his professional capacity, when I was attending a séance with my mother, who was—an ardent spiritualist. My sister, you see, died when she was very young; my mother never recovered from the shock of her death, and so—"

"I do understand, Miss Langton," he replied, still blushing, "and I assure you, I did not mean to imply—"

He was spared further embarrassment by Dora's bringing in the tea, which gave us both time to recover our composure.

"You referred to Mr. Raphael as your colleague," I said. "Are you employed by the Society?"

"No; Raphael is one of the Society's professional investigators; I am employed by Mr. Hargreaves, the architect, as a surveyor of buildings. I was intended for medicine like my father, but the dissecting-room, I'm afraid, proved too much for me. I joined the Society three years ago, in the hope . . . but perhaps you would rather not speak of this?"

"Once I would not have wanted to, but now . . . my mother died of grief, Mr. Rhys, not of attending séances; I lost her long before she died." I had never thought of it thus, but as I spoke the words I realised, with the sensation of a weight slipping from around my neck, that they were true.

"In the hope . . . ?" I prompted him.

"Well, of some communication from my father, or at least proof that such a thing is possible. . . ."

He trailed off, swirling the tea in his cup.

"And have you found it?"

"No, Miss Langton, I have not. Professor Sidgwick remarked in a lecture the other day that twenty years of intensive investigation have left him in exactly the same state of uncertainty with which he began, and that is very much my own case. Where Vernon Raphael is a complete sceptic; I have heard him say that the history of spiritualism is compounded solely of fraud and self-delusion. Which reminds me of what I meant to tell you before. The Wraxford Mystery is, I fear, a popular subject of debate at the Society—between those who think there is something supernatural at the heart of it, and the sceptics like Raphael who take the opposing view. Yet even Raphael—he has made a close study of the case—even he has been heard to say that if genuine phenomena are ever to be observed, Wraxford Hall would be the ideal place to try the question—"

I shivered at the echo.

"But those were precisely Magnus Wraxford's words."

"He is aware of that, Miss Langton . . . I see that you, too, have studied my father's testimony very closely."

I avoided answering by refilling his cup.

"Did your father leave any account—beyond what he said at the inquest—of his dealings with Magnus Wraxford?" I asked casually.

"No, Miss Langton. And you? Do you know of anything—letters, documents held by the estate—that might help my cause?"

I was tempted to say yes, but then I remembered my uncle saying, "We are withholding evidence in a murder case."

"I am afraid not," I said. "But if you would like to look through the papers at the Hall—assuming there are any; I know nothing of the contents—perhaps it could be arranged."

"That is very kind of you, Miss Langton; very kind indeed. And—if I may be so bold—might you also consider allowing Vernon Raphael, myself, and a few like-minded men from the Society to conduct an investigation?"

"What sort of an investigation, Mr. Rhys?"

"Vernon Raphael insists that, given access to the Hall, he could resolve—by way of demonstration, before expert witnesses—not only the question of supernatural influence, but the Mystery itself: that is to say, how Mrs. Bryant and Magnus Wraxford died, and what became of Eleanor Wraxford and the child—and hence, perhaps, help redeem my father's memory."

"Does he have any theory as to what might have happened?"

"I put that very question to him, and he only smiled enigmatically. Raphael keeps his cards very close to his chest, Miss Langton; I am honoured to call him my friend, but his only real confidant is St. John Vine, who works with him on all his cases; between them they have exposed several very subtle frauds, including one that Mr. Podmore himself was unable to detect. All I can say is that Raphael must be very sure of himself to have spoken thus."

"And you, Mr. Rhys, do you have a theory of your own?"

"I have wondered, I suppose, if the Wraxfords were working in concert—I mean, that the appearance of estrangement between them was contrived—to entrap Mrs. Bryant with a view to extracting yet more money from her. If so, there must have been a falling-out; perhaps Eleanor Wraxford grew jealous of Mrs. Bryant—"

"I assure you that is false," I said warmly.

"Miss Langton," he said, after a pause, "it seems to me that you know more . . . are you certain you can tell me nothing that might help my father's cause?"

"Quite certain, Mr. Rhys. Let us simply say that I have my own reasons for wanting to see the Mystery solved." I had conceived, in the last few minutes, a great desire to follow in Nell Wraxford's footsteps and see the Hall for myself.

"This investigation," I said, "how long do you think it might take?"

"From what Raphael has said, the party would need to stay only one night; two at the most."

"But the Hall is derelict; it has been empty for twenty years; how could such a party be catered for? How many would there be?"

"Half a dozen at most; they are old campaigners, Miss Langton, and would bring everything themselves: camp-beds, provisions, spirit-stoves and the like . . . do you think your uncle might like to join us?"

"No, Mr. Rhys. I should like—though 'like' is scarcely the word—to be present myself; but I do not see how I can join a party of gentlemen unchaperoned, and I have no woman friend who would be willing to accompany me."

"Miss Langton, if that is the only difficulty, I assure you on my life that I will guard you as I would my own sister."

"It is my uncle you will have to convince, sir. . . . Tell me about your sister."

"Gwyneth has just turned twenty-one; she is about your height, Miss Langton, only fair instead of dark, a great reader of novels; she plays and sings like an angel."

"Not like me, then; I can scarcely play a note, and my singing would be considered a punishment. Do you think she might be allowed to join the party?"

A shadow crossed his face. "I am afraid not, Miss Langton. My mother, you see, doesn't approve of my raking over old scandals, as she calls it; she has never forgiven my father for bringing ruin upon us—her words again—and blighting my sister's prospects."

"That will scarcely reassure my uncle; but I shall ask, and see what he says. In the meantime, Mr. Rhys, I trust that you will treat everything we have said today in the strictest confidence; I will write to you shortly."

As I rose to say good-bye, I became aware that I was trembling with fatigue—or perhaps from fear of what I had set in motion.

I could, of course, have defied my uncle, but I did not want to cause a permanent breach between us, and I dared not even hint at the possibility that I might be Clara Wraxford; I could not have said, from one hour to the next, how far I believed it myself. Nor could I speak of John Montague's death, which was often in my mind: at times I grieved for him as if he had been an old and trusted friend; at others I felt angry and betrayed; but then I would recall how ill he had looked that day, and wonder if he had kept himself alive by sheer force of will until he had appeased the demands of his conscience. And I knew, above all, that I could be at peace with his memory—and with myself—only by taking up the torch he had passed to me.

My uncle was sufficiently bohemian not to regard the absence of a chaperone as insuperable, but he lamented loudly and often that Mr. Montague had ever sent me those papers, and it cost me a hard struggle not to give in to him. Only after he had met and liked Edwin Rhys, who dined with us a week after his first visit, did he consent, and then only reluctantly.

Edwin—we were soon on familiar terms—called upon me three times during the next fortnight, ostensibly to discuss the arrangements for the investigation, which was planned for the first week of March, but I sensed that his interest was more personal. The force of my reaction to Nell Wraxford's story had made me aware that I had not, since coming to live with my uncle, really desired anything, or anyone. My only desire had been *not* to feel; never again to endure such pain as the extremity of guilt and horror that had consumed me after Mama's death. Life with my uncle had suited me because he desired only to be comfortable, and to get on with his work in peace. I had been very fond of Mrs. Tremenheere and the children, had bathed in the warmth of their household, and yet something within me had remained untouched by their affection. I had not even felt my lack of feeling; as if I had lost all appetite for food and somehow managed to survive without it.

Now I was awake again, and conscious of Edwin's covert glances, of the way his colour changed when our eyes met, of his attempts at summoning the courage to speak; approaching that scene which, according to so many novels, would be the defining moment of my existence. He was handsome, he was kind; he possessed an almost feminine delicacy of feeling. I felt sure I would not like his mother and sister, any more than they would like me; but of the all young men I had met, he was by far the most attractive.

In between his visits, I spent a great deal of time brooding over the Mystery, going over and over the papers in search of clues, until it occurred to me that I should at least write to Ada Woodward, if I could discover where she lived. Nell had said that she and Ada were no longer close; she had said, too, that she could not ask George and Ada to take her in—and that was before Magnus had died. But they had been the closest of friends since childhood; and perhaps if Ada were to read the journals, she might see something that I had missed. Though I had said nothing to Edwin, it seemed to me that the only thing which absolutely must be concealed was the final part of John Montague's narrative—and that mainly, from my point of view, because it would confirm the general impression of Nell as a crazed murderess. In the end, I decided to transcribe, for Edwin and Vernon Raphael, from John Montague's account of his first meeting with Magnus through to the disappearance of Cornelius, and deny the existence of any other papers. If it had been Edwin alone, I might have shown him the rest, but I did not altogether trust his discretion.

In my uncle's library I found a battered copy of *Crockford's Clerical Directory* for 1877, and in it I found the Rev. George Arthur Woodward at 7 St. Michael's Close, Whitby, in Yorkshire. There was no other George Woodward listed, but I could not be certain he was the right one, and so I composed a letter to Mrs. G. A. Woodward at that address, asking whether she was the Ada Woodward who had known Eleanor Unwin, whom I was anxious to trace (writing as if I knew nothing of the Wraxford Mystery) and, if so, whether she would be willing to correspond with me. But a week, and then a fortnight passed without an answer, and I did not feel I could write again. The only other possibility was the maid Lucy, whom Nell had liked and trusted, but I did not even know her surname; only that her family had lived in Hereford, and that was twenty years ago. Which left me nothing else to do but brood, and count the days until the sixth of March arrived.

From the safety of my uncle's fireside, I had imagined myself as the heroine of the expedition, led by the calling of my blood to the vital clue that all of the men who had trampled through the Hall had missed, the link in the chain that would lead me to Nell. But once aboard the train, my apprehension had grown into a hard clenched knot in the pit of my stomach. Edwin and I had shared a compartment with Vernon Raphael and St. John Vine on the early train from London. Vernon Raphael had behaved very well, betraying nothing of the circumstances in which we had met. But seeing him again had brought back disturbing memories of my time at the Holborn Spiritualist Society, and of those strange moments when I would hear myself speaking and not know, any more than my listeners, what was coming next. Mr. Raphael, I felt fairly sure, did not believe in spirits; though he refused to reveal his plans, the assurance of his manner suggested that he knew very well what was to follow. But the memories of Holborn had stirred a nagging fear that if something *was* lying dormant at the Hall, my own presence might awaken it.

Sleet was whipping across the platform as we disembarked at Woodbridge station. Edwin hurried me along to a waiting carriage, where I sat whilst boxes thudded onto the roof, wishing myself back in Elsworthy Walk. The trees were all leafless; not so much as a daffodil showed as we rattled away through the town and out onto a flat expanse of marshland from which all colour had been leached. Gusts of wind shook the carriage. I peered through the rain-streaked glass, trying to catch a glimpse of the sea, but the sky was so low that marsh and cloud blurred into greyness. The men had fallen silent; indeed, St. John Vine had scarcely uttered a word since we left London, and even Vernon Raphael seemed daunted by the bleakness of the prospect.

Monks' Wood came upon us with no warning, looming like a black wave out of the mist as we passed from grey daylight into near darkness beneath the firs. The rushing of the wind ceased, and there was only the muffled rumble of the wheels, the scrape of branches along the carriage, and the occasional gush of water from the foliage above. Shadowy outlines of tree trunks slid by, so close I could have touched them. The knot in my stomach tightened still further as the minutes dragged by, until the light returned as abruptly as it had gone.

John Montague's description had not prepared me for the sheer size of the Hall, or for the profusion of attics and gables, none of them level or square. There was not a straight line to be seen; everything seemed to have bowed or sagged or cracked; the walls were no longer a dingy green, but black with lichen and mildew, and all along the ground beneath, fragments of masonry lay heaped among the weeds.

"Do you think it's safe, Rhys?" said Vernon Raphael as we stood beside the coach. Icy air swirled about us; high above, I could see the tips of the lightning rods shivering in the wind.

"I'm not all at sure," Edwin replied uneasily. "If water has got in—as it's bound to have done—the floors may have rotted through. In fact . . . Miss Langton, I really think you should let the coach take you back to Woodbridge; there is an excellent private hotel . . . or you could return directly to London. . . ."

I was sorely tempted, but I knew that if I did so, I would reproach myself ever afterward.

"No," I said, "I have come too far to retreat."

They insisted I wait downstairs until Edwin had examined the floors, while Raphael and Vine searched out the coal cellar and lit fires in the gallery, the library, and the sitting-room that had once, for a few brief hours, been Mrs. Bryant's and where I would sleep—or attempt to sleep—tonight. The chimneys smoked badly from the wind, mingling the acrid smell of smoke with the pervasive odours of mould and damp and decay. As soon as the fires were lit, and all the boxes brought up, Raphael and Vine sequestered themselves in the gallery, to satisfy themselves that there were no concealed passages or other devices: I could hear them tapping and knocking on the other side of the wall whilst I huddled by the fire in the library, trying to shake off the chill of the journey and breathing the dank smell of mouldering paper.

Edwin had made a tour of the rooms on this level, and pronounced them safe enough, provided that no more than two people at a time ventured along any of the corridors: ugly stains on the ceilings and chunks of fallen plaster along the corridors suggested that water had indeed got into the floors above. He was, however, uneasy about the gallery floor immediately beneath the armour; there was, he said, too much play in the boards for his liking. Now he was moving about the study: I could hear him taking down volumes and opening drawers. With all this activity going on around me, the house did not seem especially sinister, and when the worst of the chill had left me, I slipped away to see the room which had been Nell's.

The shattered door hung open on its hinges; the linen had been stripped from the bed, but strangely, a pen with a rusted nib and a dried-up bottle of ink—surely hers?—lay on the table beneath the window. Puffs of dust stirred about my feet as I went on through to the boxroom where Clara—where I?—had slept. A low wooden cot, also thick with dust, stood in the centre of the floor. The room was even smaller, and much darker, than I had imagined from Nell's description, and prompted not the faintest stir of recognition—scarcely surprising, I reminded myself, when I could recall nothing of my childhood before the house in Holborn. It had a tiny window, a few inches square, set deep into the wall. The window did not open; with the door closed, which I had not the nerve to try, the little room would have been almost pitch-dark. I could see no ventilation of any kind.

I had glanced into the other rooms as I came along the corridor—all bare of furniture, but some considerably larger than these two combined. Nell must have insisted upon an adjoining room for Clara, but why had she not demanded something better when she saw what had been prepared for her?

As my eyes adjusted to the gloom, I noticed that in the corner opposite the door, the edge of the carpet had been drawn back. Moving closer, I saw a gap in the floor where a piece of floorboard about eight or nine inches long had been taken up; and there was the missing piece, underneath the cot. Dust lay thickly over everything. I knelt down and peered into the cavity, but it was too dark to see, and I did not like to put my hand into it. This, I realised, was surely the "perfect hiding place" that Nell had discovered for her journal.

I had brought the journal with me, and on impulse I went back along the gloomy corridor, glancing nervously about me at each turning, and around the landing to fetch it. Faint tapping sounds emanated from the gallery; if I had not known who was making them, I should have fled in terror. The cold had set me shivering again; I added more coal to the fire in my room and crouched before it, wondering whether I could endure a night alone in here. Nell endured several, I reminded myself, in far more terrifying circumstances; but then she had had Clara to protect.

But why had she left Clara to sleep in that dark, airless cell? (Again, I realised, I was thinking of myself and Clara as two different people—as sisters, in fact.) Because it meant that there were two locked doors between Clara and harm? The answer did not satisfy me, but I could think of no other; and so I returned to the boxroom and very cautiously slid the journal into the cavity, a little at a time, until I could see that it would fit.

Dr. Rhys said in his testimony that he had seen a hole in the floor, in the corner of the nursery, soon after the door was broken down. Which meant, surely, that Nell must have left the hiding place open when she took Clara down to her accomplice early that morning. Her journal had been found lying open on the writing-table . . . but if she had taken something else out of the cavity—papers? money? jewels?—would that not have reminded her to pick up the journal, which was in plain view?

My thought was interrupted by the sound of footsteps coming up the corridor, and Edwin's voice calling my name. I slipped the journal beneath my shawl as he appeared in the outer room.

"Have you found anything?" I asked.

"No," he said despondently. "Raphael has just expelled me from the library; he says he wants to test the influence machine. They're being very secretive, indeed; I offered to help them look for a priest's hole—there's bound to be something of the kind—but they spurned my assistance. Still, it scarcely matters; it would take weeks, or months to search this house for papers; my hope of exonerating my father seems more and more a pipe dream. This is a deathly place; I have never felt so cold."

On that sombre note we retreated to the sitting room to lunch from the hamper I had prepared. Edwin built up the fire into a blazing mass of coals, but it did not seem to lift his spirits, or mine; there was, as he had intimated, something beyond the physical chill of the house: no mere absence of life, but an active hostility to it. After a while, he left to resume his search; I meant to return to Nell's room, but instead remained huddled in a musty armchair until I fell into troubled dreams, from which I woke to find the room already dark, and Edwin tapping at the door to warn me that the rest of the party had arrived.

"Ladies and gentlemen, if you would care to take your seats, we are almost ready to begin."

Shadows darted along the walls as Vernon Raphael raised his lantern and led us toward a row of chairs arranged like seats in a theatre, facing toward the armour at the other end of the room. Coals glowed in a small fireplace nearby. Though the fire had been burning for hours, it had made little impression upon the deathly chill of the gallery. The only other illumination came from a candelabra above and to the right of the armour. Higher still, its flames were dimly mirrored in the blackness of the windows.

"Miss Langton, pray take the chair nearest the fire."

His pale face and white shirtfront dipped toward the floor as he bowed, indicating my place with a theatrical sweep of his arm. He was dressed in evening clothes, with a long black cloak draped over his shoulders. Edwin moved closer and offered me his arm, which I declined, indicating that I needed both hands to manage my own cloak. Our footsteps reverberated as if there were a dozen in the party, instead of five.

I settled myself as requested, with Edwin next to me. On his left was Professor Charnell, a desiccated, white-bearded little man, active as a monkey, and then Professor Fortesque, a florid, porcine gentleman with a confiding manner and small glittering eyes. Last came Dr. James Davenant, who stood for a moment longer, surveying the gallery. He was the tallest of the party, very spare and upright. His iron-grey hair was brushed straight back from his forehead, but the lower part of his face was obscured by a full beard, side-whiskers, and moustache. By day he wore tinted spectacles; he had, according to

Edwin, been injured in a fire whilst travelling in Bohemia in his youth, and his eyes had been permanently weakened. His voice had a slight huskiness to it, as if he were recovering from a cold. He seemed content for the most part to watch and listen, but I noticed that all the other men deferred to him. According to Edwin, he was the one member of the Society whom Vernon Raphael genuinely admired. He was also a distinguished student of crime, and had been consulted by Scotland Yard on several sensational cases, most recently the appalling murders in Whitechapel.

Vernon Raphael moved away down the room until he was standing next to the armour, where he set down his lantern, closed the shutter, and turned to face us. In the wavering light of the candles, the armour seemed to sway back and forth; reflections shimmered up and down the blade of the sword. I could just make out the wires snaking away from the plinth, past Vernon Raphael's feet, and away under the connecting door to the influence machine in the library. At his request, we had examined the machine; still, he said, in perfect working order after twenty years. It resembled a huge spinning wheel made of brass and polished wood, but with half a dozen massive glass discs side by side instead of a single wheel. St. John Vine—a dark, silent, saturnine young man whom I had scarcely seen all day—had turned the handle, slowly at first, then faster and faster until the discs were spinning blurs of light, whilst Vernon Raphael held two wires with wooden batons, bringing them gradually closer until a fierce blue spark leapt between them with a vicious spat and a smell of burning.

"Ladies and gentleman," he repeated, as if we were an audience of fifty, "you are about to witness the séance—the psychical experiment, if you prefer—that Magnus Wraxford intended to conduct on the night of Saturday, the thirtieth of September, 1868. No guesswork is required because, as we know from Godwin Rhys's testimony"—this with a sketch of a bow toward Edwin—"he described precisely what he meant to do. You may well wonder, what is the point of reconstructing an event that never took place, but for the moment I can only ask you to suspend your disbelief.

"If Mrs. Bryant had not died on the night of the twenty-ninth—we shall come to that a little later—there would have been five persons present at the séance: Magnus and Eleanor Wraxford, Mrs. Bryant, Godwin Rhys, and the late Mr. Montague. Magnus Wraxford would doubtless have asked the other four to form a circle and join hands in the conventional manner; Eleanor Wraxford, as we know, was to play (however reluctantly) the role of medium. But he also said that if no spirit materialised, he would instruct his man Bolton to operate the influence machine at full power, and occupy the armour himself—as I am about to do.

"We ask that you observe in silence, and without conferring, so as not to influence your fellow witnesses' perceptions. It will take several minutes before the armour is fully charged; I trust that your patience will be rewarded.

"One last word: the demonstration is not without risk. No matter what happens, you must not leave your seats until we have indicated that it is safe to do so; your lives may depend upon it."

He bowed to us again, turned with a swirl of his cloak, and grasped the hilt of the sword. Though the others had examined the armour in daylight (I could not bring myself to approach it), there was a collective intake of breath as the monstrous figure seemed to lunge at Vernon Raphael, its blackened plates opening like jaws eager to devour him. He stepped inside the casing, and darkness closed over him.

I tried to keep my eyes fixed upon the armour, but the movement of the candle flames distracted me. I was not aware of any draught, yet every so often the flames would sway in unison, as if someone had passed along the floor below. The heat of the fire was diminishing perceptibly. Every sound—the creak of a chair, the crackling of the coals, the occasional rustle of clothing—seemed an intrusion upon the deathly stillness of the gallery. The glittering blade of the sword (which Raphael and Vine had evidently polished during the day) was another distraction from the dark mass of the armour, which seemed to absorb all of the light that fell upon it.

Or almost all, for there was a faint yellow spark—no, two faint sparks of light side by side on the front of the helmet. They did not look like reflections, for they did not waver when the candles did, and the more I stared, the brighter they became.

A sharp intake of breath confirmed that someone else had seen it. The gleam was coming from within, shining through the slits where Vernon Raphael's eyes ought to be. I glanced at Edwin and saw my own fear reflected in his face.

The light strengthened and changed, darkening from yellow to orange to a fiery blood-red glow. As it did so, I became aware of a low, vibrant humming, like the sound of bees swarming; I could not tell where it was coming from. Edwin grasped my arm and was making as if to rise when a voice—Dr. Davenant's, I thought—said quietly but forcefully, "Do not move, upon your lives."

Dazzling white light filled the gallery, followed an instant later by a thunderclap that shook the house and left me blinded and deafened, with the diamond patterns of the leadlighting etched upon my vision. As the after-image faded I realised that all of the candles had gone out; beyond the faint glow of the fire at my side, the darkness was absolute.

Then came the sound of hurrying feet from the library. A shaft of light spilled across the floor; the connecting door flew open and St. John Vine, lantern in hand, flung himself at the armour and wrenched at the sword. The plates sprang open, the beam of the lantern steadied, and we saw that there was nobody within.

The others pressed forward; I remained in my chair, not trusting myself to stand. More lights were lit; St. John Vine was pacing back and forth in front of the armour, wringing his hands and saying, "I warned him; I warned him." Then he turned toward me and seemed to rally.

"There is still a chance. Vernon made me promise that if this should happen, we would try to summon him. We must try it, at least; Miss Langton, if you will form a circle with these gentlemen, I shall operate the influence machine. He has given up his life to bring us proof; we must not fail him."

I tried to speak, but could not. Edwin assisted me to rise whilst the others rearranged the chairs. St. John Vine, his face deathly pale, held the lantern to guide them; all of the witnesses looked shaken and fearful, excepting Dr. Davenant, whose expression was quite inscrutable. Before I had fully grasped what was happening, I found myself seated with Edwin on my right and Professor Charnell on my left. I had my back to the fireplace, so that I could see the armour, whereas Edwin and Professor Fortesque could not.

St. John Vine moved away down the room, leaving us in near darkness. He closed the front of the armour and extinguished all of the other lights, except for the four candles in the candelabra, which he returned to its shelf.

"Join hands," he said hoarsely, "and concentrate all of your attention upon Vernon. Pray, if you are minded to; anything that may help to bring him back." He passed through the door into the library and closed it behind him.

Edwin's hand was dry, and icy cold; Professor Charnell's felt like damp parchment. On the other side of the circle, I could see the glitter of Dr. Davenant's eyes, and the faint gleam of candlelight on his forehead; it was too dark to make out anything more. I was near fainting, and numb with shock, yet I could feel the vibration—was it only the trembling of our hands?—gathering in the circle.

Then all four candles flickered and went out, and we were plunged once more into impenetrable darkness. Someone—it sounded like Professor Fortesque—was gabbling the Lord's Prayer. He had reached "deliver us from evil" when a faint glimmer appeared in the vicinity of the armour, a misty pillar of light which hovered for a moment in the void and then opened, with a movement like the unfurling of wings, into a shimmering figure that detached itself from the body of the armour—now dimly visible in the glow—and glided toward us. It had no face, no form, only a veil of light floating over emptiness. I could not move, could not breathe.

I heard the sound of the library door opening, and footsteps approaching. The apparition shimmered to a halt.

"Vernon!" cried St. John Vine from the darkness. "Will you speak to us?"

"I may . . . not stay"—the voice, though faint and indistinct, was recognisably Vernon Raphael's—"but will you not . . . shake hands . . ."—growing fainter with each word—"for friendship's sake?"

The footsteps came closer; the dim outline of a man passed between me and the apparition. Light swirled; a glowing arm appeared, but there was no hand, only an empty sleeve, and when St. John Vine tried to grasp the arm, his own hand passed straight through it! With a cry of despair, he flung both arms around the apparition. For an instant, man and spirit were united; then darkness engulfed them, and I knew no more.

I came to my senses with the taste of brandy on my lips, and a lantern shining into my eyes. Coals were crackling in a grate nearby. I was lying, I realised, where I had fallen on the gallery floor, but with a cushion beneath my head. I have had a terrible dream, I thought, turning my head away from the glare. Edwin was kneeling beside me, with Vernon Raphael peering over his shoulder.

"Miss Langton, I owe you the most abject apology; I am truly very sorry. I should never have subjected you to such an ordeal."

"Indeed not!" said Edwin angrily. "If I had had any notion of what you were playing at, Raphael, I should never have allowed . . . that is to say . . ." He broke off, embarrassed, and offered me another sip of brandy.

"I don't understand," I said to Vernon Raphael. "Did you mesmerise me? Did I dream the lightning?"

"No, Miss Langton," he replied. "Everything happened exactly as you perceived—only it was an illusion, a demonstration, if you like, engineered by Vine and myself. I had planned to explain it all afterward, but you must rest now; I am really very sorry indeed."

"No," I said, becoming conscious of my disarray. "I am quite recovered, and could not possibly sleep without hearing your explanation." Lights were burning along the walls, but the floor where I was lying was still in near darkness. I took Edwin's arm and rose unsteadily to my feet.

"Well, if you are quite sure," said Vernon Raphael with obvious relief.

"Where are the others?" I asked.

"In the library," said Edwin. "I thought you might prefer . . ."

Grateful for his tact, and for the darkness of the gallery, I straightened my hair and brushed the dust from my cloak whilst Vernon Raphael went to fetch the rest of the party.

"Truly it is said, that he who attends a séance in the medium's house is asking to be deceived."

Vernon Raphael was standing beside the armour, with the rest of us gathered in a semicircle nearby.

"When I first heard of this cabinet—as, in effect, it is—I suspected it might have some further trick to it."

He grasped the hilt of the sword—I was not the only member of the party to recoil when the plates sprang open—whilst St. John Vine, who was standing off to one side, played the beam of his lantern over the armour.

"Though the back of the armour appears absolutely solid, it, too, is hinged. The trick is that it can be opened only when the front is closed, and only if this catch"—indicating the pommel of the sword beneath the mailed fist—"is in the correct position. Thus . . ."

He stepped inside once more and closed the plates. St. John Vine moved closer, and seemed to stumble; the beam of the lantern flashed across our faces.

"You see," said Vernon Raphael, appearing from behind the armour, "it needs only a momentary distraction. And if, of course, the lights should mysteriously fail—" St. John Vine strode the few paces to the library door and disappeared within. A few seconds later, the flames of the candelabra were again extinguished as if an invisible hand had snuffed them out.

"A standard magician's—or spirit medium's—property," said Vernon Raphael, "done with India-rubber tubing. The sinister glow from the helmet was equally simple: it needed only a dark lantern, concealed beneath my cloak, and a suitable piece of stained glass; your imaginations did the rest."

"But the lightning?" said Edwin. "How could you possibly . . . ?"

"Powdered magnesium, my dear fellow; all the rage with photographers, though not in quite such quantities, accompanied by a charge of black powder, and fired by a long fuse from the library window. We were lucky the chimneys smoked so badly, or you might have smelt the fumes. And whilst you were still dazzled . . ." He moved a couple of paces from the armour, one hand trailing along the wall, to the corner where the massive fireplace projected into the room, and slipped behind a mouldering tapestry, which hung almost to the floor.

There was a faint creak of hinges; St. John Vine strode across from the doorway of the library, where he had been watching, and drew aside the hanging, to reveal only a blank expanse of panelling. He rapped three times on the wall; a narrow section slid open, and Vernon Raphael stepped out.

"I was sure we would find something of the kind," he said, "though I should not care to spend any length of time cooped up in there. That masonry is several feet thick."

"Why did you not enlist my help?" Edwin sounded nettled.

"Because, my dear fellow, we wanted you to partake of the illusion. And now, ladies and gentlemen, if you would care to resume your seats, I shall give you my explanation of the Wraxford Mystery before we adjourn for supper."

Still dazed by everything I had seen and heard, I was happy to return to the warmth of the fire. My companions seemed equally subdued; whether by the force of Vernon Raphael's personality, or the sombre atmosphere of the gallery, I could not tell.

"The real mystery, in my opinion, is the death of Cornelius—rather than Magnus—Wraxford. It is plain, reading between the lines of John Montague's narrative, which Miss Langton has kindly allowed me to see, that Magnus Wraxford murdered his uncle. The question is: how?"

"Forgive me," said Dr. Davenant, "but can you explain, to those of us who have not seen this narrative, how you arrived at this very remarkable conclusion?"

"By all means," said Vernon Raphael, and proceeded to summarise the relevant passages, principally Magnus's discovery of the secret of the armour, as Magnus himself had related it on that first afternoon in John Montague's office.

"The effect of that interview," he continued, "was to convince John

Montague that his client was a practicing alchemist, and a dangerous lunatic to boot—to prepare him, in other words, for Cornelius's imminent decease by occult means, just as he was about to exhaust the last of the estate's capital. But John Montague had never met Cornelius, and knew him only by his reputation as a sinister recluse. He was therefore predisposed to believe the tale that Magnus spun for him—including Cornelius's supposed hostility to his nephew and sole heir.

"Yet in the library next door, you will find not a single alchemical work. Nor, for that matter, will you find a copy of Sir William Snow's treatise on thunderstorms, or any other work on that subject. John Montague, when he came here in response to Drayton's summons, found a quantity of burnt paper in the study fireplace. But books do not burn easily; you could not possibly dispose of an entire collection that way. I put it to you that there never was such a collection; that however Cornelius passed his time, it had nothing to do with alchemy. I say further that the manuscript of Trithemius never existed, except for the fragment Magnus contrived for John Montague's benefit; and that the story Magnus told his uncle was a very different one.

"That Cornelius Wraxford was indeed morbidly afraid of death we have no reason to doubt, if only because Magnus's scheme could not have worked if he hadn't been. Remember, too, that Magnus Wraxford was a man of great persuasive powers, an accomplished mesmerist—and possessed, I believe, of a genius for improvisation. And suppose now that he came to his uncle and said something along these lines: 'I have just learned of a wonderful new invention, with extraordinary powers of prolonging life, based upon the work of the great Professor Faraday; and it has the added benefit of affording you absolute safety during a thunderstorm. With your permission, I shall adapt the armour which, by a lucky chance, is ideal for the purpose.' One of the expert witnesses at the inquest upon Magnus argued, as you may recall, that the armour would function as a Faraday cage, with the entire charge passing around the outside, leaving the occupant unharmed. The coroner scoffed at the idea, but to an old and fearful man, whose only contact with the outside world was his nephew, it could have been made to sound very plausible indeed.

"Magnus had, with his uncle's active co-operation, constructed a seeming death trap, and one which fitted perfectly with the Hall's sinister reputation. The death of young Felix Wraxford in 1795, and the subsequent disappearance of Thomas in 1821 (I assume that both were accidents, but we shall never know), were woven into the history he was creating, no doubt with an eye to its usefulness once the Hall was his.

"But there was one serious difficulty. Lightning might strike the Hall next week; on the other hand, it might not strike for another ten years, with no guarantee that Cornelius would actually occupy the suit. And Magnus, having prepared John Montague for Cornelius's imminent decease, now had to ensure it. His plan, I am sure, was to leave his London house, ostensibly for some remote part of the country—Devon, let us say—adopt a suitable disguise, and make his way to the Hall. Once in his uncle's apartment—and I remind you, we have only Magnus's own word for the state of relations between them—he could easily smother the old man, place the body in the armour, and discharge a 'thunderbolt' from the safety of the woods nearby.

"Risky, you will say, and I agree. But, like any true artist, he was prepared to run risks in order to achieve the effect he wanted. And then Fortune came to his aid with a remarkable stroke of luck: John Montague became so anxious about the gathering storm that he wired Magnus to that effect, giving him several hours' grace in which to prepare.

"There was now no need of artificial thunder; all Magnus had to do was place the body in the armour and slip away without being seen. But why was the body not found? Even supposing that lightning actually did strike the Hall, I don't believe that Cornelius could have been vaporised out of existence; Magnus's own eventual fate is proof of that. And I refuse to believe that his vanishing so precisely on cue was mere coincidence. Yet it was plainly not in Magnus's interest for Cornelius to vanish; in the event it cost him two years' delay, and an expensive court case, before he could take possession of the estate."

He raised his hand to forestall a question from Professor Charnell.

"With your permission, I should like to complete my thesis before we debate it. During that two-year interval, Magnus Wraxford married a young woman supposedly possessed of psychic powers; an ideal accomplice for the fraud he set out to perpetrate."

I had listened, thus far, with rapt attention, but the last remark brought me up short. I was about to protest when I realised that I could do so only by revealing the existence of the journal.

"Though the evidence of Godwin Rhys, John Montague and the manservant Bolton led the court to believe that the Wraxfords had been estranged for some time, it is possible that the appearance of estrangement was—initially—contrived between them, to further Magnus's seduction of Mrs. Bryant, and also perhaps to heighten the effect of Eleanor Wraxford's powers; if she could be seen to be acting the part of medium against her will, the illusion would be all the more convincing. Magnus made the first approach, and succeeded in charming an initial ten thousand pounds out of Mrs. Bryant before Eleanor Wraxford appeared on the scene. That money, as you know, he had converted into diamonds; a highly portable and negotiable asset.

"His intention, I am sure, was to stage a séance along the lines of tonight's demonstration. Eleanor Wraxford's gift would have been brought into play; and Mrs. Bryant's late husband would surely have appeared, encouraging her to devote her entire fortune to Magnus Wraxford's Sanatorium. But by the time the party arrived at the

Hall, Eleanor Wraxford had turned against her husband. Perhaps she was jealous of Mrs. Bryant; or perhaps, as some have suggested, she meant to elope with a lover. Her mental condition, at any rate, was certainly unstable. She was estranged from her own family; her previous fiancé had died here at the Hall in mysterious circumstances; and according to Magnus, as reported by Godwin Rhys, she had foreseen his death in a vision. Magnus had sent her down here with her child, from whom she would not be parted, to prepare for her part in the fraud—"

Again I opened my mouth to protest, then thought better of it.

"He must have been very confident of his power over her. But then his plan misfired with the death of Mrs. Bryant on the night of their arrival.

"You may recall that a note was found, in Eleanor Wraxford's handwriting, inviting Mrs. Bryant to meet her here in the gallery at midnight. There are several possibilities here. It may be that she meant to betray Magnus's scheme, or simply to wreck it by frightening Mrs. Bryant out of her wits. You can see how easily, using this apparatus, a woman with a weak heart could be frightened literally to death. Of course Magnus risked killing the golden goose with his intended demonstration, but that was a risk he had to run; and Mrs. Bryant would have gone to the séance expecting to witness something remarkable, whereas here she was taken completely by surprise.

"The rest is simply told: Eleanor Wraxford managed to regain the safety of her room while the alarm was still being raised. As I need scarcely remind you"—this with a bow to Dr. Davenant—"the popular understanding of madness is quite misguided. A man—or, as here, a woman—in the grip of delusion may commit the most monstrous crimes, and yet remain lucid and to all appearances rational.

"Sometime during that night, Eleanor Wraxford staged her disappearance. She concealed her child, or murdered it—I am sorry to distress you, Miss Langton, but the latter seems most probable. A woman alone would have had a fair chance of evading the search that followed; a woman carrying an infant, scarcely any. Unless she had arranged to give the child to an accomplice, which she would have to have arranged in advance—and why, then, bring the infant to the Hall in the first place?"

I had not thought of this objection to my own theory, but I saw, with a horrid sinking feeling, the force of it.

"Whatever the fate of the child, Eleanor Wraxford managed to conceal herself until Magnus alone remained at the Hall. She confronted him with her pistol, took the diamonds, forced him into the armour, and jammed the mechanism—so much is plain from the lawyer Montague's evidence. Perhaps she meant to trap him only long enough for her to get away, or perhaps her nerve failed her at last, as witness the discarded pistol and the torn piece of her gown caught in the armour.

"And then came the final irony: lightning really did strike the Hall a day or so later. Perhaps Magnus Wraxford was already dead; I rather hope so; I shouldn't wish such a fate upon my worst enemy. I don't believe he was instantly reduced to ashes, as the coroner concluded; men have been struck in the open, after all, and survived. Most likely the heat of the blast set fire to his clothing, and the body burned slowly away, as with spontaneous combustion, so vividly described by Dickens, except that in this case the combustion occurred within a confined space, and so was more complete.

"And there, ladies and gentlemen, you have it. We shall never know what became of Eleanor Wraxford and her child; I suspect that both are lying in some undiscovered hollow in Monks' Wood."

He bowed, and the men responded with a brief round of applause, in which I did not join. The fire had burned low while he was speaking; my feet were numb with cold; the promised revelation had come to nothing. His admiration for Magnus had been plain throughout, whereas he had dismissed Nell as a madwoman who had spoiled an elegant plan. It struck me, indeed, that Vernon Raphael and Magnus Wraxford had a good deal in common.

I looked up from the floor to find the men waiting expectantly for me to rise. The thought of listening to their debate was suddenly unbearable; I was neither hungry nor thirsty, only mortally cold.

"I should like to retire," I said to Edwin. "I want nothing; only a lantern; so if you will excuse me, gentlemen . . ."

I rose unsteadily to my feet, and the room seemed to sway around me, so that I was obliged to take Edwin's arm. Accompanied by murmurs of concern, we moved slowly down the long expanse of the gallery and out into the deeper chill of the landing, where Edwin immediately began to apologise for the evening's ordeal.

"I chose to come here," I replied, "so let us not speak of it." I felt his yearning for a glance, a smile, some token of intimacy, but I was incapable of responding.

Someone had made up the fire in my room, and as soon as I had bolted the door behind Edwin, I lit the two dusty candles on the mantelpiece, dragged the camp-bed as close as I dared to the hearth and lay down fully clothed, with the lantern on a chair beside me. The smell of oil and hot metal was vaguely comforting, as was the knowledge that Edwin would be in the room next door, between me and the landing.

As the warmth crept back into my veins, I realised that what had so dispirited me, aside from Vernon Raphael's tone, was the fear that he might be right about Nell: he had, after all, deduced from what I *had* shown him that Magnus had murdered—or at least set out to murder—his uncle. I had never considered the possibility, yet it all made perfect sense; whereas his account of the Mystery, on all but a few points, had merely echoed the coroner's findings.

But if I had shown him the rest of the papers, they would only have reinforced his conviction of Nell's guilt.

Yet there was *something* he had said—something that had struck a faint chord, even as it poured cold water upon my own theory—yes; that if Nell had been willing to surrender Clara to an accomplice, why bring her here in the first place?

And why, of all the rooms she might have chosen, had she put Clara in that dark, airless closet?

Because, with the door closed, no one could tell whether there was a child in it or not.

I took up Nell's journal and John Montague's account of the inquest and skimmed the pages by the light of the lantern.

There was no record of anyone else having seen Clara at the Hall.

I turned back to the first page of the journal, the journal she said she had not dared begin in London, for fear Magnus would find it. And which she had left open on the writing table.

She had *meant* him to find it. I had been deceived; the journal was a fiction, and nothing in it could be trusted.

No; not exactly. Everything about the failure of their marriage; her loathing of him; Mrs. Bryant: everything that Magnus knew or could check; all of that would have been true, and meant to wound, to strike him on the raw, so that he would not doubt the rest.

Clara had never been at the Hall. Someone—the maid Lucy?—had borne her off to safety, whilst Nell came on to the Hall alone. That would have been the most dangerous part, getting the "child"—a doll bundled in swaddling clothes, perhaps—from the carriage to the room. No wonder she had insisted upon doing everything herself!

But why? What was the point of the deception?

To make it appear that the curse of Wraxford Hall had struck again; that she and Clara had been carried off by the powers of darkness. She had invented the final visitation to "foretell" their fate.

But the deception had not succeeded. Magnus had looked through the journal and immediately ordered a search.

Had Nell assumed that, for all his professed scepticism, he was a believer? Or that others would believe it, even if he did not? Or had Mrs. Bryant's death disrupted her own plan?

And how had she meant to escape? Without Clara, she could have got away on foot. And since the journal had been left for Magnus to find, she had every reason to escape as soon as it was light enough to see her way through Monks' Wood.

What was it Vernon Raphael had said about Magnus? "A genius for improvisation."

Nell had been so intent on creating her own illusion that she had never realised how the journal might be used against her. Magnus's letter—the one John Montague had found, addressed to Mr. Veitch—that, too, had been false, like the fragment of Nell's dress caught in the armour. Nell had never returned to the Hall, and Magnus had not died here.

Then whose were the ashes in the armour?

Not Nell's, at least; the doctor at the inquest had said they were the remains of a man of about Magnus's age and height.

To stage a convincing séance, every medium needed an accomplice. Magnus had said that Bolton was going to work the influence machine, but the machine was a mere prop. And Magnus was surely far too astute to have trusted Bolton.

No; the accomplice had been someone else entirely, a man nobody had seen, smuggled into the house at night, and hidden somewhere in the maze of rooms on the upper floor, where no one had been allowed to go. Paid handsomely, perhaps, without even knowing what was at stake—and destined never to leave the Hall alive.

There was something John Montague had mentioned . . . yes, the lightning people in Chalford thought they had seen from Monks'

Wood on the Sunday night . . . Magnus had burned the body in the armour, and then discharged the "lightning," just as Vernon Raphael had done tonight.

Or else I was wrong about the accomplice, and Magnus had brought the ashes with him; he was a doctor, after all. But in that case—in either case—he had already planned his disappearance.

I looked back through Nell's journal, at all the references to his being away from home for days or weeks at a time. Magnus had been living a double life all along!

And Nell must have known, as soon as the news of John Montague's grisly discovery had broken, that if she were caught, Magnus might well be amongst the spectators who came to see her hanged for murdering him.

My mind had been leaping from one conclusion to the next with such rapidity that I had not realised how far I had come. Because Nell had insisted that there was nothing of Magnus in Clara, I had been able to push the thought aside, imagining Nell as my true mother in a world of half belief, where ordinary relations did not apply. Now I was seized with a sudden vertiginous terror that I *might* be Clara Wraxford. Despite the two candles and the glow of the fire, the shadows behind the furniture—two musty armchairs, a wooden settle, various other chairs and cabinets—were very dark indeed. I shone the lantern around the room, striking more shadows from the peeling paper, and over the cracked, sagging ceiling, which seemed to bulge downward as the light passed over it. And how long would the oil last?

Reluctantly, I rose and extinguished the two candles. I have only to endure the hours until daylight, I told myself, and by tomorrow evening I shall be safely back in St. John's Wood.

And then what? Supposing Magnus *was* still alive? Did I not have a duty to inform the police? But they would not listen to me, any more than Vernon Raphael, who would only twist everything around until all of the evidence pointed to Nell. The only certain way to prove Nell's innocence—at least, the only way that I could see—was to find Magnus Wraxford. Who had presumably taken the diamonds abroad to sell them—which of course was why he had bought them in the first place. Like so much else in his scheme, they had served a double purpose: to assist in his disappearance, and to sharpen the jaws of the trap he had laid for Nell, long before Bolton had seen her with John Montague.

Which was why, it came to me, Nell's description of that encounter had been so perfunctory. Knowing that Magnus would read the journal, she had not wanted to make trouble—any more than could be helped—for John Montague. But by anyone else it would be taken—as perhaps Magnus himself had taken it—to mean that she was concealing a guilty liaison.

Magnus had woven his net so cunningly that every scrap of evidence turned out to be Janus-faced. Edwin, at least, would hear me out, and keep silent about Nell's journal if I asked him to; but even he, I feared, would not believe me without some tangible indication that Magnus had not died in the armour.

There was one other possibility. For me to trace Magnus was plainly hopeless; but if I could draw him into tracing *me* . . . if, for example, I let it be known that I possessed proof of his guilt, discovered here at the Hall . . . especially if rumour said also that I was Clara Wraxford. But this was madness, and to dwell upon it here would drive me out of my wits. I turned the lantern down as low as I could bear and lay awake for hours, as it seemed, with fear crawling through my veins, until I sank into an exhausted sleep, and woke half-frozen in the grey light of dawn.

Two carriages were due to return at eleven—the coachmen had, I gathered, refused to remain at the Hall overnight—to take us back to

Woodbridge. I made my primitive ablutions in icy water, and kept to my room as long as possible, even though there was nothing to do there, once I had packed my things, but brood and shiver. Though I had done my best to make myself presentable, I felt grimy and bedraggled, and the tarnished glass above the mantelpiece did nothing to lift my spirits.

Hunger and cold drove me out at last onto the gloom of the landing, and around to the library, where the rest of the party were breakfasting on tea and toast, prepared over the library fire. Feeling acutely self-conscious, I assured everyone that I was entirely recovered from my faint, and had slept quite well, and allowed myself to be settled by the fireside and waited upon by Edwin and Vernon Raphael, between whom I sensed—at least on Edwin's side—a certain antagonism.

"I wonder, Miss Langton," said Vernon Raphael, after I had declined anything further, "what you thought of my exposition last night. I was left with the impression that you did not find it altogether persuasive."

"I—I found what you said about Cornelius Wraxford very convincing," I replied, hoping he would ask no further.

"But . . . ?" he prompted. Edwin gave him an angry look, and I was aware of the other men awaiting my reply.

If I cannot be true to Nell here, I thought, I shall never be brave enough to defend her.

"I believe that Eleanor Wraxford was innocent," I said. "I think that all of the appearances against her were contrived by Magnus Wraxford—including the ashes in the armour. I do not believe he is dead." A ripple of shock ran through the room. "No doubt you will dismiss this as a woman's idle fancy . . ."

"Perhaps I might have done," said Vernon Raphael, "if you had not allowed me to see those passages from John Montague's narrative. What further evidence have you?"

"I cannot tell you that," I replied, wishing my voice did not sound so tremulous. "I am—pledged to secrecy."

"But Miss Langton, if you possess evidence to prove what you say, is it not your duty to set it before the public?"

"It is not yet enough to persuade a court; or any man already convinced of Eleanor Wraxford's guilt," I said, with the sensation of sliding toward the edge of a precipice.

"But it has persuaded *you,* Miss Langton," he persisted. "Can you not tell us why?"

"I can answer no more questions, Mr. Raphael, except to say my greatest desire is to see Eleanor Wraxford proven innocent."

There was a moment's embarrassed silence, and then, as if at an unspoken signal, all of the men rose and began gathering up their possessions.

I retreated once more to my room, intending to stay there until the coaches arrived, but found the confinement intolerable. After a few minutes' restless pacing I decided to take a last look at the room where Nell had stayed. As I came onto the landing, I saw, in the shadows on the far side of the stairwell, the study door open and a tall figure—Dr. Davenant—emerge. He glanced in the direction of the library, as if to assure himself that no one was following, strode confidently across the landing and disappeared into the corridor which led to the bedrooms. By the time I reached the entrance, the sound of his footsteps had ceased.

Pausing to listen at every turn of the corridor, I followed as quietly as I could, until I came within sight of Nell's room. Pale ligh spilled from the doorway, wavering over the dusty floor of the pas sage, and as I watched a shadow passed across it. Superstitiou dread possessed me; I turned to flee, but my foot slipped on son fallen plaster, and a board creaked loudly. The shadow darkened ar seemed to rise up the opposite wall, and Dr. Davenant appeared before me.

"Ah, Miss Langton. Forgive me if I startled you—and for taking the liberty of exploring your house. This was, I gather, the room occupied by Eleanor Wraxford?"

He was not wearing his tinted spectacles, and his eyes gleamed faintly in the light from the doorway.

"Yes, sir, it was."

He gestured toward the doorway, as if inviting me to examine something, stepping back as he did so to make room for me to enter. Politeness compelled me to obey against my instinct, and a moment later I was standing by Nell's writing table, with Dr. Davenant between me and the door.

"What was it you wanted to show me, sir?" I asked, unable to suppress the tremor of fear in my voice. His expression was all but concealed by his beard and moustache, but it seemed to me that there was a glint of amusement in his eyes, which were so dark that the irises, as well as the pupils, seemed almost black. I wondered if this was an effect of the injury he had suffered.

"I found your remarks a few moments ago most stimulating," he said, blandly ignoring my question. His voice sounded deeper and more resonant than I remembered. "You said, I think, that you possess evidence that Magnus—rather than Eleanor Wraxford—was the guilty party, and yet you are constrained by a pledge of secrecy. . . . I could not help speculating as to whom that pledge might have been given."

"I cannot tell you that, sir."

"Quite so, Miss Langton. Only it did strike me that if you had managed to trace Eleanor Wraxford, secrecy would be eminently justified, since she still faces a capital charge." His tone was courteous, even casual, but with an edge of mockery. Framed in the doorway, he seemed to tower above me.

"You are quite mistaken, sir." I was afraid to ask him to let me pass, in case he would not.

"I see." His gaze shifted from me to the cot in its cheerless alcove. "And what do you suppose became of the child?"

My heart lurched, and for a moment I was tongue-tied.

"I cannot—sir, you must not press me. Now, please—"

"Miss Langton, hear me out. Your desire to prove Eleanor Wraxford innocent is altogether laudable, but supposing you are wrong? A woman capable of murdering her child is capable of anything."

"But she did not—"

"You seem very certain of that. I put it to you, Miss Langton, that by withholding information, you are placing yourself in serious danger. If you are right, and Magnus Wraxford is still at large, he has a direct interest in silencing you. The same applies if Eleanor Wraxford committed these crimes. Ask yourself, Miss Langton, how the Whitechapel murderer has managed to evade detection with every man in London on the lookout for him—if not because the murderer is, in fact, a woman?"

"You surely do not mean, sir"—I shrank away from him—"that Eleanor Wraxford—"

"I do not say that, Miss Langton; only that a woman, once she has killed, can be as ruthless as any man—and far more adept at deceiving those around her. Which is why I urge you to confide in someone—myself, for example—expert in the appraisal of evidence in criminal cases. Anything you say to me I shall treat, of course, in the strictest confidence; indeed I would be happy to make the approach to Scotland Yard on your behalf; that way, your name need never appear in the matter. In the interests of justice, Miss Langton, and of your own safety, I beg you to trust me."

His voice had softened, and his dark gaze, as he spoke, was fixed upon mine. Confiding in him seemed, for a moment, the only rational thing to do. But even wrapped in my travelling cloak, I had begun to shiver again; and he was still between me and the door.

"I thank you, sir, but you must excuse me now; I shall—consider what you have said."

"Of course, Miss Langton."

He bowed, stepped back into the corridor, and allowed me to pass.

Troubled by this encounter, I went in search of Edwin, whom I found in the gallery, standing disconsolately at the far end of the room, contemplating the entrance to the priest's hole.

"Why could you not confide in me?" he asked as I came up. "Did you think I too would not believe you?"

"No," I said, "it came to me only last night."

"And you cannot tell me any more?"

I hesitated.

"Perhaps," I said, "but not where others may hear. What are you doing?"

"There's something wrong about this," he said. "The space within is no larger than a coffin stood on end; you could not endure more than a few hours in such confinement, whereas most of these hiding places were built to conceal a man for days, or even weeks at a time. If only I had time . . . but the coaches will be here at any minute."

I was wondering whether to suggest that he and I might remain a little longer, when matters were taken out of our hands by St. John Vine, who appeared with the news that only one of the coaches had arrived; a shaft had broken on the other when it was about halfway from Woodbridge. We followed him down the stairs and out onto the weed-strewn forecourt, where Dr. Davenant, his eyes once more concealed by tinted lenses, was conversing with Vernon Raphael. Even the nearest trees were wreathed in mist; the air was still, but so bitterly cold that breathing felt like inhaling splinters of ice. Of course they wanted me to take one of the four available seats, but I declined, on the excuse that I had promised to look for some family papers for Mr. Craik.

"Mr. Rhys has kindly offered to remain with me," I said, uncomfortably aware of Vernon Raphael's sardonic expression. "You may tell the coach to return for us at three o'clock." My heart sank as I realised that one of the others would have to stay behind as well, until Dr. Davenant resolved the difficulty by announcing that he would walk. "I need the exercise," he said, "and will probably reach Woodbridge long before the rest of you."

No one tried to dissuade him, and half an hour later, Edwin Rhys and I were alone in Wraxford Hall.

I had already resolved to tell Edwin everything—except for my belief that I might be Clara Wraxford—and as soon as I had secured his promise of secrecy, I brought out the other papers and sat with him by the library fire, wondering if I should ever feel warm again. With the rest of the party gone, the stillness of the Hall was so oppressive that I found it hard to raise my voice above a whisper. Edwin asked many questions as he read, and seemed to warm toward my theory as we talked.

"You must forgive me if I still doubt," he said, as we made an impromptu luncheon of bread and cheese and potted meat. "There is so much that I had never even considered. But supposing you are right, and Magnus was responsible for all of the deaths, including Mrs. Bryant's: how did he come and go? There must be some secret way into the gallery; it is the heart of all the devilry that has been done here. That bolt-hole that Raphael uncovered may be the entrance to it."

There was still an hour to wait after we had dined—the mist, I noticed uneasily, had grown much thicker—and so we returned to the gallery, where Edwin began to rummage through a tin box standing in the alcove near the armour.

"I asked Raphael to leave this, just in case . . . he didn't tell us he'd brought a second thunderbolt," said Edwin, holding up a greyish cylinder with what appeared to be a tarred length of string attached to one end. He replaced them carefully, took out a wooden mallet, and began to explore the hiding place. Despite the cold, I watched whilst he tapped and twisted and probed at the brickwork. The echoes sounded horribly loud. Ancient Wraxfords, their faces blurred by the grime of centuries, glared down upon us; the light from the windows above the portraits was a dim, featureless grey.

"The point about these refuges," said Edwin, "is that they were built to withstand direct assault; there are accounts of walls being half-demolished whilst the fugitive, a foot away from the pickaxes, remained undiscovered. Brute force only jams the mechanism; it is a matter of finding the trick of it."

The walls appeared to be solid brick; I could see no possible opening anywhere.

"What makes you think there is anything to be found?" I asked.

"The position of that tomb, to begin with. Why would anyone place a sarcophagus inside a fireplace?"

"Because it is not really a tomb?"

"You may well be right, though I wasn't thinking of that; those padlocks haven't been disturbed in decades; they are rusted solid. No; because it ensures that no one will light a fire. Which means there is something inside that chimney to protect."

In the exercise of his talent, Edwin was a changed man, confident and assured as he had never seemed before. He was using the mallet and a short metal bar, testing each brick in turn. I wished there was something I could do, other than wait and shiver, and try to shake off the sensation of being watched. Though he was not striking the bar especially hard, every blow of the mallet echoed like a volley of gunshots, and sometimes it seemed to me that I could hear footsteps behind the echoes. The light, too, seemed to be growing perceptibly dimmer, though it was not yet three o'clock.

"Eureka!" cried Edwin. He had worked his way down to the foot of the inside wall, and was kneeling on the floor. Now as I watched he removed a single brick, reached into the cavity (which I should not have liked to have done), and after a brief struggle drew out a scarred wooden rod about the size of a candle.

"That's odd," he said. "This is a locking pin, which you would only expect to find in place if there was someone inside. I had to crack the mortar, you see."

I did not quite see, but I caught the note of unease in his voice.

"You don't think—" I began.

"Surely not."

He grasped the edge of the opening he had made. With a rasping, grating sound, a section of brickwork like a low, narrow door swung outward; a cloud of dust and grit rolled out into the gallery, and settled slowly around us.

"Well," he said, coughing, "there's certainly no one in here—no one living, at any rate." He lit his lantern, and I saw through the floating dust a narrow stairway of brick, spiralling upward into darkness.

"You see—" His voice was cut off by a noise from the direction of the library. We stood for a moment listening; the sound was not repeated. Edwin stooped, picked up the mallet, and strode the ten paces to the connecting door. I followed, not wishing to be left alone.

There was no one in the library, and no apparent cause for the sound until I saw that the pages of John Montague's manuscript, which I had left on the seat of a cracked leather armchair, were now strewn upon the floor beneath, with Nell's journals amongst them.

"A draught, perhaps," said Edwin. But the air was completely still.

And something else had changed. Outside, where the trees should have loomed a mere fifty yards away, there was nothing to be seen at all; nothing but dense, fleecy vapour, sliding across the glass.

"Will the coachman be able to find us?" I whispered.

"I don't know; we must hope it lifts before dark. In the meantime, we may as well find out where those stairs lead."

With a last worried look around the library, he led the way back to the gallery. As he was about to step into the opening, I was seized by panic.

"What if you are trapped in there?" I said. "I won't know how to get you out."

"We can't both go," he said, "just in case . . ."

"Then I shall," I said, "at least a little way up, while you keep watch. Truly—I shan't feel so afraid this way."

I took the lantern from his reluctant hand and stepped over the threshold, into a cylindrical chamber no more than three feet wide. Dust and grit lay thick upon the stone floor. I shone the beam upward, but could see only the returning spiral of the staircase.

"I shall have to go up a few steps," I said.

"Then for God's sake be careful."

Testing each stair as I went, I moved awkwardly upward, afraid of tripping over my skirts. Musty air stung my eyes; there were cobwebs draped about the walls, but they looked old and brittle, and nothing moved when I shone the lantern over them. This, I thought, was how an ancient tomb would smell, a tomb that had been sealed for hundreds of years, where even the spiders had died of starvation.

I had completed at least two full spirals before the stairs ended at a low wooden door, set into the wall to form a ledge just wide enough to stand upon. My hair brushed against the stone roof of the chamber. I glanced back down the stairs and was seized with a fit of dizziness so that I had to grip the door handle to prevent myself from falling. The handle turned in my grasp; the door creaked open.

It was a room—or, rather, a cell—perhaps six feet by four, the roof only a few inches above my head. The door opened inward to the left, leaving just enough room for a straight-backed chair and a table placed against the opposite wall. Upon the dusty surface of the table were a decanter, a wineglass, two candlesticks, an inkstand containing half a dozen quill pens, also thickly covered in grime; and a glass-fronted case, two shelves high, containing what looked like thirty or forty identical volumes.

There seemed to be no other furniture, but as I stood staring at the desk, I became aware that my lantern was not the only source of illumination. Along the wall to my right were half a dozen dim, narrow strips of light. I took a tentative step forward, felt an icy draught upon my face, and realised that the secret room and its stairwell had been built across the width of the chimney, with slits for ventilation running through the outer wall.

Three more steps brought me within reach of the bookcase. Through the dusty glass I saw that the volumes were indeed identical, and that there was no printing on the spines; they were leather-bound manuscript books, labelled only by year, and shelved in order from 1828 through to 1866. I set the lantern upon the table, tugged at the right-hand door until it opened with a shriek of hinges, and drew out the last volume.

It was a diary, written in a crabbed, shaky hand, but legible enough.

5th January 1866

Duke and Duchess of Norfolk left this morning; due at Chatsworth tomorrow. Duchess paid me the great comp[t] *of saying that the hospitality at Wraxford Hall surpasses any she has received this season. Only eighteen left in the party until Lord and Lady Rutherford arrive on Saturday. Weather inclement, but the younger gentlemen continue to ride. Spoke to Drayton about champagne . . .*

I read on through entry after entry meticulously describing a series of grand house parties that could not possibly have occurred. The Hall of Cornelius Wraxford's imagination—for who else could have written this?—was surrounded by rose gardens, rockeries, ponds, croquet lawns, and archery fields, lovingly tended by a small army of gardeners. Grand banquets were held each night in the Great Hall, attended by the cream of English society; shooting parties roamed through the coverts of Monks' Wood. I tried several more volumes and found that they were all the same: a daily record of a magnificent life unlived, whilst the actual Hall sank deeper into decay.

Edwin's voice, muffled but plainly anxious, echoed in the stairwell. I had gone straight to the bookcase without looking round, but now as I turned and raised the lantern, I saw a bundle of old clothes lying behind the door.

Only they were not just clothes, because there was something in them; something with shrivelled claws for hands and a shrunken head no larger than a child's, to which a few tufts of scanty white hair still clung. The mouth and nostrils and eye sockets were choked with cobwebs.

I do not think I fainted, but my next memory is of Edwin's arms about me and his voice reassuring me, somewhat unsteadily, that everything was all right.

"We must not stay here," I said, disengaging myself. "Suppose someone locks us in?"

"There is nobody here, I promise you. And yes, I think it is Cornelius."

I picked up the last volume of the diary and, averting my eyes from the ghastly object behind the door, followed him shakily down the stairs and through to the comparative warmth of the library. The fog outside was as impenetrable as before.

"It is only half past three," said Edwin. "He may still find his way here." But he did not sound as if he believed it.

"And if not?"

"We have food and coal enough for the night; let us hope it won't come to that."

If I had to spend the night here alone, I thought, I should go mad with fear. He added the last of the coal—there was more, he said, in the cellar—and built up the fire whilst I told him what I had found, conscious at every pause of the listening stillness around us.

"So Vernon Raphael was right," he said, "about Cornelius not being an alchemist at all."

"And about Magnus murdering him?" I asked.

"No; I don't think so. As Raphael said, it wasn't in Magnus's interest to have Cornelius vanish. He'd gone to all that trouble to create the legend of the armour; why wouldn't he leave the body in it? I wonder, you know, if Cornelius didn't simply die up there, of a stroke or seizure, though it does seem an extraordinary coincidence; unless he was frightened to death by the storm. In fact . . . Magnus *can't* have known about the secret room, or he'd have found the body and saved himself the expense of the court case."

"Then Magnus knew nothing of his uncle's imaginary life," I said. "I never thought I would feel sorry for Cornelius, but of course the man John Montague described was Magnus's invention. Perhaps he was really quite kind; after all, he kept the same servants all those years."

"Perhaps he was," said Edwin, turning the pages of the manuscript book, "but why on earth did he huddle in that cell to write all this?"

"Because . . . because it was easier, shut away in there, to imagine the Hall as he wanted it to be," I said. "And because he had to keep it utterly secret—even from himself, in a way. Poor old man! Everything we learn about Magnus makes him seem more evil."

"And we can't, as you say, even be sure he's dead. Cornelius doesn't mention Magnus anywhere here; he seems to have kept up his imaginary life until the day he died. The last entry is for the 20th of May 1866—'Lord and Lady Cavendish expected Friday'—the day of the storm. It still seems too much of a coincidence, unless . . . let me see John Montague's account of the inquest again.

"Yes; here it is: Mr. Barrett on the effects of lightning. 'A man was rendered unconscious, and when he recovered, walked away from the scene with no recollection of having been struck.' It could have happened that way; Cornelius might have returned instinctively to his bolt-hole, and there died of delayed shock, or concussion . . . but in the meantime, I fear we must prepare for another night here."

It had grown so dark outside that the fog was no longer visible. The dingy panelled walls, and the rows of leather bindings in their cases, seemed to be soaking up what little light remained. He rose and lit two stubs of candle on the mantelpiece.

"I think, in the circumstances, we should share the room you slept in last night; we haven't enough coal to keep two fires burning all night, and in any case . . ."

"Yes," I said, shivering.

"Then what I shall do first, before it gets completely dark, is bring up the rest of the coal from the cellar. And no," he said, seeing the fear in my face, "I don't like it, either, but without coal we will freeze."

He lit his lantern, took up the coal bucket, and went out onto the landing, leaving the doors ajar. His footsteps retreated, boards groaning at every tread, changing to a muffled creak-creak, creak-creak as he began to descend, until the sound ceased altogether and absolute silence returned.

We had placed two cracked leather chairs before the fireplace, which backed onto the one in the gallery, halfway along the common wall, with rows of bookshelves receding into the gloom on either side of me. The sensation of being watched grew upon me until I sprang up and turned with my back to the fire. Even then it was impossible to see all four entrances at once. I stood glancing from door to door, straining to listen over the thudding of my heart. My twin shadows swayed across the doorway of the study opposite, seeming to move independently. I thought of snuffing the candles; but then I would not be able to see the doors to the landing at all.

I had learned at school that you could count seconds by your heartbeat. Mine was racing far faster than the measured ticking of a clock, but I began to count, anyway. Only I could not keep it up; I would reach twenty or thirty, and be distracted by some phantom sound or movement, and start again. Thus I endured an indefinite interval, while the windows darkened further and still Edwin did not return.

I knew what I must do: find the other lantern and go down to the cellar; he might have fallen and sprained his ankle, or hit his head, or . . . Only I did not know where the cellar was, and my teeth were already chattering with fear.

Edwin, I thought, had left the other lantern by the entrance to the secret room. I took one of the candlesticks from the mantelpiece and, shielding the flame with my other hand, moved toward the connecting door.

There was still a faint glow of twilight in the windows overhead, but the darkness at the far end of the gallery was already impenetrable, and the dazzle of the candle confused my eyes. The black bulk of the armour loomed between me and the entrance; instinctively, I circled around it, grit crunching beneath my feet, until I could see the mallet and chisel lying on the floor, but no lantern.

Then I remembered that when Edwin had helped me down the stairs from the secret room, I had been carrying Cornelius's journal, but no lantern, and he had lit the way with his own. Mine was still burning on the table in the secret room.

The last of my strength deserted me, and I sank to the floor, just managing to set the candlestick upright beside me. Hot wax stung the back of my hand. *You must get up, you must get up,* a voice in my head was saying, but my limbs would not obey.

I was crouching a few feet from the fireplace, almost in front of the sarcophagus, which lay just within the circle of light from the candle. *If you cannot stand, you must crawl,* said the voice. I was making another effort to rise when I thought I heard a sound from the fireplace. I clenched my teeth to stop them chattering. There it was again, a heavy, muffled, grating sound, like stone sliding upon stone. It seemed to be coming from beneath the floor in front in me.

The grating ceased; for several seconds there was absolute silence, then a faint metallic creak. I held my breath; the candle flame steadied.

The lid of Sir Henry Wraxford's tomb was slowly rising.

My heart gave one appalling lurch and stopped beating altogether. The next second, as it seemed, I was on the far side of the connecting door, with the key rattling in the lock as I fought to turn it. I could see the faint glimmer of my candle shining through the gap beneath the door. Then another, stronger light began to play about my feet; there was a creak, and thump, and the sound of footsteps approaching.

I thought of running for the stairs, but I had no light, and the visitant would hunt me down. The door handle rattled; the door shook; the footsteps moved purposefully away. In a few moments, it would be on the landing. I had not time to run and lock all the doors at the far end of the library. I thought of the weapons arrayed along the gallery wall—too high for me to reach. The tin box Vernon Raphael had left—there might be something in it I could use to defend myself, if my shaking hands could hold it, and I did not faint.

The grey cylinder Edwin had found. I could light it with the candle and throw it at—whatever was pursuing me. Most likely I would die, but if it seized me, I would die anyway, and far more horribly.

The footsteps were still receding. I gripped the key with both nerveless hands and twisted. There was a rasp and a snick, but the footsteps did not pause. I withdrew the key and slipped back into the gallery, just as a light passed out through the double doors at the other end. The beam of a lantern played across the wall beyond; then the footsteps moved off along the landing, boards creaking at every tread. For a moment I thought I might be spared, but then I heard the squeak of hinges as my pursuer entered the library. I tried to slip the key into the keyhole, but my hand was shaking so violently that I dared not let the metal touch.

My candle still burned where I had left it on the floor. There was the tin box, two paces away, partly obscured by the shadow of the armour. Footsteps moved within the library—one, two, three, and then a pause. Light flickered beneath the door. Biting my lip to stifle a moan of terror, I stole over to the box and opened the lid, but could see nothing within. My fingers touched something round, and I drew out the cylinder. The footsteps were moving again—I could not tell which way.

I moved toward the candle, almost tripping over the hem of my dress. As I knelt to the flame, I realised I had no idea how fast the wick would burn. The floor seemed to be dropping away beneath my feet. *If you faint, it will catch you,* said the voice. Better to die instantly:

I touched the end of the wick to the flame and it began to burn with a faint, sputtering, reddish spark, but crawling so slowly I could scarcely see it move.

In that extremity of terror, I saw my only chance of salvation. I darted over to the armour, grasped the hilt of the sword, and placed the cylinder inside as the plates sprang open. Then I tore at my dress, ripped away a handful of fabric, and slammed the plates upon it. The footsteps paused, and then moved rapidly toward the door. I fled blindly into the darkness until I collided painfully with a wall and had just time to huddle, only half-concealed, behind a musty tapestry before a lantern beam swept across the floor, flitted over the open tomb, and settled upon the folds of fabric caught between the plates of the armour.

The figure bearing the lantern moved into the circle of candlelight and paused directly in front of the armour. Not a ghost, but a man: a tall man in a long coat.

"Miss Langton?" said a deep, authoritative voice. "I am Dr. Davenant; I have come to rescue you."

If I had not heard him emerge from the tomb, I think I might have believed him.

"Miss Langton?" he repeated. "Come out; you have nothing to fear."

A gloved hand reached out and grasped the hilt of the sword. Searing white light burst from the armour, and for an instant the two blazing figures stood face to face, hands clasped. Then the armour leaned forward, engulfing the man, and toppled headlong through the floor.

Darkness returned with an earsplitting crash. The floor lurched and rebounded; for a moment there was silence, and then a long, low rumble, gathering power as it approached until it broke over me with a thunderous roar. Choking dust filled my lungs, and I was flung from my feet and rolled over and over like a rag doll in a storm.

There was a vile, rasping taste in my mouth and throat, and a heavy weight pressing down on the side of my head; I tried to push it away, and realised it was the floor. The boards on which I was lying were covered in sharp, gritty fragments.

A faint, misty glow appeared in the darkness away to my right. I began to crawl toward it, not knowing what else to do, brushing aside slivers of what felt like glass, until I saw that it was the light from the candle I had left burning in the library. The fear had left me; perhaps I had simply exhausted my capacity to feel anything at all. I rose shakily to my feet, made my way along the landing to the library, fetched the candle and returned to the gallery—what remained of it.

At the far end, where the tomb and the chimney and the armour had been, was a great gaping hole in the wall. Half the floor had gone; the boards ended in a jagged mess of splinters not ten feet from where I had been lying. Dust was floating up from a black pit beyond.

Edwin is down there. The thought struck me like icy water, dashing away the numbness. Suddenly I was trembling so that I could scarcely stand. Gripping the banister, and praying that the guttering flame would not blow out, I went slowly down the main staircase. The dust in the air grew thicker as I descended; faint slithering and trickling noises echoed in the darkness, but the entrance hall below seemed quite unchanged; the chimney, I realised, must have collapsed into the drawing room beyond.

"Edwin?" I called as I came to the foot of the stairs. There was no reply. I called again, louder and louder until the stairwell rang with his name. At last, from a doorway leading toward the back of the house, came a very faint sound: tap-tap, tap, tap-tap, tap. The tapping grew steadily louder as I followed it along a dank stone corridor with shadows writhing around me, until I came to a rough wooden door, set low in the wall.

"Edwin, is that you?"

There was a muffled cry from within, and the door shook slightly. I lifted the latch, and recoiled with a gasp from the hunched, blackened creature that emerged, a lantern raised in its bloodied hand, until I saw that it was Edwin.

"Constance—thank God! What happened? It sounded like the day of judgement."

"No, the chimney fell down—did you see him?"

"See whom?"

"Magnus—he must have locked you in here."

"Constance, you've been dreaming. Nobody locked me in here; I thought I'd propped the door securely, but it swung shut, and then I couldn't break it down."

"No," I said, "he was in the gallery; he came up through the tomb; he meant to kill me. I hid the charge in the armour, and it crushed him to death."

"Constance," he said, staring at me in utter bewilderment, "you've had a terrible shock. Anyway, we can't stay here; the rest of the house may come down at any minute."

He led the way back to the entrance hall, where he opened the drawing room doors and stood gazing openmouthed at the chaos within.

"I don't know what's best to do," he said at last. "We can't spend the night out of doors; you would freeze to death. I think we must risk another collapse. Your room is on the other side of the house—it should be safe enough. I shall break up some chairs to make a fire."

We made our way back upstairs to my room, and washed off the worst of the grime in icy water. I tried once more to tell him what had happened, but he would not hear me until he had got a makeshift fire going, and I had sipped a little wine and nibbled at a biscuit, while the smell of burning varnish filled the room.

"Now," he said, "were you asleep when the wall came down?"

"No, I was wide awake. I went into the gallery to fetch the lantern, and I saw the lid of the tomb start to open—"

"Impossible, I assure you; those locks were rusted solid."

"The locks didn't move." It came to me in a sudden flash of memory. "It was only the very top of the lid, where the band around the edge was. I heard his footsteps; he had a lantern. I took the cylinder out of the tin box in the gallery and lit it and hid it in the armour—you can see here, where I tore a piece from my dress, to make him think I was inside. And then—he said he was Dr. Davenant, come to rescue me—"

I stopped short at the change in Edwin's expression; he was staring at the torn fabric as if he had never seen a dress before. His eyes met mine in sudden and horrified comprehension.

"*Davenant?*" he stammered. "You—you blew up James Davenant?"

"Yes, but he was Magnus; he meant to murder me—why do you look at me like that?"

"Don't you understand? If the police find out, you could be charged with murder, or at the very least manslaughter—"

"But he came up through the tomb! Who else—"

"You *thought* he did. But you were frightened out of your wits; the light was bad; it's infinitely more likely that you only imagined the lid moving—and that Davenant came in by the front door. Which we left unlocked for the coachman."

"I did not imagine it! This morning, in Nell's room—I followed him there—he tried to mesmerise me. There's nothing wrong with his eyes—they were Magnus's eyes. He was trying to find out what evidence I had against him. And how he could he possibly have found his way back here, through that fog? He was here all along; he waited until the others had driven away, and returned before the fog came down. Don't you remember?—we heard him, in the library."

"I see what you mean," he said slowly. "The trouble is, even if you are right, no one will believe you. If you tell this to the police, you will end up in prison—or a madhouse. Whereas if you simply say that you were in the library, and then there was an explosion . . . if they ever find Davenant, they will think he set it off."

"But if Nell is still alive—" I began.

"Nell, Nell, Nell!" he cried in weary exasperation. "Don't you see the havoc your obsession has wrought? Supposing Davenant was perfectly innocent? You are putting a noose around your own neck! And besides, there isn't a single shred of evidence to suggest that Nell is still alive. *Why* are you so certain of it?"

"Because I am Clara Wraxford!"

There was a long, shocked silence from Edwin.

"You have proof of this?" he said at last.

"No, but John Montague was convinced of it—by my likeness to Nell."

"And—your parents? Did they tell you . . . ?"

"No, they did not. But my heart tells me, just as Mr. Montague's did."

"Now, Constance, this is simply absurd. The resemblance proves nothing; you and Nell were related, and a likeness can often reappear after several generations. And John Montague, if you recall, thought at first that Nell looked exactly like his dead wife. For all you know, it was your resemblance to Phoebe that struck him."

"You think I am mad," I said bleakly.

"Not mad, no, but this has been a very great strain—"

"Which is a polite way of saying the same thing."

"No! It's because I care for you so much that I—"

"If you cared for me at all, you would believe me," I said, aware that I was being unreasonable, but unable to stop myself.

"I care for you enough to risk being hanged as an accessory to murder!"

The words echoed strangely, as if I had heard them before.

"Can't *you* see," I cried, "that this is exactly what happened to Nell? I am caught in the same trap; they will think we killed him twice—" I broke off, clenching my fists until the nails dug into my palms.

"You must stop this," he insisted, "and try to rest. All you need remember is: you were in the library when you heard the explosion, and that is all you know. So long as you keep silent, you are perfectly safe."

He rose and made up the fire. My head was swimming with fatigue, my body ached all over; and in spite of the fear crawling like ice along my veins, I sank into a black and dreamless void.

The fire was still crackling when I woke, and for a moment I thought I had merely dozed, until I saw daylight at the window. The fog had cleared; Edwin was not in the room. I rose and bolted the door and washed as best I could, trying to subdue the voice that whispered, *You have murdered an innocent man.*

I found Edwin downstairs in the wreck of the drawing room, combing through the rubble. He had his back to the doorway, and did not hear me come in, and so I watched from the shadows whilst he worked. Debris was heaped several feet high against the far wall, spilling out across the floor amidst the smashed remnants of chairs and cabinets. Edwin was standing about halfway up the slope, tossing the smaller pieces behind him, lifting out the larger fragments and setting them carefully aside. His breath issued in clouds, mingling with the dust that swirled around him. He took hold of a shattered beam and leant his weight upon it; there was a slippage and a rumble, and a black barrel-shape appeared, then a metal arm and shoulder.

He knelt down beside it, and I saw that his face was deathly pale. A second later, he caught sight of me.

"Keep back!—and yes, it is Davenant, I'm afraid; he's . . . burnt, but perfectly recognisable. I was hoping against hope that you really might have dreamt it. Come away from here; there is nothing we can do for him, and the coach will be here within the hour."

"We must be clear about this," he said, as we climbed the stairs for the last time. "The best thing, I think, will be to tell them—the police, I mean—that you were in the library, waiting for me to come back with the coal—which is perfectly true—when you thought you heard footsteps in the gallery next door. A second later, there was a terrible explosion; then you came downstairs and found me; and so this morning I thought I'd see if anyone had been caught in the collapse, and that's when I found him. You don't know how he got there, or what he was doing, or how he caused the explosion—"

"But that would make you an accessory, as you said last night."

"No; I was wrong about that. I was trapped in the cellar, after all, so I don't count as a witness; I only know what you told me—which is that you heard footsteps, and then the explosion, and that is all you know."

"But if we don't—if I don't tell them he was Magnus, he'll be buried as Davenant, and Nell will never be free of—"

"Constance, for God's sake! Do you *want* to be locked away in a madhouse? If you say one word about Magnus to the police, *I* will tell them that you are delirious from shock—and which of us do you think they will believe?"

"Do you not care at all, then, about the wrong we may be doing?"

"All I care about," he said, "is saving you from yourself—and quite possibly the gallows."

A thin rain was falling as I looked back at the Hall for the last time, at the jagged rent in the side wall, and the severed cable coiled like a serpent over mounds of shattered masonry, before the darkness of Monks' Wood closed over us. The drive to Woodbridge passed in almost complete silence, while the cold ate deeper into my bones. I climbed the steps of the police station, feeling numbly indifferent to my fate; but instead of being led away in chains, I was ushered into a private sitting room, given a chair by the fire and plied with refreshments whilst Edwin talked to the sergeant, who accepted his version of events without question. An hour later, we were on the train to London, but it proved a sombre journey. We dared not speak of what was uppermost in our minds, and our efforts at small-talk faded into the clack and clatter of the rails endlessly repeating, *You have murdered an innocent man, you have murdered an innocent man* . . . until it seemed to me that parting came as a relief to us both.

My uncle's reaction, once he had got over his shock at seeing me, grimy and bedraggled, in the hallway at Elsworthy Walk, was even worse than I had feared.

"By remaining alone with Mr. Rhys," he said coldly, "you endangered your life, ruined your reputation—what do you imagine the rest of the party have been saying about you?—and embroiled yourself in the death of this man Davenant. No doubt we shall have journalists pounding on the door. As for Mr. Rhys, you may tell him he is *persona non grata* in this house. I thought you had some moral sense, but I see that I was grievously mistaken."

With which I could only agree. I retreated to my room like a child in disgrace, and lay awake for hours, staring into the dark, until I gave up and lit my candle and paced about the floor in a torment of spirit worse than anything I had endured in the wake of my mother's death. If only, I thought, I could be absolutely certain that it was Magnus I had killed, I might at least be able to sleep; otherwise I might as well give myself up to the police—but I could not do that without implicating Edwin. Again and again I relived those terrifying minutes at the Hall, but doubts kept seeping in: perhaps he really *had* feared for my safety; he *might* have found his way back in spite of the fog; he *could* have discovered the tunnel by accident; he *might* not have known I was there until he saw the piece of fabric in the armour . . . No, my only hope was to find someone who could identify Davenant as Magnus, and since he had deceived the whole world for twenty years, it would have to be someone who had known Magnus very well indeed. If John Montague had not drowned himself, I thought bitterly, he might have saved me.

There was one other person, apart from Nell herself: Ada Woodward, who had never replied to me, though that was hardly surprising; the news that Nell was suspected of murdering her child as well as her husband must have come as an appalling shock. And, of course, they had been estranged even before that. What was it Nell had said in her diary? "Even if Ada and I were still as close, she and George could not take us in: Clara and I are Magnus's lawful possessions, and he would reclaim us soon enough."

But the diary was written for Magnus to find. My mind was so clouded with fatigue and misery that the thought did not at first make sense, and I stood staring blankly at the page for several uncomprehending seconds before the implications rushed upon me, and I understood at last why Ada Woodward had not answered my letter.

The noise of the harbour floated up to me as I stood at the top of Church Lane: men shouting, canvas flapping, wheels rumbling, and above it all, the incessant crying of the gulls, piercing, desolate. Beyond the piers, the sea was a flat, steely grey; the salt air was laden with smoky smells of tar and fish and coal, and the decaying odours of mud and seaweed. Stone steps continued on up the hillside, toward St. Mary's Church and the ruin of Whitby Abbey.

No one knew where I was; I had left my uncle a note saying that I had gone out for the day and would not be back until late, and slipped out of the house before he came down for breakfast. I had dozed fitfully in the train, drifting in and out of nightmares of Wraxford Hall, and schooling myself in the intervals of waking to expect absolutely nothing of this visit.

St. Michael's Close was a cul-de-sac, curving down from Church Lane and ending at number seven, a high, narrow, whitewashed cottage, set farther below the street, with steps leading down to the front door. My self-admonition had been in vain; my mouth was very dry, and my heart was thumping painfully. I descended the stairs, grasped the heavy brass ring, and rapped twice.

The door was opened by a gaunt, middle-aged woman who must, I thought, have been very striking in her youth. Her brown hair was streaked with white, her skin was etched and crisscrossed with fine lines, and there were shadows like bruises beneath her eyes, but the eyes themselves were large and luminous; all the more striking, set in that haunted face.

"I should like to speak with Mrs. Woodward," I said tremulously.

"May I ask who you are?" Her voice was harsh, yet not unpleasant, with something of the local accent.

"My name is Miss Langton," I said.

"Wait here," she said, and closed the door in my face. I waited, shivering, for what seemed an age before the door opened again.

"Mrs. Woodward is not at home."

"Please," I said, "I have come all the way from London to see her—to give her this." I drew Nell's journal from my bag, but the housekeeper's eyes did not move from my face.

"Then I shall give it to her when she returns," she said, stretching out her hand.

"I am sorry," I said, "but I am charged to deliver it in person. Please; I shall wait in the street, if she will only come out and speak to me."

"She is not at home," the housekeeper repeated. As she spoke, a young woman emerged from a doorway farther down the passage behind her. I had a glimpse of auburn hair, dark eyes, and an alert, curious gaze before the door closed again.

There was a low stone wall at the top of the steps, and I sat down upon it, determined not to be driven away. A few moments later, I saw, from the corner of my eye, the curtains twitch at an upper window.

A quarter of an hour or so later, the door opened again, and another woman emerged; tall, like the housekeeper, but with darker hair, shot through with strands of grey that held the light. She had high cheekbones and a strong, shield-shaped jaw, and though her face was not as ravaged, she too had deep lines etched around her eyes, which were fixed upon me with extreme disapproval.

"Miss Langton?" she said sternly. "I am Mrs. Woodward. What do you want of me?"

"I wrote to you from London, some weeks ago. Did you not receive my letter?"

"No, I did not. Pray state your business."

"I inherited Wraxford Hall," I said, "from Augusta Wraxford—I am a descendant on the Lovell side. John Montague gave me Eleanor Wraxford's journals—"

"And what is that to me?"

"Please believe me," I said desperately, "I mean no harm to you, or to Nell—will you not hear me out?"

She regarded me silently, until I thought all was lost.

"Walk up to the top of the steps, and wait by the churchyard," she said at last, and disappeared into the house.

I did as I was told, and stood for another long interval amongst the weathered tombstones with a chill breeze tugging at my bonnet and gulls shrieking around me, before a cloaked figure appeared at the top of the rise and strode across the damp grass toward me.

"Now," she said, just as severely, "what is it you want of me?"

"I have come to tell you that Magnus Wraxford is dead—he died by my hand, two days ago at Wraxford Hall, under the name of Dr. James Davenant. He meant to murder me, and I killed him in self-defence, but the police do not know that; they think it was an accident. I came here to ask if you would come to London and—identify him as Magnus—"

She regarded me with horrified concern.

"Miss Langton, I fear you are not well; you should be telling this to a doctor or a clergyman, not to me."

"Your husband is a clergyman—"

"My husband died ten years ago."

"I am very sorry to hear it," I said, "but was he not the George Woodward who was once rector of Chalford St. Mary's?"

"No, you are mistaken," she said. But an edge of desperation in her voice prompted me to continue.

"If Magnus is buried as Davenant, the world will always believe that Nell murdered him, and Clara: alive or dead, she will never be free of the stain—"

"I do remember the case," she said warily, "though it has nothing to do with me. And—supposing this man you claim to have killed is not Magnus Wraxford at all—what then?"

"You mean," I said, with tears of despair welling up, "that if you come to London, and he isn't Magnus, it might lead the police to Nell, and you cannot take that risk."

"That is your meaning, not mine," she replied, but her voice had softened.

"There is one thing," I said hesitantly. "John Montague told me—it was just before he died—that I reminded him very much of Nell—and I have wondered—whether I might be Clara Wraxford."

This time there was no mistaking the shock that flashed across her face.

"Miss Langton, you must understand me: I cannot help you. Surely you have friends, family—someone you can confide in?"

I shook my head.

"A doctor, then?"

"There is no one who can help me now."

"I am sorry to hear it," she said earnestly. "What will you do?"

"I shall take the next train back to London, and then—" I was about to say, "I will go to the police and confess," but remembered I could not do that, because of Edwin.

"And then . . . ?" she prompted.

I could think of nothing to say; the prospect seemed as grey and featureless as the ocean at her back. I took Nell's journals and held them out to her, but she would not touch them.

"I am sorry," she repeated, "but I must go now. Good-bye, Miss Langton; I wish . . ."

She hesitated a moment, then turned abruptly and strode away across the grass.

I did not get home until ten o'clock that night; my uncle had retired to his bedroom, as if to say, "I wash my hands of you," but Dora had waited up for me. Edwin, she told me, had called twice at the house during my absence, and left me a note, which said only: "I shall be in the Botanic Society Gardens in Regent's Park from two o'clock tomorrow and will wait all afternoon. Please come. E."

"Don't tell your uncle I gave it you, miss, or I'll lose my place," said Dora. "When he found out it was Mr. Rhys, he said I wasn't to let him in on no account. And he said you was to look at that," indicating the evening paper, which my uncle had pointedly arranged on the hall table, with a thick pencil line slashed down the margin beside a column headed "Distinguished Scientist Dead: Mysterious Explosion at Wraxford Hall." The phrases blurred before my eyes: "Dr. James Davenant, FRS . . . following investigation by Society for Psychical Research . . . violent explosion . . . cause unknown . . . extensively damaged . . . grisly discovery. We understand that the owner, Miss Langton, was present at the time and was fortunate to escape with her life . . . Wraxford Hall, as readers may recall, was the scene of a notorious murder in the autumn of 1868 . . . Dr. Magnus Wraxford . . . Mrs. Wraxford and child . . . vanished . . . cloud of suspicion . . ."

I set the paper aside, suddenly overwhelmed by a great yearning to see Edwin; but unless I could prove, in his eyes as well as my own, that I had not killed an innocent man, the shadow would always fall between us. Through a haze of exhaustion, it occurred to me that I ought to look up Davenant's address, as I had done with George Woodward: might he not have left some trace, some memento of his former life? And if I were to visit his house, on the pretext of offering my condolences . . .

18 Hertford Street, Piccadilly, was one of a row of large, sombre town houses built of dark grey stone. I walked and up down in the sunlight—it was one of those rare, dazzlingly bright March days, the air as warm as May—gathering my courage, climbed the steps, and knocked.

After a long pause, the door was opened by a small white-haired man, dressed in a suit of mourning.

"My name is Miss Langton," I said tremulously. "I am the owner of Wraxford Hall, and—I thought I should call to offer my condolences to the family."

"Very kind of you, Miss Langton, but I'm afraid there is no family—Dr. Davenant was a bachelor, and quite alone in the world. My name is Brotherton; I was his manservant."

"I wonder," I said, "if I might come in for a moment. I am feeling a little faint"—which was no more than the truth, for my knees were shaking so that I could barely stand.

"Of course, Miss Langton. Pray step this way."

Two minutes later, I was seated in a cavernous drawing room with a glass of port wine in my hand and Mr. Brotherton hovering anxiously nearby. "This must have come as a terrible shock to you, Mr. Brotherton." I could see that he warmed to being addressed as "Mr."

"Very much so, Miss Langton; a dreadful business. I understand that you were present at the time of the accident?"

"Yes," I said, grateful for the dim light, "but I am afraid I have no idea what caused the explosion; we did not even know he was in the house when it happened. How long had you been with him, may I ask?"

"Twenty years, Miss Langton—ever since he came to London."

"And where had he lived before?"

"Abroad, Miss Langton—he was a great traveller in his youth."

"I understand he was once caught in a fire."

"Yes, Miss Langton. In Prague, it was, not long before I joined him. The hotel burned down; he was lucky to escape with his life. In those days, he wore gloves even indoors, as well as his dark spectacles, and kept his beard very full; he told me it helped the skin to heal."

"It must have been a terrible shock to his friends," I ventured.

"I imagine so, miss. The master never said, but I think he cut himself off from his old acquaintances, on account of his injuries. And of course he was away a great deal, the first few years I was with him."

I glanced around the room, my mind racing. If Magnus *had* kept something from his past, I thought, what would it be? The pictures—those that I could make out through the gloom—all seemed to be landscapes.

"Was Dr. Davenant a connoisseur of paintings?" I asked, hoping he would offer to show me around the house.

"Yes, indeed, Miss Langton; it was a great interest of his. When he wasn't in his study, you could always find him in his gallery upstairs. Mr. Pritchard—the master's solicitor—informed me yesterday that the collection is to go to the nation."

"Your master," I said, improvising recklessly, "*did* mention that he would be very pleased to show me around the gallery; of course I could not have imagined I would be here in such tragic circumstances . . ."

Mr. Brotherton drew a white handkerchief from his sleeve and dabbed at his eyes. I reminded myself sternly of all the evil Magnus had done, and waited for him to compose himself.

"Forgive me, Miss Langton; I never thought I should see this day . . . I am sure the master would not have wanted me to disappoint you. If you are quite recovered, would you care to step this way?"

He led me up a flight of stone stairs, our footsteps echoing loudly in the stillness, and into a long, panelled room, much lighter than the one below. I had naïvely expected to see canvases crowded all the way up to the ceiling, but there was only a single row of pictures hung around the walls. A great deal of thought had obviously gone into the placing of them. I set off around the room with Mr. Brotherton at my elbow and my mind racing ahead of me. The study seemed the most likely place of concealment, but what reason could I give for wanting to see it, let alone persuade him to leave me there alone? If I pretended to faint, would he leave me and go in search of a doctor? Surely not; he would ring for a maid, but I could ask if I might lie down for a little. And were there any other servants in the house? It seemed deathly quiet.

The bellpull, I had noticed, was just inside the door by which we had entered. We had almost reached the far end of the gallery, and I was nerving myself to collapse at Mr. Brotherton's feet, when we came to a picture of a large manor house by moonlight. I had been moving mechanically from canvas to canvas, scarcely aware of what I was seeing, when recognition struck me like a blow in the face: I was looking at a picture of Wraxford Hall.

Moonlight blazed over the dark bulk of the house, silvering the slates and spilling along the uneven drive like pooled water. Branches intruded in wild profusion, threatening to overwhelm the house; chimneys with crooked pots and their attendant lightning-rods hung stark against the brilliance of the sky. But the eye was drawn, most of all, to the mesmerising orange glow in the upstairs window, cross-hatched by a tracery of leading, the glow reappearing more faintly in the two adjacent windows and more faintly still in the two next to those, beyond which there was only the dim radiance of moonlight on glass. The picture had no title, but the signature in the lower right-hand corner was plain enough: J. A. Montague, 1864.

"How—how long, do you know, has this been hanging here?" I said shakily.

"Only a few weeks, Miss Langton. Dr. Davenant liked to change the pictures around, you see."

"Do you mean he bought it as recently as that?"

"I assume so, Miss Langton; he didn't say. Though he did ask my opinion, when I was dusting in here one morning. Rather sinister, I ventured to say; it seemed to amuse him."

"And did he—do you know what house that is?"

"No, Miss Langton."

"It is my own house, Wraxford Hall. Mr. John Montague, the

man who painted it, died two months ago. . . . Did Dr. Davenant ever speak of him?"

"No, Miss Langton, not within my hearing."

"Or of Magnus Wraxford?"

"No, miss . . . you don't mean the gentleman who was murdered?"

"So the world believes."

The old man was silent for a moment, gazing uneasily at the picture, and then at me.

"If you'll excuse me, Miss Langton, I really must get on now; there's a great deal to see to."

"Of course," I said. "It was very kind of you to show me the pictures."

Two o'clock was striking as I followed him down the stairs, light-headed with relief. I am free, I thought, I can go straight to Regent's Park, to Edwin; the shadow is banished.

"What will you do now?" I asked, hearing the echo of Ada Woodward's question in my own.

"Thank you, Miss Langton, I have been well provided for. Mr. Pritchard was kind enough to tell me so."

"I am very glad to hear it," I said, thinking how strange it was that a man so monstrous could be generous to his servant. I looked back through the window as the cab rattled away, and saw that Mr. Brotherton was still standing on the pavement, gazing after me.

In my excitement, I missed the way through the park, and so came upon Edwin from the wrong direction. He was seated on a bench, in sunlight dappled by the branch of a willow which was just beginning to show its leaves, all his attention fixed upon the path leading to the entrance, and did not turn until I was close enough to touch him. His face lit up; he sprang to his feet. We stood motionless for several seconds, or so it seemed, and then I found that my lips were pressed against his, with my arms about his neck and my fingers twining themselves through his hair.

"Then you love me, too?" he said when I drew back to look at him.

"Yes, yes, I do," I said, kissing him again for emphasis. "And everything is all right; Davenant *was* Magnus—I have proof of it—and now we can tell the police what really happened."

I paused at the change in his expression.

"I was so overjoyed to see you," he said, drawing me down upon the bench, "it drove all else from my mind. Tell me what you've found."

"John Montague's picture of the Hall is hanging in Davenant's gallery."

I described the morning's adventure, but, though he kept hold of my hand, the anxiety did not leave his face.

"I don't doubt you," he said, "but it isn't proof. Anyone else—including the police—would assume that Davenant bought it in a sale—it's far easier to believe. No; unless we can find someone who will identify the body as Magnus—"

"But there is," I began, and stopped, realising the difficulty. Ada—let alone Nell—would come forward only if the case were already proven. "I mean, there must be many people in London who knew Magnus well enough to recognise him, without his disguise."

"Yes, but the police won't invite them to—as far as they're concerned, he's Davenant, and I'm afraid the picture isn't enough to change their minds. Force of belief—it's what Magnus relied upon, coming back to London. He was a consummate actor; he thrived upon risk—even to the extent of hanging that picture, the moment he heard that the one man who could certainly expose him was dead—he knew, aside from the disguise, that no one would recognise him because nobody expected to see him—as far as the world was concerned, he died in the armour at Wraxford Hall.

"And even if, by some miracle, the body *is* identified as Magnus, you still mustn't tell the police, because they could still charge you with manslaughter, if they didn't believe it was self-defence—and they might well not, since we'd be changing our story. No, dearest girl, you must leave it alone. You're safe now," he said, drawing me closer to him, "Magnus is dead; your conscience needn't trouble you anymore."

"But it does," I said, "because Nell is alive; you mustn't ask me how I know, but I do—"

"And you still believe she may be your mother?"

"Yes, more than ever."

"Then—do you know how to find her?"

"Yes, but—I can't risk betraying her."

Edwin gazed at me helplessly.

"I don't know what to say, dearest, except that I love you, and will do anything to help you, whatever you decide about Nell—only you mustn't speak to the police. Will you promise?"

"I promise," I said, whereupon he began to kiss me again, and I forgot about everything else until we were brought back to earth by a scandalised harrumph from a passing gentleman.

Edwin accompanied me as far as the turn into Elsworthy Walk; he wanted to come in and ask for my uncle's blessing at once, but I told him that would only cause another explosion, a phrase which resonated uncomfortably as I climbed the steps and let myself in with my latchkey, to find Dora hovering white-faced in the hall. Two policemen, she whispered, were waiting for me in the drawing room; they had arrived not ten minutes after my uncle went out, and had been waiting for the past hour.

They were standing by the window, peering down into the street as I came in. One, massive and florid with luxuriant muttonchop whiskers, was Sergeant Brewer, to whom Edwin had spoken at

Woodbridge. The other, who might have been chosen for contrast, introduced himself in funereal tones as Inspector Garret from Scotland Yard, a tall, fleshless man with the manner of an undertaker. They declined refreshment, and took chairs with their backs to the window, so that I was obliged to sit on the sofa with the light full on my face. I saw that my hands were trembling visibly, and clasped them tightly in my lap. The sergeant produced a notebook and pencil.

"You will understand, Miss Langton," said the inspector, "that we need the fullest possible account of the events leading up to this tragic—er—accident, and since we have not yet had a statement from you . . . I wonder, Miss Langton, if I might begin by asking why you felt it necessary to join the party. It would strike many people as unusual, for a young unmarried woman such as yourself to accompany a group of gentlemen to such a remote and inhospitable place."

"Yes, sir"—feeling my colour rise, and thinking too late I should not have addressed him as "sir"—"but it *is* my house, and I was very much interested in the Wraxford tragedy—which is part of my own history—my own *family* history, that is."

"Very much interested—I see. And—er—may I ask whether there exists any understanding between Mr. Edwin Rhys and yourself—an engagement, perhaps?"

"Yes, Inspector." I prayed he would not ask when we had become engaged.

He paused, to my even greater discomfiture, while the sergeant scribbled something in his notebook.

"And had you ever met Dr. Davenant before this—gathering?"

"No, Inspector," I replied, wishing I could stop my voice from quavering.

He questioned me, step by step, about everything I had done from the time we arrived at the Hall, until the departure of the rest of the party.

"And why did you remain behind with Mr. Rhys instead of taking a place in the carriage? You said at the time"—leafing through his notebook—"according to Mr. Raphael—that you wanted to look for some family papers for Mr. Craik."

"Yes, Inspector," I said, wondering what Vernon Raphael had said to them.

"May I ask what papers?"

"I meant, papers I thought might interest Mr. Craik," I said desperately. "I did not expect the coach to be more than an hour or two."

"And what did you and Mr. Rhys do in the intervening hours—before the explosion, that is?"

Though his tone was studiously neutral, I blushed scarlet at the implication.

"I—I spent most of the time in the library," I said at last, "trying to keep warm. After I had given up looking for the papers, that is—I think I dozed for quite a while."

"I see." In the same disbelieving tone. He flicked through the pages of his notebook for a small eternity.

"Mr. Rhys says," he resumed, "that he went down to the cellar at around five o'clock to fetch more coal. Will you tell us what happened after that?"

My mouth was so dry, I could scarcely speak.

"I waited and waited—I don't know how long, until it was dark—I was afraid—I was just going to go and look for him when I heard footsteps in the gallery—"

"And where were you in the library when you heard them?"

"I—I was looking for a lantern, near the door that leads in—to where the armour was . . ."

"And the footsteps—could you tell where they were?"

"On the other side of that door."

"But you did not think they were Mr. Rhys's?"

"No."

"And why not?"

"Because—because they didn't sound like his. He would have come up the stairs and straight into the library."

"And then?"

"Then there was—a flash of light—I saw it under the door—and an explosion, and—and I started to run back through the library—and I must have tripped and hit my head—"

"So you didn't go into the gallery at all?"

I shook my head, not daring to speak.

"Then how, Miss Langton, do you account for this?"

He opened a small leather case and drew out a ragged piece of fabric, charred and blackened along one side, but perfectly recognisable as the one I had torn from my dress.

"Sergeant Brewer remembers seeing a gown of just this pattern beneath your travelling cloak when you and Mr. Rhys called at Woodbridge police station to report the—accident. We found it caught between the armour and Dr. Davenant's body."

"I don't know," I said faintly. "It must have got caught earlier in the day, when Mr. Rhys and I were examining the armour."

"Surely you would have noticed."

"I—I—I *do* think I remember something catching at my dress, but I did not know it had torn—until after the explosion—and then I assumed it had happened when I went to look for Mr. Rhys . . ."

"I see. Might we be able to examine this dress, Miss Langton?"

"I told Dora—my maid—to throw it out. She may still have it."

"That would be very helpful to us. Perhaps you could also explain the footprints—they appear to be yours—on the surviving portion of the gallery floor?"

"I—I went in after the explosion—after I had recovered from my faint—to see what had happened."

"*After* the explosion . . . I see." The note of disbelief was stronger than ever. "But there is a scuffed area, as if someone had been lying there when the dust first settled, and then a series of handprints, and then footprints—the *same* footprints, Miss Langton—but leading only in one direction: out of the gallery."

Two pairs of eyes watched me steadily while the incriminating seconds dragged by.

"I can't explain it," I said at last, "unless—perhaps I was confused about where I woke—from my faint, I mean, after the chimney fell down. I must have run all the way into the gallery without realising it . . . I'm afraid I can't remember; it was such a shock; I'm afraid that's all I can tell you."

"I see," said the Inspector heavily. "Are you sure, Miss Langton, there is nothing you would like to add to your statement?"

I took a deep breath, thinking, it must be now, or never.

"Yes, Inspector, there is. I found out this morning that Dr. Davenant was actually Magnus Wraxford. He did *not* die at the Hall in 1868, as everyone supposed—"

The two men were staring at me with utter incredulity.

"I said in front of him—before I realised who he was—that I had evidence to incriminate him—and then he must have concealed himself—he could not have found his way back through the fog—and shut Mr. Rhys in the cellar. He meant to murder us both and destroy the evidence and blew himself up instead—"

"And what evidence might that be?" asked the Inspector with heavy sarcasm.

"I did not have it then; it was just—intuition—but this morning I went to his house to—and when I found Mr. Montague's painting—"

"Miss Langton," the Inspector broke in, "you are plainly overwrought. I shan't detain you any longer—for the moment. But I shall need to speak to you again, and I must ask you not to leave London without letting us know exactly when and where you are going. Now, if you could ask your maid about that dress . . . ?"

Everything I had ever read about the horrors of incarceration came back to haunt me that night: the slamming of iron doors; the rattle of chains; darkness, cold, filth, unspeakable smells; the shrieks of my fellow prisoners; the roar of the mob as I was dragged, hooded, to the scaffold . . . until I woke at last from terrible dreams, and lay waiting, as the dawn brightened into another perfect sunrise, for the police to come hammering on the door. I had promised to meet Edwin at midday, and realised I should write to him by the first post to tell him what I had done, and why I might not be there, but the right words would not come, and after I had torn up half a dozen attempts, there seemed to be nothing left to do but try to will myself to sleep again, until Dora came up to tell me that a lady had called. She had refused to leave her name, but said she would like to speak to me privately and would wait for me by the seat at the top of Primrose Hill.

With my heart beating wildly, I crept downstairs, let myself out by the garden gate, and walked up through the wet grass, the droplets glittering like diamonds in the sunlight, until I reached the brow of the hill and saw a woman in a dark blue dress, with a travelling cloak draped over the seat beside her: the gaunt, strikingly featured woman who had answered the door of Ada Woodward's house. She rose to her feet as I drew near, and I saw that she was very pale.

"Miss Langton—we meet again. My name is—or was, until yesterday evening—Helen Northcote, but I think you might know me better as Eleanor Wraxford."

I gazed at her, unable to speak, drinking in every detail of her appearance. Her eyes, I saw, were a delicate shade of hazel, flecked with green. And there was something different about her voice, which sounded lower and more cultivated than I remembered: the Yorkshire intonation had gone.

"When Ada told me what you had said—especially after we saw the reports in the newspapers—I knew that we could not abandon you, no matter what the cost. We came down to London yesterday, but the police would not allow Ada—she insisted upon going to Scotland Yard alone—to see the body until late in the afternoon, when Inspector Garret returned from his interview with you. And then she was obliged to wait several more hours until they managed to unearth a Mr. Veitch, an ancient gentleman who had once been Magnus's lawyer, to confirm the identification. Enough to say that the Inspector has deduced—or so he told Ada—that Magnus intended to blow up the Hall, and was killed when the charge exploded prematurely."

I could not help smiling at the Inspector's appropriation of a theory he had dismissed as lunacy only a few hours before.

"And by then, Miss Langton," she continued, "it was far too late to call on you. Ada is sorry she could not be here; she was obliged to take the early train home."

"Please, you must call me Constance—do the police now accept that you were entirely innocent?"

"The warrant for Eleanor Wraxford's arrest will be withdrawn, yes. It is a very strange feeling, after twenty years of preparing myself for the worst . . . but before I say more, will you tell me your own story—since you are already so well acquainted with mine?"

And so, beginning with Alma's death, I relived for her the journey that had brought me here, with the city at our feet, and the shining thread of the river running through it, until I had come full circle: to yesterday's visit to Hertford Street, my engagement to Edwin, and the horrors of the previous night, all now dispelled.

"I do understand," she said at last, "why you thought you might be my daughter; and why you wanted to be. And if I had given Clara away, as you supposed, I would believe it, too; not only because you remind me so much of my younger self, but because of the affinity that led you to me. But, my dear Constance, you are not my daughter. She is alive and well; I think you caught a glimpse of her, just before I shut you out, as I had to do, for her sake. Her name is Laura Woodward, and she believes that Ada is her mother—and that she lost her beloved father, George, ten years ago."

Tears welled in my eyes, though I tried to blink them away. She took my hand in hers, gently caressing my fingers.

"I had no choice, you see. Everything—almost everything—happened as you divined. When Lucy and I left Munster Square for the last time with Clara, Lucy didn't come with me to Shoreditch, as I wrote in that diary; I put her in another cab to Paddington, while I drove with Clara to St. Pancras, where Ada was waiting for me. It was all arranged; she used to write to me poste restante at a dingy little post office in Marylebone, where I was sure Magnus would not go. George wasn't in Whitby then; he had a temporary living in Helmsley, thirty miles away, and that was where Ada took Clara, while I went on to Wraxford Hall.

"I never did go to the gallery, the night Mrs. Bryant died. I meant to, but my courage failed me at the last. All these years I have wondered how she died . . . and now I know."

I looked at her questioningly.

"Magnus must have forged both of those notes. And I very nearly did what he assumed I would: conceal myself somewhere nearby. And then . . . Mrs. Bryant was infatuated with him, and he was mesmerising her frequently. She need not even have read the note they found in her room; that was simply to incriminate me. He could have proposed an assignation, or implanted the suggestion in a trance. Dr. Rhys, said, I think, that she seemed to be walking in her sleep. And so she came to the gallery at midnight; and if I *had* been watching, I should certainly not have revealed myself to her, of all people. And then the lid of the tomb began to open, just as you saw that night. The shock of that alone might have been enough to kill her; or perhaps something sprang out—"

"The ghost of the monk," I said, remembering John Montague's story of the stonemason. "That was how Magnus disguised himself . . . but I don't understand. Why did he want you there? You would have denounced him—"

"Yes, and who would have believed me? By the time anyone else arrived, Magnus would have closed the tomb and disappeared into the tunnel—remember that he had gone out for a stroll in the moonlight, so he claimed, sometime before midnight—and what would they have found? Mrs. Bryant dead, and me beside her body, raving about the ghost of a monk. I should have been taken away in a strait-jacket, with Magnus playing the grieving husband . . ."

She paused, breathing deeply.

"Why did you marry him?" I had not meant to ask so baldly, and wished, when she did not immediately reply, that I could call back the question; it had sounded like an accusation.

"I believe," she said at last, "that on the one occasion he succeeded in mesmerising me, he did gain some hold over my mind; whenever I tried to muster the courage to tell him I could not marry him, an answering chorus would spring up in my head: 'but he is so kind, so thoughtful, so intelligent, so charming; how could you not grow to love such a man? And what will become of you if you do not marry him? You will be utterly alone in the world. . . .' It was not until the honeymoon," she said with a slight shudder, "that the scales fell from my eyes."

She was silent for a little, gazing at the tranquil horizon.

"I tried to persuade myself," she continued, "once it was too late—that he had married me for my gift, as he called it. I thought, you see, that his scepticism was merely another of his masks; I thought he truly believed in—supernatural powers—and sought to harness them for his own ends. Whereas in reality he saw *himself* as a god.

"No," she said, as if answering an objection, "I am sure that my visitations intrigued him; but I think he was drawn to me principally because I resisted his spell; because he had twice failed to mesmerise me; and, I fear, because he truly desired me. And so he hated me all the more, when he discovered how much I loathed him."

"And—your visitations?" I asked hesitantly. "Was the one in your journal—of you and Clara vanishing—invented for Magnus's benefit?"

"Yes, it was."

"And did they ever return?"

"No," she said wryly, "and neither did the intolerable headaches that used to follow them. That fall on the stairs: I remember thinking that it had opened a crack in my mind, just enough to let in glimpses of a world beyond—a world I never wanted to see. And then the rift closed again; I sometimes think it was the shock of Edward's death. And I will always wonder whether I should have told him about that vision, and whether he would have taken any notice if I had."

"Do you think," I ventured, even more hesitantly, "that Magnus might have had something to do with Edward's death?"

"I don't know. Edward was quite reckless enough to have climbed that cable of his own accord, but Magnus might very well have encouraged him, or even . . . I try not to think of it."

"I am sorry," I said. "I should not have asked."

"You need not be," she said. "It is always somewhere in my mind."

"How did you escape from the Hall?" I said, after a pause.

"Very much as you surmised: I left the Hall at dawn the next morning, in a gown and bonnet of Lucy's. I was enough of a mimic to pass as a lady's maid. It would have been too dangerous for me to go straight to Yorkshire, and so I had reserved a room, under the name of Helen Northcote, in a temperance hotel in Lincoln. I was still there when the first reports began to appear in the papers, and I realised that all the time I had been planning my escape from Magnus, he had been fashioning a hangman's noose for me."

"Yes," I said, "but . . . why did he kill Mrs. Bryant the night before the séance, when he had made all those preparations, and brought everyone together at the Hall?"

"Because"—she paused, as if searching for words—"because those preparations were meant to mesmerise everyone into *expecting* him to vanish from the armour. Now that I know he was living a double life as Davenant, it makes sense at last. The Hall was heavily encumbered; he had already converted Mrs. Bryant's ten thousand pounds into diamonds; that cheque was her death warrant. Another man might have gone on trying to extract more money from her, but for Magnus I think money was simply a means to an end; it was power he craved: power and revenge. If I *had* been dragged away to an asylum that night, I'm sure he would have insisted upon trying the experiment anyway. 'We owe it to Mrs. Bryant's memory,' I can imagine him saying; and Magnus Wraxford would have vanished, leaving nothing behind but ashes. But when his original plan miscarried, he saw that he could use the death of Magnus Wraxford to exact an even more terrible revenge upon me."

"Did you believe, all along, that he was still alive?"

"Yes—alive, and hunting for me. I had a waking nightmare—one of many—of standing on a scaffold, with the rope already round my neck, and seeing Magnus smiling from the shadows. I never thought I would escape him, but I was determined that Clara would be saved. And so Ada and George—at my insistence—became her parents. They let the servants at Helmsley think that Laura—as we named her—was their foster child, but when George was offered a living at Whitby a year later, they began to speak of Laura as their own, and nobody questioned it. Ada gave Helen Northcote a reference, and after three years as a housekeeper in Chester—the longest years of my life—I came to Whitby as Ada's companion."

"It must have been dreadfully hard for you," I said. "Knowing you might be snatched away at any moment, I mean."

"Yes," she said simply. "Laura knows I love her, but I have always withheld something of myself. To brace yourself for the worst, every time a stranger knocks at the door, leaves its mark, as you see . . .

"It is strange—or perhaps not—that Laura has grown to be so like Ada: sweet-natured and tranquil, with nothing of my temper, and even a natural gift for music, which I certainly do not possess. No one would ever doubt that they were mother and daughter. And now—thanks entirely to you—the shadow is gone from our lives.

"You risked your life for me," she said, taking my hand once more, "you were willing to go to prison for me; I shall never forget you. I came to London prepared to reveal myself as Eleanor Wraxford, if there was no other way of ensuring your safety. But thank God we have been spared that; the police have agreed that Ada's name will not appear in the matter, and Laura need never know."

"But surely," I said, "you must *want* the world to know who you really are. How else can you clear your name?"

She was silent for a while, gazing out across the city.

"Magnus worshipped power," she said at last, "the power to deceive whomever he chose, to make them believe, feel, even see as he directed. If they would not succumb, then in his eyes they deserved to die. And yet out of all that terror and cruelty came Laura. There is nothing of Magnus in her; blood does not always out; sometimes it is washed clean, or never tainted from the first . . .

"But the world, Constance, does not see things thus. Magnus's vision and the world's have more in common than we care to admit. I could shout my innocence from every one of those rooftops, and people would still believe me guilty of *something*. No; Eleanor Wraxford will always be 'that woman who murdered her husband'—or her child, for what could I say had become of Clara? If Laura were to learn who I really am, she would surely divine the truth."

"But—now that there is no reason to deceive her—might she not prefer to know? Would she not have two loving mothers instead of one?"

"Yes; but she would have to accept that instead of the kind and gentle man she remembers as her father, she is the daughter of a monster, who delighted in cruelty, murdered we do not know how many people, and never cared a jot for her. Would you really wish that upon her?"

"No, but—there is a way," I said tentatively. "If you would let *me* be Clara; you could say that you gave me up—exactly as you did give Clara to Ada—to protect me, and now we have found each other again. Laura could go on being Ada's daughter, and . . . I would dearly love to have you for my mother; I would never tell a soul, I promise, and then Laura could be my sister . . ." My voice broke at the last phrase, and tears welled over again. She drew me into her arms and stroked my hair and murmured the small wordless comforting sounds I had longed to hear from my own mother, and I found myself quite unable to stop until I had drenched her shoulder with my tears and lay quiet in her embrace, feeling the warmth of the sun on my back and wishing the moment would last forever.

But I knew what her answer would be as soon as I looked up.

"It is a dream of happiness, Constance, but it could never be. The secret would divide us; we should all be whispering in corners, and sooner or later, Laura would guess what we had done. I had no choice when I gave her to Ada; it would be unforgivable to deceive her a second time.

"No; Eleanor Wraxford vanished twenty years ago, and will not return. I am, and will remain, Helen Northcote, and the secret I beg you to keep—if you will—is that you and I met—here—this morning."

She rose, and drew me to my feet, and we stood for a long moment gazing at one another.

"Shall I never see you again?" I said.

"I will always think of you," she replied, and held me in a last embrace before she turned and walked away down the hill toward the sea of rooftops below, with the dome of St. Paul's rising above the haze of numberless chimneys. My fancy of the Underworld beneath the kitchen floor, with its endless tunnels stretching away into the dark, came back to me as I watched her, remembering how often, and how sombrely, I had gazed at that dome as a child. My thoughts turned to Edwin, perhaps already waiting in the gardens by the church, but I remained on the hillside, gazing after Nell's diminishing figure, long after she had vanished from sight.